"You devil... You Irish devil," she whispered.

"Oh, Tim, I've thought of you so often," Hope whispered when he finally released her lips. "I've longed for you for months and months."

"Nor was I forgettin' you, lassie. I could forget the Auld Sod sooner than I could forget you."

Ask him about Anne now—ask him! her mind prompted. She wanted to be sensible. She wanted to get things settled between them, to find out what future, if any, there was for their love. But caught up in the breathtaking assault on her senses, she couldn't even pretend to resist his lovemaking, could make no attempt to struggle against the current of desire that flooded through her.

"I love you, Hope. I love you more than I imagined I could love anybody," he whispered in a voice husky with emotion. His lips claimed hers again, and their souls seemed to meet and merge in a long stirring kiss that left her limp and whimpering for more...

Other books by Stephanie Blake

DAUGHTER OF DESTINY
FLOWERS OF FIRE
BLAZE OF PASSION
SO WICKED MY DESIRE
WICKED IS MY FLESH
SECRET SINS
UNHOLY DESIRES
SCARLET KISSES
FIRES OF THE HEART
CALLIE KNIGHT
A GLORIOUS PASSION

Bride of the Wind

STEPHANIE BLAKE

A JOVE BOOK

BRIDE OF THE WIND

A Jove Book/published by arrangement with
the author

PRINTING HISTORY
Jove edition/September 1984

ISBN: 0-515-07874-3

Jove books are published by The Berkley Publishing Group,
200 Madison Avenue, New York, N.Y. 10016.
The words "A JOVE BOOK" and the "J" with sunburst
are trademarks belonging to Jove Publications, Inc.

PRINTED IN THE UNITED STATES OF AMERICA

Chapter 1

May 1879

HOPE COX SLOUCHED in the saddle astride her pinto pony, Rollo, holding tight the reins of Star, her father's piebald stallion. They were on the crest of a high ridge overlooking the dusty bowl that contained Anderson county jail, where her father was a temporary guest of the state of Texas, charged with attempted bank robbery and murder.

The place was a hellhole. Relentless, scorching sunlight reflected off arid, barren wasteland, and for as far as the eye could see, the low adobe building was the only sign of civilization.

"Pap, you really done it this time, you really have," Hope said aloud. "Why'd you have to go get yourself all liquored up and let them Price boys talk you into taking a crack at the Bentley Bank? You never done nothing like that before."

This was the first time Pat Cox, in one of his wild drunken sprees, had tried to rob a bank—but it was also the first time he had ever been faced with a charge of murder. His appointment with Jack Ketch was quite certainly just a few days away, unless the paper safely tucked inside Hope's denim shirt could convince the warden that the governor of Texas had decided to commute her father's sentence to time already served.

"Come on, Star," she said to her father's stallion. "You'll either be carrying Pap out of here alive or his body slung over your saddle. Either way, it's gonna be over quick."

Riding down the trail toward the prison, she tried to remember exactly what Bob Kidwell, the governor's secretary, had told her to tell Warden Nugent about the pardon.

"Tell him the governor's got some new information from down San Antonio 'bout the Price brothers and is convinced your old man didn't have nothing to do with the murder," the balding secretary had said as she perched gingerly on a chair across from him and shivered inside at the way he stared at her sixteen-year-old body. "Tell him that an official messenger will be on the way with the full details as soon as they're all in order. That's official kind of talk meaning when he gets around to it."

"You 'spect he's gonna believe that?" she asked, drawing in her breath as his eyes roamed greedily over her.

"He's going to believe that's the governor's seal, 'cause it is," Kidwell said, leering at the way her only dress, which was too small for her, stretched tightly across her young breasts. "You gonna get your pa out and you're gonna come right back here to Austin, now ain't you, Hope? So I can take care of you."

Hope had a pretty good idea of how he intended to take care of her, and she wasn't having any of it. Since she had blossomed into young womanhood, several men had expressed a desire to see that she had "the best of everything," but none of them had anything she really wanted, and Kidwell certainly didn't. It wasn't her fault that he had somehow gotten the idea that if he helped her old man escape a hanging she was going to, in his words, "be nice to me."

"Sure . . . sure, I'll be right back just as soon as Pap has hit the Chisholm Trail north," she promised, without meaning a word of it.

"Then just you and me can be together," Kidwell was almost drooling. "You'll be my little girl, and I'll be your fine new dad."

"Sure, Mr. Kidwell," she said, thinking how fast she was going to shake the dust of Texas off her feet once she got her father out of the clink.

"Call me Bobby," he whispered, leaning toward her, his fat, wet lips close to her cheek. "You call me Bobby, Hope, little girl."

"Sure . . . sure, Bobby," she said, cringing inside as his fingers touched her bare arm and thinking that she would shrivel up inside if he tried to kiss her.

"'Less you want to call me Daddy."

"Daddy, if you want. Look, Daddy, I got to get going," she said. "They're gonna hang Pap day after tomorrow unless this *pardon* gets there on time."

Reluctantly he let her go, although he was aching, she could tell, to put his hands on her. Relinquishing for the moment the delights he assumed would be his, Bob Kidwell watched as she climbed out the window of his office in the State House and dropped lightly to the ground beside Rollo, who was peacefully nibbling at the weeds in back of the building.

Then she was off, riding as only an old cavalry trooper's daughter could ride, with Star galloping along behind, carrying all the worldly goods of Pat Cox, formerly sergeant-major, First United States Dragoons.

And now Hope was approaching the state prison run by probably the meanest jailer in the whole sprawling state, approaching it with a phony pardon to spring a man scheduled to hang for a crime he wasn't responsible for.

"What in the hell do you think you're doing here?" a harsh male voice growled at her from the guard tower as she rode up to the gate.

Shaking inside but moving unhurriedly and with seeming coolness, Hope looked up at the man wearing the uniform of a prison guard whose double-barreled scatter gun was pointed down at her.

"I'm Hope Cox," she said. "I've come for my old man."

"You mean Pat?" the guard's broad, moustached face showed surprise. "You planning on carrying off his corpse on that horse?"

"I'm planning on his riding off on this horse," she said, taking the paper out from under her shirt and waving it at him. "I got a pardon from the governor."

"What the hell you talking about?" he growled. "The governor don't send pardons by kids on horseback."

"Well, there ain't no telegraph, so how else is he gonna send it, less'n somebody was willing to ride all the way from Austin without stopping, day and night?"

The guard was looking at her more closely now, his hand shading his eyes from the blazing sun.

"I'll be damned!" he said. "You're a girl kid!"

"Now ain't you the smart one?" she said. "What's the matter, ain't you ever seen one before?"

The man had made an understandable mistake. Tall for a girl her age, Hope was a rangy, raw-boned female poised on the brink of budding womanhood. Her short-cropped blond hair was tucked up beneath a high Mexican sombrero, and her faded, threadbare denim pants and oversized work-shirt did nothing to establish her femininity, but as the guard scrutinized her sweat- and dust-begrimed face, he could see beneath the dirt a good complexion, a high sloping forehead, and an alluring widow's peak that formed an ideal backdrop for her arched eyebrows, shadowing eyes that glowed and sparkled like sapphires. He was looking at what seemed to be a woman . . . a woman-child. That she was youthful was obvious; but before long all her full female sensuality would burst forth like a rosebud opening in the morning sunlight. Her classic nose and chin, her high cheekbones, and the perfectly formed lips were an artist's delight.

The guard's black eyes, staring down at her from two or three feet above her head, were disconcerting, but Hope kept her nose up and her chin thrust out.

"My Lord, I'd like to—" He stopped abruptly, but Hope knew what he had been going to say. It was the effect she always had on men, from Dibby Fairfax, the dissolute English remittance man who had taught school in Medicine

Bow, where she had picked up her smattering of formal education, to the one she had just left, "Daddy" Kidwell, the governor's clemency secretary, who liked to pet little girls. She knew what the guard would like to do, but she was damned if any man was going to do it until she was sure that she got more out of it than they did.

"You want to see the warden, kid?" the guard asked. "You'll have to talk to the lieutenant of the guard first, but I don't think you're gonna get nowhere. Folks 'round here are all set on seeing a hanging, and I don't think nobody would want to disappoint them. Folk gets plumb mean if you take away their fun."

"I got this," Hope said, waving the pardon, "and I'm willing to talk to anybody I got to talk to."

"Okay...okay, I'll call the lieutenant," he said, disappearing from the parapet into the guard tower. In a moment, she heard him bellowing from the other side of the wall.

"Hey, Perkins!" A muffled answer came from somewhere inside, and the guard went on. "There's a girl kid here who claims she's got a pardon from the governor for Pat Cox." There was a pause and another mumble came from inside. "How the hell do I know why they sent it with her? There ain't no telegraph from Austin and she says nobody else was willing to ride day and night. Okay, I'll send her in with it and you can talk to Nugent."

There was more talk and shouting back and forth inside, and finally Hope heard someone rattling bars and a key being turned. One side of the double door swung open and a man came out. He had a belly almost as big as the rest of him put together, and which hung over his gun belt so far, she wondered how he could see his feet. He stood staring at her out of eyes set deep in folds of fat.

"What do you want, kid?" he asked, with none of the interest in her most men his age immediately displayed.

"I got a pardon from the governor for my pap, Pat Cox," she said, waving the paper at him.

The man took it in his two small pudgy hands and started to examine it carefully.

I wonder if he is just pretending to read, she thought. Wouldn't it be funny if we went to all the trouble to make all this official-like and nobody here could read?

"Looks like the governor's seal, all right," he said, "but what would he want to pardon that hairpin for?"

"'Cause he isn't guilty," she said.

He looked at her for a minute and laughed. "What difference does that make? They hang just as high, guilty or innocent, and we already hired a hangman, and there's lots of folks coming with picnic lunches and stuff. They gonna be damn disappointed. Nasty, maybe."

For a minute Hope felt cold deep inside, cold and scared for her pap and for herself. Pap wasn't the best father in the world, but now that her mother and two sisters were gone he was all she had. He couldn't help it if he liked a little drink now and then, could he? He couldn't help it if a couple of gunslingers had gotten him drunk and used him as the front in a bank holdup where a clerk had gotten killed trying to be a hero.

The truth was that everybody wanted to see him hanged because they were bored and needed the excitement. The fat guard had just admitted as much.

"All right," he was saying gruffly. "We'll take you into the office. Captain Nugent will have to look at this. He's the one who's got the final say."

The state prison was a long rectangular structure, with a few adobe outbuildings and a larger cell block built of the same material. Captain Sam Nugent was ensconced in an office as bleak and unpretentious as the prison and the countryside around it. He was slouched in a rough wooden chair with his feet, clad in dusty boots, propped up on a desk of raw, uncured pine. The place looked a little like one of the monk's cells she had seen down at San Antonio, Hope thought as she took in the warden, framed between two high stacks of documents, reports, and tattered folders piled on either side of the splintery desk. A twisted Mexican cheroot hung from one corner of his mouth, and his right hand cuddled a bottle of raw red whiskey.

As Hope entered the room, he took a quick swig at the

bottle, corked it, and lowered his feet to the floor. He braced his elbows on the counter, bending forward to scrutinize the girl through heavy-lidded eyes that reminded her of the venomous glint of a sidewinder hypnotizing its petrified prey, while his head swayed slowly from side to side.

"What we got here, Kramer?" he asked his clerk, peering through a cloud of smoke that briefly obscured his sinister countenance.

Hope was silent, fascinated by the cold eyes.

"Well, kid, what do you want?" He showed his snaggly, tobacco-stained teeth when he talked.

"I got a pardon from the governor for my pap . . . Pat Cox."

"The governor don't know what he's doing," the warden said. "Let me see that thing."

He stuck out a callused hand and she let go of the paper reluctantly, hoping that the warden had never seen the governor's handwriting and didn't have anything with his signature on to compare with the one she had paid to have affixed to this document.

"Don't know why the governor would do this almost at the last minute," Nugent said, staring at the paper in a way that made Hope wonder if *he* could read.

"He did it because my pap is innocent," she said, and launched into an inspired lie. "Back before the war, Pap was a wrangler for Colonel Goodnight, and Colonel Goodnight intervened with his good friend the governor on Pap's behalf."

The name Charlie Goodnight was a magical one in Texas and in most of the Southwest. Colonel was a courtesy title bestowed on a man who was one of the most active empire builders, range owners, and trail drivers in the country. His influence was almost as widespread as his reputation for integrity. Hope's story was at least partly true. Her father *had* worked for Goodnight, trailing cattle with him. But they had parted company after the war. Pat Cox had been for the Confederacy, despite his time in the U.S. Army, and had fought for the South; while Goodnight, despite the fact that he lived in Texas, had been loyal to the Union and had served only in the Rangers, who protected the state against Indian raids while most of the soldiers were fighting in the East.

Definitely impressed, Nugent sat up straighter in his chair, discarded the cigar in a spittoon next to the desk, and looked at the letter again. "Goodnight, eh?"

"Mr. John Chisum also added his recommendation to Colonel Goodnight's," Hope said, figuring that as long as she was telling a story, she might as well make a good job of it.

"Chisum, hm?" John Chisum wasn't noted for his integrity, but he was a powerful and influential man. "Chisum knows your dad?"

"Back when Colonel Goodnight and Judge Chisum was partners in trailing cattle north," she said. Goodnight and Chisum had been partners, until Goodnight had found out that Chisum was supplying him with cattle whose original brands had been blotted out, an indication that Chisum didn't inquire too deeply into the ownership of the cattle he put his brand on. So her story, if not true, was at least consistent. If Goodnight and Chisum had known about her father's plight, they might even have been willing to write letters to the governor in his behalf. But she didn't have time to ride halfway across the state and back to ask them, and neither did she possess the proof of her father's innocence she claimed to have. The only thing she could do under the circumstances was lie about it all . . . lie and hint of delights to slimy Bob Kidwell that she had no intention of delivering.

"Hm . . . I don't know about all this," Nugent said. "This looks real, and Colonel Goodnight and Mistuh Chisum are mighty big men, but I don't think you realize what kind of a responsibility it would be to stop a hangin' that's all set and folks are lookin' forward to."

"What about the responsibility of hanging an innocent man?" she demanded.

He grinned his snaggle-toothed grin again. "Well, one thing you can be sure of, a hangman ain't gonna complain, but folks who've been cheated out of seeing him hang sure might."

"My pap's old friends like Colonel Goodnight and Mr. Chisum and General Sheridan might complain, though," she said.

"General Sheridan! How'd he get into this?"

"My pap served with the general in Mexico . . . him and General Grant and—" She was really stretching things now, she realized. Her father would have to be in his sixties to have fought in the Mexican war, and he was only in his early forties. "He was just twelve at the time, a drummer boy," she said quickly. "But General Sheridan was always saying that he never would forget how that little tyke dragged him out from under his dead horse just before the Mexican cavalry charged at Buena Vista."

She had a dim idea that Sheridan had served in the Mexican war, though she certainly didn't think it likely that he had had a horse shot out from under him at the battle of Buena Vista, but she was also pretty certain that neither Nugent nor anyone else here had any knowledge of the country's history. He would swallow that if he was going to swallow anything.

"General Sheridan," Nugent said. "He's general in chief of the army."

"Yes, sir, and he's got General Terry and General Crook and Colonel Custer all out looking for Crazy Horse and Sitting Bull and their Sioux and Cheyenne that those damn fools at the Indian Bureau gave the repeating Winchesters to and let run off and kill folks." Hope Cox could look as innocent as a blonde angel while she was making up something outrageous; but what she was saying now was mostly true, and besides, no one in the West had any use for the Indian Bureau. They were willing to believe anything bad about it.

"Yeah, those stupid do-gooders won't be satisfied until the Injuns scalp all of us," Nugent agreed. He hadn't forgotten about the pardon though, and his next question took Hope by surprise.

"Your old man fought for the Confederacy, didn't he?"

"Yes, sir," she said, blinking. "He was with Hood, but—"

"Why in tarnation did your daddy leave his wife and kids and a cushy job with Colonel Goodnight to join up with the goddam Rebs?"

This was the last place she had expected to find someone still willing to wave the bloody flag, but a lot of folks in West Texas never had much use for the Confederacy and had even welcomed the California column when it had finally pushed through from New Mexico to San Antonio.

"I don't rightly know," she said. "I was just a little girl then, but I suppose he felt patriotic about his home state. A point of honor with him, I guess." There was no point in telling this man that her devil-may-care father had been blind drunk when he had signed the enlistment papers.

Nugent looked past her, toward where the guard was still standing. "You hear that, Perkins? Patriotism? Idealism? Honor? You figure that's what the bloody war was all about?"

"No, sir," Perkins said. "Supposed to have been something about abolition, wasn't it?"

The warden shook his shaggy head, uncorked his bottle, and took another healthy swig. "Abolition, my ass!" He surveyed Hope. "Young lady, your old man didn't pledge himself to Jeff Davis for all those noble motives folks talk about. He was the same as the rest of the poor suckers who went out to get shot for the Stars and Bars. He was just looking out for his own hide. They got more blacks than whites in the South, right? But they was free labor all those years, so they couldn't compete with the poor white trash sharecroppers and ranch lackeys like your old man. Now the blacks are freed, people like your old man are in trouble. Maybe that's why he took to robbing banks."

"He didn't rob that bank, Captain Nugent," Hope said. "Them other two fellows did."

"Yeah, and I'll bet they say they didn't do it but he did," the warden said.

Since that was exactly what the two gunmen from the wild Tulerosa country had said in court, Hope couldn't deny it. But she stuck to her story.

"I bet Colonel Goodnight and Mr. Chisum and General

Sheridan and General Grant don't believe that."

"So it's General Grant now?" he sneered, a more hostile note in his voice. "You got a presidential pardon tucked away under that shirt of yours somewhere?"

No, she didn't have a presidential pardon, but what she did have under her shirt, stuck in the waistband of her pants, was a deadly little Colt, and if it came right down to it, she was going to stick that in Warden Nugent's ribs to free her father.

"What, no pardon from General Grant? Well, I 'spect he would be looking for one hisself if folks knew all the crooked things going on in his administration. So maybe he didn't have time to write one for Pat Cox, the dumb bastard who robbed a bank 'cause the blacks took his job."

Her father had been out of a job for just one reason, his affection for the bottle, and from the way Nugent was gulping his whiskey, he probably would be, too. But of course he wouldn't admit it was anything he had done; he would blame it on the competition of the blacks.

"Yep, now that the blacks are free people, your old man's got to worry about them taking his work away. No more free labor. Them slaves are getting wages now and they're undercutting white men's wages by forty, fifty percent. People like your father are out of luck. And then these blacks got the right to vote now, 'cepting where the Klan is keeping them away from the polls. That there Reconstruction is ruining the South, ruining the whole country. One of these days we is all gonna be kissing the asses of black congressmen—senators, even—and next thing you know, they'll be one of 'em sitting in the White House."

Hope was getting impatient. She wanted to get her father out of here before something happened to expose the shaky plan she had devised. She wasn't interested in Nugent's racial or political ideas but knew she had to listen, or risk turning him completely against her and ignoring the "pardon."

"Yep, less'n the Democrats get back in this November, we is all going to be out of luck with them Republican crooks and their black friends lording it over us."

He took another slug from the bottle. "Yes siree, them money-greedy northern sharks sold out this nation like Judas for pieces of silver, while poor boobs like me and your pa, we fought for our rights."

He reached for the bottle again. "Who brought the slaves to this country first, missy?"

"I . . . the northerners did, I guess," she said, more to please him than for any other reason.

"You're sure as shooting they did. They brought 'em and sold 'em to the southerners so they could make more money off exploiting us all."

When she didn't comment, he went on, "Yeah, they brought 'em here and then they was overcome by a crazy religious fanaticism and appointed a Messiah, that baboon Abe Lincoln, to set it all straight in one fell swoop. Free the slaves and take away the rights of southern manhood. Goddamn! Read an editorial by a newspaper writer last week. He said that the war has plunged the United States into a decade of depression, corruption and the rich getting richer and the poor getting poorer. We're going to purgatory, and from here on, this nation is going straight down to hell! Yeah, I sympathize with your old man and all the poor sob's that can't make it no more while General Grant and his friends, the Morgans and the Carnegies, are smoking big fat cigars and eating off of gold plates while the little man's money is sticking out of their pockets."

He stared, at the pardon again, bleary-eyed. "Can't read this friggin' thing. Ain't got enough light in this place. What did you say your old man's name was, and when we fixin' to string him up?"

A cold chill was starting to settle in Hope's middle. When she had come in, the man had been at least half sober; now he was drunk. He couldn't even remember her father's name.

"Pat Cox, sir," she said. "He comes from County Down and was a corporal in the First Dragoons, USA, and a master sergeant in the First Texas Cavalry, CSA."

"Sounds like he changed sides a lot," Nugent said, grinning at her drunkenly. "When did you say he was scheduled to be strung up?"

"Tomorrow . . . I told you, tomorrow," she was getting frantic and having trouble keeping her voice down.

"Hm . . . wonder about that," he said. "Wonder if he's really the one we got on the schedule for tomorrow. We hanged a couple of fellows yesterday, you know. Maybe we got around to him early."

Hope wanted to scream, but she knew that if she did, it would be all over, so she bit her lip and prayed.

"Yeah . . . yeah. He may have been the one," Nugent said, grinning. "Maybe we better call in Old Jake, the hangman, and see if he remembers."

He sloshed the whiskey around in the bottle, a grin spreading over his face, and she realized he was teasing her. Teasing her rotten mean.

He glanced over at the guard captain and grinned. "Why don't you mosey on down to the cell block and see iffen that Cox fellow is still waiting to be hanged or if we did it the other day, Kramer?"

"Sure . . . sure, Warden," the fat man said, snapping his suspenders at the humor of the whole thing. "Now that you mention it, I don't rightly remember if that was the one we strung up the other day or not."

The door closed behind Kramer, a definite kind of sound that made Hope suspicious. She looked around at Nugent and found him leering at her the same way Bobby Kidwell had done ever since she first started hanging around the governor's office trying to get a real pardon.

That had been shortly after Ma, who was a real educated type and a schoolteacher, had gotten tired of Pap's drinking and being in jail and decided to go back to her people in Virginia. Faith and Charity had gone with her, but Hope, thinking she had a chance to save her pap's life, had been determined to hang on and keep trying. She had promised that she would stay with old family friends in Austin, but had spent most of her time camped out at the governor's mansion or hanging around his office, and that was where

Bobby Kidwell had noticed her. Bobby, an old young man, had a bald head and pinched face, highlighted by bright blue eyes that shone with birdlike brightness every time he saw Hope. He had been especially nice to her on the day she wore her one neat, clean gingham dress instead of the jeans and old shirts she usually wore. That was the day she had thought she was really going to see the governor.

But once again Bobby Kidwell had come out and shaken his head. "Sorry, sis, he says he hasn't got any time today. He's gonna meet with a group of Galveston shippers most of the morning and with cattle folks from the Panhandle the rest of the day."

"But he promised . . . he promised!" Hope had puckered up, coming as close to crying as she had since her father had been arrested and charged with murder.

"I know, sis," Kidwell had said, coming around the counter. "I know it's hard, but I been trying, honest I have."

He had sounded so nice and sympathetic, and she had felt so down and done in, that she hadn't paid much attention when he put his arm around her or noticed the way he looked over his shoulder to see if the clerk sitting behind the counter was still writing in her books.

"I really been trying to help you, sis," he said, his hand starting to slide down her back. "What did you say your ma's name was?"

"My ma is Minerva Cox. She came out here to be a schoolteacher but ended up marrying my pa, when he was in the Dragoons, hunting Apaches. His hitch was up 'bout then and he got a job with Colonel Goodnight and took part in the first cattle drive with the Colonel and Mr. Oliver Loving up to Colorado. But along came the war and he enlisted with the Rebs and—"

"And what was you telling me 'bout your sisters?" His hand came to rest on her bottom and it seemed a kind of strange place for a man to be touching a gal. Why in the devil did he want to touch her bottom? To see if she had calluses from being on horseback most of her life?

"Well, there was three of us, so Ma decided to name us Faith, Hope, and Charity."

"Faith, Hope, and Charity," Kidwell said. "Those are kind of unusual names. How come your ma picked them?"

"My ma is a woman of letters. Taught school, like I said," she told him, wishing he'd stop running his hand over her bottom. "That is, she taught school 'fore she became an indentured servant."

The fondling stopped and he looked at her suspiciously. "Ain't no indentured servants. Hasn't been no white ones for a couple hundred years and ain't no black ones no more."

Hope had snorted disdainfully. "Well, isn't that all that females are in this noble 'land of the free and home of the brave?' Second-class citizens, who can't even vote?"

She was repeating things she had heard her mother, a lady who had what were called "advanced ideas," say.

"Our main function in life," she went on, "is to slake male lust and serve as brood mares. And God help us if we produce female children rather than males. In China they used to abandon girl babies along the Great Wall at birth. Girls were considered just more mouths to feed since they'd never have the physical strength or endurance to work twelve hours a day in the fields and rice paddies. Heck, I've worked twelve, fourteen hours many a day on the hurricane deck of a bronc and done as good as any man and I ain't rightly got my full growth yet."

"But what growth you got is very nice . . . very nice indeed." Somehow, while she had been talking, he had managed to slip his arm around her waist.

"What're you doing, Mr. Kidwell? We was talking about rights and things. Why you got your arm around me?"

"I was just seeing how much growth you have, honey," he said. "How old did you say you are?"

"Sixteen, going on seventeen."

"How would you like to come live with me, Hope?" he asked.

"Live with you? I don't think I could do that without asking my pap. I couldn't get married without my pap's consent."

"Well, I wasn't really talking 'bout getting married." His round face had turned red, and the redness spread right up over part of his bald head as she pulled away when he tried to kiss her on the neck. "I was just thinking you could come live with me and be my little girl."

"I 'spect sixteen is too old to be anybody's little girl," she said. "And how about my pap? Would you want him to come and live with you, too, and maybe be kind of like your brother?"

She hadn't quite understood at first what was on Kidwell's mind, but pretty soon she did. After all, she hadn't hung around cow camps and mining towns all her life without learning there were men who liked young girls more than those their own age.

Yeah, she had known then what he was after, she had started to work fast, figuring out how she could use him to help her father without letting him do what he wanted to do.

"No, I don't think we could have your papa there," he said. "That would make it different, and anyway I don't think the governor is gonna let your pa off, do you?"

"I think he will, Mr. Kidwell, if you ask him to," she said. "Or maybe you could just stick a pardon in among a bunch of other papers you have for him to sign and he would do it without knowing what he's signing."

"You know I couldn't do that, Hope," he said. "That wouldn't be honest."

"Well, then I guess I'll just have to find some other way to get Pap off," she said, wriggling out of his embrace. "Maybe there's someone else who will be willing to help me."

"Now don't be like that, dear little Hope," he said, kissing her on the cheek.

She had started to cry, and watching him through her tears, she saw the calculating look on his face. "Supposing I did what you said. Would you come live with me and be my little girl?"

"Well, if some fellow did that for me and my pap, I sure would want to do a lot of nice things for him."

"Hope, I think maybe I can arrange for the governor to

sign that pardon without reading it. I'll put it in with other papers he has to sign."

"I would sure be appreciative of that, Mr. Kidwell. My pap really is innocent."

"Yes, there is that, isn't there?" he said, starting to shuffle through a drawer, looking for a blank pardon.

Chapter 2

AND NOW HOPE was standing in Warden Nugent's office, watching him reread the pardon Bobby Kidwell had placed the governor's seal on.

A speculative look had replaced the mocking leer on Nugent's face, and Hope kept a wary eye on him. She hadn't liked the man from the moment she set eyes on him and now she was beginning to hate him. Even Bobby Kidwell wasn't as bad as this man.

"So you think your pap ought to be let out of the picture frame we had ready for him just 'cause the governor says so, eh, gal?" Nugent asked, looking up at her. "And 'cause fellows like Chisum and Goodnight brought pressure to bear."

"No, 'cause he is innocent and has his rights, Captain Nugent," Hope replied quietly.

"I think that schoolmarm mother of yours put too many high-falutin notions in your pretty head, gal. That black Republican Abe Lincoln might have talked about rights, but most folks know there ain't no such thing." His mouth curled into a sneer around the cigar constantly rotating between his thick lips. "We got a saying down where I come from in Carolina that President Lincoln, as well as the Fourteenth Amendment to the Constitution, are full of cow manure. The way we see it is that all men are created equal, but some men are more equal than others. Get the idea, missy?"

Hope's blue eyes were ice hard as they focused on his pompous, smug countenance. "You make yourself pretty clear, Captain Nugent. Now, what about my father?"

"Well, first we got to see if he's one of them what was hanged last week or if he's one we're gonna hang this week. Powerful lot of hangin' on the schedule, and folks are really enjoyin' the shows."

He eased his considerable bulk out of the chair and walked to the window behind his desk to stand looking out into the courtyard, where half a dozen convicts were cutting wood and piling it in neat stacks against one of the wings of the fortresslike building.

"You got any idea how many people we hang a year, missy?" he asked, turning to look at Hope. "It's not just men we hang either, there's women too. We hanged two of them there female suffragettes a couple of weeks ago."

Hope's eyes widened. "Suffragettes? No one's ever been hanged for that—just beat up and spit on."

"Well, I don't rightly know if that pair was suffragettes in the strict sense of the word, but they sure as hell thought they were equal enough to men to kill a couple of fellows."

Hope breathed a little easier. She knew Texas justice could be pretty harsh but couldn't believe it had come to hanging women for their opinions.

"One of them was a big, black whore with dugs out to here." He cupped his hands way out in front of his chest to indicate large breasts. "She wasn't content with giving half the male population of Pecos the clap, she had to slip a shiv into her pimp's ribs to boot. He was a white man, so she got the ultimate—one hundred lashes and the noose. Shee-it, you should of heard her howl when they stripped her naked and laid that bullwhip on her back and big round butt. That was quite a sight, that black skin and red blood. . . . She howled and cursed and screamed when they whipped her, but she didn't say a word when they dragged her to the gallows. Guess she was half dead already. But as soon as they pulled the trap, she started to thrash around on the end of the rope, legs flyin' and that big, black hairy *hole* showin' and blood splatterin' everywhere. Don't know when I enjoyed a hangin' quite that much."

He was grinning with lascivious remembrance, and Hope, in spite of having an unusually strong stomach, was feeling a little sick.

"The other one wasn't that much of a kick. Widow woman, 'bout forty. Self-made widow, you might say. She put her husband away by feedin' him arsenic over a couple of years. Said he beat her. Beat her, mind you. Ain't that a laugh? Everybody knows there's no woman worth a damn less'n she's beaten once or twice a week. Hell, she should have been grateful to him for his interest, but no, she had to sneak around and dose him with arsenic."

He moved away from the window in Hope's direction as he continued talking. "She wasn't much fun, though. We had her most of a month and she was a plain, dried-up prune of a woman, not interested in makin' her last days more pleasant with a little canoodlin'. All she did was read the Bible, and when we got her up on the scaffold, all she said was she wanted her dress tied down so she wouldn't kick her feet and show her legs while she was stranglin'. Not much excitement in that one. Seen many hangin's I liked better'n that."

As she listened, it occurred to Hope that this was a man she could cheerfully kill. She might be a crack shot, but had never actually fired a gun at a human being, and until now she hadn't wanted to.

"Yes siree, lots of folks been hanged out there in that courtyard and lots of folks has had a good time watchin'. And here you are, honey, trying to take that pleasure away from 'em. Folks don't get much fun out here in West Texas, you know. It's an awful important decision to decide not to hang a man."

"Yes, I suppose it is, but I know you're the kind of man

who can face up to important decisions, Captain. If you weren't, you wouldn't be holding down a responsible job like this." She hated flattering the man, but it was going to be a battle of wits to free her father and she had to grit her teeth and do it.

"And, Captain, I sure am hoping you're gonna do the right thing by my pap. Even if it makes you kind of unpopular with the folks coming to see a hanging, it'll make you popular with the governor, his secretary Mr. Bobby Kidwell, and with Colonel Goodnight and Judge Chisum. I suspect that when you're running for office later on, like a man of your caliber ought to do, the voters will remember that you did right by Pat Cox and his daughter."

He was right beside her now, and her words pleased him so much that his arm suddenly snaked around her waist. She flinched as if a serpent had coiled itself around her, but that didn't shake loose the arm or stop the gross fingers from sliding upward and clumsily kneading her resilient young breasts.

"To get back to the matter at hand," he said, his face close to her ear and the reek of his cigar and booze-laden breath almost suffocating her. "Little Hope is hoping like hell to get her pa's neck out of the noose. And she tells me that good old Judge Chisum, Colonel Goodnight, the governor, and the governor's secretary all want him out too. But you know what, honey? In spite of all that, the final say-so is in my hands. Here at this little old prison, I'm the lord of life and death, you might say. If I say, 'Hang,' they hangs high and dead, and it don't matter what anyone else says."

Did he suspect that the pardon was a forgery? Had he noticed something in the way T. Edwald Shirk had written it, perhaps a secret symbol the governor included when he sent a real pardon that even Kidwell didn't know about? No, she decided, he was just teasing her, trying to get what all these beastly creatures who called themselves men wanted.

"Well, Captain, I know right well that you're the man with the responsibility, and no matter what the governor or any of those other people said after the event, it wouldn't bring my pap back. Not even if the governor fired you, or if you were indicted for murdering an innocent man, would Pap come back to life."

That brought him up short and he stopped fondling her, looked at her long and carefully, and then let go of her. He returned to his swivel chair, slouched into it, stretched out his legs full length, and swung around to face her.

"Here is the point, Hope, you lovely child." He massaged the gross bulge in his trousers with a meaty paw. "The way of life is that one good turn deserves another, don't you agree? If I decide to turn Pat Cox loose, against all public opinion in this area, it seems only fair that you reciprocate by doing a good turn for me . . . something that you might discover you like just as much as I do."

She knew what was coming and her stomach began to churn. She hadn't needed Shirk's warning to understand what most men were like, especially here, in this almost womanless country, but it came as a wrenching jolt nevertheless.

"What do you have in mind, Captain?" she inquired in a mild tone, with an underlying note of steel that he failed to catch.

"Well . . ." A self-indulgent smile lit up his beefy, flushed face. "Them pock-marked, sallow-faced whores who prowl this part of the world don't fire my burners anymore—they're old and flabby and smell like dead fish. Now you, missy, the instant you walked into this room, it was like a breath of fresh air. Young, pretty, smelling like an uncut rose . . . as sweet and pure as my kid sister—God rest her soul, she died of yellow fever two years ago down in New Orleans."

"Gosh, that's too bad, Captain," she said, thinking it was too bad it hadn't been him instead of his sister.

"Well, I try to bear up under my loss, and now that you've come along, I sort of have some of the same feelings for you I had for her." He paused, thinking, and apparently decided that his words might have suggested something he didn't intend, because he added hurriedly, "My feelings for her, of course, were of an entirely different nature, you understand."

"Oh I fully understand, Captain," Hope said, wondering just how sweet and innocent a sister of this despicable man could have been.

"Good. Now then, the good turn I have in mind for you to do me is to bring some comfort to this aching, red-hot, yearning point of mine."

Hope watched, transfixed, as Nugent spread his legs still wider and unbuttoned the fly of his trousers. She had all she could do to keep her stomach from giving up its contents as his large, purplish phallus thrust into view—the repulsive sidewinder about to strike.

"It would provide me with great relief and pleasure if you could lend surcease to this obviously critical condition." He snickered obscenely. "Ever take it into your head to make money, honey? That's an old prison joke. Only in this instance the currency of exchange is the freedom of your beloved father. I'm waiting in impatient anticipation, missy."

She gulped, trying not to look at what he was so proudly displaying, and managed to plaster a weak smile on her face. "Well, that sure is a bad condition, like you say, Captain Nugent, and I been thinking maybe I could do something special for you if you let my pap go real fast without waiting for all the formalities. You know, I brought this horse along with mine and it's waiting outside the prison right now."

"You were mighty sure of yourself, little lady. What made you think I'd obey that pardon without sending back to Austin to check?"

She chose not to answer that. "Like I say, I sure would like to help you with your affliction. I always did want to be a nurse and help the suffering."

That brought a huge grin to his face. "I think that would be a great occupation for you, honey. Why don't we start right in with your training now?"

"There's only one thing, Captain. I know you're the soul

of honesty and honor and all, but . . ."

"But what?" he asked, sitting up a little straighter.

"Well, I'd just feel a lot better about doing this nice thing for you if my pap was already out of prison and waiting for me up on the high trail."

A series of emotions crossed his face. The first, she thought, was disappointment that she wasn't more eager to enjoy the monstrous maleness of him; a second was doubt that she would carry out her promise once her father was out of his clutches. The final expression was easy to interpret: He was thinking that although Pat Cox might be gone, his daughter would still be right here in his office and later would be in his bunk for as long as he wanted to keep her without her old man having the nerve to come back and get her.

Yes, Captain Nugent was mighty pleased with himself at the prospect of having a sweet, pure sixteen-year-old he could do anything he wanted to for as long as he wanted. She could just imagine the filthy thoughts that were slithering through his rakish male mind.

"You have kind of hurt my feelings, child," he said, trying to hide a triumphant smirk, "but I guess you gotta look out for your own pa, don't you?"

"Yes, Captain. Much as I want to help you, I do have to know that my pap is safe."

"Well, you know what I'm going to do?" He smiled expansively while pushing his genitals back inside his pants and buttoning every other button. "I'm going to call the sergeant back and tell him to get Pat Cox out of his cell and give him a ten-dollar bill and grub enough to get to the nearest town, take him to his horse, and tell him to ride on off."

"Why, Captain, I think that is just wonderful . . . that is the nicest thing for you to do for me."

"Honey, that ain't half as nice as the other things I'm going to do for you after we send your pa on his way." He picked up a bell that reminded Hope of those she had seen on schoolteachers' desks and rang it. In a moment or two, Kramer stuck his head in the door.

"You want me, Warden?"

"Sure do, Seth. This little gal has convinced me that I should let her father go even though the folks roundabout here are gonna be plumb disappointed to miss the entertainment."

The other man looked at Hope and she thought his eyes registered pity. He apparently knew the price she was expected to pay for her father's freedom.

"Yes, sir," Kramer said and started to leave.

"Oh and, Sergeant, will you tell my father to wait for me at Red Rock Pass?"

"Sure will, miss."

"Yeah, tell him to wait no matter how long it takes," Nugent said, trying to keep from laughing. "And here, file away this pardon on your way out so we'll have proof that it was done all legal-like."

The man took the paper, nodded, and left. When he was gone, Hope turned to face Nugent again. "I'm going to ask one more favor of you, Captain, before we get down to ministering to your complaint."

"Sure thing, honey, what is it you want?" He sounded a bit impatient but willing to wait now that he knew he was going to have his way.

"I'd like to stand at that window overlooking the courtyard and watch while my pap is brought out of his cell and walked out the gate. I want to see him get on his horse and ride away."

"Honey, you act like you don't trust me at all."

"That's not it, Captain dear," she said, trying to keep the sarcasm out of her voice. "It's just that I'm afraid something might go wrong. You know, some jumped-up underling might take it upon himself to disobey your orders. Things like that do happen."

"All right . . . all right, sweet little pigeon," Nugent said, going to the window and raising the sash to look out. Kramer was walking across the courtyard toward the cell block.

"Kramer, this little lady wants to see you bring her pa out and watch him mount up on his cayuse and ride off. Understand?"

"Sure do, Warden, sure do," Kramer said, and grinned at Hope, making her very sure she had done the right thing by insisting on this safeguard.

"Is that what you want, honeypot?" Nugent asked, reaching out with one big hand to pull her against his drooping belly.

"Yes, but let's wait until I see Pap leave, shall we? Why don't you go on over there and relax, and I'll come over to you in just a couple of minutes and do something for you that you'll never forget."

"Sure, little dove, but you kind of hurt me when you insist on all this checking up. I don't mean you anything but good, little dove."

You don't mean anything but to turn me into a dirty little dove, Hope thought as she watched the dusty, sunlit courtyard for the first sign of her father.

It took about ten minutes before he appeared, tall and lean, looking surprisingly fit, his wild red Irish hair brushed back and several days' growth of beard on his face. For a minute he stood looking around, blinking in the light, until he saw Star and Rollo tied up outside the now open gate.

He hesitated and seemed to look around for her, and Hope sucked in her breath in fear that he might not leave without her. But he started toward the gate, and she breathed a sigh of relief. Pat Cox knew his daughter well enough to trust her to look after herself and to take her word for it that she would meet him at Red Rock Pass.

As soon as he had accepted the money and the bag of provisions from Kramer and been escorted out the gate by the fat guard, Hope turned away from the window, starting toward Nugent, looking around the room for something she could use.

"You satisfied now, sweet child?" Nugent asked, and before she averted her eyes, she saw that his erection was again bared for what he thought would be her admiring glance and worshipful service.

"I'm satisfied," she said, listening to the sound of Star's hooves as the big piebald stallion carried her father away from the prison as fast as it could move.

"Then it's time that I should be satisfied, isn't it?" He lifted the organ protruding from his fly. "Me and this poor, hurting thing."

She was staring directly at it now with the obsidian, unblinking gaze of a mongoose watching a snake. She had already spotted the object she wanted; it was a crowbar, propped up against the wall below the window.

"You gonna take care of me, honey? Please do it quick, 'cause I'm getting awful achy waiting for you."

Her voice was cooing, soothing. "Close your eyes, lie back, and relax, Captain Nugent. I am your obedient servant. Just think of me as your loving nurse who is about to tend to your terrible affliction."

"Ummmm, that sounds nice . . . that nice cool voice . . . those nice cool hands and that nice cool young girl . . ."

"You are a very lucky man, Captain Nugent," she purred, "because you are going to be the very first person I ever did this for . . . the very first. Think of it as a kind of christening."

"Ahhh, so sweet . . . such a dear child."

"I am about to favor you with sensation and surcease such as you have never experienced before in your life."

"Are you sure it's gonna be all that different? All that wonderful?"

"I don't know about wonderful, but it is going to be different," she assured him as she tiptoed to the window and picked up the steel shaft. "I'm coming, dear Captain, and my instrument is all ready for your service."

"Ah, my dear little one," he all but drooled, his eyes tightly closed as a shudder of anticipated ecstasy shook him. He was sprawled back in the chair, hairy thighs spread wide, trousers down around his ankles.

"This is really going to thrill you," she said, moving closer with catlike stealth.

Halting directly in front of his chair, she lifted the heavy crowbar high above her head, gripping it so tightly with both hands that her knuckles turned white. She inhaled deeply, held her breath, and with all her strength swung the bar down squarely beween Nugent's widespread thighs. He uttered one strangled gasp, no louder than the squeak of a dying mouse.

"Jeee-ssuss Chree-ist!" His head jerked back and he stared up at her with eyes that bulged like a bullfrog's. Grasping the arms of his chair, he tried to rise, but his arms and legs were jelly. He collapsed, and slowly, like the snake she considered him, slid off his perch and slithered onto the floor to lie unconscious beneath his desk.

Hope stood over him for a moment. "Well, Captain, I 'spect you won't be awfully functional for a while, but look at it this way. I could have used this six-gun I got in my belt and put you out of your misery for a lot longer time."

She drew the gun and gripped it as she stood looking down at him. Sure as shooting, he didn't deserve to live, not only for what he had tried to do to her, but for all the things he'd said about those two poor women he had hanged and just for being a dirty skunk of a human male.

No, better not. If she shot him, they'd be after her for murder, but they might not for just turning him into a soprano. Besides, how was he going to explain to the sheriff and local judges what he had been doing with his dong out and ready to be assaulted? Maybe when he finally came to, he'd have to make up a story about catching it in a door or something. It was better to leave well enough alone, much as she regretted leaving him alive to torment other people.

"I'm going to spare your life, my Captain," she said, "not for your sake, but for mine. I hope you're grateful even though every time you go to take a pee you find you've not got much left to pee with."

Now it was time to get herself out of this place and that might take some doing since she figured everyone in the jail knew she was supposed to be entertaining the warden in a most private way.

Well, why not reinforce that thought in their minds, she decided, and walked over to the door of the office. Pulling her shirt down off one shoulder, she opened the door a crack and peeked out. As she had suspected, there was a guard standing in the hallway.

"The warden says I should tell you he is going to be attending to some very important business for the next couple of hours and you should see that he's not disturbed by anyone," she told the pimple-faced young man.

The guard flashed her a sly grin that conveyed his lascivious understanding. "Yo' all tell the warden, ma'am, that you and him can enjoy uninterrupted privacy." He snickered. "Wardens sure do get the best of everything though, I must say."

She winked in what she hoped was a lewd way. "Thank you, my good man," she said, and gave him a look that Sissy West, the madam down in San Antonio, used. "And better luck to you next time."

"Yes, ma'am... sure do hope so."

"Hope is one thing you got to remember, big man," she purred, still imitating Sissy. "'Cause Hope is my name and bringing hope to nice fellows like you is my game."

She thought his eyeballs were going to roll right out of his eyes, so she added just before she pulled her bare shoulder and head back into the room, "Now, you stay right there and keep hoping, and maybe when the captain is through, you and I—"

She closed the door and bolted it, giggling to herself. Then she walked over to look at Nugent again. He was lying flat on his back with his mouth open and his tongue hanging out. She wondered for a moment if he was still breathing and listened until she heard a faint but reassuring wheezing.

Going to the window, she opened it as quietly as possible. The fat guard was waddling across the yard toward what looked like a mess hall. Shadows were beginning to fall in the enclosure and the sun was sinking behind the encircling hills.

She waited until the guard was out of sight and then crawled up on the windowsill and lowered herself on the outside, hanging by her hands before dropping onto her feet as lightly as a cat. A quick look around assured her there was no one in the courtyard, and not even the guard in the tower had seen her unorthodox descent. Straightening her back and throwing back her head, she walked across the prison yard toward the door, whistling "The Yellow Rose of Texas."

The guard in the tower looked as she approached and inquired if she was leaving.

"Sure am, sir," she said. "And you know what? I forgot to convey my sincere thanks to Captain Nugent. Would you do that for me when you get off watch?"

"What you thanking him for?" the guard asked, cracking open the gate.

"Oh, he'll understand," she said, looking up at him with the same lascivious smile that had floored the scrawny youth in the hallway. "Only he could possibly understand how much I owed him and how happy I was to pay back at least part of it."

"I'll tell him," the guard said as the gate opened far enough for her to slip out.

"You say it in just those words, now," she said, almost skipping toward Rollo, who stood at the hitching post under a spreading oak tree. "In just those very words."

"I will," the man said as she unhitched the pinto and swung up into the saddle.

Hope leaned over Rollo's neck and whispered in his ear. "Run, little horse. Run like you've never run before!"

And Rollo ran, heading for the pass, as the huge red ball of the sun disappeared in the west and the purple night settled in.

Chapter 3

PAT COX WAS lying in a little grassy valley with his head on his saddle and one shabby boot resting on top of the other while Hope knelt before a buffalo-chip fire, frying bacon and toasting hardtack.

Pat looked better than he had in years, Hope thought. Being in jail might have faded his tan, but being off the booze had firmed up his belly and chin and taken the red out of his eyes. But right now he was sipping at a bottle of tequila that he had bought at a little Mexican cantina on the road to Amarillo. Working hard, she thought, to rot his brain and carcass again as soon as he had gotten dried out. Her pap was a good, hardworking man, one of the best horse wranglers she had ever seen and a top-notch soldier, but only when he was sober. And now he was doing his best to become unsober, only twenty hours out of jail.

"Nice of the warden to see that we got a grub stake, wasn't it, daughter?" Pat said between swigs.

"Yeah, but I already had some grub in my saddlebags," she said. "It's forage that I'm worrying about."

She looked over toward where Star and Rollo were contentedly grazing. That was good enough for now, but later they would need hay and oats because the grass was sparse in large areas of West Texas, and a horse couldn't keep going on so little.

"What did you have to do to get me out of jail?" Pat asked after his third or fourth drink. It was almost as though he had been working up his courage to get around to asking that question.

"I didn't have to do anything," she said. "I just had to promise a lot."

"What did you promise, and who did you promise it to?" Pat's hand dropped to his forty-four in an automatic reflex.

"It don't make no difference now, Pap," she said. "Nothing happened, except that a fellow whose name we both know got hisself an awful surprise and an even worse pain."

Pat halfway got up, his hand still on his gun. "I ought to go back there and put a couple of slugs in that son of a bitch!"

"Yeah, sure you should. Maybe you ought to shoot the warden and then go down to Austin and shoot the governor's secretary and get your damn-fool neck stretched for real this time."

She started to cry. Hope just wasn't the crying sort, so Pat Cox corked up the bottle carefully, put it down, got up, and put his arm around his daughter.

"What's the matter, honey? Was it pretty bad?"

"Oh, Pap, it was awful! I thought you were a goner for sure this time."

"There, there, baby. I'm the fellow who got through Pea Ridge, the Shenandoah Valley, and Malvern Hill. Shoot, that Malvern Hill was a son of a gun if there ever was one—them green-coated U.S. sharpshooters with their repeating rifles hiding out in those rifle pits was picking us off like we were fleas on a monkey's back, and old Massa Lee just kept telling us attack, attack, attack. Sometimes I got to thinking that as fine a man as he was, he didn't know nothing but charge."

She knew he was just rambling on because he was embarrassed by her breaking up. Pat Cox was what they called a man's man in the West, and women's emotions—either those of his hypersensitive, highly educated wife or his daughters—had never been of much interest to him. But seeing the usually stoic Hope dissolve in tears had shaken him. Swallowing the lump in her throat, she eased his discomfort by asking, "Green-coated Union forces? Don't you mean blue-coated, Pap?"

"Not the First and Second U.S. sharpshooters. They wore forest green and just kind of disappeared into the foliage usually, but when Little Mac got his tail feathers singed in the Peninsula campaign and decided to get his ass out of there, he left behind them sharpshooters and some other troops, and we just kept charging and charging 'em, and they kept shooting us down with them there damn rifles that they loaded on Sunday and fired all week."

"You were lucky, Pap," she said, wiping her eyes on her sleeve and moving toward the fire, where the coffee had begun to boil. "And you were lucky when you got out of that picture frame they had all set up for you, but, Pap, you can't be lucky all the time. If you ever even think about going back and getting hunk with Nugent, you luck is gonna end right there."

She smiled crookedly, poured the coffee, and handed him a cup. "Besides, I don't think being dead would make Nugent much more uncomfortable than he is right about now," she said.

"What'd you do to him, gal?"

"I ain't saying. It's something ladies don't talk about in polite society."

He looked over his shoulder and laughed. "I don't see no polite society around here. Them horses don't much care what we say. They ain't even much interested in what they say to each other as far as I can see." Pat looked longingly at the tequila, but started sipping at the coffee.

Hope breathed a sigh of relief. This wasn't any time for him to get drunk. They had to get out of Texas and fast, and she had a plan to accomplish that, but she wasn't quite ready to break it to him until he had some chow in him.

"That food 'most ready?" he asked.

"Pretty near," she said, wishing that she had thought to steal a couple of eggs from the hens she had seen wandering around in back of the cantina. There must have been a nest somewhere close by.

"Looking forward to it," he said. "Missed your cooking, gal. That slumgullion they fed us in prison was enough to make the army food look good."

"Wish it was more, but outside of some cornmeal and canned cow that I've got in my saddlebags, this is about all we rate right now."

"Smells good," he said, accepting a tin plate of thick crisp bacon and toasted hardtack to go along with his black coffee. "Better than your ma used to fix."

"Ma was a lady of learning," Hope said, wishing they could avoid this subject. "You couldn't expect her to be a drudge around the house, now could you?"

"Might of expected her to hang around and wait for a fellow when he got hisself in jail for something he didn't do."

"Mama was high-strung—"

"I almost was," he said with a chuckle.

"The nervous type. When you was convicted and sent up, she couldn't stand the suspense."

"Nearly killed me too," he said, chewing the bacon with loud smacking sounds.

Hope sat down opposite him on her saddle. "Well . . . she felt just awful about it all. She got a chance to teach school back in Richmond and decided that she better go and take Faith and Charity with her."

"They want to go?"

"They're just kids, Pap," she said. "What with one thing or another, they hardly knew you."

"So they wanted to go, huh," he said.

"Guess they was looking forward to the big city life." She felt so miserable telling him that she didn't want to eat.

"And she went off and left you all on your own just like that?"

"No . . . no, she's not that bad, Pap," Hope said hurriedly. "She pleaded and begged me to go along too, but—"

"You always was the best of them, Hope. The best of a bad bunch. I shouldn't of never married that lace-curtain lady. They don't hold up out in this country once they find out they have to get a few calluses on their hands."

"It wasn't like that at all, Pap. Mama is a woman of learning... she just felt like this was... stifling out here, where there wasn't any books or any music or theater. She wanted to be where it was civilized."

"Woman ought to wait for her man, no matter what," he grumbled. "Shouldn't of married that fancy lady in the first place. She wouldn't of married me iffen it hadn't been for the war. Around the time that the Texas cavalry rode into Richmond in '61, I was a captain and had gold braid on my arm up to here, so she thought I looked like a catch. Ha! Some catch. A buck sergeant in the U.S. Dragoons who got promoted real fast 'cause he knew which end of a carbine was the one that shot. Which was more than a lot of them gentlemen did. But I shouldn't of married her. Knew it wouldn't last."

"It lasted almost fifteen years, Pap," she said.

"Yeah, but she was always complaining about getting her hands dirty and you gals not having no fancy dresses or a proper education."

"She taught us everything we needed to know 'bout schooling and being ladies," she said defensively.

"Yeah, and what good is it in this country?" he said. "What I taught you will do you more good in this country... knowing how to shoot, hunt, ride, brand a cow, and stick to the hurricane deck of a mustang will do you more good than all that book learning."

"Sure, Pap, I got a great future as a cowboy, 'cept I don't know noplace where they're hiring lady cowboys. That is another thing most men think ought to be left to them."

"That ma of yours taught you a lot of crazy stuff about women and their rights."

"She taught me that men get all the gravy and the women

get what's left, and it ain't ought to be that way."

"She didn't teach you to say ain't, though."

"No, I learned that and how to cuss proper around cow camps," she said, swallowing coffee that was too hot and almost choked her. "But I can talk the other way when I've a mind to. I can turn it off and on just like it was a spigot."

"Fat lot of good it will do you out here."

"You never know, Pap . . . might meet one of the Vanderbilts or Morgans riding by some day, or an English milord who'll be just that surprised by my perfect diction and grammar that he'll up and ask you for my hand."

Her father roared with laughter. "How much do you suppose one of them milords would want for a dowry?"

"Half of Texas, probably."

"Hell, I'd give it to him if I owned it," he said. "Me and General Sherman never had much use for Texas."

"Why'd you join up with the Rebs, Pap? I think you were always happier in a blue coat than a gray one."

He shrugged. "Seemed like the thing to do at the time. They had such pretty flags, such pretty songs, and such pretty women."

"Pap, those were dumb-fool reasons to go to war," she said. "When the shooting starts, the pretty flags get furled, the singing stops, and the women stay behind."

"Sure seems like you're right," he said, sipping at his second cup of coffee. "Why do you figure I did what I done?"

"'Cause you was drunk." She got up and started to kick dirt over the embers of the buffalo-chip fire and pack up their frying pan and other gear. "The same reason you got yourself in that bank-robbing mess. You was drunk."

"Daughter, I wish you wouldn't say things like that. Sure, I'm a hairpin who takes a drink now and then . . . wouldn't be much of a man if I didn't. Man and boy, I've been able to belly up to the bar with the rest of the boys and down my share without ever getting what you might vulgarly refer to as drunk."

"Pap, you have been blind, staggering drunk so many

times that I can't remember how many it's been, and before that, Ma can't remember how many times she had to drag you out of a bar."

"Daughter, you wound me . . . you really wound me," he said, reaching for the bottle.

"Not half as much as that stuff wounds you," she snapped.

"Do I hear the faint sound of caterwauling, teetotaling temperance hellcats in your voice, daughter?" he asked, taking a big swig. "Do I hear echoes of your sainted mother, wherever she might be?"

"You know blame well where my mother is," she said. "And you also know that I'm no teetotaler. I'm just trying to point out to you that when you're sober, you're probably the best hand with a horse or a gun there is in this state, but when you're drunk, you ain't worth a hang to yourself or anyone else, much less the army."

"I ought to be a good man with a gun and horse," he said. "I was brought up with a forty-four in my fist and sitting straight up on the hurricane deck of a bronc."

"Sure you were. Sure, but I'll bet you had a bottle tucked in your napkin also," she said.

He howled with laughter. "Naw . . . no chance. My mama was one of them Iowa temperance ladies. She didn't let me have a drink till I was most three years old."

"Well, you've sure made up for it ever since," she said. "I can only recall three times I ever seen you sober and one of them was when you walked out of that jail."

"There you go, just like that schoolteacher ma of yours," he sulked.

"No. If I had as many brains as my ma, I would be back in Richmond with her and you'd be swinging from a gallows tree," she said. "And I sure wouldn't have bought you that booze you are sitting there swilling when we ought to be riding out of here."

She had poured the last of the coffee into her cup and packed the coffeepot away with the rest of the gear for loading on Rollo. Star was much too proud and impractical to be asked to carry anything except his master and his master's saddlebag, but Rollo was a sound-headed, hard-working little horse who was willing to do anything she asked as long he got his feed, a sugar cube once in a while, and his ears blown into now and then.

"You're right, I shouldn't say that kind of things about you, Hope." Pat Cox had the mercurial Irish temperament and now he was feeling guilty. "I shouldn't of driven your poor sweet mother away with my beastly drinking and sexual attentions, and I shouldn't of let you stay here in Texas all alone to help me. I'm just a worthless, rundown ex-cowboy who don't deserve the things you do for me. You should have let them hang me and you'd of been free of me and could have gone back to Virginia, gotten yourself a lot of pretty crinoline dresses, and found a nice rich lawyer or cotton magnate and had one of them white houses with pillars in front instead of staying here in this wild country which no decent woman should even pass through."

"Pap, the only time I like you less than when you are blind drunk is when you're full of self-pity."

"Now, you just listen here, gal!" Pat was on his feet. "I don't got to take that kind of talk from a gal kid like you. You ain't your fancy-assed ma, who always did think she had married beneath her and was better than me or anyone else around her. I'm your father and you ought to show a little respect for me. You hear?"

"Sure I hear, Pap," she said. She finished covering all evidence that the fire had been there and called to Rollo to come so she could throw the packs over him. "I also hear horses when I put my ear to the ground like you taught me like Indian scouts do."

"Horses?" He dropped to his knees and placed his ear to the ground and then looked up. "Those ain't Indian ponies either."

"No, they're shod, and I figure there are about ten or twelve of them. Seems like they're following our trail. Got to be a posse."

"We didn't leave any trail," he said.

She raised her eyebrows. "We didn't leave any that your

average white man could follow, but how about a Tonkaway Indian scout?"

"'Spect we better skedaddle, gal," her father said, carefully corking the bottle and stuffing it into his saddlebag before whistling for Star.

Star looked up and started trotting over toward them. Rollo came obediently along behind him. Rollo admired Star and followed him everywhere. Just like she did her old man, she thought. But a least Star wasn't a drinker, although he had gotten pretty wild on loco weed a time or two.

Pat was checking to make sure she hadn't left any sign that a Tonkaway could follow, but she had spent too much time on the Stake Plains and in other Comanche and Apache country to do that. He nodded his head, satisfied, after a few moments of inspection.

"'Spect you'll make a pretty good scout yourself one of these days, gal," he said.

She tossed her bags across the pinto's back and clinched the saddle up beneath his firm belly, wondering just how long it would stay full and content if they were going to be running from every sheriff and marshal in Texas. She had a plan to get them out of this, but she wasn't ready to try it on her father yet. He would have to get the feeling of being hunted down before he would be willing to use his head. He was always a man who preferred to use his fists or his guns than his brain, although he had been a crackerjack scout back in the old Dragoon days and could speak three or four Indian languages, which was more than most white men in this part of the country or farther north could do.

"Mount up, gal," Pat said as he finished tightening his saddle. Then he looked up and saw that she was already sitting straight in the saddle and waiting to go.

"I think I can hear them without help now," he said, his hand to his ear and his face toward the wind. "They're coming fast and they've picked up something."

"When we came through the draw, I think we might have disturbed some of the brush on either side, leaving a sign a good scout could follow, even though we came across hard rock."

"There'a a little stream that flows into the Pecos down the valley a ways," he said. "We'll shake 'em there."

"There ain't no horse in all of Texas that can catch Star," Pat said. "If they get close, I want you to change horses with me so you get away at least."

"Don't bother yourself over it," she said. "This little pinto will outrun your Star in this rough country every time, even if he can't keep up on an open course."

There was a shout from down the trail, and a gun was fired into the air as though to summon scattered horsemen.

"Come on, let's hightail," Pat said, putting spurs to Star and sending him into an exaggerated leap forward.

"Right after you," she replied, whispering encouragement into Rollo's velvet ear. The little horse took after the big stallion with a surefooted gait that only an animal raised in Indian country could be capable of.

"They're coming . . . they're coming," Pat shouted as a band of horses suddenly rounded a clump of scrub timber and rode after them with a shout of triumph.

"Damnit, I can see them!" Hope said, kicking Rollo in the sides to get him to run faster.

The pinto leaped forward with a spurt of speed that swayed Hope back in her saddle, but she hung on even though her sombrero whipped back off her head and hung by its chin strap behind her neck.

Star's long strides were eating up the ground, but the little pinto was taking two strides to the big stallion's one and managing to keep up through sheer grit.

They were racing out of the hill country now, down into a long narrow canyon where they would have been caught in a trap if they hadn't been sure of their way.

"Snake Creek's a little ways ahead," Hope said. "We'll be among the trees along its bank in a couple of minutes and be able to shake them when we go upstream."

"What's to keep them from going upstream?" Pat said as they cut between several huge projecting rocks the size of miniature mountains.

"They'll go downstream 'cause they think we're headed for San Antonio," Hope said.

"I thought we were."

"So do they. That's why we're heading north toward Abilene."

"What the hell's in Abilene?" Pat demanded. "It's nothing but a dusty little town."

"There's cows in Abilene," Hope said, ducking her head as a shot rang out behind them. "And cows ain't looking for us like everyone else in Texas."

Pat Cox had pulled his revolver and was holding it in his hand, looking back over his shoulder.

"Put that away," his daughter said. "We're not going to fight it out with them."

"Why not? We're already on the hanging list of every sheriff and marshal in the state. We ain't got noplace to go."

"Sure, we have," she shouted as they entered the first of the trees that shaded the banks of Snake Creek. "We can go north."

"North? We ain't got no money and not much food. We can't go anywhere without money and food."

"I know where we can get both," Hope said.

"Well, I wish you'd tell me where," he said as they slowed, eased their horses down the steep bank of the river, and splashed into the water.

"Upstream, and hurry!" Hope urged. They were now shielded from the sight of the posse by both the trees and the banks of the stream.

They could hear shouts behind them as though those pursuing were shouting back and forth to each other. Then the voices started to fade away as they raced upstream and the others went down.

Rollo was picking his way carefully along the sand and rock bottom of the river, the two or three feet of water splashing around him. Hope was soaking wet from her boots up to her gun belt, but she was holding the Colt in her hand to keep it dry. She was determined not to fire at the men who were following them and to keep her father from doing so, but since there was always a chance of running into a rattler or an Apache, she wasn't going to let her powder get wet.

"I think we've lost them." Pat was breathless and his big horse was breathing heavily from the struggle through the water.

"Keep in the stream!" she shouted. "It's no use leaving a clear trail for whoever's scouting for 'em. The farther we go in the stream bed, the better off we're going to be."

"Yeah, if we don't catch our death of grippe from getting soaked this way."

"The sun will dry us," she said. "'Sides, you got your cold remedy in your hip pocket, ain't you?"

"No point wasting it on that. What the hell we gonna do in Abilene when we get there?"

"Tell you later." She had forged ahead of him and had to turn around to shout. "Let's make sure we've shaken that posse before we start talking 'bout what we're going to do and what we ain't going to do when we get to Abilene," she said.

"*If* we get to Abilene," her father said, pointing back to a dozen dark figures, obviously men on horseback, who were again heading toward them. "Come on, girl, ride!"

They were off into open ranchland now, but their horses were tired from the struggle along the stream, and the posse's horses fresher from having run across open country. But at least they had gained a little ground by going downstream for that short time.

"They shouldn't have figured out which way we were going so fast," Hope said.

"It's that damn Tonkaway," Pat Cox said. "They can smell a man they're after. Even the Apaches aren't as good as they are."

"Well, we have a good lead on them, and if the horses hold out, maybe we'll be able to shake them after sunset," she said, looking at clouds to the west. "Or maybe sooner if that storm that's building up breaks over us."

"Don't count on it," he said. "You couldn't shake a

Tonkaway if ten feet of snow fell after you had passed. But there's hills up ahead. Why don't I pick a good place and lay for them and put a slug through that damn Indian. They'll be blind without him."

"You leave that Indian alone," she said. "The Tonkaway are good people. He's just doin' his job. There's no call to kill him over it."

"Some people in Texas don't think the Tonkaway are such good people," he grumbled.

"There's some folks in Texas that don't think God is good either," she said.

"Texas people know who their friends are," he said. "All you got to do is look at this state and know damn well that God didn't intend any good for the people who had to live in it."

She didn't answer that. She liked Texas and she knew that Pat did too; he was just talking to keep up their morale.

Half an hour later as she looked back she could see that the riders behind them were starting to gain, and in another hour she was aware that their horses were starting to tire.

"Come on . . . Come on, gal, we can make it into them hills if that damn horse of yours can just keep up."

"Rollo's keeping up," she said. "It's your horse that is about to flounder."

"No . . . come on, Star . . . come on!"

The big stallion had greater strength and a longer stride then the pinto, but he didn't have the cow pony's stamina and heart.

"I guess you're right. Star is about done in. We got to find someplace to hole up or we're finished."

"Rollo will run till his heart gives out, but I ain't gonna push him to it," she said.

"Look, Hope . . . you be the best daughter a hairpin ever had, but there ain't no point you letting yourself be took with me or going down shooting it out with ten men. Why don't you ride on ahead and let me set up an ambush here and hold them off for a while?"

"Nothing doing. I didn't get you out of that jail in order

to leave you to die of lead poisoning out here on the prairie this way."

"Well, it won't do any good for both of us to get took," he said. "If you ride for it and I wait for them, they ain't likely to be looking very hard for you."

"You don't think so? Hell, Pap, after what I did to old Nugent, I 'spect they want me worse than they do you." She was watching the black clouds racing across the sky, and a little ray of hope was starting to spring up inside her. The hills were still a good two miles away, but the clouds and the oncoming night just might make a difference.

"Well, if they're after you, then that's all the more reason for me to turn back."

"And get your silly head shot off so I can get away?" she demanded. "There's no future in that. Either we both get away or we both get took, and we'll ask Colonel Goodnight or Uncle John Chisum to get us a lawyer who knows what he's doing."

A shot rang out, and she saw a little cloud of dust raised about a dozen yards ahead of them.

"They mean business. They don't care whether they shoot us or hang us," she said.

"Hope Cox, I am your father," Pat said, the sound of an important announcement in his voice, "and I am ordering you to ride on without me. It is my duty as a father to protect you and your duty as a daughter to do what I tell you to do."

"Keep riding, Pap . . . keep riding. Long as we keep riding, we got a chance."

"Yeah, a chance of getting a bullet in our backs," he said as another bullet winged past their ears.

"They're still a couple of hundred yards behind us and the hills are only a mile ahead," she said.

"But they're picking up on us all the time," he said. "I'm turning back."

He had drawn his pistol and started to rein his horse around to turn back to shoot it out with the posse, and she was reaching for his horse's reins to try to pull him on after her, when a streak of lightning suddenly laced across the sky and thunder like the collapsing of the heavens shook the rangeland.

Then the rain came . . . rain in blinding torrents that battered them and raised clouds of dust where the huge drops hit the parched earth.

Hope let out a whoop of delight. "The storm . . . the storm . . . we'll shake 'em now, Pap! We'll be in the hills before they can catch us!"

He hesitated for a moment and then, laughing and pulling his sombrero down lower over his face, he fired his six-shooter once in the general direction of the posse that they could no longer see and took off after her, heading for the hills and safety.

Chapter 4

THEY HAD SHAKEN the posse somewhere in the hill country as the storm flattened the grass and pounded water right through their supposedly waterproof ponchos. Finally, they had found a hidden canyon where there was grass and water for the horses and where dry firewood and twigs could be collected from beneath overhanging rocks to start a fire. Now they were sitting around the fire, hands wrapped around tin cups and bellies filled with bacon, hardtack, and beans.

"Pap, we got to get ourselves out of Texas fast," Hope said. "That posse meant business. You don't think old Nugent died, do you?"

"How in the hell do I know if you won't tell me what you did to him?" he said.

"It's a little embarrassing, but . . . well, either way, we got to get as far out of Texas as we can and as fast as we can."

"Yeah, where we gonna go? You got any ideas about that?"

"Pap, you are a fugitive from justice and I'm a fugitive

from injustice. I cracked the warden's most prized possession with a crowbar to get you out of jail. We got to get our tails out of here and head north."

"Why north?" he asked. "Why not head for the Mexican border? I knew a little gal down Nogales way—" He pulled the bottle out of his back pocket and took a big swallow.

"Pap, you know that little gal down Nogales way weighs about three hundred pounds and has got six bambinos clinging to her skirts. You want to go back there and tell everybody that you fathered the first one?"

"Well, we don't have to go to Nogales," he said. "There's lots of room in Mexico."

"There's not lots of work in Mexico."

"Oh yeah, there's that," he said as though work were a concept he wasn't quite ready to deal with.

"Yeah, there ain't no work. That is, unless you was planning on getting yourself a couple of crossbelts and joining the banditos. You got any idea to keep on knocking off banks, or maybe trying for a stagecoach next?"

"No. No, honey, you know I ain't no hardened criminal," he said. "I just got in jail because of circumstances beyond my control."

"But not beyond the control of that bottle," she said. "That bottle held up the bank along with the Price brothers. Pat Cox didn't."

"Yes, yes, Carrie Nation, I hear."

"You better hear me," she said. "I didn't get you out of that hangman's noose to see you drink yourself to death or go off down Mexico way to shoot up the poor peasants and call yourself a big man."

"I didn't say I wanted to do none of them things," he said, reaching for the bottle again.

"Then leave that dang bottle alone and listen to me!" she snapped.

"That ain't no way for no girl child to talk to her pap," he said. "It don't show proper respect."

"Oh hell, Pap, in some ways I'm twice as old as you, and it ain't showing lack of respect to try to get you to make something out of yourself."

"I done a lot of things right," he grumbled. "I'm as good a wrangler as any and I was a damn good horse soldier and scout."

"That's just what I'm talking about," she said, surprising him with her enthusiasm. "That's why I say let's head for Wyoming."

"They got work up Wyoming way?" he asked.

"Sure have," she said. "One of the kinds of work you're good at, being a horse wrangler and cowboy."

"What do you mean?"

"Up in Wyoming there is land for the staking out and it's the best cattle country, bar none. They say there's a beef bonanza coming up there that is going to make Texas cattle raising look like child's play."

"Never had much use for that cold country," he said. "Besides, where we gonna get money to buy cattle? And where we gonna sell them, when and if we get them?"

"We can always sell them to the army. And there's nothing like chasin' and killin' an Indian to make a soldier hungry for a good beefsteak."

"Maybe so, but maybe not. We still gotta get up there, still got to find land to stake out our claim, and then get ourselves some cow critters, and—"

"First thing we got to do, Pap, is get out of Texas and as far away as possible. Wyoming is a long way off."

"But like I said, we got to get there, and nobody is gonna give us no cows," he said.

"Suppose I told you that I got the first part, the getting there, all arranged for?" She was leading up gradually to this part of her idea, the part her father really wasn't going to like because it involved really hard work, trail driving.

"Yeah, that'd be good," he said. "Maybe we could hunt along the way."

"Maybe you could take the job I lined up for you with Uncle John."

"Chisum? That crook? Why, after what he did to Colonel Goodnight, I wouldn't even speak to him, much less ride with him."

She had been expecting this and knew it didn't have

anything to do with the fact that Chisum had flung a fairly loose rope and been free with his branding iron from time to time. Her pap just wasn't all that fond of hard work. Well, she liked it. She had told herself a long time ago that there wasn't any other way people like them were going to get ahead in the world except by hard work, and she had worked hard since she was seven years old and had gotten to the point where she didn't mind blisters on her hands from hauling on a lariat or calluses on her butt from long hours in the saddle. She figured there were lots of worse ways of making a living. It was a lot better than slaving in some workshop back East or being a sod-buster and trying to grow crops on land that was meant only for grazing buffalo or cattle.

"Pap, Colonel Goodnight forgave Uncle John years ago for those bloated cows he tried to palm off on him, so I figure you ought to be willing to do likewise."

"Hm . . . well, the colonel is an awfully forgiving man," Pat said. "I'm not so sure that I am."

"I thought maybe you'd get around to it, though," she said. "That's why I talked to Uncle John and his trail boss, Jeb Mason, last week, about a job for you, and one for me, too."

"You mean trail driving?" he asked.

"Pap, Uncle John is taking a herd through Wyoming, and he needs trail drivers. He knows us and he's willing to hire us and look the other way when we give him different names."

"What about this Jeb Mason?" he said. "He don't know us."

"He knows me," she said. "And he thinks my name is Clover Crawford."

"Clover Crawford? What in the hell kind of name is that?" her father demanded.

"That's the name I made up, 'cause I figured I would need a pen name like Nellie Bly if I ever got to be a big-time lady reporter like she is."

"Hm. No lady would do that kind of work," he objected.

"No lady would be a horse wrangler or a cow nursemaid

or bust the balls of a warden to get her father out of jail either," she said. "I wasn't aware that anyone had ever called me a lady. 'Sides, I hear that Nellie Bly is a perfect lady 'cept when she is flying around in a balloon or doing something else daring to get a story for her paper."

"What about this here Jeb Mason fellow? Did he believe you got a strange name like that?"

"I 'spect he did," she said. "I 'spect he didn't care 'cause he was so busy looking at my figure, he didn't have much time for my name 'cept to keep saying it over and over again in a nice husky whisper."

"You been lallygaggin' with this trail boss?" he demanded, sitting up in his saddle. "What you been doing while I had my back turned?"

"I been plotting to get you out of the state pen and then out of the state itself," she said. "Jeb—that's short for Jebel—is a real hunk of a man. Six-foot-two, with a straight nose, a chin that's kind of set like the bow of a ship, and muscles like they were made out of left-over steel cable when they built the Brooklyn Bridge."

Her father was sitting up all the way. "You been sparkin' with this here fellow Mason?"

"Jebel and I have done a little riding and walking together down by the Pecos, but I wouldn't say it was sparking," she said with a toss of her hair. "That's not to say that I might not, if he asked me."

"Now, you listen here to me, gal," Pat said. "I'm your pa and I got some say about who you gonna be sparkin' with and not sparkin' with and I don't like this Jeb fellow at all."

"I prefer to call him Jebel," she said. "It's a lot more romantic."

"Since when did you start worryin' 'bout romantic names and the like?" he asked.

"Just 'cause I mostly never wear nothing but jeans and a shirt don't mean I don't look pretty when I dress up or fellows don't notice me when I got my hair combed and all," she said, sniffling.

"Well, now look here, child. I ain't saying that you ain't

pretty...your ma was pretty, so you're bound to be. But I just don't trust no cowboy, or trail boss either, 'round my daughter, less'n I'm around to see what's going on between 'em."

"Well, you're going to get plenty of chance to see what's going on because I signed us on for that trail drive."

"Trail drive! Lord, girl, that's hard work. You ain't fit. No gal is fit for a trail drive, pushing a bunch of balky whitefaces a thousand miles through northerners and injuns and...being around a bunch of skirt-happy cowboys and a trail boss I ain't never heard of. What's his name again?"

"Mason, and you better learn to call him Mr. Mason. You know good and well that if Uncle John Chisum hired him, he's a good man with a gun and a good man with a herd of cows."

"Hm...Chisum never carries a gun hisself, but he don't need to because he can always hire other men to do it for him," Pat said.

"Well, you know there isn't anyone else who would hire us 'cept maybe Colonel Goodnight, and he ain't driving any cows north this spring. 'Sides, Colonel Goodnight wouldn't be willing to keep it secret who we are, like Uncle John is. The colonel would probably hire us a lawyer and talk to the governor about us, but he wouldn't hide us out without being sure in his conscience about it. What conscience Uncle John's got don't get sore all that much that I ever noticed."

"So you're going to be this Clover Crawford to Mason and the rest of the hands, but what about me? Am I gonna be named Crawford too?"

"Either that or we're gonna have to tell them that you are not my pop," she said. "But I thought you could probably keep your first name. Don't 'spect you'd answer too easy to anything but Pat."

"How 'bout you and Clover?"

"Oh, I'll remember. Somehow I always thought I was meant to be named Clover. Not that I don't like Hope. You might say that Clover is a lady that has a lot of hope. Hope for the future. Specially our future at the end of this trail."

"Why the end of this trail?" Pat was getting used to listening to his daughter's ideas.

"'Cause this trail ends at the Bosque Grande," she said. "That's where Uncle John and Jebel Mason are getting together one of the biggest herds ever to push up north, and they're just waiting for a couple more top hands like us."

"Some top hands for a trail drive. A sixteen-year-old girl and a thirty-year-old ex-trooper and bank robber—"

"Thirty-year-old, ha! Not unless you had me when you was fifteen, and I don't think Ma would have married no fifteen-year-old high-pocket when she was twenty."

"'Spect I forgot a few years there," he said getting to his feet. Then he put the bottle back in his pocket, lifted his saddle, and handed her the coffee cup. "Well, if that's what we're gonna do to get to Wyoming, guess we better get with it," he said. "Uncle John Chisum don't like waiting nohow, not even for a couple of top hands."

"That's the way to talk," she said, starting to pack away their gear and wrap her poncho around it to load on Rollo's back. "That's the way I like to hear my pap talk. Up and at 'em all the way!"

The Bosque Grande was a big grove of cottonwoods in a bend of the Pecos River, and in the broad meadows along the stream, Chisum pastured his gaunt cattle until he could start them north. There were soldiers at nearby Fort Sumner, so the herds were reasonably safe, at least until they started up the Texas trail toward Colorado, Wyoming, Nebraska, and the Dakotas. But anything north of Sumner was likely to get lively, from what Hope had been told, with half the Indians in the West off the reservations and traders and missionaries filling them up with whiskey and hatred for the white man and all his works.

Not that the poor devils didn't have a lot to get even for, Hope knew. Colonel Goodnight was one of the greatest of all the Indian fighters and had harried the Comanches all during the Civil War. While he wouldn't fight for Texas and the Confederacy, he didn't see anything wrong with defending the land and families of his neighbors who did. But the Colonel had told Hope that the Indians were probably treated worse than anybody in America, except maybe the Negroes.

"We ran 'em off their land and stole their hunting grounds," the Colonel had told her when she was still young enough to sit on his knee. "And I was one of the worst of the ones who did, I guess. But, you know, they never held it against me. They are brave men and they admire brave men and warriors. They ain't got no use for a coward or even a peaceable man."

The Colonel had related how during the war he had learned to follow a straight course, how he had learned to know, by day or night, every bush and shrub that indicated water. He could even tell by the flight of birds whether they were going far to water or whether it was close. When he looked at a track, he could tell how old it was, for he knew that only at night did the minute desert insects come out and leave their tiny trails.

He had been chief guide for Captain Jack Cureton and his company of Rangers and had always ridden ahead of the command. Ten Tonkaway scouts followed him, and behind them came the company of Rangers. As a dare to his Indian enemies, Charles Goodnight wore a vest made of leopardskin. Soon the Comanches came to know that spotted garment and the man who led off alone, and they named him Leopard Coat. They had also given him a second name—Dangerous Man.

"Yeah, little lady, I was plumb pizen to them Injuns, but later on they used to come down to my ranch in Palo Duro Canyon to visit me. I was plumb surprised that men I had harried, whose brothers I had killed, wanted to come 'round just to shake my hand.

"Why, there was this one old man who rode hundreds of miles just to see me, and you know what? I had shot that fellow back in '62 and left him for dead on the field. He showed me the wound where the bullet had gone through, but he told me, 'Dangerous, I bear you no ill will, you fought man to man and you did not scalp me when you could have.' But we done lots worse things then scalp them people. We took away their land and their livelihood, and they got their rights, but they probably will never win them without fighting. And you know what, little lady? If they do, I will probably be one of the first who will go out and fight against them... and they'll respect me for that, just like I respect them for fighting for their rights."

Hope thought she understood that, but she had always known that the Colonel was a very deep man, possibly the smartest as well as the straightest man in her part of Texas. She had always liked him better than she did Uncle John, but Uncle John was good in his way too, at least to his friends, and she and her pa were his friends, and now they were going to have to depend on him to get them out of Texas.

"Keep riding, Pap. It ain't so far now," she said. "It ain't so far to Bosque Grande."

"Yeah, Bosque Grande and a hard job," Pat said sourly.

Chapter 5

THE SUN WAS starting to drop behind the western mountains when they came out of a draw and found themselves looking down on Bosque Grande, nestled in a broad curve of the Pecos River, surrounded by a huge grove of cottonwoods, and with tens of thousands of cattle grazing in the broad meadows along both banks of the river.

"A mighty pretty place... a mighty pretty place," Pat said, surveying it and listening to a cowboy singing far off, not to the cows, but to let the others know where he was in case of an accident. "Always did say old Uncle John knew how to get his hands on the best of everything—horses, cows, and land."

"But not women," Hope laughed, referring to the well-known cattle-country legend of the woman John Chisum had loved and lost, the woman to whom, it was said, he had given his heart so completely that he could never look at another. As the story went, Chisum, who had grown up in Texas when it was still a republic, had fallen in love and become engaged to a beautiful young woman, and their wedding plans had been made when a dissipated lawyer had come to town and begun to court her through her parents.

The stranger was well educated and soon won over the mother and father, who hadn't liked young John to start with because of his cowboy manners and clothing. They had gone to work on the girl and finally persuaded her to marry the lawyer. The worst part of it for Chisum was that the lawyer treated the girl like a dog from the very beginning.

Chisum had never tired of telling Colonel Goodnight about this sad affair. No matter where they met on the wide plains along the Pecos or elsewhere, Chisum would keep the Colonel awake all night while he poured out his heart about this girl. He was, the Colonel had once told Hope, completely cracked on that one subject, although perfectly sane on everything else.

"That's what's warped John's life, Hope," the Colonel had told her. "It changed his nature completely and made him a miser and a thief. All he loves now is money and cows."

"Ah, Uncle Charlie, you know Uncle John thinks the world of you," she had said.

"Not so much that he wouldn't try to sell me a bunch of critters with the brands blotted over," the Colonel had said, pulling at his moustache. Obviously he had forgiven Chisum for what to him, the most honest man in Texas, was an ignoble deed, but he had not forgotten it.

"But who would Uncle John tell about that lady that he loved so much if he didn't have you, Uncle Charlie?" she had asked.

"Probably everyone else in the state," Goodnight had said. "He's told me about it enough times to cover every man, woman, and child in Texas."

Now, as they rode down the trail toward Bosque Grande with its sprawling ranch buildings, bunkhouse, barns, and the famous bar John Chisum had built for his cowboys, Pat asked Hope, "You suppose John Chisum is still watering his whiskey like he used to?"

"I hope so," she said under her breath.

It was almost dark as they rode up to the corral outside the roughly built ranch house. John Chisum didn't pay much more attention to his living arrangements than he did to his clothing. The house was little more than a shack, but the corrals were sturdily built and filled with well-groomed and frisky ponies.

Pat eyed the horses with appreciation. "One thing 'bout working for old John, there's always a good *remuda*. I rid me some of the best horses in the country the times I was riding for Chisum."

There were half a dozen cowboys hanging around the entrance to the bunkhouse and there was a smell of food cooking in the air. From the little ramshackle bar, a new institution of the ranch, there was the sound of an out-of-tune piano and voices raised in even more out-of-tune singing.

A tall black man with close-cropped gray hair, dressed in chaps and with a Stetson pushed back on his head, came down off the porch of the house and walked toward them with the typical bow-legged, rolling gait of a man who has spent most of his life in the saddle.

"Here comes Frank," Pat said. "Does he know who we're supposed to be?"

"If Uncle John knows, Frank knows," Hope said. "There ain't no one closer to John Chisum than Frank."

Frank had been a slave of John Chisum's back before the war, though he was now his horse wrangler and unofficial majordomo. A hard-riding, savvy man, he had the respect of most of those who rode for the Fence Rail brand despite the prevailing prejudice against black cowboys—or blacks of any kind, for that matter.

"Afternoon, Miz H—" Frank grinned, catching himself, "Miss Clover, that is. And who's this here gent'man?"

"This is my father, Frank . . . name of Pat Crawford," Hope said. "He's ridden for Mr. Chisum before."

"Sure, sure, now I remember," the black man said. "Mistuh Chisum, he's awaiting for you in the office. Mighty pleased to have you back. Mistuh Chisum, he's always short of good hands."

"A man with half the cows in the Southwest is bound to be short of hands," Pat said. "How many heads is the Fence Rail running this year, Frank?"

The black man pushed his hat back farther and scratched his head. "Must be somewhere 'tween thirty and forty thousand head, not counting calves and mavericks. We rounded up five thousand calves last year and found there was ten thousand more we hadn't gotten around to branding. That's a powerful incentive for a man with a loose rope, an unbranded maverick is."

"Sure is. That many, huh?" Pat said, and Hope didn't like the sound of speculation in his voice. She knew he was thinking that yearlings could belong to the first man who rounded them up and put a branding iron on their heaving flanks.

"Wyoming, Pap," she whispered as they followed Frank toward the Chisum house. "Remember, we're heading north to get us some ranch land."

"Yeah, sure, but a man could make a good living running a few hundred cows in this New Mexico country."

"If he had fresh water and the money to buy the cows," she said. The Pecos was alkaline past the point of being good for cattle. The secret of Chisum's success was a place called South Spring, a wonderful lake of clear, cold water, nearly eight acres altogether, which welled up on the nearby plain and where his tens of thousands of longhorns drank.

"Yes, suh. The judge is gonna be mighty pleased to see you folks," Frank was saying, obviously for the ears of Jebel Mason, who was sitting on the porch of the house with his brightly shined boots cocked up on the railing. It was apparent that the old horse wrangler didn't want the new trail boss to know that they had already been hired by the boss.

Jebel looked up, a wide grin crossing his tanned, handsome face when he saw Hope step up on to the porch.

"Howdy there, Miz Crawford," Mason said, getting to his feet so quickly that the chair he had been lounging in tipped over onto the porch. "Mighty nice seeing you again."

He made a little bow and took off his low-crowned black

hat, and the slanting rays of sun glistened on his curly black hair.

"It's a real pleasure to see you again, Mr. Mason," Hope responded, making the best curtsy she could manage in jeans, shirt, and chaps.

"I hope to be seeing more of you before we point 'em north," Mason said.

"Oh you will, you sure will," she said, giggling to herself because he didn't seem to know they would be going on the drive. Uncle John was never one to play any of his cards very far from his vest—but of course he was such an old miser that he never wore a vest.

Frank had opened the door to a dingy little office that was actually one of the rooms of the house, and they went in to find John Chisum sitting behind a battered old desk, with an apple crate for a chair and wearing his usual hand-me-down clothing.

"Pat! And dear little Ho . . . ah Clover," he said, a grin that was anything but miserly crossing his face. "Glad you could make it."

"So are we," Hope said. "'Specially since there was some people who didn't think we ought to come at all."

"Ah, now, is that so?" Chisum said, catching on at once. "Now ain't that just like some folks. Never want to see other folks get anywhere in this world."

Chisum took a bottle out from under the desk and two dirty glasses out of a drawer and poured a couple of fingers into each. "Don't suppose you're into the hard stuff yet, are you, sis?" he asked Hope.

"She ain't even into the soft stuff," Pat answered, reaching for his glass eagerly. "I'm clutching a bloody viper to my bosom, John. One of them genuine Carrie Nation antisaloon league types, and a real live suffragette to boot."

"Votes for females." John Chisum threw back his head and started laughing. "Haw, haw, haw, haw, haw! Now what for would women want to vote, anyway?"

"Maybe to keep you men from killing yourselves with John Barleycorn," Hope said as Chisum poured two more drinks.

"Haw, haw, haw, haw, haw!" Chisum went into another paroxysm of laughter. It was difficult to believe, Hope thought, that a man who laughed so much and always had a joke to tell was really the hard-fisted, miserly old skinflint he was reputed to be. A man who employed forty or fifty wild Texans who called themselves his "warriors," who trailed a free lasso, and were quick with the gun.

It was said that John Chisum never minded if someone stole a few cattle from him because he always knew that his hardcases would probably steal a whole herd from them. He was said to greet potential nesters with a glad hand and warm smile, and after offering to buy them out at a fair price—up to $500, anyway—he would turn his wolves loose on them if they refused his bid.

Well, it took a lot of things like that to become a cattle king, she supposed, and he had always dealt fairly with her and Pap, so she couldn't judge him too harshly. But come to think of it, Colonel Goodnight had never touched another man's cow in his life and he wouldn't keep men working for him who did. But the Colonel wouldn't have hidden them out on his cattle drive either.

John Chisum had launched into one of his stories again and her father was laughing with him.

"So this big-time operator comes here from St. Louis and he has him a good look at the fifty or sixty thousand head I'm running and at the fact that the Fence Line runs from the Stake Plains down to South Spring and beyond. And what do you know if that dude didn't up and offer me a million dollars for this place."

"A million dollars, John?" Pat was impressed.

"One million and, Pat, as God is my judge, here I was sitting in a twenty-five-cent straw hat, a hickory shirt that cost sixty-five cents, and pair of seventy-five-cent overalls, no socks, and brogans costing a dollar and a quarter—making a total of two dollars and ninety cents. But you know what I said to that fellow who was waving a million dollars in my face? I told him no thanks and then I told him why.

"'I would rather look at a cow than a dollar,' I told that

fellow. And what would I do with that much money? I can round up enough cattle before breakfast to pay every dollar I owe."

Pat Cox was leaning back in his chair, hat tilted back on his head, looking as though he was ready to settle in for an evening of drinking and bulling with John Chisum. Hope figured she'd better break that up quick as she could.

"When's the trail herd pushing out, Uncle John?" she asked.

"First of the week," Chisum said. "Figure the boys need a little free time after driving them cows in from Texas."

"Well, it can't be too soon for us," she said. "Them folks who were looking for us might drop by."

"Suppose you make camp down by South Spring, and if they come by, they won't find you. Nobody goes near my fort."

"Well now, John, I heared you were looking for men, but I ain't heared what you was paying for top hands," Pat said, becoming serious now that he knew Hope was trying to hurry things along to get him away from the whiskey.

"Seventy dollars a month and found," Chisum said without hesitating.

"Them's gunfighter wages, Mister John," Pat said, twirling the whiskey glass between his hands.

"That's what we're going to need—men who can handle a gun, to push those cows through to Lincoln with half the Injuns in the country off the reservations," Chisum said. "I hired me one of the best trail bosses, and I'm hiring me the best hands I can get, too. I'm going along myself this time just to see to things, 'cause I'll be taking some of Charlie Goodnight's cows as well as mine and my Texas friends'."

"Well now, John, trail herding is powerful hard work, and—"

"That's top wages, Pat," Chisum said flatly, showing he wasn't interested in bargaining.

"We'll take it," Hope said. "What about me?"

"Twenty dollars and found to help out Cooky," Chisum said, grinning at her.

"Cooky, hell! I'll outride any man you got at point side

or drag," she said, "and Rollo's the best little cow horse in this whole country. He can talk cow better than a cow can."

"And you'll wear the saddle right through him on a three-and-a-half month cattle drive," Chisum said. "We're talking a *remuda* along of eight horses for every man."

Hope gulped. She had heard how hard a trail drive was on horses, but she had never imagined that it would take eight months for every rider to make it to Nebraska and the Wyoming country. "I'll hold up with the rest of them anyway," she said stubbornly.

Chisum looked at her and nodded. "I know you will, sis," he said. "I'll give you fifty a month, and I won't expect you to carry no gun. I don't carry one myself, you know."

That was one of John Chisum's peculiarities. He never wore a gun. But a man with fifty gunmen in his pay didn't really have to.

When she saw Chisum pour another glass of whiskey for her father and himself, Hope gave up thinking she could get Pat away and comforted herself with the memory that all of Chisum's whiskey was supposed to be watered to keep his crew half sober and to save him money.

She had heard that at his small bar a cowhand's credit was always good, but the whiskey was always full of water. Once an outraged hand had exclaimed, "Aw, come on, Uncle John, give the fish a chance to swim. Open up a new barrel of whiskey!"

"All right," agreed Chisum, and served it straight from the keg. In fifteen minutes, every cowboy was falling down drunk. One glass of that pure whiskey had paralyzed them all, and after that the boys stopped complaining about what the fish were going to swim in.

So even if Pap sat drinking with John Chisum all evening, he probably wouldn't be blind drunk and get in trouble, and she had something else on her mind. She was thinking that Jebel Mason just might be sitting out there on the porch, looking at the rising moon and maybe waiting for her. She was real interested in that last part, more interested than she had ever been in anything any other fellow had ever done.

"Well, I guess I'll take a walk and look at what you done

since the last time we was here, Uncle John," she said.

"Take a look at that new adobe corral," Chisum said. "I built it to keep the Mescaleros from running off my horses. They must of stole a thousand horses and mules from me since I been here, but they never take a shot at me. I guess they figure that if they kill me, there wouldn't be any damn fool to keep bringing in horses for them to steal. Haw, haw, haw, haw, haw!" Chisum could go into fits of laughter even about his own misfortune.

"Did that adobe corral do any good?" Pat asked.

"Hell no, the thieving heathen just dig holes in it and sneak the horse critters out one at a time. Got me four men doing nothing but standing night guard with Winchesters, but I reckon the Apaches will figure out a way to steal horses right under their eyes one of these days."

Hope had been gradually slipping out the door and now was out on the porch looking around, disappointed to find that Jebel Mason was no longer lounging in the chair there. Before she could really get to feeling down, however, a soft voice spoke from behind her.

"Howdy, Miz Clover, you looking for something?" And there was Jebel looming over her, a very tall shadow against the rising moon.

"I was just wondering where my horse Rollo was," she said quickly.

"Well, I suspect Frank took care of it as well as the horse of that fella you were with," Jebel said, and she loved the way his soft southern drawl wrapped around the words.

"Oh yes, 'spect he did," she said. "You know, Mr. Mason, I was wondering what part of the country you came from. You don't sound like no GTT." (GTT meant "Gone to Texas" and signified that a fellow had had to leave wherever he had been more for the benefit of his neighbors than his own.)

Jebel laughed huskily, in a very masculine way that made her heart flutter. "No, I wasn't run out of anyplace up north," he said. "Raised mostly down Galveston way. My pa brought me and the other kids here from Louisiana when I was a thirteen-year-old high-pockets."

He looked to be twenty-three or so. That meant he thought he was much too old for a gal who was sixteen going on seventeen. Or did it? Men like old Bobby or Warden Nugent didn't think they were, and they were a lot older than twenty-three. Maybe, just maybe, he wouldn't think he was too old, because she sure didn't.

Frank rounded the side of the house just then. "Miz Clover, I put your horse in the corral 'long of the rest of them and saddled up a nice little filly for you if you're wanting one."

"Thank you, Frank. I would like a horse. I was thinking of riding down by the South Spring, where Uncle John says there's a good place for me and my pap to camp."

"Get you that filly right now," Frank said and hurried off, despite his rheumatism and the limp from a broken leg received when he had been thrown during a stampede and never set quite right.

"You say you're going to ride down by the spring," Jebel Mason said. "Maybe I better ride along and see that you're okay. We got some pretty tough hombres down there in what Uncle John calls his fort."

She wanted to see how eager he was to ride off in the moonlight with her, so she pretended to hesitate.

"I can take care of myself with any kinds of snakes that walks or crawls," she said, patting the forty-four she was wearing on her belt.

"Just the same, it might be better to have someone they respect along with you," Jebel said, a smile in his voice. "Then you won't have to put holes through any of them."

"Well, seeing how it cost Uncle John a lot of money he says he can't afford to keep them fellas in victuals and rot-gut, I guess I shouldn't put no holes through such expensive property."

"You wait right here while I get my horse and I'll show you the nicest little place to camp out down by the spring that you ever did see in your life. Best place to see the moon over the Pecos is there, too. It even makes that alkali water look pretty."

"I'll be waiting," she said as he hurried off and Frank

came whistling, bringing a docile little filly that followed behind him without any sign of reins.

"Here you are, Miz Clover. This is nice little hoss name of Sally," the wrangler said. "All you got to do is ask her nice and she'll do whatever you like without no bit or spurs."

"Well, she won't get any spurs from me, Frank."

"I knows that, Miz Clover. That's why I picked Sally for you to ride on for now."

She thanked the black man and nuzzled the horse, who whinnied softly, then she pulled herself up into the saddle and sat waiting, her heart pounding with excitement.

"I 'spect that handsome Mr. Jebel Mason wants to do some sparking, little horse," she whispered to Sally. "And although I ain't never done no sparking before, I'm plumb all aflutter about it and him."

Sally's only answer was another soft nicker, but it somehow made Hope think the filly understood.

Chapter 6

SALLY WAS A nice little horse, Hope decided, as she rode beside Jebel Mason along the trail beside the Pecos toward South Spring. On one side of the trail, a ditch had been dug that brought fresh, cool water from the spring to Bosque Grande itself—drinking water for the cattle and horses that roamed the range and for the people of the ranch. It had also been diverted to run under Chisum's house so the Chinese cook could dip it up in buckets through a hole in the kitchen floor for cooking and washing dishes.

"It is right nice of you to let me ride along of you, Miss Clover," Jebel said, looking at her in a way that meant he had been watching her silhouette in the moonlight.

He's interested in me, she thought happily, truly interested. Not like old Nugent or oily Bobby Kidwell, but in a nicer, more exciting way. A way that made her appreciate his soft southern drawl, his jet-black curly hair, and the way his teeth gleamed in the dark when he laughed.

"Why, I sure appreciate your wanting to see me on my

way, Mr. Mason," she replied, wondering if he realized she was only sixteen.

"Please call me Jeb," he said, his knee touching hers as their horses came closer together.

"I prefer Jebel, if you don't mind," she said. "It has kind of a poetical sound, like maybe it came out of the Bible or someplace."

"Jebel was what my ma used to call me 'fore she died of the cholera down in New Orleans," he said.

"It's a nice name."

"So is Clover," Jebel said. "Kind of reminds a fellow of a nice green valley maybe, with Texas bluebells growing 'stead of mesquite and sagebrush all around."

"Thanks," she said, a little embarrassed and wondering if he would like Hope as well and also wondering if he thought she was too young. Heck, a girl who was almost seventeen wasn't too young, she told herself. After all, lots and lots of gals got married at thirteen—even eleven or twelve out in Mormon country, people said.

A bird was singing, a low plaintive song that she couldn't identify and frogs were croaking along the river banks. The Pecos had turned to silver in the moonlight, hiding the brackish brown face it usually turned toward the world.

"You been a trail boss very long, Jebel?" she asked.

"'Most on two years now," he said. "Took a couple of herds north for Colonel Goodnight and before that, one for his partner, Oliver Loving. . . that was before the Comanches got Mr. Loving."

"Why, you must have been just a boy then," she said. "Uncle Charlie told me about his old friend Oliver and how the Comanches killed him and all."

"I didn't know you knew the Colonel," Jebel said.

"My pap used to work for him back in the early 'sixties," she said. "He made one of the runs across the Stake Plains to Trail City, Colorado."

"That's more or less the way we'll be going this time," Jebel said. "From Trail City we'll push on up to the South Platte and make a jog west to Cheyenne. The army's plumb hungry for good Texas beef."

"It sounds as though it will be an exciting trip," she said. "Will there be trouble with the Indians?"

"Injuns, northers, lack of water that drives the cattle crazy and starts them to stampeding, rustlers, and the blasted nesters who don't want anyone's cows stirring up the dust around their precious wheat and corn crops. The nesters are probably the worst of all the pests we'll be running into."

"I guess it takes a brave fellow to drive a herd as far as Cheyenne," she said, knowing she shouldn't be teasing him this way, because he would be mad as hell when he found out that she was going along and had known it all along. "You always gonna be a cowboy?"

"No. No, I suspect maybe I'll settle down up north in Cheyenne or the Dakotas. Maybe buy me a piece of land and run some cows or something like that."

"I'm going to find some land myself and build a ranch, maybe on the Powder River."

"Build a ranch?" He was incredulous. "I didn't know there were ladies in that business. Ranching is hard work, hard dirty work. Can't feature a girl like you wanting to do that kind of work."

There it was again. Men and boys always assumed there were only certain things a woman could do. That was bunk as far as she was concerned. A woman could do just about anything she set her mind to do.

"Seems to me a gal ought to be thinking about getting married, 'specially a pretty little thing like you," he said.

He thinks I'm pretty. Well, that's good, but why does that mean I ought to be thinking only about getting married?

"Seems to me you're too refined and well spoken for that kind of life," he said.

"My mother was a schoolteacher," she said. "She taught me to read and write and take down shorthand. But I guess there's a lot of ladies who are lots of things," she added. "They're not all chattels, following along behind their men like the Mormon women."

"Well, there are women like Calamity Jane—seen her use a bullwhip one time, real mean-like," he said. "But don't know if she makes any claim to being a lady."

"Well, I might not be able to drive a team of oxen or mules, but I can ride a horse as well as anyone," she said, wishing she had a more spirited mount than Sally under her so she could show him.

"Oh I seen you when you and your pap came riding in," he said quickly. "Never seen a lady who could sit a horse better, and without a sidesaddle."

"Never used a sidesaddle in my life."

"You mean even when you're wearing skirts, you don't?"

"Don't have no occasion to wear skirts 'cepting when I'm in town, and then I either walk or ride in a buckboard," she said, remembering that the last time she'd had a skirt on was when she'd hoodwinked old Bobby. But one of these days she was going to have lots of fine dresses—when she had her own ranch and was getting into politics and working for women's rights and good government.

"Bet you look even prettier in skirts than in jeans and shirt," he said gallantly.

"Well, maybe, but I'm more comfortable this way," she said, recalling the effect her pink gingham dress had had on Bobby. If Jebel Mason ever saw her in that, she wouldn't mind if he wanted to put his hands on her the way Bobby had. If he did it, it would be in a different way, nice and sweet, and his hands wouldn't be sweaty like Bobby's.

"This is the place I was telling you about," Jebel said as they moved through a shallow depression into a valley that sloped gently down toward the Pecos. The moon was so brilliant that she could see that the little vale was covered with deep, lush grass on which a few head of cattle were contentedly grazing at the far end. Cottonwood and chaparral obscured the banks of the river, but not the silvery stream itself.

"Say, this is a nice place," she said. "Bet it has a good view in the daytime."

"It's better at night," he said. "Why don't we get off and rest a spell?"

She wasn't the least bit tired, and she didn't think resting was exactly what Jebel had in mind.

"Yes, why don't we?" she said, and brought Sally to a

halt. She was reaching to grasp the saddle horn and swing down to the ground in one quick movement when Jebel's voice stopped her.

"You just let me help you down, Miz Clover." He was already off his horse, standing by Sally and holding up his arms.

Ordinarily Hope would have been insulted by a man's assuming she couldn't get down off a horse by herself, but this was different and she found that she was actually pleased and excited at the prospect of having Jebel help her.

"Here you go," he said, and his big, strong hands encircled her waist to lift her upward and over Sally's back as though she weighed no more than a feather.

He lowered her ever so slowly to the ground, letting her slide down the length of him in the process. She felt her breasts briefly touch his face in passing while the rest of her glided along his broad chest, lean belly, and hard-muscled thighs. Her nostrils filled with the scent of shaving soap and hair tonic and just plain man smell. As her feet came to rest on the grass, the moon shone right over his shoulder into her eyes, making it difficult for her to see his face clearly.

Suddenly she felt dizzy. She couldn't be sure whether it was moon madness, the nearness of Jebel, the soft breeze blowing from the Pecos, or just the fact that she was young and it was spring.

"You're awfully strong, Jebel," she said shyly.

"You're awfully light."

She laughed a bit uncertainly. "Maybe, but I'm kind of wiry, too."

"You don't feel wiry," he said softly, hands still encircling her waist.

"Don't I?" Her throat was unexpectedly dry, making it difficult to speak.

"No, you feel nice and soft, just like a gal oughta feel in a fella's arms."

She had an urge to giggle, but it stopped instantly when his arms went around her. Her heart started to pound, the dizzy feeling increased, and her mouth felt as dry as her throat.

"I'll bet your lips are just as soft and sweet as the rest of you," Jebel whispered.

"My—my lips? I—"

His head came down, his lips capturing her partly open lips, and the contact was more thrilling than she had ever imagined a kiss could be. And for some fool reason her knees kind of gave way, causing her to sag against him and his arms to tighten around her.

"Ohhh . . . that . . ." Trying to talk with his lips moving back and forth over hers was impossible.

She quit trying and relaxed, enjoying the thrilling sensation of his firm mouth taking possession of hers. Unlike her throat, her lips were moist and growing more so as the lingering caress continued. A moan of pleasure escaped her as the tip of his tongue traced a tingling path along the contour of her upper lip and then just slightly inside the curve of the pouty lower one.

This wasn't fair, Hope thought chaotically. A few little old kisses shouldn't be having such a strong effect on her. She really hadn't expected the embrace to be so exciting and unsettling. Maybe because she'd never really been kissed before. She had known it would be nicer than, say, Bobby Kidwell's sloppy efforts or the few juvenile pecks she'd exchanged with boys her own age, but she hadn't been prepared for this all-encompassing surge of feeling, this sense of weakness, and a yearning for something she couldn't quite define.

Her arms crept up around Jebel's neck and he gathered her closer, holding her so tightly that her breasts started to ache from the contact with his hard chest. Or was that what was really causing the ache? It was more as if the soft pink nipples she was used to had turned into solid, sensitive prongs that were sending prickles of insistent need back through her chest. But need for what? To be touched and caressed? She sure as blazes hadn't felt anything like that when old Bobby had fondled and drooled over her.

Of course, there was a world of difference between the governor's secretary and the young trail boss. Kidwell was damp-handed and flabby, while Jebel Mason had firm, dry skin and a hard resilient body.

"Oh, Clover honey, you smell as sweet as the flower you're named after," Jebel murmured as he released her lips for a moment and buried his face in her hair.

She couldn't think of a thing to say as he shifted position slightly and raised his head to recapture her lips. It was then that she became aware that she wasn't the only one the close embrace and kisses were affecting. The change in position had brought the swelling maleness of him right up against the soft mound at the base of her belly.

But before she had time to react, the contact was broken as he sank down onto the grass, pulling her with him. Without relinquishing her lips, he cradled her in his arms and stretched out alongside her.

And then that warm, eager mouth of his began tormenting her in earnest. The teasing tongue snaked along and between her lips, dipping beyond her teeth to meet her tongue and play twirling, twisting games with it, only to retreat and begin all over again. Her heart was beating a mile a minute and her head was swimming, making her glad she was already lying down because she knew if she hadn't been, she would have lost her balance and fallen.

"Darling . . . sweet little Clover," he whispered, his lips leaving hers to trail down the side of her neck and cause delicious shivers to run up and down her spine.

"Jebel . . . Jebel . . . what are you—I mean, why are you kissing me this way?" she asked plaintively. She was having some awfully peculiar feelings that she didn't know what to do about and wasn't sure if they were his fault or hers. She wanted to know what was causing the turmoil inside her but wasn't sure she wanted it to end just yet, wanted to feel more before she decided if she really liked it or not. It would take a while to make up her mind whether she wanted him to stop.

Besides, she wasn't sure he would stop even if she asked him to. He was breathing hard and kind of funny, like maybe he had been running or was frightened or terribly het up over something.

He was kissing her throat, pressing his lips to the pulse beating so rapidly in the hollow there. His hands had started to move over her too, and again, although the movements were similar to those Bobby's slimy hands had made, the results were startlingly different. Jebel's light, tantalizing touch set her to tingling as it ran over her ribcage to find the two little mounds. The strong fingers were almost gentle as they stroked the sensitive flesh, moving up the slopes and toying with the rigid tips. It was a lovely sensation and she found herself hoping it would go on and on. The funny thing about it was that she couldn't determine if the irresistible feeling was caused by the rubbing fingers or by the desire to be touched and caressed still more. There was a sense of expectancy, as though the erect nubbins anticipated further attention. Suddenly it occurred to her to wonder what it would be like if a fellow got so excited he wanted to kiss a girl's breasts or to draw the tender peaks between his lips and suck on them. What would *that* feel like? What would she do if such an unlikely thing were to happen? Would she tell him to stop, or would she encourage him to keep on doing it until she went crazy from the ecstasy of it? She was crazy enough already just from the way he was kissing her lips, drawing her tongue so deep into his mouth that she feared for a moment he was going to swallow it whole.

She was roused from her fantasy by the feel of his hand undoing the top button of her shirt and pulling it open so that the top half of her breasts were bared in the moonlight.

Her heart thudded and lurched. She hadn't thought about there being any undressing. Now she was in a real predicament. She had always thought she was the smartest little cowgirl in the state of Texas, one who knew how to wrap lecherous old men around her finger without getting hurt, but here she was, not knowing what to do when a nice fellow like Jebel unbuttoned her shirt. And he didn't stop with that; his fingers were dipping inside to slide along the rise of her breast until they encountered the erect nipple, and then he began rubbing his palm over it.

Hope moaned and sucked in her breath at the sensation that rippled through her as bare flesh touched bare flesh. The only thing she could compare it to was the jolt of electricity that had run up her arm once when she was a toddler and had touched the end of the wire that hooked up the transmitting keys at the telegraph office. She would never forget the frightening but not unpleasant sensation the weak current had caused, nor the way the telegraph clerk had laughed at the bewildered expression on her face.

"Darling little Clover," Jebel was whispering huskily. "You are so sweet, I could just eat you up like a sugar cake."

"Well, I ain't no sugar cake," she heard herself say, "and I'm not sure we should be doing this."

"Doesn't it feel good?"

"Of course it feels good."

"Then why shouldn't we do it?"

"Because."

"That's no reason."

"Well, then because it makes me feel so funny and dumb," she said, knowing she ought to stop that circling palm while she still could. "It makes me feel like nothing ever made me feel before."

"That's the way it's supposed to make you feel," Jebel said. "It's supposed to make you feel funny and then happy, and finally like you never want it to stop . . . until something happens inside you that is so wonderful and nice that you want to start all over again."

"I can't believe that," she said. "Nothing could make a person feel all that wonderful."

"Well, there is a little more to it than that," he admitted, unbuttoning another button.

"Hey, what are you doing?"

"I want to see these," he moved a hand across her breasts, "I want to see both of them, all of them."

"I'm not sure you should, leastwise not out here in the night air. I might catch cold there."

"Clover, I promise you I won't let you catch cold in either of the little beauties. I won't let them be uncovered long enough to get a breeze on them, much less catch cold."

"I'm not sure it's nice," she said, wishing he'd quit pressing against her the way he was. Feeling that bulge at the front of his pants made her feel funniest of all.

He finished unbuttoning her shirt and pulled it fully open to stare at her breasts, which stood out in the moonlight like two round little white muffins.

"Oh, Clover, they are so pretty." He seemed to be having trouble breathing. "They are the prettiest things I've ever seen in all my born days."

"Some girls have bigger ones," she said, his words making her unexpectedly proud of her endowment.

"It don't matter how big they are long as they're pretty, and, sweet little love, yours are the prettiest I ever did see."

"Aw, go on," she said with an uneasy giggle, wondering what was going to happen next. "I bet you're just sayin' that."

"No I'm not," he said, cupping a breast in each hand. "These are beautiful, all pink and white and perky, much prettier than bigger ones that don't stand up and out."

"How many ladies have you seen?"

"Well . . . a few," he admitted. "There are some ladies who seem to like me."

It bothered her that he was telling her about ladies who let him look at their breasts, and it made her wonder what else happened after that. Did this mean that some day he might tell some other female about the silly little girl who let him look at her on the banks of the Pecos in the bright moonlight?

"Are you going to tell everybody?" she demanded.

He look bewildered. "Tell everybody what?"

"That I got these bumps on my chest and I let you look at them."

He chuckled softly. "Sweetheart, I'm going to do a lot more than just look, and I'm not going to tell anybody." He bent his head and let his tongue flick across one nipple and then the other.

"Oh, good gosh!" she gasped.

"Doesn't that feel good?"

"I—I don't know," she said, and started shivering.

"Are you cold?"

"Y-yes," she said, although she didn't know how she could be, with his big, hard body practically on top of hers; but there was something about the smell of him blending with the smell of the cottonwoods and the grass that made her shake all over. His soft voice was almost drowned out by the sound of night birds and the chirping and croaking of all the little creatures that came out after dark wherever there was water in this desert-like country.

"Here, maybe this will warm you up," he said, and she felt his lips take a nipple into his mouth just like she had imagined earlier. It was more than she expected, but she couldn't define exactly how it felt. It didn't hurt certainly, but it was kind of shocking to have him roll the hardened button around inside his mouth, and it was getting her all het up . . . to do what?

Without meaning to, she began to squirm and wriggle against him as his mouth moved from one breast to the other. That must have been a signal to proceed to the next step, because he reached for her belt buckle and began to unfasten it.

Her mind told her that in just about a minute whatever was going to happen would happen if she didn't call a halt to it right now. She also knew that her body wanted it to happen and kept insisting there wasn't a blame thing she could do about it. But her mind kept nagging, reminding her that if she let this go on, she would be different afterward, that she would kind of belong to Jebel Mason before she was sure she wanted to belong to anyone but herself.

"Don't do that, please," she said as he started to loosen her belt.

"Shh, it's all right," he said soothingly.

"No, it's not all right. I don't want to do any more new things tonight."

"Come on, you've gone this far. You can't stop now after what you've done to me."

Ah, there it was. *She* had done something to him. Well, she hadn't done it on purpose, so she didn't feel responsible.

Reaching both hands in between them, she started pushing him away.

But he didn't intend to be pushed away. He held on to her tightly and no matter how she twisted and turned, she couldn't get away. She wasn't sure she really wanted to get away, but she had to. Someday she might actively want him to do what he wanted to do, but not tonight. The only trouble was that he was a damn sight stronger than she was, and if she couldn't figure out a way to get loose, he was going to—

Then something unexpected happened. Sally had wandered over toward them as she munched at the grass, and as she lifted a foot to move on, she put it down on Jebel's leg. Apparently thinking she had trod on a rattlesnake, the mild little horse let out a wild whinny and leaped upward, coming down several feet away and spooking Jebel's horse, which reared wildly, gave a frightened whinny, and darted off toward the river.

"What the hell!" Jebel yelled, letting go of Hope and leaping to his feet to start down the slope after his mount.

"Just goes to show you," Hope muttered to herself as she fastened her belt buckle and buttoned up her shirt, "that a horse comes before anything else for a cowboy."

She whistled to Sally, who was again grazing, having frightened Jebel's horse more than she had herself. She ambled over to Hope, and the girl vaulted into the saddle and started down the slope.

As they passed Jebel, Hope called in a voice as sweet as sage honey, "I'll round up your horse critter for you!"

Chapter 7

"HAW, HAW, HAW, haw, haw, haw!" It was John Chisum's laugh echoing through the camp that woke Hope one morning of their fifth week on the trail. They had made excellent time as far as Trail City, with the loss of only a few dozen cattle, mostly calves and the weaker creatures that made up the drag. Half a dozen prime steers had been run off by Comanches on the edges of Stake Plains, and two or three head had been lost fording the upper reaches of the Republican river. Now the icy waters of the Platte lay ahead. They were heading into the area where the Sioux and Cheyenne were on the warpath, and the cold winds were still blowing down onto the plains from the Rockies.

Pushing aside her blanket and overcoat and the poncho that covered both, she sat up and stretched, fully dressed except for boots and chaps. There was the smell of coffee, frying bacon, and beans in the air. Even now, before dawn, the camp was completely astir as the night guards came in to grab some chow and a couple hours of sleep before the herd got under way again.

"Chow down, missy, chow down!" Chou Li, the Chinese cook, was going through the camp, ringing a bell and shouting to those who were waking from a night's sleep that had been broken twice by the need to send extra men out to handle the cattle. A sudden thunderstorm had come sweeping across the plains, starting the beasts milling about dangerously.

"Be there in a few minutes, Chou. Got to wash up first," she called.

"Better eat now, wash later, missy," the Chinaman said. "Water be there, food maybe not!"

"You'll save me some, won't you, Chou?" she wheedled. "You don't want me to eat your wonderful chow feeling all grimy, do you?"

"Lady sweet talk and turn China boy's poor head," he said. "He save you a bite."

She laughed, knowing full well there would be a heaping plate of corn bread, beans, and bacon kept warm for her however late she got to the chuck wagon. Chou Li was a sweet soul with a somewhat acerbic exterior, and he was immensely fond of her, as were almost all of the twenty-five members of the trail drive.

Hope got up and went over to rub Rollo behind the ears. The other horses that had been assigned to her, including Sally, the little mare who had saved her from what might have been a terrible mistake, were with the *remuda,* where they were kept under heavy guard against Indian raids. There was nothing an Indian would rather do than steal a horse. Horses were not merely transportation to them; they were a way of life.

"Well, you're a way of life to us too, Rollo," she whispered into the little pinto's silky mane. "And no Indian is going to carry you off as long as I'm around."

She located a small bar of ill-smelling black soap in her saddlebag and started down toward the nearby creek with her only towel when Jebel appeared, tall, covered with trail dust, and as handsome as ever.

"Ah there you are, beautiful lady," he said, making one of his courtly little bows that made the other cowboys laugh at him when they dared. "It's been almost twenty-four hours since I've seen you."

"Ah now, you go on, Jebel," she said. "You've been seeing me most every day for five weeks. You must be getting a little tired of my face by now."

"Not of your face or any other part of you," he said, moving closer and pulling her behind a supply wagon.

"Careful, careful! I'm just one of the hands 'round here, you know," she cautioned. "We wouldn't want the men to know you're playing favorites or anything like that."

"Favorites, hell! I'm in love with you and I don't care who knows it."

That made her heart pound even faster than did the feel of his arms around her and his lips against the side of her neck. He smelled of horse and human sweat, dirt and hard work, but somehow there was something so completely masculine about it that she didn't find it unpleasant in the least. But the thought that she probably didn't smell much better made her pull away. A man was supposed to smell that way, but a female?

"What's the matter? Don't you like to kiss anymore?" he asked as she tried to push away.

"Are you crazy? I thrive on it when it's with you."

"Than how come you seem to be avoiding me lately?"

"Avoiding you? Well, you know, we do have a couple of tough bosses. We're here to work, not lallygag."

"I'm your boss and I'm not tough where you're concerned," he said, nibbling at her ear.

"Well, I certainly thought you were going to be when you found out I was coming along on this drive."

He chuckled, but without much humor. "I could have killed Uncle John when he told me you were going to ride herd just like the rest of us. A sweet little gal like you. It's unheard of."

"Have I been a bad point or drag hand?" she asked.

"No, no, you've been fine, but look—look at your poor little hands, they're getting as hard as mine." He took them in his, rubbing his fingers over the palms. "I hate him for letting you do this kind of work. It ain't at all ladylike."

"Mr. Boss Man, I may be a female critter, but I never claimed to be no lady type. Being a lady is something you have to learn like my ma did in one of them fancy schools back east. Out here, a woman's got better things to do than work on her etiquette and her fingernails and such-like. She's lucky if she can keep body and soul together, much less accumulate a trousseau in matching colors and keep her toenails polished."

"Don't be silly," he whispered, squeezing her closer. "Of course you're a lady, and that's why I was so upset when I heard you was going to be the only woman among twenty or more wild trail drivers."

She shrugged. "What could happen to me?"

"Well . . . some of these boys are pretty wild, you know. Uncle John doesn't usually hire Bible students to do his trail driving."

"Look, even if I wasn't perfectly capable of taking care of myself, I've got my pap, Uncle John, and you to look out for me, don't I? Now who's going to take on a combination like that?"

"Maybe you're right, but you can't blame me for getting upset when I heard you were coming along."

"So upset you wouldn't even talk to me for the first three or four days?"

"All right, I sulked for a while, but I was a little angry. You hadn't told me you were going to be on the drive."

"But you hadn't asked me," she said, knowing that wasn't exactly a valid excuse.

"And you walked out on me that night down by South Spring," he went on.

"Well, I'll tell you, Mr. Boss Man, if I hadn't walked out on you after the horses got their tails in an uproar, you never can tell what might have happened."

"No, but it would have been what I wanted to happen," he whispered. "I wanted to love you. I still want to love you, but it seems like you're always thinking up some reason to avoid letting me do it. Some silly excuse, like you've got to check the feed for the horses."

"Well now, that ain't silly. I love all those nice horses Uncle John supplied for me to ride, and I like to see that they're as happy as can be while they're working so hard."

"Clover, you know that isn't the real reason why you keep avoiding me."

"No it isn't. It sure isn't," she admitted. "It's just that I don't trust myself when I'm alone with you."

"Well, you can trust me. You know that, don't you? I love you, and if a gal can't trust the man who loves her, who can she trust?"

"Her father and mother, maybe," she said, and laughed. "It isn't that I don't trust you. It's just that I don't trust you not to do what I want to do as bad as you do."

"Do you really want me as much as I want you?" he asked in wonder. "I can't believe it. If you did, you wouldn't be able to stay away from me the way you do."

She pushed away from him because she could tell that he was becoming aroused again and she wasn't exactly in a state of peace and quiet herself. "I better get down to the creek and get washed up. Chou Li's saving me some breakfast, but he can't keep it forever and the herd is moving out in a couple of hours."

"How about I come along and wash behind your ears?" he proposed, laughing and trying to hold her.

"Thanks, but I can reach behind them quite well," she said. "What do you think, they're as long as a jackrabbit's or something?"

He was still laughing as she hurried around the supply wagon and headed down a path that led upstream from where the three or four thousand cows were having long morning drinks of water before starting out on the trail. Here in Colorado there was much more water than there had been during the first phases of their drive. Then the cattle had been half mad for a drink for days on end and had been likely to bolt toward the smell of it, no matter in which direction it lay or what kind of water it was.

A lead cow or smart bull or steer could smell water ten

to fifteen miles away, but they didn't seem able to tell the difference between sweet water and alkali that would sicken or kill them outright. It was only the fact that John Chisum and Jebel were experienced trail masters, and most of the hands were veterans of the Texas cattle roundups, that had enabled them to avoid that kind of problem and come as far as they had with as little loss as they had.

When she reached the creek, surrounded by reeds on either side, and sloshed through the mud along the banks, she could hear the cowboys whooping it up a little way downstream, but during the three days they had rested here for the good water and grass, she had discovered a secluded clump of bushes where she could have a little privacy. She was willing to work and even sleep in public, but when it came right down to bathing or even just washing up, like she intended to do now, she liked to be completely private.

Feeling grimy beyond bearing, she took off her boots and socks, sat down on a flat rock, and stuck her feet into the cold water, shivering at its coldness. Her feet were caked with trail dust, as was everything but her face and hands. They had been three days off the trail, but she hadn't been able to wash all the dust off because even at rest the riders had been on constant alert, keeping the restless cattle from spooking at the smell of a coyote, a buffalo, or the occasional mountain lion that had wandered down from the high country. To add to that, there had been the all too frequent thunderstorms that had required every hand except Chisum and the cook to be in the saddle from dawn till dusk and part of the night as well.

The water was cold but still tempting, and as she washed her feet, she couldn't resist any longer. It was deep enough here so that if she took off her shirt and jeans, she could plunge in, soap herself down fast, and be dried off and back in her clothes in less than fifteen minutes. Cooky would keep her food that long, she told herself.

She was undressed in a moment, and pausing only to glance quickly at her slim white reflection in the clear water, she stepped in and sank to the pebbled bottom, yelping at the cold. Then she was scrubbing herself with the black soap in pleasure that couldn't be dimmed by the fact that the frigid water was turning her nearly blue. "Oh, to be clean . . . really clean for the first time in five weeks," she muttered to herself. "It's so good."

But time was passing, and if she stayed much longer she would be shaking so hard she wouldn't be able to get back into her clothes. She was just about to get out when a stick cracked behind her.

"Hey there, little missy. Look what I got!" The unpleasantly familiar voice made her jump in fright. She whirled around and looked toward the bank of the stream. Standing there was the swarthy, moustached cowboy known as Cajun Joe. He wasn't an Acadian, as the name implied, but a half-Indian French Canadian. He was a good hand with the rope and branding iron, but a troublemaker. However, half the men John Chisum hired for the Fence Rail outfit and as his warriors at the fort were troublemakers. Many had left Texas under circumstances not much more auspicious than hers and her father's.

But Joe was different from the others. They were only wild. He was mean. Mean clear through, and she had been wary of him from the first day, when she had seen the way he looked at her with his glittering black eyes. Once or twice she had almost mentioned him to her father and Jebel, but had avoided it because she had known he was the kind with whom a disagreement would have only one ending.

"I got me some girl-size clothes up here, is it not so, *chérie?*" he said, holding up her jeans, shirt, and towel.

"Those are my clothes, Joe," she said, trying to keep her voice firm through chattering teeth.

"You know, somehow Joe he know that," he said laughing, "seeing how no one else wear this small a size."

"Get out of here and leave me alone, Joe," she said. "I got to get dressed and get back to camp."

"Why? What is it to hurry for?" he said. "Pretty soon the camp will be moving on and it will be quiet and peaceful 'round here and we could have some fun, no?"

"I'm not interested in having fun with you, Joe," she

said, staying up to her shoulders in the water so he could see as little as possible of her nakedness.

"Why not you want fun with Joe? The girls in town knife each other for the privilege of have fun with Joe."

"I'm sure they do, Joe," she said, trying to keep calm. "But I'm different."

"How you different?" He wasn't laughing anymore. "Maybe you too good for Joe. Is that it?"

This man was like a rattlesnake, she told herself, but she had dealt with rattlesnakes before, and she could deal with him if she just had the time. If she had the time, she could just stay here in the water and wait for someone from the camp to come to look for her. But that might take a while, especially amid the excitement and confusion of breaking camp and moving on. And by then she might be quite literally freezing.

The best thing she could do, she decided, was to appeal to his loyalty to John Chisum.

"Uncle John wants to get under way as early as possible this morning, so we can camp on the banks of the Platte tomorrow night and have all next day for crossing," she said.

He shrugged, holding her shirt up and smelling it, as though enjoying the woman smell of it. "That is his problem, no Joe's, hey?"

"That is your problem, too," she said. "If Uncle John comes looking for you, he'll be furious."

"What difference his anger? He not carry a gun. He depends on other men to do his fighting for him. That means he is not a very brave man, no?"

"No, it doesn't mean anything of the kind," she said. "John Chisum is as brave as any man. He just doesn't feel that he needs a gun to run his outfit, even on a trail drive."

He laughed. "Chisum no carry a gun 'cause he know that no man draw down on an unarmed man. Joe not afraid of him."

Appealing to this man's loyalty was obviously a lost cause, Hope decided. She would have to think of another tactic before she froze to the smooth rocks under her feet.

"Jebel Mason knows where I am, Joe," she said, trying not to make it sound like a threat. "I told him where I was coming just before I left."

His face was black with rage. "Ah, so that is it, is it? That is why you no like Joe. You not like Joe because you go off into woods with Mr. Trail Boss himself."

"That isn't so," she said, reminding herself that everything depended on keeping calm. "I haven't been into the woods with anybody on this drive and I'm not going to. So please put my clothes down and leave."

"Ho, Joe is not stupid," he said. "Cajun Joe see what is in front of his eye. He see the sheep's looks you give Mr. Trail Boss. He see the way the Mason lust for you. He know what going on."

"That isn't true, Joe," she said. "There isn't anything going on. You've got to believe that. You've got to believe it because it is the plain simple truth."

"It may be simple, but it ain't the truth," he said. "Joe, he not simple, he know that where one man is getting it, another man can too, and Joe he is the man who is here to get it now."

"You're not going to get a damn thing!" she snapped. "I'll stand here in this water and freeze to death before I'll give you so much as a soft look!" She had lost her temper, and she shouldn't have, she realized the second she saw the look on his face.

"So, she is too good for Cajun Joe, but she give it to Mason and old man Chisum and probably that Chinaboy, too," he snarled. "Well, she is mistake if she think Joe not going to get his share."

"Those are lies, damn dirty lies!" She was yelling, furious at the unfairness of the accusation. "You go away, or you're going to be damn sorry!" she shouted.

"You come out or you're going to be damn froze," he shouted back. "Come on, you like it with Joe. You see."

"Let me have my clothes."

"Come on out and I give them to you," he said. "Afterward."

"You have no right to even touch my clothes. They are my property, and if you don't let go of them, I'm going to—"

"You're going to what?" he sneered.

Yes, what was she going to do? Scream? Cattle were bellowing and the cowboys were shouting. No one would ever hear her.

"What you gonna do? Hey, little gal, what you gonna do?" he mocked her.

What could she do? Throw rocks at him? Threats didn't mean a thing. He was too sure of his masculine powers and obviously thought that once she had enjoyed his "favors" she would be so thrilled she would never think of telling what he had done to her.

"You get out of here, or you are damn well going to be sorry that you ever tangled with me," she warned.

He roared with laughter and sat down beside her boots, still holding her clothing in his hands.

"You have no call to do this," she said. "I've never given you any indication that I might have anything to do with you, here or any other place or time."

"Ha, that is because you do not know what is good for you," he said, sniffing at her clothing again, this time at the crotch of her jeans. If she hadn't been so blue with cold, she would have turned red with embarrassment.

"Ha, woman, she always smell different, always smell good even when she is dirty and sweaty and wears no perfume like the fancy ladies do at the houses in Trail City and Cheyenne."

"You better save yourself for the fancy ladies in Cheyenne," she said, "and leave me alone. I ain't no lady."

He snapped his fingers. "So you are no lady. I will forgive that and make you very, very happy."

"The only way you can make me happy is to put down my clothes and get the hell out of here so I can get out of this damn ice water and get dressed and get some chow and go to work."

"I let you do all that," he said. "Right afterward . . . and as horny as old Joe is, it will not take long. I promise you that. I also promise you after that first time, you will want it more and more, all the way to the end of the trail."

You conceited bastard, she thought. I'll freeze to death before I let you lay a hand on me.

But thinking things like that wasn't doing any good. Time was passing and she was going to catch her death of something or other if she didn't get out of this water, get dressed, and eat some food. She had to think of a way to convince him to leave her alone. So far neither threats nor pleading had worked. Maybe promises would, and she saw no reason why a promise made to a man who was behaving so outrageously should have to be kept.

She had already discovered that he was inordinately vain. Maybe if she convinced him that just because she objected to his present behavior she didn't necessarily find him personally repulsive, he might settle for a promise of a later assignation. And it would be a whole lot later, if she had her way.

"Yes, *chérie,* these sure nice jeans you wear. Maybe I just keep and give to my gal in Cheyenne." Joe was fondling her pants as he talked.

"Look, can't we talk this over?" she asked, making her voice sound pleasant and conciliatory.

"Sure, you come on out, we do it for a while, and then we talk long as you want."

"But, Joe, the herd will be pulling out and if we miss it, both our asses are gonna be in a sling."

"Joe good with rope and branding iron. He can always get job, job with less work than this one."

"But I can't, Joe, and neither can my old man. We got to have this job to get up to Wyoming and to give us a stake to get started up there."

"Not my problem," he said with a shrug.

"But it is mine. Don't you care what happens to me?"

"There's only one thing I want happen to you, and you know what that is, sweet little bird."

"Well, maybe we could arrange that."

"Hey, you mean you willing?" He got up onto his knees

to stare at her, his little black eyes glittering with lust.

"Well . . . you know." She was shivering so hard she could barely get the words out. "Y-you know I—I have n-noticed you around camp a l-lot, and have kind of th-thought maybe I would l-like to—"

"You want do it with me, hey? That make you smart lady. Why you been horsin' 'round about it then? I'm here and this your chance. Come on out. I give you good time like you never had before."

"I didn't like the way you went about it. You shouldn't have grabbed my clothes that way."

"Hey, look, I give them back right after we do it. That a bargain, right?"

"No, not right. I do want to do it with you real bad, never saw a fella I wanted so bad, but gee, if we do it now, I won't be with the herd when it pulls out."

"So? What is lost? You catch up later."

"Yeah, and lose my job."

"A woman? What for they care if woman ride herd or not?"

His male arrogance made her heart pound with rage, but she kept her voice level and friendly. "I'm a good hand, and I don't want to lose my job. I've got an idea how we can do what we both want to do and still keep my job."

"How?"

Now it all depended on just how conceited he really was. If he actually thought no woman could give up a chance to have sex with him, then he might believe her proposition.

"Look, you put my clothes back where they were and get along over to the camp, then I'll get out and dress and follow you."

"Yeah? How that get me what I want?"

"Tonight, as soon as we make camp again, you and I will take a couple of blankets and sneak away. We could have the whole night together, not just an hour, and still have our jobs."

"You keep promise?" he asked. "You keep promise and sneak away with me?"

"Yes, that's what I'll do. And, Joe, it wouldn't have to

be just one night. We could do it as many nights as we wanted after that."

"You give Joe lots of fun, huh?"

"That's right, Joe, all the fun you can stand. When I really go for a fella, I'm the kind of gal who'll do just about anything he wants...and do it better than any of them honky-tonk gals, 'cause I do it for fun, not for pay."

"You do for fun, eh?" He was standing up now, still fiddling with her shirt and pants. "You really do anything I want? What kind of things you do?"

She hadn't the faintest idea what kind of things honky-tonk girls did, so she had to stay as vague as possible. "Oh, just about anything...some of it I don't much like to talk about, but, man, when it comes to doing them, I ain't backward at all."

"You do but you don't talk, is that right?"

"That sure is right. And every night for as long as you want to."

He tossed her clothes into the air and let them fall to the ground. "Joe probably not want to bother with you after we reach Cheyenne. There lots of gals there who like Joe big much, and you kind of skinny for his taste."

"That's fine, Joe. Once you want to get rid of me, I wouldn't make no trouble," she forced herself to say, although she was gritting her teeth at his arrogance. "I'd just go my way and you could go yours."

"All right, we do it," he said, kicking her clothing in her direction. "I go join the trail now and you follow. Later we have our fun."

Thank God, she thought fervently as he turned and strode off through the cottonwoods. He had fallen for her ploy. And the next time they met, she'd make sure she had a gun in her hand.

She dashed out of the water, shivering violently in the cold wind blowing off the snow-covered Rockies, and darted toward her clothes. She was bending over to pick up her pants when a twig snapped behind her and she felt arms suddenly encircle her in a steely grip.

"Ha! You think you fool Joe, huh? You think he dumb cluck who take a kiss and a promise. Well, Joe take the real thing!"

Then she was being thrown naked onto the ground and he was on top of her, pinning her arms and forcing her legs apart.

Chapter 8

THE CANADIAN'S FETID breath was in her face, his mouth close to hers. His hands felt as though they contaminated her body with their evil touch, and the scream that tore from Hope's throat was pure reflex. She had no more control over it and the shrieks that followed than she did over the way the rest of her body reacted to his attempt to violate it. Her fingers turned into claws that raked at anything within their reach, her feet and legs became weapons of another sort, lashing at him with all the strength weeks in the saddle had given them. As he gripped her arm and tried to pin it behind her, she sank her teeth into his wrist, drawing blood and a howl of anger and hate from Cajun Joe.

"You dirty little beast, I show you. I show you how to treat me!" he snarled, drawing back a fist and aiming a blow at her head. "I make you crawl!"

But the blow didn't land. Like a wildcat fighting for its life, Hope clawed and twisted away from him, kneeing him in the stomach and causing his breath to whoosh out explosively as he staggered away from her.

Flipping over onto her hands and knees, she scrambled away from him and was lurching to her feet when he reached out, grabbed her by the heel, and yanked her back. Desperately, she kicked out with the other foot, connected with his chin, and knocked his head back on his shoulders. He cursed, and twisted her foot until she thought her leg was going to tear out of its socket. She tried to roll away from his grasp, but he followed and flopped on top, knocking the wind out of her. His weight held her helpless and his vile breath filled her nostrils, while a smile of triumph and hate wreathed his face.

"Ha, you bitch, I got you now! First I split your cunt, then I split your throat!"

The thought of death before dishonor had never crossed her mind before, but as she lay defenseless under this shaggy brute, she knew she would rather be dead than submit to him, and if he ravaged her, she wouldn't care if he killed her afterward.

"You all nice and naked and ready for Joe, hey?" he gloated, and then his bewhiskered face touched her, his mouth lapping at her flesh and his fingers caressing her in a way she found utterly revolting.

Pinning her legs to the ground with his and holding both her wrists above her head in one big hand, he unbuckled his belt and started to unbutton his pants. Hope sucked in her breath for one last screech and a final desperate effort to fight him off.

As the scream burst from her lips, there was a shout, and Joe half turned to look behind him.

"Now, I'll be troublin' ye to get yourself off the young lady," said a voice thick with the accents of counties Cork and Down. Over Cajun's shoulder Hope could see a black stallion carrying a tall, red-haired young man in a Stetson, checked shirt, and denims faded almost white by washing.

"Go 'way, stranger," the Canadian growled, his hand snaking toward the pearl-handled revolver in his holster. "Lady no want you around. Lady want what I got for her."

"No I don't!" Hope yelled. "Please stay!"

"Shut up!" Joe said, and backhanded her across the mouth. "You got no choice."

"Let her be, you bastard! Let her go!" the Irishman shouted. "Get away from that girl, or I'll—"

Joe was on his feet with the speed of a catamount, hand streaking toward his gun.

The redheaded cowboy was faster. He wore his holster on the left hip, and his six-gun seemed to appear in his right hand almost by magic. The echoing bark drowned out the crack of Cajun Joe's weapon as it fired into the ground and dropped from a relaxing hand.

The half-breed tumbled over backward, a neat red hole appearing on the front of his dirty shirt. Hope got to her feet, dazed, and stared down at the dead man as his mouth fell open and his eyes glazed over. A few moments ago this creature had been threatening her with rape and death, but now that he was sprawled dead at her feet, she couldn't help being appalled by the swiftness of his passing.

Another scream was building up, but she clamped a hand over her mouth to stifle it as she heard the redheaded cowboy's horse trotting toward her and saw three more mounted men behind him, their tanned faces almost invisible beneath pulled-down Stetsons and neckerchiefs drawn up against the dust. For some reason they and the yellow sun climbing up the sky seemed to swirl before her eyes.

Hope was not the fainting kind, but she felt herself swaying and started to go down. A strong arm in a checked sleeve swooped down to catch and lift her up onto the big black stallion, and a handsome freckled face with startlingly green eyes was looking down into hers.

"Why, the poor lassie is plumb tuckered out from strugglin' with that fellow." The brogue was strong and had a warm lilt that seemed to go with the feeling of confidence and realiability his arm gave her. "Tuckered out and as naked as the bird they call the jay."

Before she could say a word, he was whipping his oilskin poncho from the roll behind his saddle and covering her with it with as much care as her own mother might have done.

"Poor wee chickie, out here all alone and attacked by that black-haired, black-hearted rascal."

"I say, what's going on, O'Callahan?" asked an older man, dressed in a spick-and-span jacket and riding britches. He was mounted on a thoroughbred horse with an English saddle and had a strong British accent. "What was that shot, and where did you get that young woman you're holding on your saddle?"

"Trust O'Callahan to find a woman! He'd find one in the middle of the Sahara Desert if you gave him a chance," said one of the other horsemen, a sallow-faced, moustachioed man with crossed gunbelts and two pistols.

"'Tis nothin' at all, Mr. Fenwick," O'Callahan said to the Englishman, who seemed to be the boss of this outfit. "I just killed me a rattlesnake. A mighty mean one, too, with fangs at both ends."

All three horsemen were close enough now to see Hope clearly as she lay in a half-swoon in the Irishman's arms.

"What happened to the girl?" the Englishman asked. "Where are her clothes?"

"Looks like they're scattered all over the ground," O'Callahan said. "That snake had them just before he grabbed the girl." He swung in his saddle and addressed the sallow-faced man with the two weapons that marked him for a hired gun. "Cal, quit gawkin' like an ape and bring the lady her clothes, will you?"

The gunman hesitated for a moment, his hooded eyes seeming to measure the redhead. Then he shrugged and clicked to his horse, stooping from the saddle to pick up the articles of clothing one at a time. If Fenwick was the boss of this group, the big Irishman seemed to be the foreman who gave the orders.

"Are you all right, young lady?" Fenwick had ridden closer and was looking down at Hope, through a monocle of all things. "I say, you do seem to have had a bad time. Are you hurt?"

"No, sir. I'm all right, thanks to this gentleman," Hope said, sitting up and pulling the poncho more tightly around herself.

"Timothy O'Callahan of Kilkenny the town and Kilkenny the county, in Wyoming by way of the Dakotas and a mining dig that ran out, plus six years on the hurricane deck of a Colorado bronc workin' for the Auld Triple Cross, a right proper name for an outfit that threw a long loop when they got near to other people's cows. This is Mr. Morton Fenwick of Sussex Ranch, named for the county in merry old England. He's the only local Powder River chap whose name is in that *Burke's Peerage* they keep over in London town so they can tell who has the most blue blood."

"Kilkenny must be beautiful countryside," Hope said. "Are its horses as handsome as its men?"

"Well now, lassie, would ye be havin' a bit o' the colleen about ye?" O'Callahan asked.

"No, not really, but my father kissed the blarney stone a time or two in his day. I had the misfortune to be born in Texas instead of on the Emerald Isle meself."

"Sure now, and you had me fooled," he grinned. "And that rattlesnake ye was wrestlin' with, he'd not be from Ireland even secondhand, I'd wager."

"No, he was French Canadian, but don't hold that against the other people there. He's the kind that create their own meanness wherever they're from."

"And what are you doing out here in this wilderness all alone, young lady?" the Englishman asked.

"I am not alone. I'm with the Chisum trail herd, which is just over the rise there."

"Ah ha!" O'Callahan said, glaring at the man he had called Cal. "And you tell me you know this country? How is it then we were going the wrong way and would have been fifty miles past the herd if we hadn't heard this lassie screaming her little heart out?"

"Mr. Fenwick," Cal Harris said. "You hired me for my gun, not my trail-breaking. I did my best. O'Callahan should have hired a guide."

"You mean you are looking for the Chisum trail herd?" Hope pulled away slightly from the arm around her, instantly suspicious. Some of the Powder River outfits had a reputation for rustling even down in Texas. She didn't want to be responsible for leading a band of rustlers into Chisum's herds.

"We are indeed, young lady," the Englishman said. "The winter on the Powder River was an especially hard one and we are in need of heifers and yearlings. We are interested in buying as many head of cattle as Mr. Chisum will sell us."

"Well, he may have pushed on by now." Hope was still a little suspicious. It seemed like too much of a coincidence that she should be rescued by riders from an outfit that wanted to buy Chisum cattle. "I came down to take a bath before we hit the trail and that—that varmint was lying in wait for me."

"What we gonna do with him, Mr. Fenwick?" asked the fourth man, an older cowhand with a gray beard.

The Englishman looked at the corpse. "I suppose we ought to do the decent thing and bury him. But we haven't got a shovel, and I must say—"

"The buzzards will take care of him," Harris said. "That's as good as he deserves."

O'Callahan looked up at the half dozen carrion hunters already circling the area. "Sure now, in this wild country, they take care of most of us sooner or later, don't they?"

"Well, I hardly think he deserves a Christian burial after what he tried to do," Fenwick said. "Was he one of Mr. Chisum's hands or a stranger to you, young lady?"

"He's one Uncle John hired at the last minute because he was shorthanded when it came time to move out. Most of that kind skipped, but Cajun Joe was still with us, unfortunately."

"Well, it was certainly unfortunate for him," Fenwick said. "Perhaps Mr. Chisum will send men with shovels to bury him. We should press on to his herd at once."

O'Callahan raised his hand and the three cowboys who

were sitting and watching from a distance formed up behind him and followed as he and Fenwick and Harris led the way.

"And what was a wee sweet blossom like you doing ridin' along of a trail herd in the first place?" O'Callahan asked as his big black horse ate up the distance toward the cloud of dust that could now be seen marking the trail herd's path.

"If I were a 'wee, sweet blossom,' I wouldn't be with this or any other herd," Hope laughed.

"Are you Mr. Chisum's niece?"

"No, not really. I've known him a long time. Almost everyone in Texas calls John Chisum Uncle, and it's not always complimentary."

"I had an uncle back in the auld country everyone called Uncle except me. A man o' dark moods and hard fists he was, so I preferred to address him as Squire."

"Well, Uncle John is not a man of dark moods. He's a great laugher, but you can't always be sure what's behind the laugh, because even when it seems he's got nothing to laugh about, he still keeps right on chortling."

"Knew a captain like that during the Rebellion," O'Callahan said. "Always a-laughin' and yellin' 'Charge!' Seemed like *charge* was the only word he knew. A wee bit like that Custer fellow who got his arse shot off by the Indians up in the Dakotas. The man I knew got his shot off at Spotsylvania Courthouse, chargin' when he should have been retreatin'. Nice fellow, though. Sure had himself a pretty little wife."

"Horsemen coming our way," Harris reported and put up a hand to shade his eyes. "They ain't Indians."

"Well, that is fortunate," Fenwick said sourly. "If they were we'd all have been scalped by now, thanks to our sharp-eyed scout."

"Didn't hire out to be no scout," Harris said with a shrug.

"Mind your lip now, mon!" O'Callahan said. "Englishman or not, *Burke Peerage* or not, he's the boss man."

"That's my father and Mr. Chisum," Hope said. "And my friend Jebel Mason."

O'Callahan looked down at her, his expression half sad and half whimsical. "Oh, 'tis a 'friend' you'd be after havin', is it? Well, 'tis the way it goes for a poor Kilkenny boy so far away from home. Just when he thinks he's found a delicate prairie flower, she turns out to have a 'friend'!"

Was he teasing her, or was he serious? The Irishman seemed to speak in a mock serious way even when giving orders to his men.

How could a girl tell about a fellow like that? Jebel was serious and hardworking, and she always knew exactly where she stood with him. On the other hand, Timothy O'Callahan was devilishly handsome and just the kind of man she had dreamed about, the few times in her life when she hadn't been working too hard to dream about anything.

Now, as Pat, Uncle John, and Jebel approached, Hope was wishing she had thought to put her clothes on instead of carrying them clutched in one hand and being bare under O'Callahan's rubber poncho. Pat and Uncle John, and especially Jebel, would wonder and be shocked to find her with no clothes on among strange men, but it couldn't be helped.

"Greetings, gentlemen," John Chisum said. "Seems like you must be following our trail."

"'Specially since you seem to have found my wanderin' daughter," Pat Cox said. "Where you been, girl?"

"I was taking a bath and—" That was hardly the right way to start an explanation, but how else could she start except at the beginning?

O'Callahan was even more blunt about it. "The little lady had some trouble with a skunk," Timothy said. "One of your skunks, I understand, Mr. Chisum."

"Who? What happened?" Jebel demanded, his face dark with anger. "I looked all over for you, Clover. What happened?"

"Cajun Joe sneaked up on me while I was in the creek, grabbed my clothes, and wouldn't give them to me. Then after I thought I had gotten rid of him, I came out of the water and he—he jumped me and tried to rape me. Said he was going to kill me afterward."

"Where is he?" Pat demanded. "Where is that half-breed devil? I'll personally—"

"No need, Pap," Hope said. "This gentleman took care of Cajun."

"He's lying back there by the creek," the Englishman said, "with a bullet through his heart and the buzzards circling round."

Jebel Mason looked at O'Callahan, inclined his head stiffly, and muttered, "I must thank you, sir, for being there to help her." Then he reached out to take Hope. "I'll carry my fiancée now, though."

"Oh 'fiancée,' is it?" O'Callahan said, the quirk at the corner of his mouth not quite as humorous as his voice sounded. "From friend to fiancée in one easy step, is it now?"

"That's right—fiancée," Mason said, looking angry as he reached again for Hope. "And I'll take her now, if you don't mind."

The Irishman seemed disinclined to release Hope, but finally did so when she looked up pleadingly. The last thing she wanted was a clash between these two.

"We are not really engaged, but Mr. Mason has—" Not knowing how to finish, she let her voice fade away.

"We plan to be married when we get to trail's end," Jebel said.

"Well, that may take a while," Fenwick said. "I'm hoping to buy all the cows you can sell me, Chisum, and I want them delivered on the hoof to Fairfax on Powder River."

"Well, we planned to sell most of 'em to the army," John Chisum said. "But first come is first served. The first comer always get first choice from John Chisum. Haw, haw, haw!"

He wasn't laughing at what he'd said, Hope knew, because in truth the army usually did get first choice for the very good reason that the army was willing to pay more than anyone else. Anything to get away from the bully beef that came in a can and tasted like the wrong part of the cow had been discarded. This might be a chance for Uncle John to make a real killing. The Englishman looked rich and he said he needed cattle because a hard winter had wiped out most of his herds. That was the kind of situation made for John Chisum's sharp dealing, and the army could always look elsewhere.

"Are you all right, Clover?" Jeb asked anxiously under cover of the dickering. "That swine didn't—"

Hope shook her head, wondering how he would have reacted if she had been raped. Would he have been as tender and comforting as now, or would his attitude have been accusatory? She knew some men tended to blame the woman when one of their fellows behaved like an animal. They seemed to feel that the woman had somehow brought it on herself. Well, maybe she had by doing something so outrageous as going off by herself to take a bath. It wasn't her fault if that beast had followed her.

"I'm all right, I really am," she told Jebel as he set her on her feet. She wondered why it had taken so long for someone to come looking for her. Surely she must have been missed when the herd started to move out. Hadn't anyone noticed a side man was missing to push the cattle along?

"What are you paying for prime cattle these days, Mr. Fenwick?" Chisum asked, with a friendly chuckle that gave the impression he was doing nothing more serious than passing the time of day.

"Probably twice as much as we should be," O'Callahan interjected. "Considerin' that their tails have been about walked off and they're so scrawny they hardly have the strength to moo."

"Under the circumstances, we have no choice but to buy or close down the ranch," the Englishman said.

"These cattle have been better fed than we have," Chisum said with another of his demented laughs. "Ain't that right, boys?"

"Sure is," Pat said.

"I surely hope they are," Mason drawled. "They're bad off if they ain't."

"Now, now, Jeb," Chisum chided. "You had your chance at the chuck wagon just like everyone else when we butchered two yearlings back a week or two ago."

"There was too much fat on them cows," Mason said. "I like my beef lean."

"Perhaps we should have a look at some of these overfed cattle," Fenwick said. "I like cattle that are fat and happy on my range."

"Boys, you think maybe this fella don't trust me?" Chisum asked, and went into such a fit of laughter that first Pat, then Jebel, and finally the rancher were laughing with him.

This was, of course, just the usual buildup Chisum went through before he started talking price and delivery. Hope wondered, not for the first time, if Chisum's laughter was as spontaneous as he liked people to think. But if nothing else, it was a way of relieving tension and getting folks into a more friendly mood.

Jebel stopped laughing abruptly, and Hope could see out of the corner of her eye that he was looking from Timothy O'Callahan to her and back. He was jealous, she realized. Had he noticed the way her head had been resting on the other man's chest and the way his arm had just seemed to fit around her waist? He must have, because he was scowling and chewing at his lower lip in a way that meant trouble of some kind. And she and Pap didn't need trouble. All they wanted was to find some land they could stake a claim on, settle down, and make a home for themselves.

Hope liked Jebel and found his kisses exciting, but Timothy was handsome and thrilling. Perhaps it was just because he was a newcomer; she didn't want to be forced to choose between them, at least not yet. She was young and there was plenty of time for getting serious and deciding which man, if any, she wanted to marry and spend the rest of her life with.

"Aren't you going along with Mr. Fenwick to inspect the herd?" Jebel asked O'Callahan as the others rode off.

"'Twould do no good," the Irishman said with a shrug. "Fenwick is the one who knows cows. My job is to get work out of the cowboys. We didn't raise longhorn steers in my part o' the Auld Sod, and 'tis solderin' and gun-totin' I've done this side o' the ocean."

Hope looked at the six-shooter strapped to O'Callahan's hip and noticed again the quick-draw way he wore it. He wasn't as obvious to spot as Harris, but apparently had also been hired as a gunman. Why did a nice quiet English gentleman like Mr. Fenwick need two gunmen siding him? Of course, one heard strange stories about rustlers and such in the vicinity of Powder River, but surely things couldn't be that bad.

"Aye, 'tis not much I've done but tote a gun since I got off the boat. First in the Rebellion and then in the West."

Jebel eyed him coldly. "Where I come from, it is customary to refer to that conflict as the War Between the States."

He was trying to pick a fight, Hope realized. He was going to pretend to be insulted as a southern partisan and use that for an excuse. She'd better find a way to stop it before it got started. She liked both of them too much to have them blazing away at each other.

"Sure now, and I've never heard that ruckus referred to in precisely that way," O'Callahan said, the lilt gone from his voice and an undertone of steel showing through.

"I assure you it is called that by anyone who makes any pretense to being a gentleman."

Hope heard the same deadly silkiness in Jebel's voice as she had in that of a man who'd shot down another in an Austin bar without bothering to determine if his opponent was armed.

O'Callahan's smile was grim as he, too, recognized the menacing intonation. "Gentleman, eh? Well, I never was one with pretensions o' that kind, but 'tis sure I am that I learned during the Rebellion the difference between a true American and a turncoat."

Hope found her voice. "Why don't we go down to the chuck wagon and see if Chou Li has saved something for us?"

"Stay out of this, Clover," Jebel said, reaching to push her out of the way.

"You down-South gentlemen in the habit o' handlin' womenfolk that way?" Timothy asked. "Do ye treat them the same way you treat your black folks?"

"Why, you son of a—" Jebel paused and looked at Hope. "If you'll pardon me, Miz Clover, I have occasion to use language that I would prefer not fall on your ears, so I must request you leave us."

"You'd do best to mind your mouth, Mason," Timothy said. "It could get ye in a lot o' trouble."

"Why, you—"

"Oh, my . . . oh, I feel . . . so faint," Hope said, swaying and putting a hand to her forehead. "I've been through too much today . . . can't stand . . ." She toppled sideways, relaxing completely and hoping to fall onto grass.

But instead of soft sage, she landed on a patch of prairie prickly pear and had to grit her teeth to keep from crying out as two spines pricked her bottom and another stuck in her thigh. Ladies who fainted, she reminded herself, did not feel pain, so she didn't dare let a sob or whimper escape her lips.

Her ploy was successful. Both men leaped from their horses with exclamations of concern and rushed to her.

"Clover, my darling!" Jebel knelt beside her and lifted her head. "Are you all right?"

"Little lady, are ye conscious? Can ye take water from me canteen?"

"Don't bend so close, O'Callahan," Jebel snapped. "A *lady* needs air when she's fainted."

"Then why don't ye fan her with your hat?" O'Callahan said. "Kneelin' there bitin' your lip will do no good at all."

"Why, you stupid, clodhopping mick! I'll have you know that I—"

They were about to go at it again. What could she do now? She couldn't faint all over again, and if they drew down on each other now, she would be right in the middle of it.

"Please stand aside, gentlemen," a voice said, "and let me tend to my daughter. Can't you see you've distressed her beyond her delicate strength?"

Thank God Pat had his wits about him and had decided to play the concerned parent.

"I'm right sorry, Pat, if I did anything to cause our sweet Clover distress," Jebel said. "That was not my intention."

"'Tis sorry I am, too, sir. She's as sweet a colleen as I've seen since I left the auld country, and the last thing I'd be wantin' to do is distress her now that I've found her."

"What is that supposed to mean?" Jebel demanded. "It sounds as though you were looking for her. I've told you, she is my—"

"Please, boys, please. Can't you hear her moaning even in her swoon? Your harsh words are getting through to her."

"'Tis that sorry I am, sir," Timothy apologized.

"Sorry, Pat," Jebel muttered.

"Poor little Clover. Poor, dear girl. I'd better carry her to the wagon, where I can tend to her proper," Pat said, lifting her in his arms. "She is subject to spells of giddiness in crowds or where there is unnecessary violence. Can't say what might happen to her health if anyone were to get into a shootin' match over her."

"Please ask her to forgive me," Jebel said, gathering up her clothes and placing them atop her limp form. "Tell her my gun will stay in its holster as long as she wants it to."

"And I'll be savin' my bullets for snakes like that Cajun," O'Callahan said as Pat turned and walked away.

Hope heard one more exchange before their voices faded.

"That's not to say I have to like you, O'Callahan."

"Nor I you. Haven't met anyone I liked less since I hit this Wyoming country," came the response. "But ye're not a rattlesnake, so I'll be keepin' my gun in its holster."

Pat looked down at his daughter. "Figured it was time I took a hand before those young bulls locked horns over your swooned body."

"I hope they don't stay back there and think of something else to fight about," she murmured.

Pat glanced over his shoulder. "No, they're following at a discreet distance, glarin' at each other but not talkin'. Long as they keep their mouths shut, they ain't insultin' each other, and besides, I've removed the bone of contention."

Hope smothered a giggle. "For a minute there I thought they might rip me apart and each take half. I like that redheaded cowpoke, don't you, Pap?"

"He's likable enough, but I don't cotton to that gun he carries," Pat said, heading for the chuck wagon, where an anxious Chou Li was waiting. "Don't like the talk I hear 'bout Powder River country either. Hear tell Fenwick is as rich as he is English and he's stayed out of the disputes up there. Still, he keeps gunmen on his payroll to guard that wooden castle of his, and it looks to me like they take orders from O'Callahan."

"Then I guess poor Jebel is lucky I stopped their quarrel."

"You'd better hush. You're supposed to be in a dead faint."

"I am," she said, shutting her eyes and letting her head fall against his chest as Pat strode more rapidly toward the Chinese cook.

"Poor missy, poor missy," Chou Li said, shaking his head mournfully as he came to meet them. "Who shoot her? I get meat cleaver and chop him up."

Hope's eyes flew open. "No, Chou, no! I'm all right. I just had a touch of vertigo."

"Vertigo? Like cholera? Chou nurse missy back to life. Know all about cholera and how to take care of her."

"Chou, I'm all right. I just ran into an excess of pigheaded maleness and had to stop a gun fight before it happened."

"Ah, missy come back to life! Thank Christian God . . . thank Buddhist god . . . thank Taoist gods . . . thank Indian Great Spirit . . ."

"Calm down, Chou, calm down. Don't waste your thanks on gods who did nothing. I wasn't dead, and nobody had to raise me from the grave."

"Ah, missy only play dead like 'Melican possum," Chou

said. "Bring into wagon. Chou save breakfast for her. Maybe she faint from lack of chow."

Reminded of food, Hope realized she was famished. Pat lifted her into the wagon and she was out of O'Callahan's poncho and into her jeans and shirt almost before the cook could bring out the plate of food he had kept warm for her. She ate ravenously, while the smiling Oriental watched and her father walked back to meet her two admirers, assure them Hope was recovering, and suggest that they return to their individual duties.

Having no choice, the pair thanked Pat, glared at each other, and took off in opposite directions.

Chapter 9

IT TOOK THREE days for Fenwick to inspect the vast herd, but finally he nodded his approval. "They are in better condition than I expected. I must congratulate you, Mr. Chisum. I will buy every head you deliver to my ranch by the end of this month."

"Fine," Uncle John said, with a warm-up chuckle. "Fine, but you haven't mentioned money yet, and I always say money talks."

"Fifteen dollars a head."

Chisum began laughing as though he would never stop. He had confided to Hope that he thought he would be lucky if he got twelve dollars a head for the cattle that would have sold for five in Texas, and now here he was laughing as though Fenwick's offer was the funniest thing he'd ever heard.

"Haw, haw, haw, haw! You're trying to take advantage of me because no one else has seen this fine herd. I was going to sell part of it to the army. They'll go over fifteen and I'd be helping my country. No siree, fifteen just ain't enough. Haw, haw, haw, haw!"

"It is a very good price, sir," Fenwick said stiffly. "There is no reason to treat my offer with levity. I am willing to pay a premium price for the whole herd delivered on the hoof."

Hope looked away, embarrassed. Someday Chisum was going to be getting into that laughing scene of his and someone would pull a gun and put a bullet right through his roar. Even this gentlemanly Englishman seemed irritated, and she wondered if Uncle John hadn't brought the whole sale to a sudden end.

"Fifteen dollars a head? Haw, haw, haw! For magnificent beasts like these? If it wasn't so funny I'd be insulted. In fact, I think I am insulted." Still laughing, Chisum turned his back on Fenwick.

The rancher looked uneasy and glanced at O'Callahan. The Irishman shrugged as if to say he knew nothing about the price of prime beefs.

"I guess that water we filled them cows with ain't foolin' Fenwick," Pat whispered to Hope.

She looked at him, startled. She had always known that, generous as he was to friends, John Chisum drove a hard bargain when it came to business deals, but she had never known him to deliberately bloat cattle to make a bigger profit. And it didn't seem to be working, because as Chisum walked away, Fenwick just stood there kicking at the dirt with his fancy British boots.

Chisum turned around and looked at the Englishman. "You know, I ought to be so insulted I wouldn't make you a counterproposal, but I'm not one to let pride stand in the way of doing business or helping out a fellow man. How about eighteen dollars a head?"

Fenwick had just cut a cigar with an expensive-looking knife and placed it in his mouth. Now he gulped audibly and snatched the slender roll of tobacco from his lips to stop himself choking on it.

"Haw, haw, haw, haw, haw, haw!" Chisum slapped his thigh in apparent glee.

Timothy had strolled over to stand beside Hope and now he asked, "Does he always do that crazy laughin'?"

She nodded. "Most often when he's taking somebody into camp on a business deal. That really seems to tickle his funny bone."

"Aye, I can see why," O'Callahan said, watching the play of expressions on his boss's face. Fenwick was obviously considering the possibility of returning to Sussex Ranch without the cattle needed to restock his spread and then discovering that some of the neighbors he didn't always get along with had bought up Chisum's herds after he had refused to buy them because of the inflated price.

"Which puts a rancher out of business faster, not having cattle or paying too much for those he buys?" Hope asked.

O'Callahan shrugged. "Either way, Fenwick's got too much money to go bankrupt, but he likes to run his hobbyhorse spread like a real ranch."

"Once more women come into this country, cows won't be the be all and end all of existence. Settlers will mean farms, and men will think more of raising crops than cattle."

"If the day comes when a fella has to push a plow to make a livin', I'll go back to Ireland. You and your pa seem to be cattle folks. Why do you want to see more settlers in the area?"

"'Cause when I'm old enough and there's enough people out here to vote and Wyoming becomes a state, I'm going to run for Congress."

O'Callahan grinned down at her. "Are ye, now?"

"Yes, after I become an actress, a lawyer, and a hoochie-koochie dancer."

His grin broadened. "'Tis the last I'd like to see first."

"I doubt you could afford the price of a ticket on a cowpuncher's pay."

"Then I'd best be workin' on me target practice. In this part o' the country, they pay a man better for how well he can shoot than for punchin' cows that can't punch back."

"Gunslinging isn't an occupation with much of a future."

"Ah, 'tis true, 'tis true. Perhaps a gambler, then. They

wear fancy vests and have gold chains on their watches."

Hope giggled and turned back to the bargaining in time to hear Fenwick say reluctantly, "Well, suppose I were to offer sixteen?"

"Not as insultin' as fifteen," Chisum said, "but almost as bad. Why don't you try eighteen or nineteen?"

"My good man, that is outrageous. I will not pay it—but I might go to seventeen."

"Done!" Chisum said before the Englishman could be sure he had actually made the offer or had merely been speculating aloud.

"Well . . . all right," he finally agreed. "Will you deliver before the first of the month?"

"You planning on going somewhere after the first of the month?" Chisum asked with the usual volley of laughter.

Fenwick looked around at the cowboys from both outfits, whose ears were trained on the negotiations. "Let's just say I happen to have very good reasons for wanting to have my ranch fully stocked as soon as possible."

"Wouldn't have nothin' to do with the railroad pushing a spur line through up toward Buffalo, would it?"

"If that line goes through, it will mean ruin for ranchers south of it," Fenwick said. "Personally, I don't believe it will go through because some very powerful men do not want it to. But just in case, I would like to be ready."

"Smart move. A man without cows wouldn't be in a position to ship them back east if the chance should come, now would he, Mr. Fenwick?"

"No," O'Callahan said, "but a lot of folks are going to be in that fix after the terrible winter this year."

The deal was made—Fenwick would buy all but the few hundred head Chisum had promised in writing to the army, and that group would be delivered to Fort Abraham Lincoln first. The cattle would be started northeast instead of northwest and would cross the North Platte River closer to its junction with the South Platte, then head on through Nebraska into the Dakotas.

Inevitably, and long before Hope wanted it to happen,

the time came for Timothy O'Callahan to depart with Fenwick and the Sussex Ranch cowboys.

"Are there many big ranches along the Powder River?" Hope asked the Irishman as they walked out away from the camp toward the area where the night watch was holding the herd. A huge prairie moon created shadows from the rocks and stunted trees and they almost seemed to dance in the breeze.

"Outside of Fairfax, almost none," he told her. "Most are small spreads that run a hundred to a hundred and fifty cows and hire two or three hands. A lot of folks up there have the reputation with the big ranchers to the south of being free with other people's cattle."

"Is that your opinion too?"

He shrugged. "Like most folks anywhere, there are good ones and others you wouldn't trust your wash with unguarded."

"Would you say it's a good place for a person to start their own ranch?"

He looked at her closely, but she couldn't read his expression because the moon was behind him and his face was in the shadow. "Well, there's lots o' land, good grass for grazing, and lots of water even though 'tis said Powder is a mile wide, two inches deep, and a thousand miles long. The summers are hot, though, and the winters sheer hell."

"Then you're saying it's not a good place?"

"Miss Clover, I'd sure like to have you livin' someplace where I could climb on a horse every couple o' days and ride over to see you and spend a few hours sittin' on the porch sippin' lemonade and—"

"Is that the strongest thing you drink?" she asked, looking up at him, half laughing.

Timothy started to answer but paused to look at the way the moonlight brought out highlights in her honey-blond hair. He reached out and put a big hand on each of her shoulders, and for a moment she thought he was going to kiss her. Her heart started to beat faster and her stomach muscles tightened as she wondered what it would be like to be kissed by this big, handsome redhead.

But he let go of her and turned to walk on. "How old did you say you were, Miss Clover?"

"Sixteen... but I'll be seventeen in four months."

"Sixteen, eh? Well now, 'tis a fine age for a colleen, but I'm pushin' twenty-seven meself, and that's kind o' a big gap, wouldn't you say?"

She smiled and tossed her head and avoided answering by reminding him, "You didn't answer my question about whether lemonade was the strongest thing you drink."

"No, I wouldn't be sayin' it was. I've been known to take a drop o' the hard stuff now and then. You wouldn't be one o' them Carrie Nation ladies, now would you?"

"No, but Pap has his troubles with the bottle," she said. "If I find a place in the Powder River country and you come to see me, I'll serve you a mint julep, if I have any mint."

"And julep."

She laughed. "There's no such thing as julep. It's only a name."

He grinned down at her. "That so? Now I'll tell you something. No one who lives anywhere near it ever calls it *the* Powder River... just Powder River."

"How odd," she murmured. His hand had found hers as they walked through a small grove of trees toward a stream.

"Powder River folks think they are different, and maybe they are. I know they sure don't think much about throwin' a rope around somebody else's calves."

"Down in Texas we say that a maverick is a motherless calf and whoever puts a brand on it first owns it."

"Well, in Wyoming the cattle barons feel like the mavericks belong to them and when they hold roundups, they portion out the mavericks accordin' to the number o' cattle a fellow has to start with."

"Does your Mr. Fenwick agree with them?"

"He kind of falls halfway between the two sides. After all, he is Powder River people even though the others live in sod huts and he lives in kind of a castle."

"A castle?"

"Compared to what everyone else lives in, even the big boys down to Cheyenne, 'tis a castle."

"What's it like?"

"Well first off, it's located on the Sweetwater a few miles below the point where the three forks of Powder River come together. Fenwick bought out the seventy-six brand from a rancher name o' Tim Foley and drove the first big herd up into Powder River country in '73. As for the castle itself, 'tis not exactly like the buildings we called castles in Ireland because 'tis built mostly of logs, but for that country, 'tis a humdinger. There's a great hall with a fireplace at each end and hung all about with Indian trophies, buffalo robes, and heads of elk and deer. A solid walnut staircase goes up to the second floor, where the bedrooms are, and about halfway up there's what they call a mezzanine—his lordship calls it the musicians' gallery—and Mrs. Fenwick has it filled with potted plants and vines that cascade over the railing into the hall below. Besides the great hall, there's a dining room, a library, an office, and a great big living room, plus the kitchen and pantry downstairs."

"My, it sounds wonderful," Hope sighed.

"Sure now, and 'tis a proper house."

"Do you live there with the Fenwicks?"

"No. I've a snug little cabin between the house and the bunkhouse, where the hands stay. Nobody stays in the house with the master and missus but Sara, the cook, and a right proper English butler, although he's really from Ottawa, where he learned not to tell folks to do it themselves when they ask him to bring cigars and brandy."

"Oh, it all sounds so grand," Hope said. "Someday I'm going to have a house like that all my own."

He laughed. "When? After you get through being a hoochie-koochie dancer?"

"No, when I'm a cattle baron."

"Baroness."

She nodded. "A cattle baroness and a political power in Wyoming after it becomes a state."

"The number of folks who pass through would make it

a state real quick if they stayed, but they're all on their way to Oregon or Washington or California and don't see anything in Wyoming that makes 'em want to stay."

They had come to the bank of the stream now and stood watching leaves that were dark against the reflected moonlight skipping over the surface of the water as the soft breeze hurried them on.

"I think I'm going to love Powder River country," Hope said dreamily.

Tim squeezed her hand. "Love it or not, ye'll be makin' it the lovelier."

She turned her head and saw the way he was looking at her and for a minute was a little afraid of him. She had known him only a few days; he wore his weapon like a gunslinger and that was the capacity in which he served Fenwick—foreman, bodyguard, and chief gunman in a rough territory known for its rustlers.

But she forgot all that when she saw his crooked smile and felt his hands on her waist as he lifted her off the ground and bent his head to touch his lips to hers. The kiss was gentle at first but gradually turned passionate and Hope let herself become lost in the sweetness and excitement of the moment.

"Oh, Timothy . . . Tim," she whispered breathlessly when his lips released hers for a moment.

"What is it, darlin'?"

"Nothing—just Timothy." Her arms crept around his neck and her lips met his again. This kiss was harder and more demanding, and he folded her so close to his chest that she could feel his heart pounding against hers, its powerful beats vibrating through her ribcage and causing tremors of desire to ripple along her nervous system as deep inside as they could go.

When he finally let her go, she was breathing so heavily that she could hardly talk and was surprised to feel his fingers shaking as they smoothed back her hair.

"Are you sure you're only sixteen?" he asked unsteadily.

"Yes, but I'm almost seventeen," she said, taking his

hand in hers as he set her down and kissing the knuckles one by one. "And twenty-seven isn't all that much older than seventeen, is it?"

His laugh was husky with emotion. "Maybe not, but it might be best for a big grown-up Irish lad to be walkin' out with a woman his own age."

"Like who?"

"No one in particular. I didn't have a specific person in mind," he said.

"Do you have to leave tomorrow?" she asked, wishing they had more time to work out this feeling between them. It was different from what had happened between herself and Jebel, and that wasn't worked out either, even if Jebel thought it was.

"His lordship wants to get back to her ladyship. They've only been married six months, you know, and she's a real beauty."

"Is she now?" Hope felt an unexpected pang of jealousy.

"Now, now, Miss Clover, don't go gettin' any ideas about me and Miss Anne. I respect her and her husband a great deal."

"Yes, and I've heard about you Irishmen. My pap is one, you know."

"And I've heard about southern beauties with hotheaded friends who claim to be fiancés."

Hope laughed in spite of herself. "He really isn't, you know. He hasn't asked me. He just says we're engaged."

"And if he does ask you?"

"Well . . . he'll be going back to New Mexico soon, and it'll be some time before he returns with another herd. I figure, I have time to think about that later."

"Do you have time now to think about my kissing you again?"

"You didn't ask the first time."

"No, so I guess I won't this time either," he said, gathering her into his arms and capturing her lips.

After long minutes of breathtaking, soul-searching kisses, his lips moved along her cheek to nibble at an earlobe and slide down her neck to the open V of her shirt and back to her lips before he broke the embrace and lowered her tingling body to the ground again. "God, I wish you were at least twenty-one."

"You spend a lot of time worrying about age when it's what a person is that really counts."

"Aye, I know, but—" he said in a strangled voice.

"What would you do if I were twenty-one?"

"I'm not going to tell you. Someday when you're all grown-up I might."

"You're the one who needs to grow up," she said as he took her hand and kissed the palm. "I know what you want to do and I'm not going to let you. But I'm kind of glad you want to."

"Why, you know-it-all little devil! You're as brash as a fisher lass in Galway."

"Maybe on the outside, but inside I'm shaking like a little girl at her first party. Not that I know too much about that because I never had a party."

"Ye never had a party?" He sat down on a flat rock and settled her in his lap. "Ah, 'tis a fine party I'd like t'be givin' you. One like we used t' have back in the auld country, where everybody danced to the fiddle till the sun was like to come up, whirlin' around and laughin', dizzy from havin' so much fun, not to mention a wee drap o' poteen."

"Oh, I would love to dance with you all night long," Hope said, putting her head on his shoulder and looking up into his sparkling green eyes.

"And I would love to do anything at all all night long with you, mavourneen," he said, stroking her hair with one hand while the other one ran up and down her spine. "Even if 'twas only a barn-raisin' up Powder River way."

Impulsively, she kissed the side of his neck and along his firm jawline. He shuddered and then they were kissing again, straining together and communicating their mutual passion and need with touches and caresses that only fanned the flames higher.

When she heard herself gasping and moaning, Hope became frightened. She wasn't used to feeling herself driven from within to do something she knew she shouldn't do, something that would only mean a lot of trouble for them both.

She pulled free of the torrid embrace and stood up, saying shakily, "I—I'd better be getting on back to camp. The moon's sinking low, and—"

"And what?" he asked, making an obvious effort to get himself back under control.

"Well, pretty soon the day riders will start getting up. Cooky is probably already up, heating the water for coffee and slicing the bacon. And when they smell that, the night guard will start to drift in and—"

"And what?" he asked again in a much calmer tone.

"Jebel is in charge of the night guard, and I don't want him to see you come in with me."

"Clover honey, I am in no way afraid of that curly-haired terror from below the Red River."

She put her hands on his shoulders and looked into his eyes. "I know you're not. In fact, I'm afraid you'd kill him if it came to real trouble."

He grinned halfheartedly. "Sure now, and ye know I'd not be doing that if you asked me not to."

"But he's quite capable of forcing a fight on you."

"Then I'd have to wing the Rebel, or shoot him in some part of Dixie he doesn't absolutely need."

"Shhh!" She put a hand over his mouth only to have him hold it there while he kissed the palm and licked it.

Her blue eyes widened as he did it again. "What is that for? What does it mean?"

He laughed recklessly. "That's the question you've already given me the answer to."

She drew in her breath. "Maybe—maybe the answer won't always be the same."

"For now it is, because we ride out in two or three hours."

"And you'll be going back to a woman who has a different answer for you."

"Back to a woman who has never heard the question asked."

"Neither have I."

"No, but you're the lass who answers before she hears the question," he said with a grin.

They were strolling back toward camp now when all she really wanted to do was cling to him, to go back into the grove of trees, and do more of the long, sweet kissing. But the camp was astir, and even though it was only Chou Li, who worshiped her and would never tell a soul, she didn't want to be seen returning at this hour with Tim.

"Let me go on in by myself," she whispered as he swung her up in his arms again and bruised her lips with hard kisses. "Ah!" She was so breathless she couldn't continue.

"Why, sure now, me darlin', I wouldn't be compromisin' ye in front o' the cows or anyone else," he said huskily, and let her go as she ran toward the camp.

Thankful for the darkness that still covered all despite the faint light that was starting to appear in the east, Hope hurried on and had almost reached the place where she was supposed to be bedded down when she stumbled over a saddle and went sprawling on the ground, causing the nearby *remuda* to start milling around and the guard standing watch on the horses to call out. She lay still, hardly breathing, until in the gradually increasing grayness of dawn she became aware of a man standing over her and recognized his boots.

"Good morning, Uncle John," she said.

"'Mornin', Hope," Chisum said dryly. "Been out doin' a little sparkin', have you?"

"Uh... well, yes."

"Mmmm. And you were with that O'Callahan fella instead of Jebel?"

Hope sighed. There was no use lying. "Yes, I was."

He cackled quietly. "You women! Fickle, every one of you! Did I ever tell you about the woman who broke my heart?"

"No, sir, but I heard you tell Uncle Charlie Goodnight about it a couple dozen times."

"Haw, haw, haw, haw. Well, you better get yourself some chow and saddle up 'cause we're pointing these cow critters north just as soon as Fenwick and his boys ride off."

Two hours later the cattle were starting slowly northward, the hands spread out around them in a half circle, and Fenwick and Chisum were shaking hands while Hope stood watching with her father and O'Callahan.

"Two months at the longest then, Mr. Chisum," Fenwick was saying. "I want the cattle settled on the range before the fall rains start. Winter comes early up at Powder River."

"Two months it is," Chisum said. "If you ride horseback all the way home, you won't get there much before we do."

"We'll ride across country to Omaha and take a train from there to Cheyenne. Even going that far out of our way will save us a couple of weeks."

"One of these days we'll be able to bring cattle north by rail and old trail drivers like me will be out of work."

"You'll be retired and watching your grandchildren growing up long before that," Fenwick said.

"Haw, haw, haw, haw, haw! Not me, not old John Chisum."

Hope quit listening, acutely conscious of the way Timothy was looking at her as he edged his horse closer to hers.

"Well, lassie, time to say goodbye."

"I—I thought we said that last night."

"Always time for one last kiss," he said, and lifted her halfway out of her saddle, his mouth seeking hers in a long, lip-bruising, tongue-tangling kiss.

When he set her back on her mount, he was no longer laughing but staring as though he were seeing her for the first time. It didn't surprise her, because she felt that way every time he kissed her.

"Begorrah, lass, if you're not a continuous revelation to this poor Irish lad."

She was having trouble regaining her own composure, not having expected such an ardent embrace right out in front of everyone.

Timothy tipped his hat to Chisum and Pat Cox and said sotto voce to Hope, "I'll be seein' you up Powder River way, macushla, so don't go and get married till we have a chance to work this out."

Hope watched him ride off, touching her lips and muttering to herself, "You'll be seeing me all right, you red-headed so-and-so."

"What's going on?" Jebel asked, riding up behind her, looking handsome enough to start any girl's heart fluttering with his curly black hair falling down over his forehead and his dark eyes flashing.

"I—I was just saying goodbye to Mr. Fenwick and his men," Hope said.

"Any particular one of Mr. Fenwick's men?" Jebel's voice was tense and angry.

"No, to all of them."

"Did it take all of them to bruise your lips like that?"

"Yes, Mr. Mason sir, it surely did," she drawled in her best Deep South manner. "'Cause you know what? I simply had to kiss every one of those po' cowboys who haven't seen a woman in months, and they all was mighty appreciative."

Jebel wheeled his horse around, and as he rode off she thought she heard him swear, a very unusual thing for a southern gentleman to do in the presence of a lady.

Chapter 10

"THEY'RE RUNNING!" The shout came from the guard in the middle of the night and brought Hope out from under her blanket and poncho instantly. She had been sleeping fitfully during a raging rainstorm. Now it had turned into a fireworks display that had stampeded the herd, or at least part of it.

Soaking wet, she grabbed for her boots and chaps and whistled for Rollo, who would be close at hand, storm or no storm.

"They're running! A third of the herd! Heading for the Platte!" It was Jebel's voice, fighting to outshout the rolling thunder.

Cringing as a particularly bright streak of jagged lightning lashed across the sky directly above Hope's head, she emptied the water out of her boots and pulled the cold, slippery things onto her feet.

"Everybody out! They're heading for those coulees over toward Plumo Creek! Get 'em milling, boys! Get to circling 'em or we're up a creek!"

The lightning was almost continuous now, the sky bright with it and the ground shaking from the tremendous bombardment of thunder. There were few things in nature as spectacular and awesome as a thunderstorm in the northern plains. Hope had experienced many a norther in Texas, but that had been mostly hard cold winds and blowing sand. This was a whole lot more dramatic than that.

"Hope! Hope!" her father called as he milled around with the other figures in the alternating dark and light. "You stay here at camp! This is nothing for you to get into!"

She made a face, got her chaps laced on, grabbed up her saddle, which had been serving as her pillow, and raced to throw it on Rollo's back.

The little cow pony had his ears back but hadn't budged from the spot he had moved to in response to Hope's whistle. While the other hands were running around trying to get their panicked horses saddled, Hope was swinging up into the saddle.

"Keep those other cattle steady!" Chisum bellowed above the storm. "You night guards, don't let the rest of them go or we'll lose our ass for sure!"

"They're headed northeast, Uncle John!" yelled a cowboy whose voice Hope didn't recognize. "They've got their tails between their legs. They're running flat out."

"Take after 'em, boys!" Chisum shouted. "Take after 'em, and ride like Comanches was after you!" He had managed to get on his horse and was heading with half a dozen of the night guard in the direction the stampeding cattle had taken.

Hope let out a whoop of sheer excitement and turned Rollo's head to follow them, praying the smart little horse could avoid gopher holes, especially after she saw one night guard go flying over the head of his mount when the animal went down.

"Look, there they are!" someone yelled as Hope caught up to the group led by Chisum and Mason.

"Get ahead of them, boys, get ahead of them!" Jebel was yelling, waving one arm at the bunched herd the lightning revealed ahead of them.

"Get up front and turn the lead critters, boys! Circle 'round from both sides and turn them in on themselves! Get them circling! Geth them milling!"

That was always the tactic in a stampede. There was no way of stopping a stampede short of a barrier the size of the Grand Canyon; they would run right through anything else. But it was sometimes possible to get a few of the lead cattle confused and frightened enough to turn in on the rest of the herd.

Hope and her horse were both wet and miserable, but the excitement of the chase through the stormy night was rapidly warming their blood. Rollo's nostrils flared and he let out a whinny that sounded almost like a shout of defiance.

Hope's hands were cold. She had forgotten her gauntlets in the rush to get mounted. That might turn out to be a serious oversight if she had to use her lariat. Her hands would be cut and bleeding before she could get the rope wrapped around the pommel of her saddle.

The first riders was gaining on the cattle, and behind them they could hear the shouts of other hands coming to their aid. Those in the rear probably wouldn't make too much difference unless the chase continued for several miles. Hope prayed silently that it wouldn't because every racing step brought the danger of a broken leg for the horse and a broken neck for the rider, certain death for both.

There were two horses close to her, and in the flashes of lightning she could see Chou Li mounted on one and a Mexican boy named Juan on the other. The boy had apparently leaped onto his horse with no saddle or spurs. He had only the reins in his hands and a blanket under him, which meant that the slightest misstep could unseat and throw him.

"Go back, Juan, go back!" she shouted as she maneuvered Rollo between two large jutting rocks, hail pelting down all the while. "It's dangerous—too dangerous!"

"Where you can go, señorita, Juan can go. Juan is a man, you are a lady, no?"

"Lady, no," she said, leaping a small arroyo and turning on almost the proverbial dime when the fleeing cattle suddenly changed direction, as though every mindless one had had the same flash of inspiration.

"Holy Moses, it's like the devil was telling 'em what to do," she muttered. Rollo's iron-shod hooves skidded and threw off sparks as they raced across flat rocks not far from the banks of a dry riverbed where the Platte had changed direction some time in the past.

"They're heading for the big coulee over to the southeast," Chisum was shouting. "Get ahead of 'em, boys! Turn 'em or there'll be fifteen hundred dead cows and the Limey will never see his new herd."

"And Uncle John will be out his seventeen a head," Hope said to herself as the smaller, more agile Rollo darted ahead of the others by dogging his way through a stand of cottonwoods and jutting rocks to get an angle on the stampede.

Hope was almost alone now, perhaps five hundred yards ahead of the others, with only Juan following her. She was moving at an angle to the cattle that could put her between them and the coulee.

Her chances of turning back the herd all by herself were practically nil, but she let her riding whip drop to hang from her wrist and reached for the revolver in her holster. It was still there, thank God, and if she could get ahead of the herd, she could at least attract the attention of the leaders with it. Of course that might lead to them and her being overrun by the crazed beasts behind.

"Let's go, Rollo! There's just a chance we can slow 'em!" she said, and the little horse responded with an extra burst of speed and heart, no whip needed to drive him onward.

There were shouts on the other side of the herd, that sea of heaving backs and plunging heads, and she thought she could make out Chisum, her father, and Jebel perhaps half as far behind her as she was behind the herd that was running toward the coulee and certain destruction.

"Don't try to get ahead of them by yourself!" Her father's shout carried faintly across the rumble of the stampede and then was drowned by a blast of thunder that almost seemed to rock the mountain to the west of them.

The cattle were stumbling over themselves, steers were

going down, and smaller, weaker animals were being run over by those behind them. The loss would be severe even if the herd was turned short of the coulee.

"Run, Rollo, run!" she whispered to the horse, who was already moving faster than he had ever run before.

A shout from behind told her Juan was still following her, with Chou fairly close on their heels. The Mexican boy was on an inferior horse, but his expert bareback riding was making up for it, and Chou was managing to stay in sight by sheer grit. He was carrying a shotgun in one hand and a pistol in the other, holding the reins in his mouth, but that was nothing new; the Chinese cook had always been an inventive horseman.

"Keep going, missy," his voice came to her through the clamor of the storm and the thunder of the herd. "We come to help you, Chou and Juan!"

His voice was swept away on the wind, and Hope was nearing the leaders of the herd, big, bull-like steers with five-foot-long horns and the dispositions of mountain lions. Their eyes glinted white in the flashes of lightning, their mouths hung open, tongues lolling out and sides heaving.

Closer and closer she came, her Colt drawn, her quirt in the other hand. She was guiding Rollo with her knees and trusting to the pony's cow sense to keep him out of danger.

Rollo not only had cow sense, he had a lot of spunk. He kept pushing nearer the outriders of the herd, his sides almost touching those of a steer whose fearsome horns could have impaled him in an instant.

Hope's heart was in her mouth as she began shouting and waving her hat in an effort to turn some of the outer animals in toward the center. She wasn't sure, but she thought the coulee had a drop of perhaps twenty-five feet to the bottom and very sheer sides. It was less than a mile away, and the steers were showing not the least sign of faltering in their mad rush to destruction.

"Whoa! Back there! Back! Whoa!" she screeched at them, trying to nudge the nearest beast with her foot against its side, waving her whip, doing everything she could think of to turn them before she had to make the fateful decision to cut in front of them.

Rollo had the speed on them now. The small horse seemed tireless, his feet beating a constant tattoo that could only be heard in rare moments through the ear-shattering thunder of the herd that almost matched that in the sky.

Hope's efforts were having no effect on the leaders of the stampede. They plunged right on, ignoring shouts, her waving hat, and the pony's presence at their flanks.

"We're going to have to do it, Rollo. We have to, even if we get trampled," she whispered, shuddering at the memory of the terrible thing she had seen after a stampede in Texas. A horse and a man had been trampled by a herd that nothing would halt, and all that had been left of the horse was a carcass sheared by thousands of hooves. The cowboy had fallen under the horse and there wasn't enough of him left to tell the difference between human and horse flesh.

"Come on, Rollo!" She barely had to twist the reins, because the pony seemed to know by instinct what was needed now. His head went up. He nickered, then cut so close in front of the first steer that the long horns almost raked his flanks and Hope thought she could feel the beast's fiery breath.

As they dashed across the front of the herd with about twenty paces to spare, Hope aimed the Colt in the air and pulled the trigger.

The sound of the gun echoed above the pounding hooves of the stampeding animals, the heads of several of the leaders went up, and they made as though to turn away from this new menace toward the north. But they were packed shoulder to shoulder and rump to rump, almost locking horns and pushing against each other.

"Back, back! Turn, you bloody beasts, turn!" Hope yelled, firing across in front of them during a break in the lightning, firing so they could see the flash of the pistol as well as hear its loud crack.

She thought she saw some falter, but the herd was coming closer and so was the coulee. Although she didn't dare turn her head to look for the jumble of rocks and trees along its bank, she could almost feel the menace of the death gully on her right as Rollo hurled them across the path of the stampede.

There was still time, she thought, for them to escape those menacing horns and hooves if they rode straight across, shooting and shouting but not slowing down. With Rollo's speed and sure-footedness, they could probably make it. But she was doing this to turn the herd, and was determined to succeed even if it meant riding back in front of it from the other direction.

She had to use both hands to reload, and gave herself up entirely into the pony's safekeeping. Rollo had to maintain a few feet of space between them and total disaster.

"Clover, get out of the way!" It was Jebel yelling now from the far side of the herd. Behind him were her father and, a little farther back, John Chisum. Beyond him were the shadows of half a dozen men strung out to the rear.

Hope waved. With the gun reloaded, she suddenly drew rein, turned Rollo away from the leaders to give herself a bit more room, and started back across the front of the stampede.

But in turning she saw the coulee almost within rock-throwing distance and realized that it would be almost impossible to make it back across before they all reached the banks and went over in one squealing, dying mass of girl, horse, and steers.

For a minute she regretted her decision, but she was too busy to think about it as Rollo flew along almost in the faces of the leaders, with Hope shouting and firing at their feet, and the pony snapping at the closest beasts.

Again there was faltering among the leaders and those directly behind them, but time was running out so fast that Hope could feel the icy hand of death on the back of her neck.

The cattle in the rear kept pushing against those ahead, still in the grip of panic, since they hadn't yet had to face the gunfire or the fiery little horse and its rider.

Shouts and shots were coming from behind Hope now,

and she knew Jebel and the others must have rounded to the front of the herd and would soon be reinforced by the riders trailing behind. Maybe they would be able to save part of the herd. Perhaps as she and Rollo went over the embankment with hundreds of steers, the men could turn the left flank and get the remaining part of the herd to milling. It was too late for her and Rollo, all but among the cattle, threatened by horns that scratched the pony's sides. It was only her nimbleness that had saved them so far. Reloading had enabled Hope to continue blazing away at the feet of the animals and into the herd itself. Several steers stumbled and went down to be trampled by those behind, but it wasn't enough. The brink was only a few feet away now.

Suddenly there was a tremendously loud blast and then the lesser crack of a pistol. Looming before her were Chou, blazing away with the shotgun, and young Juan, firing a pistol and waving a cape that made him look like a matador down in Mexico.

The herd began turning away. The shotgun blast was as awesome to them as the rage of the storm that now was pelting horses, humans, and cattle with hailstones that felt big enough to batter a skull.

"Back, you idiots! Turn! Turn!" she yelled as Chou blazed away again. The horns of death were only inches from Rollo's flanks, but the horse was undaunted and the menace was slowly swinging toward the center of the herd, pushing and shouldering the others aside, confusing the beasts to the rear, starting all of them into a struggling, mooing, rumbling mass that ran into another mass coming from the opposite direction as the riders with Chisum and Pat turned the stampede in from that angle.

"Oh, my!" Hope said, leaning forward to hug Rollo, whose flanks were heaving. "We did it, boy, we did it!"

Chou and Juan were beside her, their horses circling the herd and proving to the stupid animals that a smart cow horse was a match for any twenty of them, snapping and lashing with its hooves at those reluctant to turn.

Chapter 11

"BABY . . . CLOVER . . . are you all right?" Pat Cox asked anxiously as he rode up to her on Star.

"Yes, Pap, I'm fine," she said, "thanks to Chou and Juan. Dear Chou, you're the one who did it."

"Shotgun more better than little pistol," Chou said, raising the double-barreled weapon above his head.

"You right, you no lady," Juan said, flashing her his white-toothed smile. "You a devil on a horse."

"Thank you, Juan," she laughed. "That's the nicest thing anybody ever said to me."

Jebel rode up, his face strained in the diminishing flashes of lightning. "Clover, you little fool. You came closer to getting yourself killed than I've seen anybody do and live to tell about it."

She grinned up at him defiantly, head thrown back, her sombrero hanging down her neck and her hair blowing in the wind. "We did it, didn't we? Rollo and I did it! We knew we could!"

"Clover, honey, you did mighty well. You made an old

man very happy," Chisum said. "You also gave me a few dozen more gray hairs, but without you, I think we would have lost them all."

Hope knew the prospect of losing a herd worth seventeen dollars a head was what was making John Chisum wax sentimental, but still she was appreciative of his praise, just as she was touched by her father's concern. Jebel was the one who troubled her, because he seemed more angry than worried.

"That was a silly thing to do," he said. "A herd of cattle isn't worth your life."

"Oh, now, Jebel, I wouldn't say that," Chisum said, his usual laughter ringing out. "Guess it depends on whose cattle they are."

"They're runnin'! They're runnin' again!" A shout from one of the men on the left side of the herd jolted them all out of their jubilance.

"They're headed north toward the Platte!" someone else yelled. "Look at 'em go!"

"Yeah, there they go," Jebel said, pointing to where perhaps two hundred head had darted out of the main body of milling cattle and were headed into scrub brush and broken rock terrain near the bend where the North Platte joined the South.

"Let's go get 'em!" Hope shouted, preparing to spur Rollo into action again.

"No, let 'em go," Chisum said. "That's only a couple hundred. Boys, hold the rest of the herd. That's more important. It'll take a couple of days to dig those critters out of that jungle."

"We can get them, Uncle John," Hope said. "I know we can. Let's round them up and bring them back."

Chisum paused to study the situation, from the gradual paling of the horizon in the east to the slackening wind and rain, the fading lightning, and the excited bellowing, pushing, and shoving of the cattle. "No, honey, I can't spare the men. We got to keep this herd closed up or they'll get their wind up again just from the sight of daylight."

"Those runaways are halfway to the Platte by now," Jebel

said as the animals began disappearing into the broken, jumbled land with its thickets of scrub timber and cottonwoods.

"You're right, John," Pat Cox agreed. "Better to let the few go to save the many."

"Then I'll go get them by myself," Hope said stubbornly. She hadn't risked her neck to save a bunch of cattle only to watch part of them race off into the wilderness, where they'd eventually be rounded up by Sioux or Cheyenne and be butchered.

"You're crazy, girl," Jebel said. "Those steers are lost for good. We got to get this bunch back to the main herd."

Hope ignored him as she reloaded her Colt and cinched up her saddle. "I'll get them, Uncle John, don't you worry."

"Girl, it would take an army to round up them critters," Chisum said, scratching his chin.

"Uncle John, this here pinto of mine is the best cow horse, bar none, in the whole country. He don't look like much, but he can just plain talk cow. He don't whinny when he's after a cow, he moos. He could round up those crazies all by himself if we had the time, but since we're in a hurry to get on the trail, I'll go along to help."

"Clover Crawford, you are the most braggy girl kid I ever run into," Chisum said. "You can no more round up them critters in that hell's acre over there than you could fly up and around the moon."

"You just watch me!" she said, checking that her saddle was on tight before leaping up into it.

"Clover, listen to reason. It just can't be done," Jebel said. "Besides, we need you to help with these cattle."

"Aw, come on now, Jebel," she teased. "A big fella like you ought to be able to run a couple thousand tired-out cows back to the main herd all by yourself without help from poor little me."

Jebel looked as though his dignity had been mortally offended, but Hope gave him one of her more dazzling smiles and he shrugged and turned to give orders to the men to keep the cattle milling for a while longer before starting them back toward camp.

"I'll tell you what I'll do, Uncle John," Hope said on a sudden inspiration. "Let me go after those steers and if I'm not back with most of them by noon, you start on along the trail and I'll catch up with you."

"More likely you'll catch up with a Sioux who'll take you or your scalp back to his hogan," Pat said. "You stay right here with the rest of us."

But she had sparked John Chisum's interest. She could tell by the way he was stroking his chin and looking in the direction in which the runaways had disappeared into the thicket.

"Tell you what, honey," he said finally. "If you and that cow-talkin' horse of yours can round up as many as fifty head by noon, I'll give you the pick of one out of every five."

"That's ten cows," Jebel said, looking angry again. "Don't do it, Clover. You'll break your neck for nothing in there."

But Hope was already whooping and waving her hat above her head. "Uncle John, I'm gonna bring back at least a hundred and fifty of them critters and thank you for thirty head to start a little spread of my own."

"Daughter, don't do it," Pat said.

"Don't be foolish, Clover," Jebel warned.

But Chisum was grinning and waving her on with his Stetson. "Get going, girl! I'll be surprised if you show up with ten, but good luck and don't break your fool neck!"

"No, sir," she said, setting out at a gallop toward the thicket as full daylight began to brighten the sky over the dangerous jumbled acres of brush and rock.

"Come on, Rollo, we are going to get ourselves a start in life," she whispered into the pony's silken ear. "We'll teach those fellas that people who can talk cow make better nursemaids for the critters than any five big strong males."

Rollo responded with a whinny that seemed to say he understood and agreed.

"That's a boy! Let's go get 'em!" Hope said, and then turned to look over her shoulder at the sound of horse's hooves.

Thinking it was Jebel Mason coming to talk her out of

her enterprise, she spurred Rollo forward. Unused to this kind of treatment, the pony neighed in protest.

"Sorry, boy. I know you're tired, but you're the only one who can do what I need right now, and I promise after this job I won't ride you for at least a week."

Looking behind her again, Hope could now see her pursuer and it wasn't Jebel. It was Juan, still riding bareback and grinning widely.

"Señorita, you need help. Juan help," he said as he caught up with her.

"I don't need any help."

"But, señorita, I want to help you get herd of your own, then maybe some day you own ranch and give Juan a job, no?"

"Well, it is sure that I'm gonna have my own spread before you can say jackrabbit, but I don't know how long it will be before I can afford to pay wages."

"Juan work for found till we all get rich and have great house and many horses, then he be your foreman."

She grinned at him. "All right, Mr. Foreman. You can hold the cattle when I bring them out. That old gray mare of yours couldn't walk through a thicket, much less run down cattle in it."

The youth's spontaneous laugh echoed after her as Rollo suddenly spurted ahead, and Hope wondered if he'd been taking lessons from John Chisum. She entered the thicket and branches brushed against her face and body while Rollo half-pranced and half-danced between the rocks and scrub trees.

There was a path of sorts made by the two hundred crazed cows that had just gone crashing through. Rollo snorted as a young steer appeared unexpectedly ahead of them, legs spread, eyes glaring, and head lowered menacingly. The pony whinnied threateningly and bared its teeth. The steer had been around cow horses all its short life and knew who was boss between horse and cow. It turned and trotted off in the opposite direction.

Hope let out a whoop and went after him. "That's my Rollo," she said proudly. "Not only does he talk cow, he can buffalo a steer until it does what he wants it to do."

She caught up with the steer in about five minutes and discovered a dozen others with him. Taking off her hat, she waved it as she rode toward them. They milled about and scattered a little, but Rollo circled them like a sheepdog, dodging among the rocks and trees and keeping them together.

"Come on, you critters, you're going home!" Hope shouted, and started them back along the rough trail to where Juan was waiting.

It wasn't easy, but they got it done. She turned that first dozen over to Juan and plowed back into the brush again, fighting the lashing branches and getting drenched in occasional gusts of rain and hail as she searched for cattle, finding them in groups of two, three, or four, and sometimes alone. Twice she had to resort to her lariat to drag a squalling brute out of a bog into which it had fallen before she could head it in the right direction.

Then as the sun began to show through the remaining clouds scudding across the heavens, she located almost fifty of the creatures, now grazing contentedly on the banks of the Platte. But it was marsh grass they were eating, and some were sinking into the soggy earth almost up to their hocks.

"Come on, Rollo, we've got our work cut out for us this time," she said, guiding the pony around the group toward more solid ground on an embankment overlooking the stream.

The embankment was about three feet high, and steep. Rollo had to hunch down in the wet slippery earth to haul them up onto the rise, but they were able to work their way around the cattle. Then Hope shouted and rode at them. "Get going, you dumb things! Get out of here before you get bogged down to your haunches!"

Most of the cattle began to move in the direction she wanted them to go, but there were a few hungry, stubborn beasts that didn't want to stop chewing on the lush, tasty grass. When she had about half of them started down the trail toward Juan, she rode back to work on the dozen or so that were still grazing. Several were cows with dogies staying close around them, the type of animal that made up the drag. Weaker and smaller, drag animals usually arrived at watering and grazing areas hours after the point creatures. At the moment, this group seemed to have found paradise and saw no reason to leave it.

Hope could see a lot of reasons why they should, one of the most pressing being the rapidly climbing sun. Another was that some of them were sinking deeper into the mud as their hooves broke the crust that had formed under the trampled grass.

"Come on, you white-faced boobies!" she yelled, waving her hat and laying her quirt lightly on the back of a balky beast.

Some of the animals went on grazing, others started reluctantly along the newly made path. One young cow with her dogie headed off in the wrong direction and Hope had to swerve Rollo around to go after her. This cow didn't want to be pushed around. She slapped her head into Rollo's flank and the horse promptly bit her on the shoulder.

Letting out a bellow of fear, the cow turned and made off the way Hope wanted her to go, but her dogie slipped and went down, sinking into a section that was completely waterlogged. When it was in up to its shoulders, it began howling for its mother.

The rambunctious cow turned back and came at Rollo on the run. Of its own accord the pony spun out of the way but slipped and threw Hope to the ground.

For a minute she sat there, half-stunned, but thankful to see Rollo quickly recover her footing, apparently unhurt.

Now the problem of the rebellious cow and her trapped dogie had to be dealt with. The calf's terrified squeals filled the air, and the mother was angry enough to lower her head and dash at Hope, whom she obviously blamed for the plight of her little one. Hope scrambled to her feet and tried to jump aside, only to slip and be shoved off balance by the beast and sent sprawling into a spot that was like a real swamp. She was in deep trouble now, covered with mud and unable to pull herself out of the sticky, sucking stuff she had fallen into.

"Rollo, help me!" she called, struggling to reach an overhanging branch.

The obstreperous cow had nudged and pushed her bawling offspring out of the watery hole, and the pony was busy doing his duty by trotting at their heels to make sure they took the right path to the trail, but he turned back at once in answer to Hope's cry.

"Over here, boy, where I can get hold of your stirrup."

The horse picked its way carefully to her side, turned so she could get hold of a stirrup, and then stood with spread legs while Hope hauled herself out of the bog and onto solid ground. Then they both went after the creatures who had almost led them to disaster.

The rest of the morning went the same way, and finally, at about eleven o'clock, an exhausted Hope and Rollo stumbled out of the morass with five more cows and found Juan waiting with the previously collected hundred and ten.

"That's it," Hope said as they reached the Mexican boy's side. "Neither horse nor human can do any more."

"Already you do more than the rest could," he said. "I work for you from now on, huh?"

"You did a good job too, keeping these critters from wandering off with only that nag of yours. Yes, if Uncle John keeps his word, and me and Pap stake a claim and start our own spread, you'll be our first hired hand, although God only knows how we'll pay you."

"With found and part of profits when they come," he said with another of his dazzling smiles. "With that I bring my mama, my papa, two brothers, and sister from New Mexico. They all work for you and I will be foreman."

"Sure," she said tiredly, doubting for the moment that it would ever come true.

When John Chisum saw how many cattle she had brought back, he pushed his hat back on his head and stood staring. "Well, I'll be damned! You actually did it, didn't you?" he said, and burst into another of his bouts of laughter.

"What's so funny, Uncle John?" Hope asked, wondering why she had never asked him that before.

"Well . . . haw, haw, haw. You know, Clover honey, I

just never expected you to bring back that many cow critters."

"Didn't you, Uncle John?" Her voice was soft but held an undercurrent of anger. She knew he was looking for a way to renege on his bargain.

"Well, honey, you know them cattle are worth seventeen dollars on the hoof at Fenwick's Sussex Ranch, don't you?"

"Yes."

"Well now, honey, if I was a rich man, I could spare these cattle, but—"

"You are a rich man, Uncle John. Did you forget?"

"Well, yes, I suppose you could say I'm rich in land, in cows, and the love of my friends, but—"

Hope looked around at Jebel, her father, Juan, and half a dozen cowboys who were watching their exchange intently. "Uncle John, you're looking to lose the love of your friends because of your love of the silver dollar."

John Chisum had the grace to gulp and look a little sheepish. "But, honey, you know how these things are. A man brings a herd of cattle this far and manages to sell them for a good price—"

"An exorbitant price," Jebel put in.

"—and then has to give away twenty-three of them. That ain't hardly fair now, is it?"

"It ain't fair to make a promise you don't intend to keep, Mr. Chisum," one of the cowboys said.

"You know, Uncle John," Hope said, "Uncle Charlie Goodnight once told me that as far as he knew you had done only one dishonest thing in your life, and that was when you tried to sell him those cows with the brand blotted out. That's why he forgave you."

John Chisum looked as though he was standing on hot coals. Caught between his cupidity and his better nature and real affection for this girl he had often treated like a daughter, he was in torment.

"All right, all right!" The words seemed torn from him. "They're yours. The cattle are yours—one out of five."

"Thank you, Uncle John. I knew you would do the right thing," Hope said, and then added quickly, "You know what else I need to start my own spread? I need a bull and I saw one back in those canebrakes and bogs."

"Bull? What bull?" Chisum demanded.

"It must be Caesar, Uncle John," Jebel said. "He's the only one missing."

"But he's my best bull. I planned on taking him back to Texas with me. We only brought him along to act as a leader and to service some of the heifers who come of age."

That was probably true, Hope thought. Some trail bosses did take a bull or two along for just those reasons and then returned them to the home range afterward.

"He was a leader, all right," she said. "He led that group right into the bog. He did you out of seventy-five cattle I couldn't find, Uncle John."

"I'm also out twenty-three you did find," he said, kicking at the dirt with one badly scuffed boot. "Oh, go ahead, you keep him if you can find him. You might as well get a good start in life as a halfway one."

Hope got that bull, but it wasn't easy. After a short rest and some food, she mounted Sally instead of the exhausted Rollo and returned to the boglike area with her father and Jebel. When she came on the bull, she managed to get a lariat around him and hang on while he first plunged at the horse and then tried to get into a canebrake. Pat came up in the nick of time and got another rope around him and finally Jebel managed to throw him with a third. Then they made their way back to camp with the big, black fire-breathing monster trailing reluctantly behind with three stray cows, which found him immensely attractive, and their dogies.

John Chisum took one look at the three cows and the pair of calves and practically blew his top. "You're robbin' me blind, girl! You're worse than all the rustlers I ever ran into in Texas."

"But, Uncle John, you always said that you didn't mind if someone stole a few of your cows because you stole whole herds. I thought you meant that," she said, dimpling at him.

He roared this time, and for once she was sure he was really laughing inside out of humor and the joke on himself.

"Take 'em, damnit, take 'em," he said. "And with your talent for trailing a loose rope, you'll probably be the biggest rancher in all the Dakota territory before you're twenty."

"Wyoming, Uncle John. I'm going to file for a homestead in Wyoming. The territorial legislature in Cheyenne gave women suffrage because they have so few folks living there they can't get up a quorum without the females."

"What you figure on doing, honey, voting at sixteen?"

"No siree, Uncle John. I'm figuring on running for office when I'm twenty-one."

Even John Chisum had no answer for that.

They crossed the North Platte the next morning, the hands swimming along with the horses and cattle. The current was swift and the water cold, but Chisum and Mason had the fording of a river down to a science by then, and as long as the cattle didn't panic, they seemed to know instinctively what was required of them.

Sitting beside Jebel on the opposite shore, watching the men bring the last of the herd across—those in the drag needed more help than the others, and the weaker dogies had to be dragged bodily through the water—Hope shook her head. "I swear I never would have believed cows were such good swimmers if I hadn't seen it with my own eyes half a dozen times on this trip. And not just cows, but Texas cows that are more used to doing without water than swimming across it."

"Heard tell there was a couple of young fellows, brothers by name of Saunders, who back during the War Between the States took eleven hundred head east to sell to the Confederacy. Swum them across the Mississippi, they did."

"Jebel, the Mississippi must be a mile across in some places. Do you believe that story?"

"More than a mile in lots of places," he said, "but I got to believe their story because they were southern gentlemen."

"And you're a southern gentleman, too, aren't you, Jebel?"

He drew himself up in the saddle. "Although I was not

old enough to wear the gray, I hope to be thought worthy of that title."

"I was born in the Confederacy, Jebel. My mama was a Virginia lady and my pap fought for the South. Does that make me a southern lady?"

He mulled that over for a few minutes before replying. "You come from a good background, certainly, and have many, if not most, of the virtues sought in a woman of the old South. But you have a kind of devil-may-care attitude and resourcefulness that is not usually considered to be a facet of southern womanhood. On the other hand, you speak very well when you set your mind to it—but you do dress in a way that..."

He hesitated, and she waited patiently for him to go on. She was sure in her own mind that she didn't really give a hang whether anyone considered her a southern lady or any other kind of lady, but she was interested in his opinion.

"...but...well, I think when all your virtues are counted, as well as your undeniable physical attractiveness, I could not possibly feel the way I do about you if you were not a worthy person."

"Why thank you, Jebel. That is very kind and I appreciate how broad-minded you are being about this."

"I don't believe one has to be broad-minded to appreciate your many charms and virtues."

"Well, I'll tell you what I figure," she said, letting him put an arm around her and kiss her warmly. "The way I see it is that lady or not, I'm a woman, and just as good as most men, better than a lot of them, and I'm going to carve out the kind of life I want for myself and let folks judge me when they see what I've done."

That took some hard swallowing on Jebel's part, but he did it manfully and then pulled her halfway off her horse to kiss her more passionately. "I hope that kind of life doesn't leave out something for us together."

Hope pulled away from him, laughing and settling back into the saddle. "No, not necessarily. I figure the good Lord made men and women different for some reason, and it wasn't so they could do without each other."

There was a reason why there might not be a life together for her and Jebel, but she didn't have to tell him that right now. She would keep to herself her dreams of a six-foot-four redhead with a warm, lilting Irish voice and a laugh that sent shivers up and down her spine, not to mention what his kisses did. She was already eagerly looking forward to seeing him again when they reached Powder River country.

The herd forged its way northeast, coming into lusher prairie land every day, so lush that the hands were kept busy moving the cattle along to prevent their grazing during the daylight hours as well as all night. More and more signs of civilization appeared as they passed through Nebraska—cattle spreads, large farms, and nesters. They also saw numerous bands of settlers heading west toward the Bozeman road to Washington and Oregon and the others that led south to California.

Chapter 12

THE CHISUM TRAIL herd had trouble with nesters close to Sioux City and lost a dozen head of cattle, including two of Hope's that she had marked with a makeshift brand the blacksmith had made for her. The nesters and farmers raged at the very sight of a trail herd that might knock down their fences and trample their crops.

It was only John Chisum's ever-present good humor and gift of gab that got them through without considerable bloodshed, although twice Jebel had to draw down on a farmer with a shotgun, and once Pat winged an enraged nester who was firing at the herd with a Winchester. Hope bandaged up the man and tried to conciliate him.

"We're not trying to trample your crops on purpose," she told him. "We're delivering beef to the army and to a big ranch up in Wyoming. Without the beef, the army won't be able to protect you folks."

"Lot of protecting we get anyway," the man grumbled. "I got me a wife and six kids and another on the way, and they're all like to be scalped any day with the agency Indians eating government food one day and killing the folks the next."

"I guess the army is doing its best. What do you hear about Powder River country?" Hope asked, her mind not only on the area they were making for but the redheaded cowboy who was also headed there.

"The rustlers are running wild and shooting things up, and the cattle barons are hiring gunmen to do more shooting," the farmer said. "Far as I'm concerned, they can do each other in. Got no use for nobody who nursemaids a cow."

Hope smiled at him, as friendly as could be, and offered him some broth, which he accepted eagerly. "'Spect we might be able to round up a good side of beef for you and your missus and kids," she said. "Kind of make up for any trouble we caused you."

The man's eyes lit up. "Meat is hard to get in farm country. It would surely be appreciated."

"Maybe you could do me a favor in return," she said. "If you're grateful to me for fixing you up, don't say anything about the trouble in Powder River country around the cowhands."

He grinned nastily. "Well, I could sure get even for this hole in my shoulder now, couldn't I? If I spread the word around that you might be riding into a range war, you wouldn't have a hand left to drive cows over folks' property, would you?"

"No, and the army wouldn't get its beef," she said, "and I might have to put a bullet through you in a much more vital place than the one my pap put in your shoulder."

"There ain't no need for that," he said sourly. "I'm not gonna say nothing. I seen you trying to turn the cattle aside before they trampled my corn. I ain't got nothing against you or your old man either. He could have shot me in the gut, 'stead of the shoulder, and he might as well have done it. I won't be able to work and my kids will probably starve as it is."

"Suppose we left you a whole beef. Would that help out any?"

"You runnin' things in this outfit? Seems like a mighty big job for a little girl."

"No, I ain't runnin' things, but I got twenty-six cows of my own, and I do with 'em what I want," she said. "And if you need one to feed your kids—"

For the first time, the farmer looked a little less sour. "I'd be powerful grateful to you, sure would. With a whole beef, I can trade for flour and sugar and other stuff we're going to need."

Pushing on, they sighted the Missouri near Fort Rice, and Hope sucked in her breath as she stared at it. "Lordy, that is the biggest bunch of water I've seen since the Gulf of Mexico. I sure as shootin' wouldn't want to swim no herd of cows across it."

"We won't have to," Pat said. "Fort Lincoln is on this side of it, and we can deliver the army beefs and then head west toward Wyoming to deliver the cows that's going to the Sussex Ranch on the Powder River."

"And the place we're going to stake out our own claims, Pap."

"Hope honey, you know it's awful hard work, ranching is," Pat said. "Why don't we just sell them cows of yours and put the money in our pockets and take off?"

"I earned them cows, Pap, and we ain't selling them. Soon as we get settled on our land, you won't mind the work at all. Why, I read this pamphlet about the beef bonanza and how anyone with a few cows who's willing to work can start up a herd that will make him rich. All the country up there is an empty paradise of waving grass; a cowman's paradise with the Indians out and no one else much in. There ain't nothing there but the Sussex place, some small spreads, and one army post called Fort McKinney."

"What book did you say you was reading?" Pat asked.

"*The Beef Bonanza,* or *How to Get Rich on the Plains,* by General S. Brisbin, U.S. Army."

"Never had much use for get-rich-quick schemes," Pat said.

"This one is a sure thing. You should read that book. Some of the things it said really stuck in my mind about the lightness of snowfalls, the mild climate, and the abundant grazing. Unlimited opportunity with at least a twenty-five-percent growth, few risks, and—"

"Still sounds like a get-rich-quick scheme," Pat said grumpily.

The truth of the matter, Hope knew, was that Pat Cox, for all of his virtues and his ability around cows, just wasn't all that fond of hard work.

"We gonna do all this ranching by ourselves?" Pat asked.

"Nope. Juan and Chou Li are going with us, and the land I have in mind is going to be rich with grass and have lots of water. You're going to have more money to jingle in your pockets than you ever had before, Pap."

He jingled the cartwheels Chisum had paid them. "I think we maybe have more now than we're ever going to have."

"That's nothing compared to what we're going to have," she told him. "We're going to build ourselves a house like the one Tim tells me Mr. Fenwick and that English lady of his live in."

"Lordy, girl, you sure do have fancy ideas," Pat said.

"If you knew how fancy, it'd scare you half to death," Hope laughed.

They finally arrived in early August. The area was dusty, the grass tinder dry, and the cattle took off for the river as though they had never seen water before.

"They'll be needing fattening up, Mr. Fenwick," Chisum told the Englishman, while Hope searched for Timothy with her eyes and Jebel watched her, his black eyes brooding.

"Where's that young ramrod of yours, Mr. Fenwick?" Pat asked. "He said he was going to show my daughter and me some good government land when we got here."

Fenwick's eyes flickered in their direction, and the slim, dark-haired beauty in a fashionably cut riding habit who stood a few feet behind him looked at Hope with an intensity that took the girl aback.

"O'Callahan has a job of work to do for me down Cheyenne way," the Englishman said. "I'm not sure he'll be back before you folks head on south again."

"Oh, we're not going south," Hope said. "We came here to settle and raise our own cattle."

"Really?" The news didn't seem particularly pleasing to Fenwick. Hope wondered if he found the possibility of competition distasteful or if he had other reasons for reacting coolly to the idea. Whatever it was, he apparently decided not to let it prevent his acting the genial host now he had inspected the heads he had bought.

He summoned his straw boss, a big Oglala Sioux who wore a white man's jeans and gun belt, but also a single white feather in his flat black hat. "Show Mr. Chisum's hands to the bunkhouse, will you, Joe, while I see that our friends here get a chance to wash and change clothes before dinner."

He turned to the woman who stood with her head held high, dressed in an English-style tophat, gray coat, and riding skirt, twisting a whip in her long white hands.

"This is Anne, my wife," Fenwick said, holding out his hand to the woman. "This, my dear, is Mr. John Chisum, who is quite an institution in the state of Texas, I understand."

John Chisum removed his hat and took the hand Anne Fenwick extended to him. "Pleased to meet you, ma'am," he said. "Don't pay no mind to that institution talk. I ain't embalmed yet."

Then he turned to Hope, Pat, and Jebel. "And this here, Mrs. Fenwick, is my little gal helper and her father, Pat, and this here is my trail boss, Jebel Mason."

Hope noticed that Uncle John had neglected to mention her name, and since she was going under a false one, she was sure it hadn't been an oversight. John Chisum never did anything by accident.

"Well, ladies and gentlemen, please come in," Fenwick said. "We're rather proud of our little house in the wilderness and we'd like you all to see it, if you would care to."

Anne Fenwick merely bowed slightly when she gave her hand to Hope, but studied her as though she were something entirely out of her ken. "I hope you had a good journey," she said to Pat and Jebel, and looked at Hope again.

She doesn't like me, for some reason, but she is interested in me, Hope thought. But how can she dislike me when she doesn't know me? Could Tim have told her about me? She wondered what he could have told Anne and why it made her look at Hope with such chilly disdain. It made her even more sorry Tim O'Callahan wasn't here. She wanted to see him, and not just because he had promised to show them the best government land to be had for staking out and filing on. She wanted to see O'Callahan because she had been comparing him with Jebel all the way from the spot on the river where they had parted to the Sussex Ranch.

Some of Fenwick's cowboys appeared to move the cattle into a pasture, where there was water and lush grass along the riverbanks. Juan and Chou Li cut out Hope's twenty-six cows and ran them into a holding area where they could be kept for as long as they stayed at the ranch.

Chisum, Pat, Jebel, and Hope were escorted into the house that Tim had, with good reason, called a castle. It was bigger than any house Hope had ever seen, although she had heard there were bigger ones in New Orleans and St. Louis—and way back east, of course. The great hall was everything Tim had said it was, and Hope was struck particularly by the pegged hardwood floors that shone with a gloss almost like ice.

"Golly, maybe we ought to take our boots off," she said.

Fenwick laughed. "Young lady, if your boots go through the wax on this floor, I'll make sure you're provided with some new ones."

"Of course," Anne Fenwick said, "we seldom have the opportunity to entertain young women who wear boots."

Oh, meow, meow! Hope said to herself. The claws were out, and on a great lady like Anne Fenwick they were not only unbecoming, they didn't make a great deal of sense. Why had she got it in for her? Hope certainly didn't have eyes for that husband of hers, rich as he was. Something else was upsetting her, but what?

They were shown upstairs by a real butler in real butler's garb, just like a picture in a magazine. Hope thought he must be the one Tim said had been trained in Ottawa to shine people's shoes instead of telling them to do it themselves. She noticed that he didn't have nearly as much of an English accent as did the lord and lady of the manor.

"The guest rooms have baths with running water," the butler told them. "You'll probably want to take a bath, miss, so I'll send one of the maids up to draw it for you."

"Running water in a house? Well, I'll be darned," Pat said.

"Oh, this house has things that nobody west of the Mississippi has seen, like that tel-e-phone in the master's office."

"A tel-e-phone?" Jebel said. "Why, I never saw one of them even in New Orleans!"

"Where's he call to on it?" Pat asked.

"Oh, just down to the 76 store Mr. Fenwick owns and the post office twenty miles downriver," the butler said. "But it certainly is a novelty for people who comes to Sussex House."

"I 'spect so," Hope said, not much impressed. What good was a machine that let you talk twenty-five miles away when there was no one to talk to?

"I'll send one of the maids up immediately to draw your bath, ma'am," the butler said.

"Thank you, but I can wash behind my own ears," Hope said.

The six of them dined in the great hall, dwarfed by the size of it and the table on which dinner was served. Hope had put on the pink gingham dress she had bought in Austin and discovered it was almost too small for her. She was embarrassed when she saw the magnificent robin's-egg-blue bodice and bustled skirt of black taffeta that Anne Fenwick was wearing.

"Why, my dear, you have quite outdone yourself," Fenwick said to his wife. "If I had known you were going to be so formal, I would have put on something more appropriate."

That dress was intended to make me feel like two cents, and it sure has succeeded, Hope thought, but she bounced back with her usual ebullience. To heck with her. Someday she was going to have dresses just as fancy as Anne Fenwick's, she was going to look even better than Anne did in hers.

But when she turned her attention to the food, which was served in a seemingly series of endless courses, she was dismayed. Most of it she couldn't even put a name to. This was not the usual beefsteak and fried potatoes of the ordinary ranch house. There was something called hors d'oeuvres—dainty bits of fish and cheese on tiny toast rounds—chicken pâté, glazed ham, and too much of everything, especially the wine, which neither she nor Pat was used to. It made them giddy, and John Chisum glum and moody instead of his usual jovial self. Only Jebel, who was used to New Orleans ways, seemed able to cope with the situation. While his friends fell silent he chattered away with Anne, throwing in a word of French occasionally and comparing the cooking with that of Louisiana. Anne Fenwick brightened up considerably and, fortunately, quit scowling at Hope.

Jebel said one thing that Hope noticed even through the wine-induced haze. "When Clover and I get married, we hope to have a house, not quite as elegant as this, but at least a respectable place where we can entertain."

After that remark, Anne became far more friendly to her and even insisted that they stay on at the house until Tim returned and could carry out his promise to show them some really good land on the other side of Powder River.

"Do you know, my dear," Anne remarked, "they say that Powder River is a mile wide and an inch deep? Too thick to drink, too thin to plough. But there is also the fact that there isn't a fence between here and the Arctic Circle."

Fenwick was talking to Jebel and the morose Chisum. "If two hundred thousand dollars were to be invested in Texas cattle, it would double itself in this country in four years and pay a semiannual dividend of eight percent."

Hope and Pat didn't have two hundred thousand dollars, didn't have even two hundred, but she had a herd of twenty-six good Texas cattle and figured that between them, she and her pap knew as much about cows as anyone in Wyoming, and certainly more than this English dude, who had paid John Chisum almost twice what his cows were worth.

The men settled in for some good solid talk about cattle and water rights over brandy and cigars. Hope and Anne were supposed to make conversation in the drawing room over tiny cups of coffee, but Hope excused herself, saying she was tired, and went up to her room. She was tempted to take another bath in the tub that sat in the middle of the bathroom on sturdy little legs, but the bed was even more tempting; she hadn't seen one in months. She crawled out of her dress, petticoat, and drawers and into her only nightgown, a cotton one with pink roses on it that was badly wrinkled from having been wadded up with her gear since they had left Bosque Grande. Wondering sleepily how Jebel and Anne found so much to talk about, she slid between the cool, clean sheets and was instantly asleep.

The next morning she heard a sound through the open window that made her sit bolt upright in bed. It was Tim O'Callahan's voice, and he was yelling for breakfast.

"Hey, Cooky, I didn't ride a hundred miles for nothin'! Get me some chow! I want six slices o' bacon, three eggs, pan fries, biscuits, and a whole pot of coffee, and I want it in a hurry!"

Hope pushed open the window and leaned out. "You sure got a big appetite for an Irisher raised on potatoes and grass!"

Tim looked up, a huge grin on his face. "Oh, so there ye be. I came a-ridin' like the wind 'cause I heard you were here."

His clothing was covered with dust and his face was so gray with it she might not have recognized him if she hadn't heard his voice.

"How did you know I was here?" she demanded. "You been trailing us all along, fixin' to steal our horses?"

He whooped with laughter. "No, 'tis trailin' you I was to make sure you weren't going to steal our cows."

"Oh, you make me so mad! If I had something to throw at you, I would!" she said, laughing.

"Please, don't, me lady, leastwise not till I get washed

up. I wouldn't want to be found dead with this much dirt on me!"

"How did you really know I was here?" she asked.

"I heard about it on the tel-e-phone," he said. "Called up from the post office to talk to the boss and he told me the herd had come in and you were with it. So I rode harder than an Irishman passing through Ulster."

"Just to see the cows," she suggested.

"Just to see you."

"Oh, come on, don't give me any of your Irish blarney. That might work with the girls back in Kilkenny, but I know you glib micks too well to fall for that."

"Well, how's this then? I'll go wash up, and you get yourself decent and come down and have breakfast with me and then I'll take you for a ride and explain it all to you in a proper Irish way."

"To be polite, I ought to eat with the Fenwicks," she said.

"I'll fix it with the boss."

"But if you've ridden a hundred miles, you must be tired."

"I won't be once I get washed up, get some food in me, and close enough to you to—" He finished the sentence with a kissing motion, and laughed exuberantly.

"I'll be down as soon as I get dressed," she said. "Remember you promised you would show me the best free government land about these parts."

"'Tis only an hour's ride," he said. "We'll go this morning."

"You got a deal, pardner," she said, and withdrew her head from the window to search among her gear for her best jeans and shirt.

By the time Hope was dressed and had her hair combed, Tim had washed up and changed clothes. His red hair neatly slicked down, he was waiting for her at the foot of the steps from the front veranda.

"Well, you look good enough to have for breakfast yourself," he said as he led her off toward the mess hall, where smoke was rising from a chimney and delicious smells were wafting their way. "'Tis sorry I am I ordered all that food now."

"You keep your mind on what you're supposed to have for breakfast and forget about other things," she said. Then, suddenly sensing a movement behind and above her, she looked up at the house. A curtain that had been drawn aside was quickly dropped, and she knew someone had been watching them.

Hm, she thought. I'll bet that was Miz Fenwick's room and it was her a-watching us. Now why do you suppose a great fancy lady spies on her husband's foreman? Or is it me she's keeping an eye on?

Chapter 13

BREAKFAST WAS GLORIOUS. Not only was Hope hungry, but she felt much more at home eating in the mess hall, with the cowboys from the Sussex and 76 ranches tramping in shouting, roughhousing, and joking. It was also pleasant just watching Timothy eat. He didn't wolf his food like most of the cow folks she had known, but consumed it with a calm enjoyment that she thought would make a person want to cook for him.

Better watch out, she warned herself. When you start thinking like that, you are taking a fellow too seriously.

"How much land do you plan to file on?" Tim asked between mouthfuls of egg.

"As much as I can, or rather, as much as Pap and I can together."

"You can have pretty near as much as you want. Land is the one thing in this country there's plenty of, but you have to ride down to Buffalo, the county seat, to do the filin' once you stake out your claim amd take up residence."

"Residence? Would a tent do?" she asked.

"A tent, a barrel, a box. Most anything you can spend the night in. But you don't really need a couple thousand acres to pasture twenty-five cows and one bull."

"I plan on those twenty-six being a hundred and twenty-six by next year, and from then on, the sky's the limit!" She grinned and licked some syrup off her lips.

"Hm, I've a feeling you read *Beef Bonanza,* or one of the other books the first fellows in this territory used to write."

"Yes, I read the *Beef Bonanza*. What about it?"

"Well, it wasn't exactly truthful in everything it said."

"What do you mean?" She was starting to feel belligerent. She had put a lot of faith in that book. "What are you talking about?"

"Well, what the fellow said about there being plenty of grass and lots of water is true . . ."

She breathed a sigh of relief, but he went on.

". . . in the autumn, the spring, and mostly the summer, but winter is another matter. We have some real humdinger winters around these parts. That's why we lost so many cattle and had to buy more at those outright thievin' prices your so-called Uncle John charged."

"What do you do about the cattle in the winter?"

"Most winters they survive, but along comes one like last year and it's sheer hell. People are lucky if they can survive themselves. With twenty-five cows and a bull, you could lodge 'em in a barn and feed them hay and fodder; that is, if you had a barn."

"Right now, I don't even have a cabin," she said. "Pap and I and the boys will have to build one."

"That will take care of you. What about the cattle?"

"I don't know."

"Well, you got about four or five months to make up your mind and get it all done," he said.

"Yeah, and that will take some doing, won't it?"

He laughed. "It can be done if you have help, and there's one other thing. The place I thought you might like to start your home range has a pretty sheltered pasture down near the banks of the river, where you can chop through the ice for the cattle to drink."

She smiled, convinced he had just been joshing her about the hard winter and had relented enough to explain how all her problems could be solved. He didn't smile back. "That will help, but it won't make Wyoming the paradise you've been told it is," he said. "Summers are often dry and dusty, and winters are hard. Cattle can be raised successfully in this country, but it's hard work, just like it is any other place."

She grinned. "All right, Mr. Sobersides, I've been warned. Now how about showing me this great ranch site you've got picked out for me?"

"You got a horse that is fit to ride after that cattle drive?" he asked.

"When you ride with John Chisum on a drive, you are provided with eight horses."

"Well, if he took as good care of his cattle as he did his horses and cowhands, we might have a bargain after all," he said, getting up and taking his plate over to one of the cook's helpers.

Hope followed him, thinking this was one of the biggest ranches she had ever seen, and she had seen some big ones down in Texas. Imagine having a whole building for a mess hall and a cook with three helpers working full-time as the cowhands came off the night guard and day roundups. Someday when she had a lot of money, she not only wanted a home like the Fenwick place but a ranch as big as this one.

She had bragged about the condition of the horses, but Rollo was a little worn down and needed a rest, so she sent Juan to saddle up Sally, and he soon arrived with the little filly, who was frisky and ready for a romp.

Timothy appeared on the same big black stallion she had first seen him on the day he had saved her from being raped by Cajun Joe.

"Where to?" she asked.

"Across Powder at the ford and then north up the far

bank for about fifteen miles, and you'll see the finest pastureland going, and no neighbor for twenty miles or more in any direction except this."

"Oh? I was hoping to have places nearer than that, so when fellows come a-sparkin' they can stay late."

"Turn around!" Tim bellowed. "We'll go in the other direction! I know a place that is fifty miles away from everything else and the only fellow who could possibly reach it in less than a day's ride would be me."

She giggled, and he gave her a big freckle-faced scowl but kept on riding in the same direction. After about two miles, they came to a low spot in the bank of the muddy-looking river where wagon tracks and horses' hoofprints led down to the water.

"This is the ford," he told her, "and 'tis here I'll be makin' me stand many a night to see that no laddie bucks come a-courtin' at the new ranch, which, by the way, hasn't a name as yet."

"Oh, we'll call it the Lazy H, I think," Hope said.

There was no response, and she suddenly realized that she had never told Tim her real name.

"Lazy H means nothin' to me," he said, looking at her closely.

"No, because you think my name is Clover."

"And it isn't?"

"My real name is Hope Cox and my father is Pat Cox. We left Texas in kind of a hurry, and Uncle John let us travel with his trail herd under what you might call false names. But we didn't really commit any crimes, Tim."

Timothy smiled. "That's good enough for me. Hope kind of fits you better than Clover anyway. Clover has kind of a placid sound to it, but Hope is full of bounce."

They had stopped on the far bank of the river to let the horses rest for a moment, and on impulse she reached over and put her hand over his two on the pommel of his saddle. "You're a good Irishman, Tim," she said.

"All Irish are good, Hope girl. Some are just better than others," he said, and kicked his big stallion Shamrock to start him on the way.

"There it is! There's the Lazy H spread," Tim said after about two hours' ride. They had come to the top of a low line of hills and were looking down into the craterlike area that slanted toward the river.

"Oh golly, it's beautiful!" Hope breathed, looking at the brook that ran down through the deep grass of the meadow to empty in a miniature waterfall into Powder River. The grass along the banks of the creek was almost blue in its lushness, and there was a hillock in the middle of the pasture land shaded by half a dozen trees standing on its crown.

"That's where we'll build the house. Cabin first, then later a great big house." Hope was fairly bouncing up and down in her saddle.

"Well, for starters, we could have a picnic over there under those trees," he said.

"We sure could, if we had anything to picnic with," she said, amazed she could feel so hungry after their huge breakfast.

"Well, to tell the truth, we do," he said, reaching into one saddlebag to bring out something carefully wrapped in napkins and into another for a bottle of dark red wine.

"I had Cooky make up cornbread and fried chicken and borrowed a bottle of wine from the boss's cellar."

Hope clapped her hands. "Wonderful! We'll have our first meal in my new home."

He looked over at the hill. "Nice-looking little place you got there, Miss Cox. You figurin' on entertainin' a gentleman friend there this afternoon?"

"I might consider it since he brought victuals and wine," she said, and suddenly spurred Sally forward. "Come on, I'll race you for the first sip of wine."

"You're on!" he said, and urged his stallion after the little filly. But it was an up-and-down half mile to the top of the rise and Sally was more surefooted than the bigger horse. Hope was already off her horse, on her feet, and laughing at Tim when he dismounted in a single bound, his Stetson flying off to rest on the back of his neck and his red hair glistening in the sun as he grabbed her in his arms.

"Hey! Hey, what's this!" she yelped as he pulled her to him and kissed her.

"You won," he said. "You get the prize."

"The prize was the first sip of wine," she said, holding him off for a minute while he tried to gather her closer.

"Hey, you shouldn't—" She was struggling but not very seriously. In fact, before she knew it, she was kissing him back with a great deal of enthusiasm.

"I knew you hadn't forgotten how to do it," he said, dropping down onto the soft lush grass with her in his arms. "I knew you still know how to kiss better than any girl I ever met."

"You sure do know how to spread the blarney," she whispered against the strong line of his neck, feeling the pulse that beat there and tasting the slightly sweaty, masculine flavor of his tanned skin with her lips and tongue.

"Mmmmm . . . you're pretty good at teasing, aren't you?" he said as her hands ran up the sides of his face and tangled in his hair.

"But not as good as I am at kissing," she murmured, and this time it was her lips that sought his, roving back and forth across his firm mouth and flicking at his lower lip with a greedy tongue that couldn't seem to get enough of him.

He rolled over partially on top of her, pinning her down in the sweet-smelling grass, his chest flattening her breasts and causing the nipples to rise and harden in a way that she was sure he could feel through the thickness of both their shirts.

"So sweet," he said as he ran a string of sizzling kisses down the side of her neck and across the base of her throat.

"Tim . . . Timothy . . . Timmy," she repeated his name until his mouth claimed hers again, bruising it, penetrating it with an insistently probing tongue that burned her mouth, causing it to seek more and more of his kisses.

"Oh darling—darling Tim," she whispered as his lips ran down the front of her throat, slipping under the neckline of her shirt and stroking the upper curve of her breasts even as his fingers undid the buttons that held it in place.

"Tim, I don't think that—" she protested weakly, but it was too late, the shirt had fallen open and her breasts were revealed, white, firm, and upturned, the pink peaks already aroused and waiting for his kisses.

"They are pretty . . . so pretty," he murmured huskily, kissing one nipple and then the other, sending thrills of pleasure racing through her entire body and causing her to surge up against him as though seeking something more.

"My darling, I never expected to find you," Timothy was whispering. "When I rode down to Colorado with Mr. Fenwick, I never expected to find the most beautiful lass in all the West struggling for her virtue by the riverside. Nor did I expect to fall for her the moment I laid eyes on her."

"Oh, if I could only believe you." She was running her fingers through his hair, watching his mouth move avidly against her breasts and feeling a sensation she had never known existed.

"Oh, Tim. Tim, I think we better stop while we still can," she gasped.

"Why?" he asked. "We love each other. Why not prove how much?"

"That isn't the only way . . . that's not the only way, is it, Tim?" she whispered against his ear while his fingers tenderly stroked and rubbed her tingling breasts.

"It's the most direct and sweetest way I know of."

"How many girls have you proved it with?" she demanded.

"Not as many as you might think, and they were different. Not like you at all. No one has ever been like you. Nary a one had a turned-up little nose, sweet, natural-perfumed hair, such a wonderfully kissable mouth, and beautiful little white pigeon breasts that seem to bloom when I kiss them."

"Oh God! That feels so good . . . that feels so wonderful . . . I don't know what I'm doing . . . I don't know what I want . . . or what I don't want. I don't know anything."

"Let me show you, lass. Let me show you, macushla," Tim whispered, his fingers on the belt of her jeans.

"Please, please don't . . . oh, darling . . . don't." He was kissing her bare midriff now, his hand slipping under the waistband of her pants, and she felt his knowledgeable fingers—too knowledgeable, perhaps—caressing their way down over her stomach.

"Oh, Tim, please don't do that."

"Why not, love? I want to do it and I think you want me to, and sweetheart, that isn't all we're going to do."

"Yes, it is. It's got to be. Please stop, please. You're getting me all . . . all . . . Oh, Lord, I don't even have a name for it!"

Then her jeans were down off her hips and she could only moan, rolling back and forth and tossing her head until her blond hair shimmered against the grass like a halo.

Slowly he was moving over on top her, his weight forcing her bare bottom into the grass and soft earth beneath it. She was acutely aware of his smooth-skinned body and of the size and strength of his maleness. It excited her and yet made her want to cry out that she couldn't—couldn't—but she didn't have the words to say what she couldn't do, and before she could say anything, she discovered that she not only could but that she was reveling in it. Staring at the intensely blue sky of Wyoming over his shoulder, she loved it also because it had brought her this moment . . . this most supreme of all the moments of her life.

Afterward, she clung to him with both arms and legs, clung as though begging for more of what she had never known she wanted until now.

"Oh, Tim, I think I'm in love with you," she said a few minutes later, when she had finally let him go, pulled her jeans on, and was sitting with her arms folded across her bare young breasts.

"Only think? I like my women to be sure," he said, grinning his big, heart-wrenching grin.

"I think I *know* it," she said softly.

"Well, maybe by the time we have lunch you can be sure. Even if I didn't cook this magnificent repast meself, 'tis delicious you'll be findin' it."

"Oh, Lord, how can you think of food at a time like this?" she asked, looking up at the blue sky and remembering how she had been gazing deep into it while he had made love to her.

"A fellow works up an appetite making love," he said. "Besides, we ought to have a little wine to drink a toast to how wonderful it is to love someone like you."

"And you," she said, taking the tin cup he handed her after filling it with wine.

"To me lovely lass from Texas," he said. "If I had known what Texas girls were like, nothing would have brought me to Wyoming in the first place."

"A fine story that is," she laughed, sipping the red wine. "If you ever saw what other Texas gals look like, you wouldn't give me the time of day."

"Sure now, and I wager I would," he said.

"What are you gonna bet?" she asked, and drank more deeply from the cup.

"A chicken drumstick and a big chunk of buttered cornbread," he said, holding the food out to her.

"Seems like a shame to eat after something so wonderful," she said dreamily.

"Well, love takes strength, and to keep up one's strength, one needs food," he said, holding the cornbread up to her mouth for her to take a bite.

"Hmmmm . . . good, but I'm not really hungry anymore," she said, sipping the wine again. "I just want to think about us and what we did."

He gave her an odd look. "You know, love, thinkin' about things too long isn't always good."

"It is when it's the most marvelous thing that has ever happened to you."

He looked away toward the river and seemed to be thinking.

"It was that way for you, too, wasn't it?" she asked, a little worried.

"Sure and it was, but I wish you'd eat," he said. "I don't want to take you back to the ranch drunk on wine. What would your father think?"

"That I was a chip off the old block," she said, but to please him, she nibbled at the drumstick she was holding in her hand and took another bite of cornbread.

"That's better," he said, grinning at her in his usual way. "We can't starve ourselves for love. Frenchmen may do things like that in operas and plays, but in Wyoming there's too much work to do for anyone to spend much time mooning over it."

She paused with the chicken halfway to her mouth and took a sip of the wine instead. Somehow it seemed to her that Tim wasn't giving as much importance to this as she was. But she had to face the fact that he had done it before. This wasn't his first experience with the soul-shattering miracle of loving and being loved.

She supposed she should be conscience-stricken rather than ecstatic. Everything she had ever heard or read implied that once a girl took the step that she had just taken she was forever lost as far as society was concerned. She was a fallen woman and should be properly chastised for her stumble into depravity. Even her schoolteacher mother, as "modern" and free a woman as she thought herself, had looked down on Victoria Woodhull for her views on free love, even while admiring her advanced opinions on the subject of women's votes and women running for office.

"A woman doesn't have to be a trollop like Vicky or a courtesan like George Sand to be for women's rights," her mother had often said. "She can be both virtuous and assertive."

But Hope didn't feel as though she had lost her virtue. She felt she had gained something, something very precious. She was damned if she was going to sit around and mope about it. It was really something to celebrate. Then why wasn't she celebrating? The answer came to her almost at once. She wasn't celebrating because Timothy wasn't. Something seemed to be bothering him. Was it that he hadn't found it as thrilling as she had? Well, he ought to remember that she didn't have the experience of some of the other women he had been with. That gave her something else to think about. Who were those other women? Was one of them more important than she to him? Was he in love with someone else?

No, that couldn't be. If he were in love with another woman, he wouldn't have been able to make love to her so passionately. Or would he? Men were supposed to be different from women, weren't they?

She took another bite of the chicken, but swallowed it with difficulty. She looked at Tim, who was comfortably eating chicken and cornbread and taking occasional sips of wine.

"Timothy, are you in love with some other woman?" she demanded.

He looked up, startled, and almost dropped his chicken leg. "In love with some other woman?"

"It's a fairly easy question to answer, isn't it?"

"Well, yes, of course 'tis easy," he said.

"Then why don't you answer it?"

He didn't say a word, only carefully put down his chicken and cornbread and reached for hers.

"What are you going to do?" she asked, her heart starting to pound again.

"Answer your question," he said, pulling her into his arms and searching for her lips with his. "I'm going to answer it the only way I know how."

"Oh, Tim . . . it's a wonderful way," she said, yielding, surrendering completely to his arms and lips.

"This is how I love you," he said, his mouth starting a fire in hers that threatened to consume her. "And this is how I love you," he said again, kissing first one eye and then the other. "This is how I love all of you, every single inch and every nook and cranny of you."

"Oh, Tim, I don't know if I can stand that much love. I'm not used to it—it might be too rich for my blood."

"You'll learn to get used to it if it takes me a hundred years of working, day and night."

"I hope you don't expect double wages," she said as he gently eased her down into the grass so that she was again looking up at the clouds drifting in the blue sky beyond the spreading branches of the tree under which they lay. This tree would always be their very own tree, she thought contentedly.

They became completely absorbed in each other. Her whole being was responding to his every kiss, to every caress of his hands and lips, to every whispered word and murmured endearment. So totally absorbed were they that they heard neither the approach of a horse nor the exclamation torn from the lips of its rider.

They didn't hear a thing until the horse was within a few feet of them. Suddenly a woman leaped from the saddle and let out a groan of pain and astonishment.

"Timothy! Oh God, Timothy! How could you?"

The words cut through the sweet fog that had enveloped Hope. She felt Tim pull away from her and sat up abruptly, trying to button her shirt and pull her denims into place at the same time.

"Oh, how could you! Damn you! Damn you, you saddle tramp!" Anne Fenwick stood over them, her beautiful face distorted with fury.

"What the devil are you doing here, Anne?" Tim demanded hoarsely, getting to his feet and slowly buttoning his jeans and tightening his belt.

"I followed you! Haven't I the right? Didn't it give me the right when I let you—"

"Damnit, Anne, you didn't *let* me do anything!"

The woman screamed at him. "I sacrificed everything, my honor, my wifely virtue, and this is what I get! It wasn't bad enough that you and that Ella Watson—"

"Shut up, Anne! Goddamn you, shut up!" Tim growled, his face black with anger. "You have no claim on me, now or ever!"

"Haven't I? After all I've done to please you? Even after that Watson woman I took you back! I risked everything to be with you! And now I find you with this female hobo in our place—under our tree!"

That was all Hope could stand. Everything was clear to her now. She had been used, used in a vicious, evil way for the pleasure of a man who apparently made a practice of using women. No wonder Anne had acted so strangely when Hope had come to her house. No wonder she had watched them. Tim O'Callahan had seduced a married woman and then betrayed her with someone called Ella Watson. And now he had done the same thing to Hope, had used her, had told her he loved her. Without a word, she darted away toward Sally, who was contentedly grazing.

"Hope! Hope, wait a minute! 'Tis not the way it looks!" Tim caught up with her, grabbed her hand, and tried to pull her toward him.

"Let got of me," she said through clenched teeth. "Let go of me, you seducer!"

"'Tis not the way it looks, Hope," he pleaded. "Believe me, macushla! If you'll just listen for a minute, I'll—"

"I don't want to hear anything you have to say!" she sobbed and struck at him with her quirt. "I don't want ever to see you again or hear your name. I don't even want to think about you!"

Riding back to Sussex Ranch at a full gallop, Hope closed her mind and her heart to any further thought of Timothy O'Callahan, focusing instead on her plans for her future. She gathered up her personal belongings, rounded up her father, and rode on to Buffalo to file on the land she was determined to have, silently vowing never to see or speak to her seducer again. They bought what supplies they needed, and she sent Pat back to get Juan and retrieve her cattle while she and Chou Li went directly to the site to pitch a tent and begin work on a tiny cabin.

When it was time for the Chisum group to start back south, she met Jebel Mason to say goodbye.

"Clover honey, it's in my contract that I have to return to New Mexico with Uncle John and bring another herd north in the spring. Come with me and we'll be married."

"I've filed on three thousand acres of prime ranch land and I've got my herd started, Jebel," she said gently. After the episode with Tim, she had been tempted to rush into Jebel's arms and offer him the marriage he wanted. But after a week of thinking it over, she knew she wasn't going to do it. Just because one man had turned out to be a two-timing, treacherous skunk didn't mean that all men were. But it was still too soon. She wasn't ready to trust another man, not yet. The six or eight months before she would see Jebel again might enable her to decide if she loved him. "I'm staying here. And, Jebel, there's something I have to tell you before you go."

"What is it, honey?"

"My name isn't Clover—and it's not Crawford, either."

"What?" His eyes became saucers.

"My pap and I were fugitives from injustice in Texas, so we changed our names and got out of the state fast."

"I don't believe it. You, my sweet little Clover—"

"My real name is Hope, Jebel. Hope Cox."

"Hope Cox," he repeated, seeming bewildered. "But what did you do? What was your crime?"

"It wasn't a crime, Jebel. I just administered a little justice, rough justice, you might say, but justice."

"I don't understand. What happened?"

"Well, there was this fellow, a certain Mr. Nugent, sometimes calling himself Captain Nugent, and he had what you might call designs on me."

"Designs?"

"Yes, he wanted me to perform an act a woman wouldn't engage in after one such short acquaintance and that a lady would never engage in."

Jebel's face flushed slightly. "I see. But what was your—your act of justice?"

"I busted his balls for him, Jebel," she said, smiling sweetly. "'Cause if any man ever deserved it, he did."

"You did *what?*"

"I busted his balls with a crowbar."

"Oh my God! My sweet little Clover?"

"Hope, Jebel."

"Hope," he said, swallowing hard.

"Not a very southern ladylike thing to do, was it, Jebel? My mama would never had done anything like that and I'm sure your mother and sister wouldn't, either."

"Well, I suppose it all depends on—"

"So now that you know I'm a hardened criminal, you won't be wanting to see me when you get back with another of Uncle John's trail herds."

Jebel shook his head as though trying to clear it of the effect of a hard right to the jaw, but he smiled bravely and took her by the shoulders. "That isn't so, Clo—Hope. Whatever happened back in Texas, I know you are what you are and I like what you are. For a while I thought you were going overboard for that redheaded Irishman—"

"O'Callahan? Never!" she said. "That guy has been in the hay with half the women in Wyoming and I never want to see him again. Not ever."

"Well, I'm glad, because when I come back I want to ask you again and I don't want no one else hanging around when I do."

"There won't be, believe me, there won't be. Especially no Timothy O'Callahan."

He pulled her into his arms and his lips came down on hers. It wasn't like it had been with Tim—maybe nothing would ever be like that again—but it was nice. His lips were firm and eager, and in a minute she was warmly returning his kisses. But before there was a chance for things to get out of hand, she put a stop to it.

"I expect Uncle John and the others are waiting for you, and my pap and my cows are waiting for me."

"Where will I find you, Hope?"

"The first three thousand fenced acres on the other side of Powder River," she said. "Just ask for the Lazy H ranch and that will be me."

"Lazy H," he repeated and laughed, remembering the H lying on its side that she had used as a brand on the cattle she had earned from Chisum. "Seems like you think of everything."

"Not quite," she murmured to his retreating back, wishing she had had the foresight not to fall in love with a man who considered himself a sultan, with all the women of Wyoming for a harem.

Chapter 14

"VOTES FOR WOMEN! Votes for women!" Hope chanted, raising high a piece of cardboard attached to a stick on which had been lettered WOMAN SUFFRAGE TODAY OR MEN SUFFERING TOMORROW.

She was pacing up and down outside the building, which resembled a shed, where the territorial legislature was scheduled to meet. There were half a dozen other women with her, ranging in age from Hope's twenty to Amy Andrews's eighty. All were wearing home-sewn calico dresses, and they had washed and curled each other's hair so they'd look as presentable as possible for the demonstration. But they were now in the third day of marching back and forth; their hair was starting to look a bit limp, and their dresses had lost their freshly starched appearance.

"Give us the vote, or we'll give you the air!" shouted Amy Andrews. She lived on a small sodbuster's spread up Powder River from the place where Hope and her father had put down stakes three years before. "Give us the vote or there won't be anyone left in Wyoming!"

The population of Wyoming Territory had been expected to swell with the coming of the Union Pacific, but the railroad had proved to be only another means of traveling through and beyond the area. People looked out the train windows and remarked on what a barren countryside it was and how glad they were that they weren't getting off until they reached California.

"Get off your rumps and follow your hearts!" another woman yelled at the handful of legislators who were watching, along with perhaps fifty other men and a few women and children. Sixty people was a large crowd in Wyoming, since its population had fallen in the past five years and at a faster rate than ever in the last twelve months.

The Indian troubles to the north had resulted in the virtual closing of the Bozeman road to Oregon except for full-scale military operations, and the massacre of Major Fetterman and his troops along the trail had discouraged settlers. Another factor that had made a lot of people move on was that the land that had been thought to abound in natural resources had turned out to be good for nothing but grazing cows or sodbusting.

That was the argument that Hope and the other ladies were hoping would influence the all-male, all-Democratic territorial legislature and the appointed governor, who was a Republican.

"We want our rights!" Hope shouted. "We want the vote, and we want it now."

"Get yourself some pants!" yelled a barrel-bellied man, chewing on a burned-down cigar, a derby tipped back on his bullet-shaped head.

"I've got pants, and I know how to wear them when I ride a horse," Hope retorted, "but that doesn't mean I can't vote without having them on!"

There was a chorus of boos and the man hurled his cigar at her. She shrieked in outrage and leaned over to pick something off the ground. "Why, you lousy, double-chinned, potbellied boob, I ought to crack that thick skull of yours!"

"Yeah? You and who else?"

"Me and this rock!" Hope said, and raised her hand to throw.

Amy Andrews grabbed her arm before she could loose the rock. "No, Hope, you promised! You promised to keep the peace, remember?"

"I'm sorry," Hope said, "but when I agreed to leave my Colt at home, I didn't promise not to use something else to let the sawdust out of an ignorant man with a mouth that matches his big belly."

"Why, you nasty little cat, I ought to turn you over my knee and redden your saucy ass for you," the big man said, starting toward her and beginning to roll up his sleeves.

"Come on and try it," Hope said, hefting the rock and trying to decide how much force it would take to knock him out.

"Now, you just take it easy, Bull," Jim Pulver, the town marshal, said. "We don't want no rough stuff here. These ladies has got the right to make fools of themselves if they want to."

"They're doing worse than that," said a handsome, graying man in a dark coat. "They are going against the will of the Lord."

"That's right, Reverend Potter," a woman in a sunbonnet said angrily. "They're trying to turn this town into Sodom on the Plains with bloomers for women, a red-light district, and a saloon on every corner!"

Since Cheyenne already had a saloon on every corner, the crowd didn't seem up in arms over that, but the Reverend Edgar Potter seemed bent on changing the situation.

"Ladies and gentlemen," he said, taking a Bible from a pocket of his long, dark coat and holding it over his head. "I hope most of you recognize this book."

"Sure do, Reverend," said Bill Bright, a saloonkeeper from South Pass City who happened to be a member of the legislature. "I always keep one right on the bar so the boys can use it to swear on when they're drunk enough to make a vow to give up the demon rum."

That brought a laugh from the crowd and somewhat

spoiled the effect of the reverend's dramatic opening, but unfazed, he continued holding the Bible aloft, turning slowly as though showing it to each and every person present.

"You all know it by sight, I assume, but I'm not sure very many of you have ever opened it and looked inside."

"Come on, Reverend, we don't need no hellfire-and-brimstone sermon," Bright said.

"Don't we, brother Bright?" the minister asked pointedly, reminding Hope that Bill was usually referred to as Colonel Bright because he had served with the rank of major in the Quartermaster Corps in Washington, D.C., during the Civil War.

"So now you have all seen the book, even if you haven't looked inside it," Reverend Potter said with a grim smile. "Well, let me tell you something about this book. It's called the Good Book. You all know that, do you not?"

"Sarcastic so-and-so, ain't he?" Hope said loud enough for everyone to hear.

"Shhh," Amy said. "He's trying to start a new church and has to work hard at it 'cause this town has hardly got enough people for one church."

"Do you know what the Good Book says about women voting?" Potter demanded.

"No, and neither do you," Hope said. "The subject had never come up at the time it was written."

That brought a few laughs but more frowns. Folks around Cheyenne didn't have much use for preachers and tried to avoid them, but they did not like to hear them mocked.

"The Book tells us that the place of women is in the home," Potter thundered, his deep-set eyes intense. "*In the home*, tending to tasks of the hearth and bearing and rearing children."

"Oh my God," Hope groaned. "Next he'll be telling us that we belong flat on our backs, serving our lords and masters."

That was outrageous enough for Potter to turn his full attention on her, and she was shocked by the fanatical blaze of his black eyes as they met hers. "You seem to have strong opinions on this matter, young woman. May I inquire how old you are?"

"I'm twenty, your honor," she replied mockingly. "Begging your august pardon."

"Well now, my dear child," Potter said in a pitying, condescending tone as his glittering gaze swept her from head to toe. "Are you aware that if, God forbid, this ill-conceived measure should be passed by our territorial fathers, you would not be included in the franchise?"

"Of course I know that, but I won't stay underage forever, and in the meantime, other members of my sex would continue to be able to vote on measures that affect all of us."

"Why has it stopped at white women?" Bull Collier shouted. "Why not put 'All nigger women and squaws' instead of 'women' in that bill?"

This was greeted by a roar of laughter confined to the dozen or so men who stood near Collier.

"Brother, I can understand your trepidation in this matter," Potter said, "but we must maintain the verities even in these troubled times in which we live."

Bull Collier nodded, but turned to whisper to the man next to him, "What the hell is trep'dations and verities?"

Potter had taken possession of center stage again and was making the most of it. "We must remember that a woman's place is in the home. The dirty business of politics, in the vile—"

"It doesn't have to be dirty," Amy Andrews interrupted. "That's why we're voting, to take the dirty out of politics."

"Tell me, madam, and I bow in respect to your gray hair," Potter said, "do you have a husband?"

"Of course I have a husband. What do you think I am, a fancy lady at eighty?"

"Do you vote the same way as your husband?"

"How do I know?" Amy said. "Never did ask Joe how he voted."

"Ah, but suppose he ordered you to do so," the minister said. "Suppose he ordered you to vote against the Anti-Saloon League, for instance?"

Mrs. Andrews put her hands on her hips and stomped her foot. "My Joe has never taken a drink in his life. Why would he order me to vote against the Anti-Saloon League?"

"The whole question is ridiculous and beside the point," Hope said, feeling that the older woman was being tricked into giving only the answers the preacher wanted. "How would her husband know how she had voted? If she wanted, she could vote just the opposite to the way he voted and he'd never know because the ballot is secret."

"Ah ha!" Potter exclaimed, holding up a finger. "Are you telling me this lady would break God's commandment by lying to her husband about the way she had exercised the franchise he had voted to give her?"

"He wouldn't be giving her anything," Hope said. "The Constitution would be giving it, because everyone is created free and equal."

"All *men* are created free and equal is the way the Constitution actually reads, and rightly so, in my opinion."

"The founding fathers, with the founding mothers right at their elbows, were speaking rhetorically," Hope said, using one of the arguments her mother had taught her.

Potter looked puzzled, apparently not knowing the meaning of *rhetorical,* and immediately shifted the argument. "God tells us right in the Good Book that women are not to be allowed to vote!"

"Quote the exact passage, if you please," Hope requested. "I want to know what there is in the Bible about politics in a republic, whether they preferred the bicameral or unicameral legislative system and which type of ballot—"

Bull Collier had moved up beside Reverend Potter and was now standing so close to Hope that she could smell the tobacco and whiskey on his breath and clothes. He bent forward to peer at her, his little pig eyes buried in folds of flesh and his liverish lips pursed angrily.

"Young lady, that sounds like atheism, ungodliness, and lack of respect for the Good Book to me. We good citizens don't hold with that kind of thing around here."

"Easy, Mr. Collier, easy," Potter said placatingly. "The

little lady has a right to her opinion in this here democracy of ours, but—"

"It's not a democracy until women can run for office just like men," Hope said.

"How about children?" asked a roughneck leaning against the door of the barbershop. "Do kids get to vote too? I got a couple of good-for-nothings back at the cabin I think ought to get the vote since they ain't got the good sense to come in out of a norther. They ought to do as good as the already elected people like Grant and them senators who can't hit the spittoons in the Senate chambers."

"That's exactly why we women need the vote," said Violet Mechin, the half-French schoolteacher, a little mouse of a woman who seldom spoke up. "We need it because of our greater sensitivity. We will not send men who use spittoons to the Senate."

The lounger in front of the barbershop looked puzzled. "I wasn't sayin' nothin' against spittoons, only about dudes who can't hit them on the first try."

Some of the men sent up a cheer for that sally.

"Well, we seem to have drifted away from the heart of the matter," Potter said. "What we should be addressing here is whether the Good Book is in agreement with this female suffrage nonsense."

"All right," Amy said. "Where does the Bible say women shouldn't vote?"

"Nowhere," Hope answered quickly. "It doesn't say it anywhere because in the days when the Bible was being written they didn't have political parties or presidents or senators or congressmen, nor even state legislatures. All they had were kings and princes and satraps who ruled by force and didn't need anybody to vote them into office. Neither men nor women voted then, so I say it's just plain silly to talk about what the Bible says in regard to women voting."

"Young lady," Potter said, "it seems to me you're just too smart for your britches, but—"

"I ain't wearing britches today, Reverend. I got a skirt

on so nobody will have any doubt as to which side I'm on."

"Seems to me you're on the side of ungodliness," Collier said, looking very holy, Hope thought to herself, with the stub of a cigar in his mouth and his fat belly heaving against his dirty undershirt and the suspenders that were having trouble holding up his pants over the downslope of his ponderous belly.

"Well, Bull, you sure as hell ain't the one to be tellin' us who's godly and who ain't, are you?" Hope said. "I understand you're one of Madam Marge's regular customers. Do you get Reverend Potter's blessing every time you come out smelling of cheap perfume?" Now she had definitely gone too far. Madam Marge's was Cheyenne's favorite and only brothel.

"Now, Hope, you stop saying things like that," Marshal Pulver ordered. "You know Madam Marge is a nice lady who does her best to run a decent place."

Yes, she had overstepped the mark, Hope knew. She hadn't meant to disparage the small group of slightly wilted prairie flowers who labored hard and long to keep body and soul together in the wilderness. She had allowed Bull Collier to anger her with his sudden religiosity, but he wasn't the real problem. The good people were the real problem, the good men of the territory specifically. It was they who, out of a sense of mental and moral superiority, felt that women were either too silly and flighty, or too easily seduced into evil ways, to be permitted to have a say in making the laws they had to obey. A woman in Wyoming, after all, was as liable for hanging as a man if she shot someone in the back. A woman who held up a stagecoach or put her brand on someone else's cows got the same treatment as a man did for the same offense.

Or maybe a woman didn't get the same treatment. She hadn't wanted to think about the last time she had seen Tim O'Callahan, because that was the day when the lackeys of the cattle barons, the Cheyenne Ring, as she usually referred to them, had hanged the woman called Cattle Kate along with Jim Averell, her lover.

Cattle Kate hadn't had a vote in deciding who the judges

would be who permitted the cattle barons to get away with her murder. No, she hadn't had a say in that, any more than had Amy Andrews had a say in deciding how many saloons there would be per block in Cheyenne. And Violet Mechin didn't have the right to decide what would be taught in her school. Nor did Hope Cox have a vote in deciding how land titles should be confirmed or whose cattle should run where. That wasn't right! If women were not allowed to help make the laws, why should they be expected to obey them?

Those were all good arguments, but Hope had the feeling they wouldn't convince many men—lordly men who felt that a woman was a chattel, just like a horse or a cow, and should sit quietly at home while her master decided whether she should serve his coffee on her knees or come crawling to him on her belly like women and other slaves did in Araby.

"This ain't Arabia!" Hope shouted, so agitated that she didn't stop to think that nobody who heard her could possibly have been following her train of thought.

"I do not believe anyone suggested it was," Reverend Potter said, sounding very reasonable and half amused.

"Then why do you treat us like slaves?" she yelled. "What are you going to do next, put rings through our noses?"

Chapter 15

THE LOOK POTTER gave her made Hope think that was exactly what he would like to do to her, and not merely for political reasons. Reverend Potter might have a wife at home, but that didn't keep him from having an eye for pretty young women.

She was a little surprised. She had handled men like him before. While not as shamelessly lecherous as Bobby Kidwell or as openly obscene as Warden Nugent, he had the same thing on his mind. And now that she knew, she'd be careful not to be left alone with him in a dark room, or even a well-lighted one, for that matter.

The arguing had become more general now, with one of the ranchers, Philip Wallace, and Mrs. Sara Friedrich, a tall, handsome, stern-faced pillar of Potter's church, taking the side against women's suffrage, while Violet Mechin spoke for the women's side in her quiet, meek way.

Potter took the opportunity to edge closer to Hope while other voices echoed up and down the street. "My dear young lady, I hope you do not take my stand on this matter personally. It is, after all, the welfare of you women and girls I am concerned with, not any loss we men might suffer from granting this privilege—"

"This *right!*" she interposed.

"—this *privilege* being granted. I hope you understand that my belief on this subject does not mean that you and your father would not be perfectly welcome in my church whenever you are in Cheyenne."

"My pap isn't a churchgoing man," she said. "And I have moral scruples against sitting in the same pew with members of the Cheyenne Ring."

"The gentlemen who belong to the group you call the Cheyenne Ring do not consider themselves members of a gang," Potter said mildly. "They consider themselves just the opposite, honest businessmen defending their right against those whom they see as rustlers."

"Is that why they hanged the woman their bought-and-paid-for newspaper pinned the name Cattle Kate on?" she demanded, wishing that subject would quit coming up because she didn't want to think about that day.

"Hm, that was a most unfortunate affair, and yet the grand jury failed to indict any of those who were active participants or any of the honorable men who employed them."

"No, because those same honorable men also employ the grand jury and own the *Cheyenne Sun* and its editor Ed Towse, who not only told most of the lies that got the mob started, but hung the name Cattle Kate on the poor woman."

It was plain to Hope that Potter was uneasy about the "crime of the Sweetwater," as it was becoming known throughout the West, after the little river whose banks had been the scene of the lynching.

"There is a great deal of rustling in Johnson County and along Powder River," Potter said.

"Look, Reverend, me and my pap have staked our claim to three thousand acres of good ranch land. Since we arrived here three years ago with four horses, two hands, twenty-six cows, and a bull, we've been working like dogs. We built ourselves a cabin, just me, Pap, our Chinese cook, and our Mexican cowboy. We also built ourselves a barn and used the money we earned from our wages as trail hands, plus a couple hundred my friend Judge Chisum loaned me, to get a good start. We worked our tails off to get what we have and nobody like Philip Wallace over there, or the other cattle barons, is gonna take it away from us."

"And yet," Potter said, "brother Wallace is a churchly man, a pillar of the religious community, and a strong proponent of an end to the outlawry and rustling on Powder River."

"Yes, and Wallace was one of those behind the gang that hanged poor Cattle Kate and her man without cause. He's also one of the big cattle owners who turn purple every time they think about us small ranchers and farmers up along Powder River and would like nothing better than to do to us what they did to Cattle Kate."

"The ranchers claim some of the people who have settled around Buffalo are rustlers, not ranchers," Potter said, his intense black eyes staring fixedly at the pulse beating in Hope's neck.

Hope shrugged. "Well, one man's rustler might be another's man's honest small rancher, as Colonel Charlie Goodnight used to tell me."

Hope had a fairly respectable herd of cattle now. She had sold off all the steers from her original group, which had left her with Caesar, the big black bull, ten cows, and five yearlings. Caesar had done his best with his faithful harem, but most of the hundred cattle she currently owned were from another source.

It had surprised her that, when they said goodbye, John Chisum had given her Sally, the little mare, as well as loaning her two hundred dollars. He had also made Pat a present of a cow pony, wished them well, and promised to see them on his next drive. That two hundred had gone mostly for building supplies, food for the four humans, and fodder to get the cattle and horses through the beastly Wyoming winter when they had been snowed in for weeks at a time. So it hadn't been possible for her to buy any additions to the small herd.

No, the increase had come by other means. Charlie Goodnight had always impressed on her the fact that another man's cows were sacred, while John Chisum had held a less rigid attitude toward that. To Hope, a branded cow or steer was one thing, yearlings and dogies were another. If a maverick yearling was wandering about all by his lonesome, who was to say he wasn't one of yours who had strayed? And if you found a calf mewling after a branded cow, that didn't necessarily mean the calf belonged to the man who owned the cow. To avoid disputes, the best thing to do was to get your brand on that calf quick as you could. Hope had never stolen a cow in her life, but she had twirled a pretty loose rope when it came to mavericks and unbranded dogies. Who didn't along Powder River and vicinity? But that wasn't the way the big ranchers—Hope called them the cattle barons in imitation of the steel and railroad barons of the East—saw it. They were used to having the range to themselves and liked to think that everything with four hooves that crossed it belonged to them. Hope and her friends disagreed.

Someday they might have to disagree with guns if the Wyoming Stock Growers Association, as they called themselves, or the Cheyenne Ring, as they were called by the residents of Johnson County, didn't change their tune. The people who lived along Powder River, which, as Anne Fenwick had remarked years before, was a hundred miles long, a mile wide, and an inch deep, were not like the people of Cheyenne or southern Wyoming. They were more independent, less under the thumb of the big ranchers, and were hated and feared by the latter because of it.

There was a sudden stir in the crowd as several men came out of the hotel and headed for the old building in which the state legislature was to meet. One of them was Ed Towse, the strident editor of the *Cheyenne Sun*, who acted as mouthpiece for the Stock Growers Association. It was Towse who had been the leader in the blacking of the reputation of Ella Watson, the woman lynched along with her lover on the false charge of cattle stealing. He had invented the name Cattle Kate to convince people the murdered woman had been a real outlaw.

Another man in the group was Edward M. Lee, the man appointed by President Garfield as secretary of the Wyoming Territory. He and Governor Campbell were the only Republicans in the territorial government.

Walking behind Lee and Towse, who were deep in conversation, came most of the legislators. At the rear of the group was Mrs. Morton E. Post, a friend of Susan B. Anthony's and the leader of the group of women who had determined to seize the opportunity of pushing the suffrage bill through the legislature while the area was still a territory, so that it would not require a constitutional amendment as it would once Wyoming became a state.

A cheer went up from those gathered near the door of the building, and people moved aside to let the officials enter.

Hope was glad of their arrival. She had managed to wangle the right as a landowner and taxpayer to testify for ten minutes before the legislature sitting as a committee of the whole to consider the opinions of its constituents before voting today.

She was particularly glad that the meeting was about to begin, because while she was arguing with the others she had thought of a point she intended to put forward that had nothing to do with altruism or justice, only with self-interest. It seemed to her that for the most part people acted out of self-interest.

"Get in there and vote, boys!" someone yelled, and it sounded to Hope like Tom Adams, secretary of the Stock Growers Association. He and H.B. Ijams, another of the stalwarts of the Cheyenne Ring, were sitting in a buggy nearby with half a dozen other big cattlemen. "Get in there and vote that bill down!"

It hadn't occurred to Hope that the stockmen might take a stand on the suffrage vote, because she knew some of the big ranchers' wives were in favor of it. But it made sense all of a sudden. As long as the ranchers controlled the territorial government, they could get away with lynchings like that of Ella Watson and Jim Averell. If women got the vote and elected a new group of legislators, that kind of thing might be ended.

"Don't give in to them females!" yelled a bearded, dirty old prospector. "Don't let them get their claws into our hides!"

"Jake, if any woman got her claws into that mangy hide of yours, she'd sure as shooting snatch them out again before gangrene set in," Bill Bright said as he joined the other lawmakers entering the building. "Every time you pick up a glass in my bar I have to rinse it in cow dip to get the stench off."

"You better be careful, Colonel Bright," Jake growled. "There's other saloons in town besides yours."

"I know, but most of them won't even let you through the door, much less extend you credit."

Laughter accompanied Bright as he went through the door. Sticking out of his pocket Hope saw a folded, official-looking document that she had noticed Secretary Lee placing there. It was the suffrage bill. And she had noticed the forty-eight-year-old Bright's twenty-six-year-old wife whispering earnestly to him just before he started toward the building. The bill was going to be presented, and if she had anything to do with it, it was going to pass.

"I understand you are going to testify, young lady," Potter said to Hope, rubbing his long white hands together. "You certainly are a precocious young person."

"Reverend, my pap and I never owned a damn thing till we came up here to Wyoming and we'd like to see no one takes what we made away from us."

"And who do you think would do that?" Potter asked, his eyes wandering to the group around Tom Adams and H.B. Ijams. They were all talking to Ben Sheeks, the only one of the lawmakers who hadn't gone inside yet.

"You're looking at them, Reverend."

"Ah, so you are of the opinion that the Stock Growers Association is behind the move to block the suffrage bill."

"What do you think, Reverend? You must know something about it. They're on your side, after all."

He looked a bit troubled by the accusation, and his fingers

drummed on the leather-bound Bible as he shook his head. "You do me an injustice, Miss Cox. I am opposed to the female vote for only one reason—well, for two reasons, actually. One is that it is against the teachings of the Good Book, and the second is that politics, in my view, is so utterly vile that it will besmirch the sacred honor of our womanhood."

"You better save that for the boys inside," Hope said. "You can't sell it to me."

"Ah, so you know I am going to speak also."

"Yes, you, Editor Towse, and H.B. Ijams against the bill, and me, Mrs. Post, and Mr. Lee for it. You're not in very good company, Reverend, if you're not working for the association."

It was all beginning to come together for Hope now. She had thought at first that the opposition to the suffrage bill was merely the usual bull-headedness of men. Now she was able to see that men from the Powder River area and recently arrived easterners like Lee were in favor of the bill. It was those who took their orders from the association who were its main opponents.

She couldn't be sure about Potter. He was a newcomer and active in charity work, friendly to the Indians, and liberal in his view of the squatters and Mexican families who had settled along the river valleys and were constantly harassed by the ranchers. Did the fact that he was opposed to the franchise for women reflect the standard attitude of churches on the subject, or did it mean that despite his display of sympathy for the poor and downtrodden, he was shifting his support to the stockmen? Well, that remained to be seen. For the present, it was enough to get that bill passed.

"You are a surprising young woman," Potter said, his black eyes speculative. "Not yet twenty-one and already a leader among the women of this area."

"You ain't seen nothing yet, Reverend," she said with a laugh. "One of these days, I'm going to be governor of the state of Wyoming."

Potter smiled tightly. "What you will be is a dutiful wife to some man."

"Maybe I will, Reverend, but I got a lot of anger, a lot of ambition, and a lot of hope inside me, too."

Chapter 16

"I AIN'T A fellow to be prejudiced, but I'll tell you right here and now that there ain't no woman in this territory or in this country or in any country of Europe who knows enough about the world to know the difference between right and wrong where—"

"What in the devil you talking about, Ed Towse?" shouted Madam Marge, a portly, red-faced woman with peroxide-blond hair, at the editor of the *Cheyenne Sun*. "You know damn well my girls know right from wrong because you're always trying to talk them into doing something wrong."

The whole legislature, and the three or four dozen people who had managed to crowd into the barnlike building, broke into laughter at the embarrassment of the pompous editor of the *Sun*. There wasn't anyone there who didn't know that Towse and his paper were at the Stock Association's beck and call. The only person in the whole territory Ed Towse ever fooled was himself when he pretended to be publishing an impartial, accurate account of local happenings. Everyone else knew he was writing, editing, and publishing nothing but what the Cheyenne Ring told him to. To most Powder River people, if not to everyone in the state, that made even the weather reports in the *Sun* suspect.

"You just go on now, Marge. You know I ain't never been in that place of yours 'cept on business, and—"

Marge kicked one leg up in the air, displaying a huge yellow bow just above the knee on a pair of shockingly pink stockings. "Oh, oh, that's a good one, Ed! That's a good one! Never in the place 'cept on business, boy, that's a good one!"

"Order, please!" The speaker of the house pounded his gavel. "This is to remain a dignified and proper meeting or it will be closed to the public."

A chorus of hoots and catcalls answered him, but the boisterous spectators quieted down when Marshal Pulver tapped on the board laid across two barrels that served as the desk behind which Towse was reading his testimony from a clipping of one of his own editorials.

"Go on with your testimony, please, Mr. Towse," the speaker said as soon as silence prevailed.

"Why?" Amy Andrews shouted. "We already read it in that rag he calls a newspaper. We know what he thinks."

"Amy, you be quiet too," Bright said. "This is for the record, and we got to know what the Growers Association, I mean the *Cheyenne Sun,* thinks about this thing."

Another roar of laughter was suppressed by dint of gavel and pistol butt, and finally Towse went on with his reading, while Hope grimaced and clenched and unclenched her fists in rage at his overblown phrasing and ridiculous reasoning. "If that's what they call newspaper writing," she muttered half to herself, "I might just start out as an editor instead of a lady reporter."

"Is it your opinion, young lady, that you could write a better editorial than Mr. Towse?" asked Reverend Potter, who had managed to slip into a seat on the bench next to Hope. "He is noted for his flowery phrasing and well-turned sentence structure, I understand."

"But who can understand what he's saying 'cepting that

he don't like women unless they're working in the kitchen or at Madam Marge's?"

"Well, of course I don't approve of the soiled doves at Madam Marge's, but on the other hand," the clergyman evidently felt he was being very reasonable and fair-minded, "what other occupation than wife can a woman of upstanding morals aspire to?"

"Well now, I tell you what, Reverend, I figure that a woman can be a nurse like Clara Barton or Florence Nightingale, a politician like Miss Victoria Woodhull, a newspaper lady like Nellie Bly, a poet like Elizabeth Barrett Browning, a mule-skinner like Calamity Jane, a bandit queen like Belle Boyde, a cowgirl and rancher like me, or even a queen and empress like that Victoria who's got that soft job over there in London."

Potter showed his teeth as his mouth fell open. Obviously he had never thought of any of the women she had named as having occupations.

"And they do tell me that back in Roman and Greek times, and even farther back, they had ladies like Juno and Venus who were worshiped as goddesses, and some of them had jobs higher up the ladder in the Pantheon than some of the men had."

"Ah, but they were heathen," Potter said as though that proved his whole point.

"They may have been heathen, Reverend Potter," she said, "but they created some of the greatest art ever seen, built the finest buildings, and had cleaner, purer water and better-paved streets in their cities than we do."

"Ah, but they didn't have God."

"No, but they had pretty potent goddesses," Hope said. "And they seemed perfectly happy with what they had."

"Sometimes I am of the opinion that education is not suitable for women," Potter said. "They have too many weapons already to use against us poor men."

Hope took that for a compliment and tried to concentrate on the proceedings as Towse finished his long and generally pointless tirade, and Mrs. Morton E. Post rose and adjusted her pince-nez. After announcing that her friend Susan B. Anthony had promised to campaign to get women to move to Wyoming if the women's suffrage law was passed, she began to speak.

But her words were spoken over an excited murmur, and Hope noticed that it was mostly men who were chattering, especially the bachelors, who were obviously pleased by the announcement.

After all, Wyoming was a place where there were five or six men for every woman, and a young fellow who didn't have a wife or girl had nothing to look forward to but the company of Madam Marge's girls or of free-lance scarlet women like the late Cattle Kate. So that had been a good move, and Hope felt Susan B. Anthony would be as good as her word and influence some women to come westward.

Now Mrs. Post was going on to explain logically why it was not only morally and constitutionally right, but also to the benefit of the soon to become state of Wyoming for women to be on an equal footing with men.

"Gentlemen, do you really think that the woman who has stood beside you in the storm and against the enemy, who traveled over the river and desert, faced heat, rain, and snow, suffered through privation, hunger, and thirst at your side, isn't fit to stand beside you in the voting booth and cast—"

"No she ain't! No woman is!" Bull Collier roared, and Hope wondered if even one of Madam Marge's girls would be willing to stand next to a disgusting creature who went around in a dirty, sweaty undershirt, sagging suspenders, and with a stogie stuck in his mouth.

"Are the women who bear your children and nurse you in illness, who keep your house and cook your food, unfit to vote for your politicians?"

"They got enough to do already!" someone shouted. "Iffen they started politicating, they wouldn't get nothing done that needs to get done 'round the house."

"The kids would be runnin' wild," another man said.

"The filth of politicians would rub off onto the clean

skirts of our women!" another man shouted.

"Women are too good to vote!" a woman yelled, adding her voice to the uproar.

"Women are too good *not* to vote!" Mrs. Post shot back. "If women are what you say they are, then women will not be demeaned by politics; they will elevate them. They will uplift the whole range of political life; they will turn this great country into the shining example it should be from sea to sea. They will end political corruption, they will end poverty and crime, and with the power of their vote, they will send to Washington men—and, yes, women too—who will make our democracy the envy of the world."

"It already is," someone said.

"That is only because of what other countries have to offer," Mrs. Post said. "We are corrupt, but they are more so. If America is first, then England and France and then all of the other democratic countries will follow, until even the autocracies like Russia, Austria, and Prussia will come to see that universal suffrage is the way to the future."

Hope believed in women voting, and she believed most of what Mrs. Post was saying, but in her almost twenty years she had seen too much of the orneriness of men, and sometimes of women, to be quite ready to believe that the millennium was going to arrive on the day that ballot boxes across the country were bulging with the votes of virtuous women. What she did believe was that men had done such a rotten job, especially in the years right before and after the war, that the addition of millions of new, dedicated voters couldn't help but improve the way things were going.

But she didn't think men were going to be persuaded to give women the vote because they thought women would do better than they had. No, you had to give them a better reason, a reason that fitted in more with their self-interest. She thought she saw a way to do that.

Mrs. Post had taken her seat to the applause of most of the women and a few of the men, and now Reverend Potter was getting to his feet and clearing his throat before walking toward the board that passed for a desk.

"You stick to the truth now, Reverend," Hope encouraged him. "Remember what the Good Book says about the truth."

He pursed his lips and glared at her for a moment, but then smiled as he moved to the front of the room. "My friends, in this matter as in everything else, I take my stand on the Good Book. I speak not out of lack of respect, not out of a feeling of superiority toward women, but out of the heartfelt belief that womanhood, especially American womanhood, especially Wyoming womanhood, is sacred. To be a woman is to be sent to earth on a mission of the good Lord Himself to bring hope and beauty into the life of us males."

"Oh golly, he is really going to sling it, ain't he?" Hope said loud enough for her neighbors on either side to hear. Amy heard and shook her head vigorously.

Don't worry, Amy dear, Hope said to herself. Little old Hope knows what she's doing and she's got a surprise for these boys that is gonna have them all eager to vote the way we want them to.

"We have all felt the need of the company of good women in this far frontier land," Potter was going on. "We have all wondered if we could attract ladies of quality if we were to offer them a bribe—a bribe in form of the vote. We have heard here today that Susan B. Anthony has promised to campaign for women to come to Wyoming to settle *if* we pass this—this mistaken bill.

"Well, I ask you, my friends, what kind of women will those be? What kind of women will listen to this apostle of modernism? They are a new type of womanhood, unlike the devoted helpmates we have known in the past, unlike the mothers and sisters we remember from our childhood. Tell me, friends, would your mothers have wanted to vote?"

"My ma sure as hell wouldn't of wanted to vote," Bull Collier shouted.

"Your mother was a gorilla," Hope shouted, and brought on a flurry of gavel and pistol butt and hurt looks from Amy Andrews and Violet Mechin.

"Stop that! I'll not have any more of that! You, young lady, if you make any more outbursts, I'll have you ejected from this meeting," the Speaker said.

"Hope, please!" Amy Andrews said. "You're hurting our case more than you are helping it."

The older woman was right, of course. But the concept of Bull Collier having a mother was just more than she could stand without crying out in anger.

Potter had hardly allowed himself to be interrupted. He was going on at the same measured pace, talking the same kind of nonsense as before, his sonorous voice echoing through the building.

"Would your sisters have wanted to vote? Would you want to marry the sort of women whom Susan B. Anthony could influence into coming to Wyoming?"

"No!" It was a roar from the benches at the back of the room, where most of the town loafers had taken their places. "Hell, no!"

"We want good women!" Bull Collier said. "We want women who will stay home and take care of the children. We don't want no women who will be running around politicking!"

Hope had to close her eyes and put a hand over her mouth to keep from yelling one of the several choice answers that popped into her mind. But she remembered the look on Amy's face and sat with her fists clenched and her mouth firmly closed while Potter went on with his rabble-rousing.

"That is not to say that there may not be perfectly decent women who feel that they would like to vote." Potter pushed his long hair back from his forehead and nodded gallantly toward Mrs. Post and Amy. He also smiled at Hope, and she struggled to keep from sticking her tongue out at him.

"But, friends, those ladies are mistaken in their desire. They believe that they are seeking something that will improve our territory, our country. Of course they are not. They are seeking something that is unnatural, something that was not meant to be, something that they were not placed on earth by God to worry their little heads about."

"I'm going to kill him!" Hope muttered to herself. "I'm going to pull every hair out of his head, one by one, and then I'm going to make him eat those words, one by one, without any catsup."

"Please, please," Amy whispered, putting a hand on Hope's arm. "You know we must be careful not to seem too aggressive. That is just the picture of suffragettes they are trying to paint. We must show them that we are decent, God-fearing women who simply want the rights that the Constitution was meant to give us."

"The rights that *they've* been taking away from us ever since," Hope hissed. "The rights they grind our faces in every time we ask for them nicely and politely."

Amy looked shocked. She ran a nervous hand through her gray hair. "Hope, dear, you're not one of those women who really hate men, are you?"

Hope patted the other woman's hand reassuringly. "Amy, there are a lot of men I hate some of the time, some men I hate all the time, and a few others I can't bring myself to hate any of the time."

Amy nodded, reassured. "You know, I hear about some women back in the East who are running around after men with hatchets and things like that, and I just thought—"

"Amy, that is Carrie Nation and the Anti-Saloon League people, not the suffragettes, and any time I take after a man with a hatchet, he will really deserve it."

"Oh, that makes me feel much better."

"If I'm just ordinarily mad with a fellow, I'll use a Colt forty-four." Hope had a feeling that some men needed a gash cut in their skulls before any new ideas could be inserted.

One of that type was talking right now. Handsome, and brimming with charisma that she would be willing to bet would get him as far as the famous Henry Ward Beecher, whom Vicky Woodhull had exposed for the lecherous hypocrite he was. Yes, Edgar Potter had the technique down to a T, and his ravings against female suffrage would probably have been employed just as fervently in its favor if that had seemed to him the side his bread was buttered on.

"Picture yourselves, my friends, coming home from a

hard day off the range, soaked with sweat of honest labor, and looking forward to a hot tub of water to soak in and a good home-cooked meal to comfort your belly and finding—" He paused dramatically.

"Yeah, what would we find, Reverend?"

"Finding that the little woman, that helpmate in time of trouble, that homemaker, that comfort in your travail, was gone! Gone where, you ask?" He was really warming to his argument now. "I'll tell you where she's gone, leaving the little ones to shift for themselves and leaving you supperless! She's gone out to a meeting of Tammany Hall, that's where she's gone! She's wearing trousers like George Sand, that writing woman, and she's got a big cigar stuck in her mouth and her boots up on a table, with a glass of raw whiskey in her hand, and she's jawing away with a bunch of other females who have lost or given up their femininity to become second-class men trying to decide matters that women, thank God, don't know anything about! And if this body, in its wisdom, votes no, women will never have to know anything about!"

The building exploded with applause. The men were standing, stamping their feet, and cheering. The faces of Amy Andrews and Mrs. Post fell. The legislators weren't cheering, but most of them were smiling.

"Oh dear, we've lost, I just know we've lost," Amy said, dabbing at her eyes with a lace handkerchief.

"Don't give up yet," Hope said. "I've still got my say coming and I think I know just how to appeal to the better nature of those gents."

"Better nature?"

"They're political animals," Hope whispered as the speaker called her name, and she got up to go down to the front. "I'm going to give them a political reason to do what they ought to do out of a sense of what's right."

Amy opened her mouth to say something, but Hope was already heading toward the makeshift podium, her skirts swinging and her pigtail bouncing up and down. The eyes of every man in the place swung in her direction almost automatically, following her lithe, active body as it moved smoothly toward the front.

A couple of young cowboys whistled as she went by, but Reverend Potter frowned them into silence. He did not take his own eyes off the easy swing of the girl's legs and hips, however.

Reaching the board on two barrels, Hope leaned on it casually and faced the members of the legislature, rather than the crowd as Potter and the others had.

"Well, boys, I know you and most of you know me. You fellows from up Powder River way know me as a neighbor more than three years now. The rest of you know how I stand on this votes-for-women business." She paused to let that sink in, hoping a few moments of quiet might help them shake off the spell of Potter's flowery rhetoric.

"You've heard what the reverend had to say about how your wives will all run off with a drummer from the East if you give them the vote, how your children will be homeless, and you'll have to go a dozen years without a bath or a home-cooked meal while your wives plot with the Tweed ring to bring down America. You've heard all of that, but I don't think that most of you fellows believe it for a minute."

She paused and let that sink in also.

"I wonder if even Reverend Potter believes it. If he does, he's got a mighty poor opinion of women. Personally, I figure that no woman who has the courage to come out to this godforsaken land is so weak and flighty that the mere fact that she got herself a vote is going to make her throw herself into the arms of corruption and join Boss Tweed and his gang in looting the Treasury."

There was silence from the legislators, but no hostility, so she plunged ahead. "So if you don't believe Reverend Potter, you don't have any good reason to vote against the suffrage bill, do you?" She paused again and then went on, speaking quietly, not orating as Potter had done.

"But that doesn't mean you've got good reason to vote *for* it either, does it? And I figure that a fellow who hasn't got good reason for voting for something, even if he's got no good reason to vote against it, is more likely to vote no, or not vote at all. So I thought that I would try to give you a good reason for voting yes instead of no."

They were beginning to show interest, sitting up in their chairs.

"Now I'm not going to insult you by telling you that a vote for women's suffrage is the right thing to do. I'm not going to plead with you by telling you that it is only just that women have an equal say with men in the running of this territorial government. I know you brush aside arguments like that and say to yourselves, 'Well, what's in this for me?'"

A gasp went up from the spectators, and one or two of the legislators looked insulted, but Hope knew she had come too far to turn back, so no matter what the result, she had to plunge right on with her idea.

"Yes sir, that's what any sensible man would say, isn't it? What's in this women's vote for me? Well, I won't tell you that if you vote to give the women the vote they'll all vote for you next time they get a chance. I don't know how that would go. They might all vote for other women. So if I can't tell you that, what can I offer to gents who are mainly thinking about their self-interest—about getting reelected?

"Well, I came up with an idea that might interest men of the world like you, free-spirited sons of Wyoming who don't take orders from nobody and vote their consciences and their pocketbooks at all times. Well, this is it."

They were interested now, all leaning forward and listening to every word she was saying.

"You're all Democrats here in the territorial legislature, aren't you, boys? Each and everyone of the gents who have been voted into office in this state has been a Democrat, and that's what most of the folks around here are also, 'cepting maybe some of the folks who call themselves the Stock Growers Association—never understood that word *growers,* seems to me that a calf grows itself, with some help from its mama and the good rich grass of this territory—but anyway, most folks are Democrats, saving those big fellows in the association. In fact, there are only two public office holders in this state who are Republicans."

This was hardly an astonishing statement. The Garfield administration had appointed John A. Campbell governor of the territory and Edward M. Lee secretary. The people of the area, many of whom had come up from Texas, had quite naturally elected an all-Democratic council and house to oppose them.

"Does that suggest anything to you gentlemen of the council and House of Representatives?" she asked, and went right on without waiting for an answer.

"Well, it does to me. It suggests to me that if you stand together and vote for female suffrage and it passes, then it will be in Governor Campbell's lap. We all know Republican mucky-mucks back east are opposed to suffrage at least as much as they probably would have been to the whole Bill of Rights if they had been around at the time."

She paused for a minute and glanced around. She saw a look of admiration on Edward Lee's face. He seemed to have a glimmer of what she was up to. She grinned at him and went on.

"So what do you suppose Governor Campbell is going to do when he gets that suffrage bill dropped in his lap by his all-Democratic legislature? Why, he's going to wonder what President Garfield, Secretary Stewart, the House of Morgan, and all the rest of them are going to say to him if he signs that bill. Why, they're going to say to him, 'John, you let us down. You let us down real bad. You let them females out west get the vote and now they're *all* gonna be asking us for the right to vote. And, John, that is gonna really upset the way things are. That's going to upset the way we've been running the country. You're not going to have a job very long, John. No siree, you opened the floodgates and the water is running all over us.' Now, gents, you know old John Campbell isn't going to want to hear things like that from his bosses back east, so he's gonna veto that bill you're going to pass so fast that your hats will spin on your heads."

She paused to let that penetrate and then, grinning broadly, she continued in a confidential tone.

"And, boys, where is that gonna leave you, with the governor's veto staring you in the face? That is going to leave you in the cat-bird seat, 'cause you can say to the ladies of this territory that you tried. You can go home to your little wives and say, 'You see, Ma, I did just what you wanted me to do. I voted to give you the vote. I can't help it if old John Campbell, that hidebound Republican, vetoed it, now can I?' and you can look at your little daughters and say, 'Honey, I was thinking about nothing but your future when I voted so when you grow up, you'll be on the same level with your husband. But that gang in Washington, those crooks around President Garfield, they don't want women to vote. But, honey, your papa does.'"

Hope heaved an inward sigh of relief that it was over and walked away. There was no applause. The legislators were all putting their heads together and talking. Those who had come to protest for suffrage were staring at her open-mouthed.

Only Amy Andrews followed her as she walked out of the building and looked around for Juan and her horse. "Hope, I never thought you'd turn against us that way. I just don't believe it. I can't believe that you would say anything so cynical."

"Amy, we were beaten after Potter got through giving them the direct word of God on the subject. I thought the only thing I could do was to mobilize their worst selves on the other side."

"I don't understand. You mean that—"

"I mean that right now those good old boys in there are voting their political futures instead of their consciences, and they are passing our bill."

Amy stared at her. "Hope child, how can you know that?"

"I know that, Amy, 'cause I think I know how men's heads work," Hope said. "I'm not like you or any of the other ladies, 'cause I was raised in army camps and on cow trails, and most of the time there wasn't any woman around but my ma and she didn't trust men at all."

"And you don't trust them either," Amy said.

"Sure I do. I trust 'em to be men, not something else,

not some Prince Charming out of the fairy tales."

There was a loud cheer inside the meeting hall; it sounded as though most of the voices were women's.

Amy's mouth fell open, and she looked at Hope in awe. "Sometimes, child, I think you are smarter than any twenty-year-old has got a right to be."

"It's not so much being smart, Amy," Hope said modestly, "as it is seeing what you look at. If you look at something and see what you want to see rather than what's there, you're not ever going to get along in this world."

Then the doors of the meeting hall burst open and Edward Lee came running out, putting something in his pocket as he went. He waved at Hope and clasped his hands over his head like a pugilist claiming victory before he dashed to his buggy and drove off toward the governor's house.

"What was all that about?" Amy asked.

"I think Mr. Lee was telling me that the legislature just voted to give women the franchise," Hope said, "and he's taking the bill to the governor."

"And now the governor will veto it."

"The governor's not going to veto that bill, Amy."

"But you said yourself that he would."

"Oh golly, did I say that?" Hope grinned.

"I heard you say it, and so did those men in there," Amy said. "Some of them might have even voted for that bill thinking the governor would veto it and they would be able to have their cake and eat it too."

"You know, Amy, I wouldn't be surprised if they did." Hope grinned. "And if they did, I think they deserve just what they get."

"Why are you so sure that the governor isn't going to veto the bill? What you were telling the legislators sounded like pretty good sense to me. You know that stuff about his not wanting to start a trend that would spread to the East and offend the big boys in the Republican party."

"It did kind of make sense, didn't it?" Hope said. "But you know, Amy, I made all that up. I don't think President Garfield gives a plug nickel whether or not women are voting out here in Wyoming. I don't think it will even make the front page in the papers back east. But I'll tell you what, Amy. The women will hear about it and they'll start asking themselves, if women can vote in Wyoming, why can't they vote in New Jersey?"

"But are you sure the governor is going to sign that bill, Hope? Why should he?"

"Because the secretary of the territory, Edward Lee, is a strong supporter of women's suffrage and he is going to be talking to him, pointing out that, after all, Wyoming isn't going to be a territory forever, that someday it is going to be electing a governor and that the man who approved the suffrage bill could start out with the votes of every woman in the state in his pocket. Why, he might even become the first elected governor of the Equality state."

"The Equality state?"

"Sure, that's what I think we ought to call Wyoming when it gets into the Union. That will be about the time I'm old enough to run for office, and maybe if John Campbell gets to be the first governor with the votes of women behind him, I'll be the second."

"Hope, you amaze me. You just plumb amaze me, and you're hardly more than a child."

"Amy, you know what the Good Book says—'and a little child shall lead them,'" Hope said laughing.

"Yes, and speaking of the Good Book, here comes the fellow who thinks he wrote it."

"Ah yes, the fellow who almost lost us the vote and may have come close to getting the legislature to rule that we all ought to wear rings through our noses for men to lead us around by," Hope said.

"Well, I'm certainly not going to stay here and talk to him," Amy said. "And from now on, I'm going to old Reverend Carlson's church, not his."

The old woman hugged Hope and hurried off toward her wagon, giving Potter a look of distaste as she passed.

"Well, now," Potter said, running his hand through his silver-streaked hair, "I think Mrs. Andrews is taking some of my remarks personally. I hope you haven't, Miss Hope."

"Oh, no! Of course not, Reverend," Hope said. "I don't

mind being compared to a creature who just swung down out of the trees and shouldn't be given the right to breathe, much less vote."

He looked surprised. "Why, I don't believe I said any such thing, Miss Hope."

"Didn't you, Reverend Potter?" Hope asked. "Do you really think we women have the right to breathe?"

"Why, of course I do," Potter said, looking at the way her breathing was causing her breasts to rise and fall. "I think women have a great many rights, in fact."

"I'm so glad to hear that, Reverend. It makes me feel a great deal better about all of this."

"Miss Hope, I don't think you should take this sort of thing to heart," Potter said. "I bear you nothing but goodwill and admiration."

"How nice," she said, thinking that he was a handsome devil, even if he did pretend to be a saint. "I'll remember that the next time I hear you preach a sermon about how dumb and flighty women are and how we're all going to end up down at Tammany Hall smoking cigars and drinking red-eye."

"Well now, you have to think of that as being rhetoric in a large degree, or at least as a description of what might happen to some of your weaker sisters. I would never expect you to fall into the hands of Tammany Hall."

"That's good," she said. "Because if Tammany Hall or a similar political machine ever moves to Wyoming, I'm going to be running it, not controlled by it."

"You know," he said, "I can almost believe that after the way you maneuvered the legislators into voting yes in there a while ago. I can almost believe you might become a political power in this state . . . or at least the power behind the throne, you might say."

"You believe it, Reverend," she said, "because when I get to be governor of this state and you come looking for a job, I'll make you the chaplain of the board of sanitation."

"Oh? Why would you think of that position for me, assuming you should ever attain that power?"

"Because as I see it, Reverend," she said, "one of the

main jobs of the board of sanitation is to keep the state as free of shit as possible, and I never met anyone in my life who could shovel it the way you do."

The man's face turned beet-red, his mouth hardened into a thin line, and his eyes flashed dangerously. "You shouldn't have said that, Miss Hope. I was offering you the hand of friendship and you chose to reject it. That was not a good thing to do. It might even be a dangerous thing to do."

"You gonna have that vengeful old God of yours strike me dead, Potter?" she asked.

"God has ways of punishing enemies and the enemies of His people other than with lightning bolts."

She burst into laughter. "You mean you're gonna dry-gulch me, Reverend? Does your God approve of shooting in the back?"

"Young lady, you are insulting, and I can only promise you that you are going to regret it."

He turned and stalked away, his back very straight and his head in the air.

"I'll watch my back from now on, Potter," she called after him. "And you watch your front, because if I ever have occasion to use a gun on you, I'll do it while you're looking!"

Chapter 17

HOPE LEFT CHEYENNE in the same fashion she had come, on the back of the Andrews's buckboard. She hadn't ridden in on horseback because of wearing a dress for the demonstration and her speech, but before they started for home, she had changed into comfortable denim pants and a plaid shirt and now lay with a broad-brimmed black sombrero shading her eyes, sucking on a straw as the wagon rattled along one of Cheyenne's better but nevertheless rutted streets.

As fate would have it, one of the impressive buildings they drove past was the Cheyenne Club, the luxuriously appointed headquarters of the Wyoming Stock Growers Association. It was said to have the finest chef west of the Mississippi and the finest wine cellar west of New Orleans, but in Hope's opinion its members were the worst cutthroats and murderers west of everywhere.

Albert J. Bothwell, Tom Sun, and Ed Towse were all members. They dined and wined there dressed in fine black suits, white shirts with stiff collars, and elegant black ties, and every one of them had blood on his hands. The blood of Ella Watson, Jim Averell, and at least five others should have poisoned the premium wines when that gang sat down to dinner, and justice would have been served if they had choked on their choice steaks in retaliation for the way they had choked Ella Watson, Hope thought.

Her mind returned to those dreadful events eight months before, when it had all begun—the tragedy that still hadn't ended, the struggle that might be only beginning. It was a time that would live forever in her memory because its emotional content had run the gamut from rapture to horror.

Reluctantly but inevitably, she recalled asking Juan to saddle up Rollo early one morning so that she could ride out to the western limits of her ranch in search of six cows that had been missing when she had checked the herd of three hundred the day before.

"I'll find 'em and run 'em back to the herd in a few hours," she had told Pat. "They can't have wandered all that far."

"Naw. Cows don't have all that much initiative on their own," he agreed. "Of course, someone coulda run 'em off and be busily blotting out our brand right now."

"Now, Pap, who would do that to us? People hereabouts are our friends."

Pat snorted. "Yeah, sure they are. They also got the reputation of being the busiest bunch of brand changers and maverick branders in the whole West."

"And you know as well as I do how they got that reputation, Pap."

"Either by doin' it or by folks lyin' about them doin' it," Pat said. "You pays your money and you takes your choice."

"I've made my choice," Hope said. "I'll stand by Powder River people every time against the Cheyenne Ring, and I'll stand by Johnson County against Wyoming Stock Growers Association-types every day of the week and twice on Sundays."

"Is that why you couldn't give Jebel an answer when he came north this spring? Is it Powder River you love, or is it that Irisher?"

"If you're talking about Timothy O'Callahan, you know

I don't see him and have no intention of doing so ever."

"Yeah? Good thing," Pat said. "Them Fenwicks ain't our kind of people."

"What kind of talk is that?" she demanded. "What has Tim to do with what kind of folks the Fenwicks are? He only works for them. He ain't one of them."

Pat smiled knowingly. "Well, not yet, but I hear he eats at the big house, has a room there, and has been seen riding with pretty Mrs. Fenwick. He—"

"Pap, your mouth is too big for your own good!" she snapped, more irritated with him than at any time since he'd given up the bottle and become almost as hardworking as she was. Stalking out of the house, she leaped up onto Rollo and kicked the little horse in the sides so hard that he looked back over his shoulder to make sure he had the right rider on his back. "Go, Rollo, go!" Hope shouted, snapping her quirt. "We're headed for the southeast pasture down Sweetwater way."

Contrary to her prediction, it took longer than a couple of hours of riding to round up the missing cows. She was glad Pat hadn't been right in saying she'd find someone in the process of obliterating their brand, although she did find the beasts in the wrong pasture, mixed up with another herd, and couldn't tell whether it had happened by accident or design.

She had topped a rise and was starting down the other side when she spotted El Blanco, a noticeable animal with a white head and a black-and-white body, feeding on succulent summer grass. Beyond the cattle was a small cabin she had never spotted before.

"Wonder who that belongs to," she said to Rollo. "I thought this was Al Bothwell's land. Leastwise, he claims it. Never knew him to allow anyone to build on his land. And what are my cows doing over there in that pasture acting like they were invited to dinner? Guess I better ask some questions before I cut them out."

Loosening her Colt in its holster, she rode up to the cabin, noting that there was only one horse and a mule in the corral in back and taking care to make enough noise so the occupants wouldn't get the idea she was sneaking up on them.

She was within twenty feet of the shack when the door was thrown open and she found herself staring into the double barrels of a shotgun.

"I got buckshot in this thing, if anyone is interested in knowin'," a woman's voice said, and Hope saw a sturdy, rather handsome woman in her late twenties who was holding the shotgun like someone who knew how to use it.

"Oh," the woman said, looking relieved. "You're a girl . . . not one of them."

"That's right," Hope said, letting her pistol slide back into its holster as the woman lowered her weapon. "I'm a girl, and I'm not one of them, whoever they are."

The woman peered around cautiously as though checking to make sure no one else was in sight and then sighed with relief. "I'm sorry, ma'am, but there's talk that some folks are out to get me."

Hope didn't know what to say, so she turned her gaze to the herd in the pasture, wondering again how El Blanco and the others had gotten onto this woman's land.

"You heard any talk like that?"

Hope shook her head. "No, but since I don't know who you are, I wouldn't be likely to know if folks were talking about you, would I?"

The woman's broad face lit up with a big smile. "Guess not. My name is Ella Watson."

"And mine is Hope Cox. Glad to—" She broke off in midsentence. She had heard that name somewhere. Then she remembered. That was the name Anne Fenwick had hurled at Tim O'Callahan that day under the trees on the hill where her ranch cabin now stood. Reluctantly, she took the woman's extended hand and nodded. "Glad to meet you. I came here looking for some cows of mine that have strayed."

"Oh, you lookin' for cows too? Seems like everybody who comes around is lookin' for cows. Guess that's because of what that Ed Towse has been sayin' about me in the *Sun*."

"I don't read the *Sun*," Hope said. "It's the mouthpiece of the Cheyenne Ring."

"'Spect so," Ella Watson said. "That's why that Mr. Towse calls me Cattle Kate and says I'm a rustler."

If the *Sun* was out to get Ella Watson she couldn't be all bad, Hope decided, and slid down off her horse. She couldn't help wondering, though, if Tim had really had an affair with this woman. Ella wasn't unattractive, but she was rather common-looking and coarse in a down-country way. Women weren't all that numerous on the frontier, and Anne had made it clear that she was available to Tim, so it didn't seem logical that he would have taken up with Ella also.

Or was she grasping at straws? She had not been happy since the day she had parted from Tim in anger. Even the prospect of her long-delayed marriage to Jebel Mason couldn't make her forget the ecstasy she had found in Timothy O'Callahan's arms.

Hope shook her head impatiently. This was no time to be thinking about Tim. She had come here for her cows. "You say Ed Towse accuses you of being a rustler?"

"Sure does, and he hung that name Cattle Kate on me when it ain't my name at all. He says my gentlemen callers," she said with a self-conscious smile, "bring me stolen cows."

"And that's not true?" Hope asked, looking over at her own cows again.

"Not any way so," Ella said. "He's just sayin' those things because old Albert J. Bothwell wants my land along of that of my friend Jim Averell."

"They say Jim Averell is free with a wide loop and running branding iron," Hope said, bringing her gaze back to Ella and finding it impossible to imagine Tim with this busty wench, kissing her big full mouth and listening to her rough endearments. It didn't seem to fit, and she began to wonder if she had made a terrible mistake in believing the things a jealous woman had said.

Ella shrugged. "Everybody along Powder River does a little maverickin' now and again."

"Well there's branding mavericks, and then there's rounding up other people's cows," Hope said.

"That ain't what they got against Jim. They don't like him 'cause he's educated and a surveyor and he's discovered that old Bothwell is occupying some fine meadowland that he don't got no right to. A lot of those fellas have claimed public land they got no right to. Jim, he's outspoken, and calls Bothwell and the other Stock Growers Association men tyrants and usurpers and land sharks. I've said a few things about them myself from time to time and they don't like it much."

Hope was sure everything the woman was saying about the members of the Cheyenne Ring was true, but there was also the troubling matter of her cows being in Ella Watson's pasture.

"Would you like to come in for a cup of coffee?" Ella asked in a wistful way that touched Hope. It was probably lonesome living way out here all alone with nothing but cowboys for company. Ella probably needed female companionship, but there was still the matter of the cows to be resolved.

"Thanks, maybe some other time," Hope said. "Today I just came for my cows." She pointed to El Blanco and the others.

"Oh, is them critters yours?" Ella asked with a disarming smile. "I was wonderin' where they come from. They just wandered in and stayed and I didn't rightly know what to do with 'em."

"Well then, why don't I just take them off your hands . . . the ones that have my Lazy H brand on them?"

"Why, Miss Hope, you do as you please about that. I'll take your word that them cows is yours. You don't have to check no brands or nothin'."

"Thank you."

Hope turned and started to walk toward the herd, leading Rollo, but on an impulse, she turned back and grinned at Ella. "Just between you and me and this horse, how did my cows really get into your pasture?"

Ella Watson kicked the dirt with her heavy grogans.

"Seein' as how you ask so friendly-like, I guess it won't hurt to tell you."

"I'd sure appreciate it."

"Well, you see, it's like this." For a minute, Hope thought Ella was starting to blush, but then realized she was struggling to control a giggle. "A fella I know gave them to me, and I didn't bother lookin' to see if they was branded or not."

"He gave them to you?"

Ella nodded. "Yeah. You see, I sometimes entertain cowboys and other menfolk here at my cabin. There's no end of lonely men in this here territory, you know, no end."

"So I've heard," Hope said. So it was true that sweet Ella was running what was known in these parts as a hog farm. "You see lots of these fellows?"

"Sure do. Guess that's one reason old Bothwell wants me out of here. He don't like me sparkin' his cowboys 'cause they talk, you know. They tell me things Jim Averell says is real interestin'. I like picking up information for Jim 'cause I'm kind of sweet on him."

The woman was an odd mixture of sophistication and naïveté, Hope thought, steeling herself to ask the next question. "Among these fellows you see, is one of them Timothy O'Callahan, the foreman over at the Seventy-six ranch?"

"You mean the Sussex Ranch?"

"Yes," Hope said, suddenly aware that her fists were clenched, the fingernails digging into her palms.

"Yeah, I remember him. Big, tall Irish fella with red hair. Whoooooee, he's some man!" Ella grinned and rolled her eyes.

Get on with it, damnit, get on with it! Hope fumed silently, dying inside inch by inch.

"Yeah, I remember him real well. Nice fella that one is, real nice."

Hope's heart seemed about to drop through her boots, and the woman half closed her eyes as though recalling intimate details of encounters with the man Hope loved.

Then, suddenly and incredibly, Ella was shaking her head. "No, never did spark none with him. Sure would have liked to, but he's got a gal somewhere and I guess he's faithful to her. I seen him once with Jim Averell gettin' information about Bothwell and his land-grabbin'. That even affects the Sussex Ranch, though Mr. Fenwick was here before anybody. Bothwell, Bob Galbraith, and some of the others have been grabbin' up pieces of Sussex land for years, and Fenwick is finally gettin' fed up with it and set O'Callahan to lookin' into it for him."

"Did you say O'Callahan has a girl he's being true to? Do you know her name?"

Ella shook her head. "No, just heard it from Jim. Cowboys don't tell things like that to gals like me. Guess they don't want me to know that things like being faithful exist."

She looked sad for a moment but soon burst into a fit of giggling. "Maybe they're scared I might try it. No danger of that, I reckon. Not for the likes of me."

Hope's heart had leaped on first hearing of Tim's constancy as she thought that perhaps it might be she he was being faithful to, but a nagging second thought told her it was probably Anne Fenwick who had inspired such behavior. But how could a man remain faithful to a married woman?

He certainly hadn't been faithful to Anne the day he'd gone out with Hope and seduced her. The whole thing had been gnawing at Hope ever since she'd ridden off and left Tim standing there with the Fenwick woman screeching at him. What she ought to do was forget him and marry Jebel Mason. She could be happy with Jebel. He was a gentleman, had ambitions, and had talked about reading for the bar with old Judge Wise down to Cheyenne and maybe running for office once he and Hope were married and settled down.

"Do you know Timothy O'Callahan?" Ella was asking, and Hope shook herself out of her unhappy reverie to answer.

"I . . . yes . . . I mean, everyone on Powder River knows Sussex House and ranch and all the people who live there."

"You ever seen that palace of Mr. Fenwick's?" Ella asked wistfully.

"Yes. I spent one night there with my father and my old

boss, Colonel John Chisum of Texas. It's not really a palace, but it is about the finest house I was ever in."

"And that Mrs. Fenwick, she must be just like a queen."

"No, not exactly. She is pretty and dresses well and has a lot of dignity, at least when she's entertaining guests, but I wouldn't compare her to a queen."

Again the picture of Anne yelling obscenities and accusations at Tim and shamelessly flaunting the fact that he had been her lover flashed through Hope's mind. No, that had not been queenly behavior. Queens might have lovers, in fact they probably did, but they didn't scream and act like fishwives about them.

"I heared they got a tel-e-phone in that house. That true?"

"Yes, but I don't see much point to it since the only two others in the whole territory are at the post office that serves Sussex House and another of Fenwick's houses."

Ella shook her head in wonder. "Some folks seem to have more money than they know what to do with."

"More money and more cows," Hope said. "And speaking of cows, I'd better get mine cut out of your herd and start on back. I got a couple of hours' ride and there's clouds gathering over there in the west. I don't want to get caught in a storm with six frisky cow critters."

"'Course not," Ella agreed. "You just go on ahead and pay no mind to me. I want to stand here and watch. Never seen no girl cut cows out of a herd."

So this is the notorious Cattle Kate, Hope thought with grim amusement as she took her lariat off its hook and started toward the pasture. She doesn't even know how to cut out a cow, but according to the *Sun,* she's the queen of Johnson County outlaws.

Hope and Rollo went to work while Ella watched, and as the little horse separated the Lazy H cattle from the others, Hope became aware that they were being watched by someone else. She sensed it at first almost like a physical touch between her shoulder blades and, turning quickly, caught a glint of sunlight reflected off what might be binoculars coming from a mesquite-covered hill about a half mile from Ella's cabin.

"What do you suppose that is all about?" she asked Rollo as she put her through the intricate maneuvers it took to turn a cow away from those with which it was peacefully grazing. "Who is watching us, little horse?" Hope had all but one cow and El Blanco cut out and the herd was milling around discontentedly when it occurred to her that there might be a Winchester as well as a pair of glasses aimed in her direction.

"Come on, you old-so-and-so!" she yelled at El Blanco, whacking him on the rump with the rawhide lariat and sending him moseying over toward the small group of her cows. That was when she noticed the assortment of brands on Ella's herd. It looked as though the woman had been entertaining a lot of young gentlemen and that every cowpoke had brought one of his employer's cows along to pay his tab.

Once her cows were all together, Hope left Rollo to hold them in place and walked back to Ella.

"I'm much obliged to you for feeding my cows for a night and a day, Ella," she said.

"Why, you sure are welcome, Miss Hope. It wasn't no trouble at all."

"Thank you. I see you're taking care of some other people's cattle also."

"Well, I can't stand to see no cow go hungry," the woman said. "Guess I'm just soft-hearted that way."

"Well, if I were you, I'd be careful whose cows I took in," Hope said, "because someone is watching this place from over on the hill."

"There is?" She put a hand up to shade her eyes from the sun and stared in the direction Hope had indicated. "Funny, I don't see anybody."

"Maybe not, but I saw the sun reflect off his binoculars and he seems mighty interested in what's going on over here."

Ella shrugged, seemingly unalarmed. "Probably one of Bothwell's cowhands. They're always pokin' around hoping they'll see me pinching somebody else's cows. They think I'm a lot more stupid than I am."

"Just the same, you got a lot of brands in that small herd of yours, and those Cheyenne Ring boys are plenty mean, meaner than a hungry coyote. Just the fact that you got other people's cows in with your own might be enough to make them take a shot at you with a Winchester."

"Oh, I 'spect they'll be more direct than that. That's why I got this shotgun. I don't think they feel they have to bushwhack me 'cause they figure they got the law on their side."

"Do they have the law on their side, Ella?"

"That depends on who can afford to pay lawyer men the most, don't it, Miss Hope?"

Hope shrugged. "Sometimes men don't wait for the law. They make their own with the help of a Winchester."

"I don't think I'll get dry-gulched. Folks are kind of afraid of Jim Averell, 'specially since the papers been buildin' him up. Why, they say he's the most dangerous man in the whole county. That Towse fella has got a powerful imagination and he's writ that Averell threatens death to those who interfere with him, that he's killed a man—two men—several men, and that he shot one of them in the back. If he keeps on writin' stuff like that, he'll have every hardcase in the territory walkin' wide of Jim."

"Well, you be careful," Hope said. "Everyone doesn't take as free and easy a view of lost cattle—some folks can be awful mean about it."

"I thank you for the advice, Miss Hope, but I got this," Ella said, patting the shotgun, and then stood waving as Hope started her cattle up the trail northward.

Keeping one eye on the gathering clouds and another on El Blanco to make sure he didn't take it into his head to light out and stampede the whole bunch, Hope crossed the low-lying hills that sheltered Ella's cabin and pasture from northers and was passing through a grove of cottonwoods when she saw a man in a derby hat and store-bought suit sitting astride a gray horse in a patch of shade. A field-glasses case hung from his shoulder and a Winchester rested in the crook of his arm.

"Hey, you," he shouted. "Whose cows you herding?"

"Whose business is it?" she asked, her hand resting on the butt of her Colt.

The man rode out into the sunlight. "What the hell, you're a female."

"So I've been told. What are you?"

He guffawed. "You better hope you never find out. Now, I asked you whose cows those are?"

"And I said who are you to ask?" she said, her pistol out and resting against her saddle without his being able to see it because of the sun in his eyes.

"My name is George B. Henderson," he said, making the name itself sound like a statement of importance. "I am the manager of the Seventy-one Quarter-Circle Ranch."

"I've heard of the Quarter-Circle," Hope said. "It's up by Three Crossings. But your name means nothing to me."

"Maybe it will when I tell you I used to be a Pinkerton back in Pennsylvania and a member of the Coal and Iron Police. Maybe you've heard of the Coal and Iron Police?"

"Sure have," she said, looking with distaste at his thin face and the full, drooping moustache that was stained with tobacco juice. "They were always shooting down miners and iron workers, weren't they?"

He scowled. "They enforced the laws of—"

"Of the coal barons."

"Look, sis, you're too fresh for your britches. I asked you whose cows those are, and I want an answer."

"Do you, Mr. ex-Pink?" She moved just far enough that he could see her Colt was not only drawn but cocked and aimed. "Well, I want to know what business it is of yours."

"There's cows being rustled hereabouts, and we think we know who's doing it."

"Then go ask them whose cows they got," Hope said. "These ain't Quarter-Circle critters."

"Maybe I ought to see that for myself," Henderson said, spurring his horse closer.

"You try that," she warned, "and I'll drive that fancy belt buckle you're wearing right through your backbone."

The Colt was held steady right on his middle and he eased up on the spurs. "Seems like you're awful jumpy, little lady. I ain't accused you of anything yet."

"That's mighty white of you," she said. "I always get jumpy when I know someone is watching me through field glasses and has a Winchester trained on the back of my head."

"I didn't know you was a woman," he said, half-apologetically. "I thought you were another of them cowboys who are always visiting Ella's hog ranch."

"Well now you know, and if you'll get yourself and your horse out of my way, I'll be driving my cows on home before the storm hits."

"Those your cows? Is that why you were rounding them up in Ella's pasture?"

"She was keeping them for me overnight. And if you keep fondling that Winchester, you're likely to get the stock shot off it along with your hand."

"You talk pretty tough for a gal kid still wet behind the ears."

"And you ought to learn to remove your hat in the presence of a lady, Pinky," she said, and put a bullet through his derby, sending it flying off into the mesquite. "Especially a Texas lady."

Henderson was swearing a blue streak as his skittish horse danced around looking for a way to buck him off. His idea of control was to dig his spurs cruelly into the animal's flanks, and that further infuriated Hope.

"Drop that Winchester and your gun belt," she ordered, lifting her Colt again. "Shut your foul mouth and keep your spurs to yourself. It's not your horse's fault you made a fool of yourself."

"Why, you dirty little bitch, I'll put so many holes in you that—"

Hope's gun cracked again, and this time the stock of the Winchester shattered and left Henderson staring open-mouthed at the crease across his hand.

"Now, drop it! Be quick about it! Unhook that gun belt!"

"All right, but you don't know what you're getting into, lady. One of these days you'll be right sorry for this."

"What I'll be sorry for is that I didn't put a bullet between your eyes while I had the chance. Nobody would ever believe you didn't try to steal my cows if I stretched you out proper."

He turned pale, apparently convinced she was capable of killing him on the spot. "All right, all right... the rifle's gone... the gun belt's gone."

"Fine. Now you can go look for your hat, Mr. Henderson. And just so you'll know, my name is Hope Cox and these are my Lazy H stock. I don't let anyone inspect their brands unless they ask me nice and polite and show me a badge."

He turned away, cursing her but not very loudly, seemingly not wanting to take a chance on goading this Texas wildcat into a killing rage. "I'll be seeing you again," he muttered finally.

"You'd better not be wearing that hat," she warned. "I never put a bullet in the same place twice. It's a waste of lead."

Then she and Rollo were urging her cows on up the trail, taking their time and not bothering to look back. She thought she knew a properly cowed bully when she saw one.

Instead of worrying about what Henderson might do, she was thinking about Tim O'Callahan and the fact that Anne Fenwick had lied about him and Ella Watson. Was it possible that she had also lied about Tim's being her lover? If so, then Hope Cox had been the biggest damn fool in the whole of Wyoming Territory.

Chapter 18

LYING IN THE soft hay in her neighbors' buckboard, Hope recollected that it had been five days after her first and only meeting with Ella Watson that she had seen Timothy O'Callahan again.

It had not been by accident. She had sought him out deliberately by riding into the area along Powder River where the 76 had its line camps. On almost any given day, she knew Tim would be riding between the camps to check on the operations of the straw boys who managed the many cowboys needed to nurse Sussex Ranch's numerous herds.

She was sure now that Tim and Ella had never been involved with each other and that that part of Anne Fenwick's accusations had been a lie, but she wanted to know about the rest of it. Actually, she wouldn't turn her back on him forever just because sometime in the past he had been his boss's wife's lover. The unforgivable thing would be if he had gone on with the affair after declaring his love for Hope. That would be intolerable. She had no intention of playing second fiddle to any woman, let alone a high-

and-mighty aristocrat like Anne Fenwick. What she wanted was for Tim to tell her that there was no more truth to that part of Anne's jealous ravings than there had been to the one about his alleged intimacy with Ella.

But in order for him to tell her that, she had to meet with him alone. She was sure it wouldn't be easy to reestablish a close relationship after the way she had rushed off in a cold rage and ignored his very existence all these long months, but she was determined to try.

"It's not as bad as it sounds, Brick," she told the reddish cow pony she had bought from a Sioux on the run and which had become one of her favorite work horses. "I have no intention of waylaying the man and forcing him to confess at gunpoint that he has nothing to confess."

Brick's ears pricked up as he listened, but he didn't seem to feel her statement worthy of a reply.

"Oh, so you still think I'm a designing woman, do you? Well, that's because you're a male and don't understand a woman's heart. I should have ridden Sally today, but I thought you might be restless and want a bit of a gallop."

Brick whinnied in anticipation and Hope laughed, touching his sides with her heels, giving him the signal to stretch his legs. He whinnied again and broke into a canter along the dusty, rutted road that led to Three Crossings and the place where the 76 Ranch land touched that of the Quarter-Circle. It was along that rough boundary that the Sussex Ranch line camps were strung out.

Brick was at a full gallop by the time they reached the crossing she and Tim had used the day they had ridden to the site where her ranch house now stood. It was one of the few places along the shallow, soft-bottomed, quicksand-filled Powder where there was a granite shelf solid and wide enough to cross on. Reining in the horse, Hope held her Winchester, cartridge belt, and Colt over her head as they splashed across the stream.

"Easy . . . easy, Brick, boy. Don't step off that stone ledge or we'll be in sucking sand up to our ears in nothing flat." The horse was intelligent and well-trained enough to curb his impatience until they had reached the opposite shore and he could scramble up the soft dirt of the bank.

Hope put her weapons and ammunition back in place as they rode on toward the East Bend line camp, the largest of the camps, used mostly for hands engaged in keeping the cattle out of the thorn thickets and loco weed patches of Diablo Canyon. She had decided beforehand to use the excuse of looking for lost, strayed, or stolen dogies, and when the cook came out of the rough-hewn board shack that served as bunkhouse and mess room, she hailed him.

"Hiya, Cooky! I'm Hope Cox of the Lazy H. Seen any of my cows 'round these parts?"

A sour-faced man, the cook wiped at the flour and biscuit dough on his arms with his apron and shook his head. "Got no time to look at brands. I climb out of my bunk at three in the morning to get chow down for fifteen men at four-thirty. Got to start fixin' dinner right after that for twenty-five hands, and supper after that for fifteen. That don't give me no time for lookin' at no brands on whitefaces, does it, sis?"

"My name is Miss Hope Cox," Hope said. She was a ranch owner and saw no reason to let a camp cook address her as though she were a saddle tramp of a kid. "I own the Lazy H and I'm looking for strays."

"Ain't seen any, and wouldn't be like to. Better ask someone else."

"Who?"

"The line boss, Curt Harbot, or the man himself."

"And who might that be?"

"The boss. Tim O'Callahan. If anything is happening on this range, he knows about it. Ask him."

"I'll do that. Where can I find him?"

"Reckon he's over to the northwest range gettin' yearlings and heifers out of the rough terrain and movin' 'em out onto the winter range."

"Thanks. I'll go talk to him." Hope turned Brick's head and lit out westward, her heart doing flip-flops at the mere thought of seeing Tim again.

The ground started to rise up toward the higher ranch area around Buffalo Creek and the Middle Fork of Powder. Ahead of her loomed the Big Horn mountains, their crests topped by snow, clouds crowding about their higher peaks. The wind coming off them was cool even in the middle of summer. They would have another early autumn and cold winter, she thought, not the mild, salubrious ones that had been promised by *The Beef Bonanza*. Not one of the winters they'd been here for had been mild.

She spotted the tall, straight figure on the big black stallion soon after fording the Middle Fork and climbing to the highest point of the 76 ranch.

"Tim!" she called when she was within hailing distance. "Tim O'Callahan!"

He whirled from where he had been studying the foothills of the Big Horns for strays and stared at her in wonder as she rode up. "Hope? Faith and 'tis you!" A wide smile lit up his face, erasing the worry lines that had been there when he first turned toward her. "What brings you to the Seventy-six Ranch—to this side of Powder River?"

"I told the cook at your East Bend line camp that I was looking for strays."

"Have you been losing cows, Hope?" he asked, real concern in his voice. He looked unbelievably handsome, Hope thought, with his red hair showing under the Stetson pushed back on his head.

"No, none, except for a few I found at Ella Watson's place a few days ago."

"Ella Watson? Hope, I wish you would let me explain about Ella and Jim Averell," he said, riding closer.

"You don't have to. I talked to Ella. She is a great talker, that lady. I like some of what she had to say, but I'm afraid she's going to get into trouble pasturing other people's cattle because, as she puts it, she 'doesn't like to see a hungry cow.'"

"Aye, she and Jim are both already in trouble with Bothwell and Sun and the rest," he said. "But why did you tell Cooky you were looking for cows if you're not?"

"Because I wanted to find you and talk. I've been thinking about us—"

"Nary a day has passed that I haven't thought about you," he said, green eyes smoldering as they locked onto hers. "'Tis nearly two years since we parted, and many has been the times I've wanted to come by and see you, but . . . well, you were so definite and determined when you rode off that I despaired o' talkin' you out of it."

"Maybe you should have tried," she said, feeling her heart begin to pound as his horse edged still closer to hers in response to the pressure of his knees. "Maybe I just went off half-cocked and was unfair to you."

"'Tis not that I blamed ye, after the way Anne acted, but I wish ye had given me a chance to tell my side of it."

"Well, I'm here now."

"Yes," he said, reaching to lift her out of the saddle and onto his horse. "You're here and at last I can look at you and hold you in my arms and kiss your sweet lips."

The comforting strength of his arms around her, the warmth and firmness of his chest against her breasts, and the intoxicating nearness of his lips made her tremble with excitement.

"Oh, Tim, Tim, it's been so long . . . so very long," she whispered huskily.

"Forever," he murmured just before his lips closed over hers and her arms went around his neck.

Timothy's lips were burning with the same insistent passion Hope remembered from the past. The movement of his mouth against hers and the darting, teasing torment of his tongue were like a brand searing her soul. She forgot that she had come to talk about his involvement with Anne and what he intended to do about it, forgot everything but the intense need he was arousing in her.

"Oh, Tim, I've thought of you so often," she whispered when he finally released her lips. "I've longed for you for months and months."

"Nor was I forgettin' you, lassie. I could forget the Auld Sod sooner than I could forget you."

Ask him about Anne now—ask him! her mind prompted, but she couldn't bring herself to do it with his kisses along the contour of her jaw and down the sides of her neck creating prickles of mounting excitement.

She wanted to be sensible. She wanted to get things settled between them, to find out what future, if any, there was for their love. But caught up in the breathtaking assault on her senses, she couldn't even pretend to resist his love-making, could make no attempt to struggle against the current of desire that flooded through her.

She was kissing him with a fervor as great as his own, nibbling at his neck and earlobes, while her hands stroked his shoulders and back.

"I love you, Hope. I love you more than I imagined I could love anybody," he whsipered in a voice husky with emotion.

"I love you too, Tim. I guess I have ever since that first day, when you came to my rescue."

He smiled down at her. "Sure and a man would've had to have a heart o' steel not to fall in love with you after all I saw."

She tweaked his ear gently. "You had no right to look."

"Begorrah, I'd have had to be blind not to have looked and gloried in the beauty of that perfect young body." His lips claimed hers again, and their souls seemed to meet and merge in a long stirring kiss that left Hope limp and whimpering for more.

"You devil—you Irish devil," she whispered as his lips moved down the column of her neck to the pulse beating so rapidly there, before nuzzling under her open shirt collar to caress the sun-warmed flesh of her shoulder. "You are doing things you shouldn't be doing—making me feel things that are positively sinful."

"Nothing is sinful between two people who love each other."

"Oh? How do you know?" she asked with a sharp intake of breath as his hand moved up along her ribcage until it encountered and enclosed the outward swell of her breast.

Her body was strained against his and her thighs were throbbing at the touch of his powerfully muscled legs. His grasp on her loosened slightly and then tightened again, molding her belly to his and causing his engorged maleness to pulse against her soft woman's flesh, and even through the layers of cloth between them the touch was like flame, quickly bursting into a prairie fire that consumed all in its path.

They were falling down together onto the fragrant grass, and while she planted passionate kisses on his neck, he covered her breasts with kisses, sucked at the eagerness of her nipples, and buried his face between them.

"Hurry. Please hurry," she begged, pressing herself hard against him.

"Yes, my darling, yes." His hands were fumbling with her belt buckle, and he cursed under his breath when he couldn't get it undone until she helped him.

"Oh, Hope . . . Hope, my dearest girl," he moaned as she yanked the belt off and rolled onto her back to strip off boots, jeans, and underpants.

"Hurry, hurry, hurry," she was whimpering as he got out of his own clothes and then brought their bodies together again.

She felt the bigness of him and his need for her. She allowed her fingers to search every line and plane of him, every strong taut muscle of this man she loved with all her being.

"Timothy, my darling . . . my love . . . my lover," she whispered as she opened to him and felt the pressure of his conquering manhood entering her welcoming softness.

A muffled scream, halfway between pain and extreme pleasure, escaped her lips as he eased all the way in and his hands slid under her buttocks to lift her toward him.

But she was beyond the need for urging. She surged up against him, rolling her hips, closing her eyes and moaning in pleasure as she felt the fullness and driving strength of him possessing her.

They had been apart too long, had spent too much time

thinking about each other and about each other's bodies, brooding about how wonderful they were together. He seemed to have an insatiable need to touch her, to know her completely. His hands were moving all over her body, stroking and caressing her shoulders and arms, the arch of her back, her sides, the tightened muscles at the back of her thighs. And as his hands moved downward, hers came upward along his flanks, over his buttocks, up his back, across his shoulders, and finally locked behind his neck to hold him ever closer.

"All of you, Tim . . . I want every inch of you," she panted. "Give yourself to me, love, give me all of you. Oh my God, Timothy, I love you so much I can't bear it."

She turned to fury beneath him, bouncing and wriggling, rocking from side to side and gasping for breath as she soared into the throes of completion.

He followed her quickly, bursting inside her like a sky-rocket. This was joining, she knew, a union of two bodies and, she hoped, two hearts and souls. There was a long, luxurious silence.

"Hope, me darlin', that was wonderful. Nothing like it ever happened to me before. There's never been anyone like you . . . no one in my life like you."

Still delirious with passion though she was, Hope thought about his words. He wasn't saying she was the one and only woman in his life. She couldn't be entirely sure he meant she was the only current one. But her doubts faded in a resurgence of desire she made no effort to restrain. "Tim, don't go, don't leave me yet," she whispered as he stirred. Kissing his chin and the corner of his mouth, she tightened her arms and wrapped her legs around his hips, locking her ankles at the base of his spine.

He raised himself on his hands and smiled down at her. "Well now, ye are a lovin' lass, aren't ye?"

"What's the matter?" she teased. "Is a little country girl from Texas too much for the big bad boyo from Kilkenny?"

"No, but sometimes a fellow needs to slow down just a bit."

"I don't believe it," she said, rolling her hips slowly and

lifting her bottom off the ground to bring their love flesh into searing contact again.

"Ah, you are a lass who knows what she wants."

"I wouldn't have come all the way to Wyoming looking for a ranch if I didn't. And I couldn't have gotten my herd together if I hadn't known what I wanted. Nor would I be here with you if I didn't know what I wanted."

"Aye, you'd not have done any of it without a real determination in your head," he agreed.

"And in my body," she said, moving sensually and feeling his quick response.

He laughed and kissed her. "Sure and it has been a long time since we were alone like this."

"Seemed like forever to me," she said, biting the lobe of his ear lightly and rolling her hips again. "And once after forever isn't enough."

"Whoever said it had to be?"

"That's what I'm trying to find out."

He pretended not to notice her undulations, teasing her with inaction and light butterfly kisses on her nose and chin. "Well now, ye are a lady who goes after what she wants, and I've an idea I know what it is you be a-wantin' right now."

"It's marvelous the way you read my mind," she said, prodding him on the rump. "I guess it's true you lads from the Auld Sod are lacking in initiative and need a little pushing to get to the task at hand."

"Ye must have heard that from some Ulsterman who knows not how hot flows the blood in the veins of the men of Kilkenny and Cork."

"Quit bragging and show me!"

"Ah, now ye've gone and asked for it, and 'tis sure ye'd better be that ye want it, because I'll not stop till you're after cryin' uncle."

"Never, never... not if it takes all day!"

He stretched her arms wide and pinned them down with his own, captured her lips in a wild tongue-tangling kiss, and began moving with tantalizing slowness, making each thrust and withdrawal an experience of almost agonizing pleasure. Then, when she thought she could bear no more, he picked up the tempo and drove at her in a sudden fury of passion. Hope responded to him fully, and heard his groan of ecstasy as she used newly discovered muscles to squeeze and encourage him, demanding his best and glorying in his vigor and stamina.

Chapter 19

LATER THEY RAN the horses away from the banks of the nearby stream and plunged into the water, laughing and splashing and ducking each other, finding a different pleasure in bathing. Thoroughly relaxed and momentarily satiated, it was a delight just to look and touch, to enjoy the smooth skin and taut firmness of youthful bodies.

Hope was fascinated as her hands roamed over him, exploring his lean, trim physique, examining his maleness to learn exactly what God had been up to when he created the creature called man.

"You're so different from me," she said, almost in awe.

"Vive la différence! as the French say."

"Do the French know a lot about love?" she asked, running her hands over his buttocks and down well-developed muscles of his thighs, realizing now where the strength came from that enabled him to be so good for her.

"I'd say they probably know about half as much as they'd like other people to think they know," he said as he leaned over to lick drops of cold water off the tips of her breasts and chase more of them trickling down her belly.

She tried to keep her tone casual as she asked, "Have you been with a lot of Frenchwomen?"

He looked up at her and grinned. "'Tis not gentlemanly to keep a tally."

"But you must have some idea," she insisted, even though she knew she probably shouldn't let herself become obsessed with his previous affairs. It hurt her to think of other women sharing the wonder of his lovemaking. It wasn't ordinary jealousy, she told herself, it was just that he belonged to her. She loved him so much that she didn't want to think of his having been with anyone else, although reason told her he had. "There must have been at least one."

"Well, I couldn't rightly say I was ever with a French lassie."

"What does that mean?"

He grinned at her crookedly. "Are ye sure you want to know all this?"

"Yes," she said. "I want to know."

He shrugged and kissed her lightly. "Well, all right, then. I was but a slip of a lad, only fifteen, when me brother and me came from Ireland. We traveled in steerage, and there was a French lady on board. No better off than us was she, with our shoes full of holes and the seats of our pants patched by our mother the day before we left, but she had a trade at least."

"Ummm," Hope said, climbing up onto the bank to let the warm sun dry her. "I think I can guess what it was."

"No, 'twas not what you're thinkin'. The lady was a seamstress and had great expectations for her life in America."

"Was she older than you?" she asked as he clambered up onto the bank to sit beside her.

"Aye, and 'tis a shameful fact to admit to, but I was still a virgin and she seduced me."

She looked into his twinkling green eyes and wondered if this was one of his jokes. "I sometimes wonder if you were ever a virgin."

He laughed outright at the expression of doubt on her

face. "Why, lady love, everyone is a virgin to begin with. Even you, me darlin'."

"Yes, until I met you," she said as he helped her to her feet and they went back to the cottonwoods to dress.

All the time she was getting her clothes on, she was working up the courage to ask him about Anne Fenwick. She wanted to get that settled before they parted. That he had been the woman's lover in the past she could live with, but if he still was—well, that was a different kettle of fish.

"It wasn't really the French lady I wanted to ask you about," she finally began.

"Then what was it?" he asked, pulling on his boots, and she could tell by the expression on his face that he suspected what she was going to ask and wasn't particularly eager to answer.

Hope pulled on her boots and stood up, trying to find a way to phrase the question so she wouldn't sound like a jealous witch.

Then suddenly time ran out and they heard the sound of a galloping horse pounding toward them, while a shout broke the peaceful afternoon quiet.

"Tim, Tim O'Callahan! Tim O'Callahan!" The man's voice sounded frantic.

"What the devil is this?" Tim said, tucking in his shirttail and picking up his Stetson.

"I can't imagine," Hope said, trying to smooth her hair. She finally put on her sombrero in an attempt to hide its tousled condition.

"Tim! Tim O'Callahan!"

"Why, 'tis Frank Buchanan," Tim said, shrugging into his denim jacket and starting forward. "What's he doing way up here ridin' like the devil was after him?"

The man on horseback had apparently spotted Tim's horse, because he was coming directly toward them, still yelling.

Hope was close behind Tim when he emerged from the cover of the cottonwoods and waved his hat at the oncoming cowboy.

The man returned the wave and shouted. "Tim, something terrible has happened!"

He was close enough now that Hope could see he was a short, slender, sandy-haired man in his middle twenties and that his horse was flecked with foam from hard riding.

"What is it, Frank?" Tim asked as man and horse came to a halt near them. "What's the matter?"

"Al Bothwell . . . Tom Sun . . . and several others," Buchanan panted, "they grabbed Jim Averell and Ella Watson. They're lynchin' 'em, Tim, lynchin' 'em!"

"What?"

"They took Ella away from her house, then went to get Jim," Frank babbled.

"Slow down, boy, slow down," Tim said, his face dark with anger and his hand hovering over his gun belt. "Tell it like it happened."

"Can't, Tim. They need help—might still be alive."

"Where are they?" Tim asked, whistling for his horse.

"Down by the Sweetwater," Buchanan said as the big black stallion came running, with Brick trotting after him. "I saw it, Tim, but couldn't get nobody to help. There were at least six of 'em, all armed with long guns, and me with only this peashooter."

"Hope, ride on to Casper and get the sheriff," Tim said. "I'll got with Frank and see if there's anything I can do."

"I already sent Tex Healy to Casper," Frank said. "Can't find anyone willin' to help . . . all afraid of the cattle barons."

"I'm going with you," Hope said, checking the cinches on her saddle and the Winchester in its case. "Three guns are better than two."

"Hope, stay out of this, please. You don't even know Jim and Ella."

"The hell I don't. I told you I met her the other day. She had half a dozen of my cows in her pasture. She seemed harmless enough, and I'm not going to stand around and let that bunch lynch her."

"We better get going if there's going to be any chance to help at all," Frank said, and Tim and Hope mounted up. Tim turned to say more about her not going but only shrugged when he saw the look of determination on her face.

"Tell me about it now," he said to Frank. "Tell it as we ride."

"I was at Ella's place," Frank said, giving Hope a sidelong glance, "along of John de Corey, who works for her, and that kid, Gene Crowder. Ella had just come back from buying new moccasins from a party of Indians camped down by the river when the six of 'em rode up. There was cattle in the pasture, and John Durbin took down a piece of wire and drove the animals out while Ernest McLain and Bill Connor kept Ella from going into the house for her shotgun and made her get in the wagon they'd brought with them."

"So they came all ready for it, did they?" Tim said.

Frank nodded. "They were out for a killing for sure."

"That poor woman," Hope said. "She seemed like such an innocent no matter what they say she's done."

"They pulled their guns on that fourteen-year-old kid Gene Crowder and made him go in the house and stay. I was far enough away that they didn't see me, and I sneaked up behind the house, lookin' for some way I could help, but there were too many of them. I didn't know what they intended and I didn't want to pull anything right then."

They were passing through a gully and the echo of the horses' hooves on the rocky ground was so loud that Frank had to raise his voice.

"While I was behind the house, I heard Ella ask what they were going to do with her, and Bothwell said they were taking her to Rawlins as a receiver of stolen property. I think she knew they was lyin' 'cause when she asked if she could go inside and change clothes, McLain laughed and said he didn't think she needed to get gussied up for where she was going."

"Those bastards!" Tim said. "Then what happened?"

"I followed them to Jim Averell's place and he was just settin' out for Casper with a team and wagon. They ordered him to put up his hands and said they had a warrant for his arrest. When he asked to see the warrant, Durbin and Bothwell drew their guns and said shootin' irons were all the warrant they needed. They forced him into the buckboard with Ella and set off toward Independence Rock. I got this gun out of Averell's store and told Tex Healy to ride for the sheriff in Casper while I went after the lynch party to see what I could do."

"With only yourself against six armed men?" There was respect in Tim's voice as he looked at the young cowboy.

"Actually, it turned out there were seven of them. That ex-Pinkerton guy, who's the ramrod at the Quarter-Circle, George Henderson, joined them before they hit the Sweetwater."

"I know him," Hope said. "Found him hanging around Ella's place when I got my cows. He was watching her through field glasses."

"You met him face to face?"

"Sure did, and I drew down on him when he tried to inspect my cows. He's got rattlesnake eyes."

"He is a rattlesnake," Tim said. "You were lucky he didn't try something."

"He did and I shot his gun out of his hand."

Tim's eyebrows shot up and he looked from her to Buchanan. "Seems like I'm ridin' with a couple of bloody heroes. What am I doing here?"

"I followed them down to Independence Rock and kept them in sight as they went toward the river; saw them drive into the ford and followed up the bed of the stream for about two miles. They stopped then and argued for a while, but I wasn't close enough to hear what they were saying and... well, pretty soon they dragged Jim and Ella out of the wagon and I knew for sure what was going to happen, and I guess they did too, because they were kicking and fighting as they were dragged to a tree, and—"

"Go on," Tim said. They were approaching the Sweetwater now and his eyes were roving restlessly, looking for trouble, his gun hand never far from his holster. "What happened then?"

"They had a rope around Jim's neck and it was tied to a limb," Buchanan said. "Bothwell told him to be game and jump off the rock they had dragged him up on, but Jim spit in his face and cussed him out. Henderson smashed his pistol in Jim's face and Ella screamed and . . . well, that was when I opened fire on them with this."

Frank pulled the little thirty-two he was carrying out of his belt and showed it to Tim. "I don't know whether I hit anybody or not, but they kept on trying to put another rope around Ella's neck and she was dodging her head from side to side to keep them from doing it and yelling for help.

"I tried to help them, Tim, honest I did, but then Henderson and three others spread out and started trying to pick me off with their Winchesters and I figured the best thing I could do was to skedaddle out of there and get help. You're the first one I could get to come back with me, though the whole countryside seems to know about it now."

Tim was cursing quietly but steadily as they reached the Sweetwater and started upstream. The Irishman had his rifle in hand and was throwing the lever to insert a round into the chamber.

"If we run into Bothwell and Henderson and their gang of murderers, there'll be long guns on both sides of the argument," he said grimly, his lips set in a hard, tight line.

Hope had never seen him like this, not even the day he had killed Cajun Joe and almost drawn on Jebel. Then he had had a grin in his eyes as though he had known it would come out all right in the end. This time he seemed to expect to find the worst, but then so did she.

"Don't suppose I could talk you into hidin' in the bushes, Hope, and lendin' Frank your Winchester?"

"Don't suppose so. Try me on a target and I'll bet I'll place ten out of ten closer to the mark than you."

"Maybe so. I was thinkin' more about what we might see than how good a shot you are."

"Oh. Well, I can stand it if you can."

He shrugged and they rode on, splashing through Spring Creek, the walls of the canyon, rising high on either side of them, beginning to block out the sun.

"It's not far now," Frank said. "Up along the gulch over there is where they took 'em."

"All right," Tim said. "Don't suppose they're still there, but be careful."

All three had their guns out as they moved through the rocks, sagebrush, and scrub timber of the gulch.

"Right around those big rocks over there," Frank said. "That's where I hid when I shot at... oh God!"

They had come to a stunted pine growing on the summit of a low cliff where Spring Creek joined the Sweetwater. Hanging from the limb of the tree were two swaying bodies.

"Mother of God, they used ordinary cowboy lariats," Tim growled as they rode closer. "They strangled them! The dirty, murderin' bastards! Even Sassenach don't do things like that."

Hope was staring at Ella Watson. The pretty, smiling face had been transformed into a grotesque mask by her terrible death. The skin had turned purple and her tongue was lolling out. Spittle and vomit had run down her chin and dripped onto her dress. The man Hope had never met. In life, he must have been a stalwart, handsome fellow with receding hair, but his face, too, was now discolored and contorted with pain and terror.

"Shall I cut them down?" Frank asked.

Tim shook his head. "No, the posse should be here before too long, and we want clear evidence that there was a lynchin'." As he moved around the lifeless bodies, he bent over to pick something up off the ground.

Frank's voice was shaky as he said, "Those are the moccasins Ella bought from the Indians."

Hope stared at the pitiful bare feet, knowing that Ella must have kicked off the moccasins during her desperate struggle to stay alive. Feeling nauseated, Hope's first impulse was to run off somewhere and vomit, but she had told Tim she could take it, so she fought down the urge.

Tim was still examining the corpses, lifting one of Ella's limp hands and then one of Averell's. It was the same in both cases: the tips of the fingers were torn and bloody. "They ripped out their nails trying to claw the ropes away from their throats," he said in a voice choked with anger. "Of all the barbarous pieces of work it's been me misfortune to see, this is the worst. We treated Mosby's guerrillas better than this when we caught them redhanded during the war."

Standing in front of the two dangling bodies, he bowed his head as the sun disappeared behind the rim of the gulch. Hope realized he was praying. Stumblingly, she tried to remember a psalm her mother had taught her.

After a few moments, Tim turned and came toward her. "Guess we better make camp and light a fire so the posse from Casper can find us," he said to Frank, and handed Ella's moccasins to Hope.

As her hand closed on the soft leather, the enormity of the crime that had been committed hit her full force. "Oh, that poor soul, that poor harmless soul! How could they do it? Those beasts! Those unspeakable beasts!" The tears came then, a veritable storm of sobbing and crying, composed equally of sympathy and anger. Tim put an arm around her and led her about twenty feet away behind a clump of brush. He held her tenderly, murmuring soothing, comforting words, while Frank began collecting dry twigs and fallen branches for a fire.

"What do we do now, Tim?" Frank asked later, when Hope had calmed down and they were sitting around the fire listening to the horses stomping about looking for night shelter and some tasty grass.

"We wait for the posse, and then we go get those murderers," Tim said. "They may think they're above the law, but I don't. I came from a country where the law doesn't mean much, but I think it does here. If it doesn't, then 'tis our business to make it work. I want justice for Jim and Ella and I'll see that they get it."

Hope leaned against his shoulder and gazed into the fire, thinking about Ella and wondering what kind of future there was for anybody in a territory where a small band of rich, ruthless men could murder anyone who opposed them.

"That gang won't get away with it, will they, Tim?" she asked.

"No, they won't," he said grimly. "They won't get away with it if I have to bring every one of them to justice myself."

She looked at him in alarm. "Not by using their tactics,

Tim. Not by brute force. We need law."

"Aye, and we'll have it eventually, but in the meantime it may take a bit of pushing here and there."

"But isn't that what Bothwell and his gang are up to? Doing a bit of pushing here and there?"

"Yes, but they do it to make it easy to grab land, not to support the law."

"Ella told me the big cattle people and the *Cheyenne Sun* have been claiming she was receiving stolen cattle as payment for her, uh, services."

"Those people have been trying to pin a rustlin' tag on Johnson County for years," Frank said.

"Well, there is a lot of mavericking going on in these parts," Hope said. "Though not as much as there was in Texas, where it's more or less considered a part of the game. Why, even a straitlaced man like Charlie Goodnight was prepared to turn a blind eye to that."

"That isn't the real problem," Tim said. "Here we are dealing with cattle companies from the East and England, where shares and partnerships have been sold. Those people are interested only in profits, and the local leaders are convinced that the only way to go on producing higher and higher profits is to drive out all competition—all the small competition, that is. Later on they'll probably get around to cutting each other's throats, but right now 'tis the little man on the other side of Powder River who is their target. Jim and Ella were the first to get the full treatment because they knew more than the rest and were louder in talking about land-grabbing and the other schemes the Cheyenne Ring is promoting behind a smokescreen of accusations against the little fellow."

"Fenwick can hardly be called a little fellow," Hope said. "Where does he fit in?"

"Morton hasn't been well the last few months and leaves all the business dealings and managing the ranch to Anne and me."

Here was her chance. He had brought the subject up and given her the perfect opening to ask about Anne, to demand to know what their relationship was, but Hope knew she couldn't do it. Somehow it wouldn't be right, not with poor Ella and Jim swaying in the wind so close to where they were sitting.

Conversation fell off after that and in a few minutes Frank Buchanan proved he was as discreet as he was brave by casually suggesting that he would curl up with his saddle on the far side of a large boulder, where he could keep an eye on the horses and watch for the approach of the posse.

Alone by the fire, Hope and Tim stretched out under Tim's blanket and lay staring up at the stars, aware of each other's nearness but, by silent mutual consent, not making love.

In a way, Hope thought, it was just as wonderful. Lying with her head cradled on his shoulder, the quiet of the night punctuated by the yelping of prairie dogs or the occasional howl of a wolf, she was content. This was what it must be like to be married. Of course there was still the hideous reality of what had taken place here that would have to be dealt with, but there was nothing they could do about that until the posse from Casper arrived.

Again it could have been a time to talk about Anne, but Anne seemed a million miles away, and Hope didn't want to do or say anything that might cause Tim to remove his arms from around her. She never wanted that to happen, she realized as she nuzzled her nose into the open neck of his shirt, breathing in the warm male smell. She wanted to lie here forever, watched over by a million stars and listening to the night birds and Tim's quiet breathing, shutting out all thought of Bothwell and Sun and their hired killers.

On toward dawn, Hope felt Tim shaking her gently and awakening her with a kiss. "Up with ye, lassie. The posse is finally coming."

"What?" She sat up and looked around. "Where? I don't see anybody."

"I heard them," he said. "With me ear to the ground like I learned when scouting against Morgan and Mosby. I heard lots of horses, coming fast."

"Hey, Tim! Miss Hope!" Frank called from his side of the boulder. "Horsemen coming up the creek bed! Must be the posse."

Looking toward the east Hope saw the faintest glimmer of light, but the shadows in the canyon they were in seemed to grow thicker. She wondered if her father would be worried and send Chou Li or Juan out to look for her. She had spent nights out on the range before, but this time she had left no hint that she would be gone so long.

She was still brushing twigs and leaves off her clothes when the posse, twenty men strong, guided by Tex Healy, came riding up. Some of the men were holding lanterns aloft to help them find the way. The sheriff wasn't with them, Healy told Tim, because he'd had to go to the other side of the state to pick up a prisoner. Cy Carter, justice of the peace and acting coroner, was in charge of the group.

A stoop-shouldered, bowlegged old ex-cowboy, Carter had a wad of tobacco packed in one jaw, the juice from it trickling down into his gray whiskers as he called two of the lantern-bearers to go with him while he went to inspect the dead bodies. "Bad job. Damn bad job," Hope heard him muttering. "Sloppy work. Can't abide a man who never learned to tie a decent hangman's noose."

After examining the victims from every angle and asking questions of the Crowder boy and Frank Buchanan, he seemed satisfied for the moment. "All right, boys, cut 'em down and load 'em in that wagon we brought along. We'll take 'em back to Averell's and hold the inquest general in his store and bar."

Fourteen-year-old Gene Crowder murmured a short prayer and the members of the posse cut down the two corpses just as the first rays of sun penetrated the canyon. Wrapping each in a blanket, the men carried them to the wagon, where two horses impatient for breakfast were stomping and snorting in the early morning mist.

"All right, boys, and you, Miss Hope," Carter said. "We'll ride behind the wagon like a proper funeral procession 'cause I suspect they won't get one otherwise."

Slowly, the melancholy little caravan wound its way back

to the crossroads general store and bar that Averell had run in conjunction with his ranch. The bodies were laid out in the icehouse to await burial, and then Carter empaneled an impromptu jury and began to take testimony. First Gene Crowder and John de Corey testified about the seizure of Ella Watson, and Frank Buchanan and several others related the kidnapping of Jim Averell. Later Frank was called back to the improvised witness stand and informed by the justice of the peace-cum-coroner that since he was already sworn in, he should go on and tell what he had seen of the hanging on the Sweetwater. And finally, Hope and Timothy were called to verify the finding of the bodies and the condition they were in.

"Poor Miss Watson had torn every one of her fingernails out trying to rip that noose from her neck," Hope told the jury. She had cried when Gene Crowder had related how Ella pleaded to be allowed to change her dress, but was clear-eyed and steady-voiced now.

"Wasn't no proper noose," Justice Carter interposed. "It was a strangler's rope, no better than those thugs in India use. Not civilized, not civilized at all."

As though lynching was ever civilized, Hope thought, going back to her place beside Tim.

The seven-man coroner's jury didn't take long to come to a decision. Gene, Frank, and John had seen the men who had done the deed and named them. Now the verdict was in.

"We, the coroner's jury, find that the late Ella Watson and Jim Averell came to their deaths by means of a felonious hanging committed by the following individuals," the foreman reported, and read off the names. "Albert J. Bothwell, W. B. Connor, John Durbin, R. M. Galbraith, Ernest McLain, and Tom Sun."

"Everybody but Henderson," Hope whispered to Tim. "Why not him?"

"Probably because the other witnesses didn't actually see him in action and only Frank could testify that he was involved."

"He and Towse and the entire staff of the *Cheyenne Sun*

should have been on that list if justice was to be done," Hope said out loud.

"Shhh!" Tim said, nudging her in the ribs with his elbow as the justice of the peace began to speak.

"Those men, having had a true bill found against them for lynching, will be subject for arrest, and I so order," Carter said, striking the bar with the butt of his pistol and emphasizing his sentence by taking a quick sip of whiskey.

"That drink is on the estate of the late Mr. Averell," Justice Carter declared as the jury and most of the witnesses followed his example. "Thereby, we should proceed to the matter of arresting the men who did him in."

"That might be easier said than done, Mr. Justice," said a short, round-faced man who was a storekeeper in Casper. "Al Bothwell and Tom Sun are two of the biggest ranch owners in the state. Bothwell alone must have thirty cowboys working for him, and a lot of them are quick on the draw. How do we go about arresting them?"

"I'll swear out warrants," Carter said, refilling his glass.

"Who's going to serve them, with Sheriff Wentworth away across state?" asked a stooped, balding man.

"Sam, ain't you Wentworth's deputy?" Carter asked.

Sam Arco looked around. "How many of you boys is ready to form a posse to go pick up Bothwell, John Durbin, and the others?"

Nobody said a word except Frank Buchanan, who immediately volunteered.

"You can't go," Carter told him. "You're our main witness, and I intend to place you under a five-hundred-dollar appearance bond for the trial."

"If you'll be deputizin' me, Mister Justice," Tim said, "I'll be servin' those warrants in person backed up by enough Seventy-six cowboys to see that they stick."

"Hm, you're one of the witnesses too."

"Yes, but not an important one," Tim said. "Besides, unless someone arrests those men, there won't be a trial for any of us to testify at."

"Well, we could wait for Sheriff Wentworth to get back," Carter said, but it was obvious the crusty old veteran didn't place much faith in the sheriff's being willing to go up against men backed by the full power of the Wyoming Stock Growers Association and the Cheyenne Ring.

"My father and I will go along with Mr. O'Callahan in this important move toward supporting law and order in the territory," Hope said, ignoring the look of distress on Tim's face.

"So will I," Gene Crowder said.

"No, kid, you better get back to your pa's ranch when this meetin' is over."

Carter waited a minute or two, but there were no more volunteers, so he turned back to Tim. "Well, O'Callahan, it looks like you're the only man here with the damn-fool courage to go after them criminals. If my rheumatiz didn't give me fits on a horse, I swan I'd go with you. You got the job if you really want it, and it ain't one I envy you."

"I'm not much worried about it, Mr. Justice."

"No, guess not. Hardly seems likely any of them fellas would draw down on *you*."

"No, it doesn't," Tim said with the same grim smile and air of quiet competence Hope had seen him display at other times of crisis.

"Guess all you got to worry about is gettin' bushwhacked then," Carter said, producing a sheaf of papers and a pen from a pocket and starting to write out warrants.

Chapter 20

"WE'RE MAKING OURSELVES enemies we don't need, gal," Pat Cox said to his daughter as they rode behind Tim O'Callahan and his group of cowboys from the 76 ranch toward the home ranch of Albert Bothwell. "Powerful enemies."

"They were already our enemies, Pap," Hope said. "They are the enemies of every person who lives north of Powder River, and some who don't. Their hands are set against all the little people of Wyoming, and we have to show them we're not going to let them run roughshod over us and our rights."

"One of these days I'm gonna wake up and find you've got a banner nailed to the front door with DON'T TREAD ON ME! painted on it."

Hope laughed. "I just might, Pap. But more important, I'm going to get into politics, just like I've always said I would. This kind of thing will keep on happening as long as that gang in Cheyenne is running things. We had lots of big ranchers in Texas, but they were different. Here most of the large spreads are owned not by those who live on them but by investors back in New York and Boston, sometimes as far away as England and Scotland. Investors like that don't give a hang for people, only for the profits they can make from the land."

"Bothwell lives here."

"That's where he made his mistake. If he had ordered Jim and Ella hanged from some fancy office back east, he might have escaped the consequences, but he put the rope around their necks in person and now he'll face the courts for it."

"Yeah, and the courts will turn him loose 'cause his gang owns them," Pat scoffed. "What I'd like to see is for him to draw down on Tim O'Callahan. That way he'd get justice quick and sure."

"And we'd have gun law instead of democracy and justice."

"We got democracy now," Pat reminded her. "And what good does it do? When we vote, they ignore it."

The fifteen men in the posse pulled up as Tim raised his hand for a halt. They had come to a slight rise from which they could look down at the Bothwell ranch. Early morning cook fires were burning and the wranglers were rounding up the day's work horses. Smoke was also coming from the large, pretentious house Albert Bothwell had built for his family.

Hope sat looking at the place, counting the number of horses being made ready for work, and hoped that all would go as well here as it had when they arrested Tom Sun an hour earlier. The posse had passed through the deep cleft in the rocks called Devil's Gate and ridden up to the clapboard ranch house just as Sun came out to go to work. An oldtimer, Sun was the only actual westerner in the group that had committed the Crime on the Sweetwater, as it was coming to be called.

He hadn't seemed a bit surprised when Tim had served the warrant on him. Nor had he seemed concerned.

"Sure I was there with Al Bothwell and the others when those two rustlers were hanged. What about it?"

"You mean lynched," Tim had said, his hand making no

move toward his gun although Sun was armed.

"One man's lynching is another man's justice," Sun had said with a shrug.

"I think you'll learn the difference this time," Tim said. "We have witnesses."

"You don't need witnesses. I ain't got nothin' to hide, and I'll tell anybody who wants to know exactly what happened."

"Includin' how that poor woman slowly strangled to death while tearin' her nails out tryin' to free herself?"

For the first time, the white-haired Sun had looked troubled and pulled at his moustache. "The boys were in a hurry and didn't want to take the time to find someone who could tie a proper hangman's noose that would've broken their necks."

"In a hurry, or because Bothwell and Henderson enjoyed seeing them die in agony?"

Sun said, slightly shamefaced: "I thought we should have waited for a proper rope."

"Take him to Casper, boys." Tim had ended the discussion, detailing three men to escort the arrested man.

Now they were at Bothwell's, and Hope knew that here there would be trouble.

"All right, let's go get him," Tim said, and the posse rode down the slope and through the double gates of the Slat A and up the road to the house.

Six or seven cowboys came out of the bunkhouse wearing gun belts. Hope loosened her Winchester in its case, and Pat got out the Spencer repeating-carbine he had carried during the war and held it like a cavalryman.

A man wearing a flat black hat, a vest, and store-bought pants came around the house and met them at the foot of the steps to the porch. "What do you boys want?"

"We've come for Albert Bothwell," Pat said.

"Mr. Bothwell? What's all this about? I'm his business manager—"

"Get out of the way," Tim said, pushing the man aside with his horse and riding up the steps. He slid out of the saddle onto the porch just as the door handle started to turn.

Taking three quick steps to the side, Tim was standing behind the door when it burst open and a tall, slender middle-aged man with black eyes like slits and a black moustache that drooped around his small mouth came out holding a double-barreled shotgun in one hand and pulling his suspenders up with the other.

"Drop the gun, Bothwell," Tim said quietly, stepping into sight but still not drawing his Colt. "Drop it. I have a warrant for your arrest."

Bothwell whirled and started to bring the shotgun up, only to have it knocked down by a sideways swipe of Tim's arm.

The cowboys near the bunkhouse started forward, and Pat leveled the rapid-firing carbine at them. "Hold it, boys! Hold it right there!"

"You men would do well to stay out of this," Hope added, drawing her Winchester. "We have a warrant for Bothwell's arrest and are taking him to Casper for arraignment on a charge of lynching."

"Lynching?" Bothwell roared. "What the hell are you talking about?"

"In case you've forgotten," Tim said, "the day before yesterday, you strangled Ella Watson and Jim Averell to death down by the Sweetwater. That's against the law, and we're takin' you in."

Bothwell hadn't dropped the gun and was watching Tim as though trying to decide whether he could bring it up before Tim could draw.

"You're Timothy O'Callahan from over at the Seventy-six, ain't you?"

"You've heard of me?" Tim said with the tight little smile Hope had seen before when there was likely to be shooting.

"I've heard of you," Bothwell acknowledged, "but even red-hot guns can't get into trouble when they're on the right side of a fight."

"Why don't you try it with that scatter gun, Al?" Pat Cox called. "You might get it halfway up before O'Callahan puts three bullets between your eyes." A general fight was hanging in the balance, and Hope wished her father would keep his mouth shut instead of aggravating the touchy situation.

But all Bothwell did was turn and look at Pat as though fixing the man's face in his memory for future revenge. Then he let the shotgun slide gently to the floor of the porch and turned toward his men. "Forget it, boys. I'll take care of this. Go back to your breakfast."

"That's right, boys, put your tails between your legs and skedaddle!" Pat gibed.

"Pap! You're not helping any!" Hope hissed. "Do you want a gunfight?"

"I want Bothwell dead," Pat said. "Otherwise he's gonna be after us from now on. You don't step on a rattlesnake and then walk away so he can get you the next time."

"He's going to jail."

Pat snorted. "For about ten minutes, until that crooked lawyer and crooked newspaper get him out."

Already the *Cheyenne Sun* had started a campaign to blacken the reputations of Jim Averell and Ella Watson, Hope knew. Yesterday, the day after the murders, a rider had come into Buffalo with copies of the paper. It had been an education in the power of the press.

Ella Watson, with her calico dress, sunbonnet, and moccasins, had been changed by Ed Towse into "Cattle Kate Maxwell," a former Chicago dance-hall queen who wore silks and diamonds, rode like a demon, imported race horses to the prairie, and shot a drunken Mexican dead for insulting her. She was accused of having held up a faro dealer at Bessemer and robbed him of his bankroll. She was also accused of poisoning her husband, shooting a colored boy who had made off with her diamonds, and winging one of her cowboys for having the nerve to call her Katie instead of addressing her as Miss Maxwell, as the arrogant Queen of the Range demanded. According to Towse and the Cheyenne Ring, she had stolen more cows than any man in the West. The *Laramie Boomerang,* which didn't kowtow to the cattle barons, had poked fun at the Sun's transformation of a simple country girl into a gun-toting Jezebel by editorializing: "Farewell, Cattle Queen Kate! Thou didst never exist, but *vale* anyway."

Towse had worked Averell over in the same way, and it was all meant to cast credit on the murderers and aspersions on the murdered pair.

"Will you let me go in and put on a coat at least?" Bothwell was saying, and Hope realized he had agreed to be taken without resistance.

"Seems to me," Tim said, "that Ella Watson asked for a chance to change her dress."

Bothwell glared. "Surely you're not comparing me to that woman."

"No, I wouldn't do that," Tim said, adding, after a pause, "to Ella."

Bothwell's face turned scarlet. "You will regret this till the day you die, O'Callahan."

Tim laughed in his face. "Then it makes no difference how I treat ye, does it? If I shoot you in the back, I'll not be any worse off."

For a moment Bothwell looked frightened, but then he laughed. "You won't do that. Fools like you will shoot a man in a gunfight but won't kill him in cold blood."

"Go get your coat," Tim ordered, "and don't get out of sight of that window. And if you want to find out if I'll shoot a man in the back, try runnin' for it."

Bothwell moved with great care, leaving the door open and staying in view as he went inside the house. He spoke briefly to a long-faced woman and a hulking youth, took down a coat from a wall rack, and returned. A wrangler brought a prancing, beautifully curried palomino, and he mounted up. Then he looked at each man in the posse, committing their faces to memory.

"Take a good look at every tree you pass on the way to Casper, boys," he said. "You'll be seeing lots of other rustlers swinging from them in the future."

"Maybe a few murderers too," Pat said.

As they rode off the Bothwell place, Hope's thoughts returned to the way the *Sun* had described the double murder, making it sound like the heroic struggle of a few honest, decent men to save their ranches from the ravages of hundreds of ravening rustlers.

"Word was passed along the river," Towse had written, "and early in the night, ten to twenty men, made desperate by steady loss, gathered at a designated rendezvous and galloped to the Averell ranch. They approached the place cautiously, for Averell had murdered two men and would not hesitate to shoot, while the woman was always full of fight.

"Within the little habitation sat the thieving pair before a rude fireplace. The room was clouded with cigarette smoke. A whiskey bottle with two glasses was on the deal table, and firearms were scattered around within easy reach. . . ."

Towse had gone on to describe how Averell "showed himself a cur. He begged and whined and protested innocence, even saying that the woman did all the stealing. The female was made of sterner stuff. She exhausted a blasphemous vocabulary upon the visitors, who essayed to stop the vile flow by gagging her, but found the task too great. When preparations for the short trip to the scaffold were made, she called for her own horse and vaulted from its back to the ground."

"Lies! All damn lies!" Hope said aloud. "They're not content to murder people, but have to tar and feather them in print as well."

"Yeah, pretty sickening, ain't it?" Pat said. He knew what she was talking about, because he had seen one of the copies of the *Sun* that had been passed around among the posse before they started out. He hefted the Spencer and looked at Bothwell's back. "And now he's threatened all of us. What do you suppose would happen if this carbine just happened to go off?"

"We wouldn't be any better off than we are right now," Hope said quickly, afraid he might actually pull the trigger.

"And what do we do if we don't use guns?"

"We use ballots."

"That why you let Jeb go on to Washington without a wife? So he could get a head start in state politics?"

"Jebel made his own decision," Hope said, her eyes on Tim's broad shoulders. "I had nothing to do with it."

"Except to say no when he asked you to marry him."

"I said maybe," she snapped, "and I'm tired of hearing about it."

"What's he gonna say when he hears you're gonna be a delegate to that woman's suffrage thing?"

"He'll say it's my own business," she said, wondering what Tim thought of women in politics. Probably, like most men, he had never given it a thought.

The arrest of the remaining four killers was accomplished without incident. Ernest McLain, William B. Connor, Robert Galbraith, and John Durbin all surrendered when confronted by the posse and Tim O'Callahan, with his reputation as the fastest gun on Powder River, an area not noted for men who were slow on the draw.

Justice Carter was waiting when they trailed into Casper and ordered the suspects to jail to await trial.

"I'll be out in two days," Bothwell told Tim. "Just as soon as the news reaches Cheyenne."

"If you are, you'd better stay out of my way," Tim replied.

"Careful, love, careful," Hope whispered when the man was gone. "Don't give him anything he can use against you."

"To my mind, that man is no better than one of Mosby's guerrillas, and we used to hang them soon as we caught them down in Kansas and Missouri."

"But there's no war on now."

"Not yet, but I've a feelin' there will be."

They rode back from Casper feeling as though they had at least taken a step in the right direction that day.

As they neared Powder River, Tim dropped back to ride beside Hope while Pat was busy exchanging war stories with another rider who had served on the Confederate side. "Supposin' I leave the Seventy-six men off at Sussex Ranch and ride on up to the Lazy H with you," he suggested. "Would ye whip me up some supper and sit with me afterward to look at the moon?"

Hope glanced at him and smiled. "Well, we have a very good cook, so I don't do much more than brew up some coffee, but Pap goes to bed early and I like to look at the moon."

Fenwick met them at the entrance to his ranch. He looked much paler and thinner than Hope remembered, but he was polite and pleasant to her. Not so his wife. She had been standing on the front veranda as they rode up, but on seeing Hope she turned and went inside the house.

"Did everything pass off all right?" the Englishman asked his foreman.

"We got them all," Tim replied. "Bothwell was the only one who put up any fight."

"Unfortunately, they gave us no excuse to shoot them," Pat said.

"Well, I'm glad there was no violence and that it will be settled in the courts," Fenwick said. "Will you be here for dinner, Tim? The boys brought in a dozen partridges and the cook has prepared them in a special sauce. Anne thought you might like it."

"'Tis kind of ye both to ask," Tim said, "but I was thinkin' on seein' Miss Hope home . . . 'long of her father, of course."

"Yes. Yes, I see," Fenwick said, and Hope thought he looked relieved. Did he know about Tim and his wife?

If so, he gave no further indication as he continued the discussion. "You know, Tim, I'm of two minds about this affair. We've lost cattle also and are the biggest outfit in the area. I belong to the Stock Growers Association, and I really should—"

"Morton, we'd best be on the side of law and order or we'll find it impossible to operate a business in this country. If we turn our neighbors against us, we might as well close up shop and move back to the old country."

"Yes, yes, but it will get around that it was my men who . . . well, no matter. At least no one was injured, and I'm thankful for that."

"'Tis thankful ye might also be that six murderers are in jail tonight."

"I know, lad, I know, but the entire state of affairs is most worrisome," he said, turning to enter the house. "It was pleasant to see you again, Miss Hope, Mister Cox. Good night, Tim. We shall discuss this again when I have had more time to think."

"Good night to ye, sir," Tim said, and turned to Pat and Hope, his face expressionless as they heard a woman's voice, shrill with anger, begin to berate his employer. "Shall we be on our way, then?"

"What was that all about?" Hope asked Tim as they rode away.

"Oh, 'tis just that Fenwick feels he should stand shoulder to shoulder with those of his own class, and I can't convince him that those in the Cheyenne Ring are not of his class. It is a bit of a worry for him."

"I didn't mean that," Hope said. "I meant Anne Fenwick. It sounded like she was raising hell with him about something."

Tim shrugged. "Like most married folk, they have their problems."

"Does it have anything to do with what she said that day we rode out to choose my ranch site?"

Tim glanced at Pat, who was riding slightly in front of them but listening to their every word. "'Tis a long, hard day we've all had, Miss Hope. Could we not talk of something more pleasant?"

"We're going to have to—" Hope began, but broke off as her father dropped back to join them.

Chou Li did himself proud with the evening meal, and after it was over, Pat began to yawn and soon went off to bed.

Hope and Tim sat together on the porch swing Pat had made from scrap lumber salvaged from the abandoned shacks of would-be placer miners along the river. Although not noted for her housewifely skills, Hope had managed to cover some old pillows with a pretty chintz print, and the seat was a comfortable and private place from which to watch the moon rise.

With Tim's arm around her and her head resting on his

shoulder, Hope was content. She had put on a dress for supper and he had been properly complimentary; now it was nice just to sit and think and to reflect that one small part of her dream was coming true. She had her own ranch and house, small as they were, and was sitting with the man she loved under the moon.

But how did that fit in with her other dreams of a big cattle ranch and a political career? Had she seen a man beside her in all those dreams? For some reason her vision was clouded in that respect. The rest was very clear, but she couldn't tell if a man was involved or who he was.

She knew she loved Tim O'Callahan and would marry him in a minute if he asked her. And if he didn't ask her, maybe she'd ask him. But she still couldn't see how he fit in with all her grandiose plans to fulfill the dream she'd had ever since she was a kid.

"It's beautiful," she murmured, looking out at the wonderland the moon was creating. "Even the sagebrush looks magical tonight."

"I ordered it special for ye, darlin'," Tim whispered, lifting her hair to kiss the back of her neck.

"Sure you did. You Irish are magicians when it comes to weaving spells in the moonlight, although I must admit you did a fine job of rounding up those lynchers."

"That I learned in the army," he said, sliding a hand inside the neckline of her dress and pushing it off her shoulder so he could kiss the dimple where collarbone joined breastbone. "This, on the other hand, just comes naturally."

"Are you sure you didn't learn it from that French lady who stole your virginity?"

"No, lass. More interested she was in the fundamentals than the preliminaries."

"And so, it seems, are we," she said, removing his hand from her breast and holding it in hers. "We always seem in a hurry to get down to basics."

"Ummmm," he said, kissing her eyelids and nose. "We never do have all that much time for the frills. Maybe someday we will."

His lips closed over hers, sending sparks of desire shooting along her nerves and making her head spin. She felt his hand on her knee and then it was creeping up her thigh. She knew she should stop it, but the fingers were so gentle and loving that she couldn't resist letting them do as they pleased.

"When do you figure we'll have that extra time?" she whispered dreamily.

"Ah, who can say? Perhaps after the next roundup."

"You bastard," she said against his lips. "I thought you meant..."

"'Tis possible I did. Perhaps I meant just what you thought I meant, but there are a couple of difficulties standin' in our way," he whispered, and then plunged them both into the vortex of another irresistibly sense-stirring kiss.

Now his fingers had found what they sought, and she felt all sense of reality fading away as they crept under the edge of her drawers to caress the soft flesh where her thighs joined her body.

Chapter 21

REMEMBERING THAT NIGHT, Hope could still shiver with pleasure as she lay staring up at the fleecy clouds on the way home from Cheyenne. The Andrews' buckboard was bouncing steadily toward Powder River and she could hear Amy and Joe excitedly discussing the momentous meeting of the territorial legislature.

That night had been one of the most memorable of her life, Hope thought, but all the times with Tim were indelibly carved on her heart. Oh God, how had it all come to naught . . . all the love she had felt, all the love she had been so sure he returned? It was all over now and she was alone, alone and yearning for what she could never have again.

The very next day after that night of moonlit magic, everything they thought they had accomplished the day before began to fall apart and they had plunged downward toward tragedy as though drawn by an unseen but irresistible force.

She had heard the first bad news when she was still aglow with Tim's kisses, those kisses that seemed to burn on a dozen places on her body—the tips of her breasts, her knees, the inside of her thighs...

Bad news travels fast, and it took no time at all for word to come that Justice Carter had been taken off the case of the Sweetwater crime and been replaced by Superior Judge Joseph Blinden. The judge had reviewed the case, keeping firmly in mind the money and power of the Cheyenne Ring. Although first-degree murder was not subject to bail under the law, the six accused stockmen were granted immediate bail at what to them was a trifling sum, $5,000 each. To top his performance and further secure his career, kindly Judge Blinden permitted the six killers to sign one another's bonds.

"There should be a new arraignment," Amy Andrews had said. "If there is any justice in this territory, those men deserve to be in jail."

"They deserve to hang," Joe said, "but you mark my word, they'll never spend another night under lock and key."

"Then none of us in Johnson County is safe," Hope said in despair. "They accuse us all of being rustlers or worse."

"You wait, honey," Amy had tried to console her. "You just wait until we get the vote and we'll put judges like that out on the street selling pencils for a living."

The killing of Jim and Ella made the papers all across the country, and two weeks later Hope read about it in the eastern press, which took its cue from the larger Wyoming papers that were owned or influenced by Bothwell and Sun's friends.

The *Chicago Interocean* reported that Ella had remembered her dear mother during her last minutes on earth and had requested that her ill-gotten gains, jewels, and other expensive trinkets be used to found a home for wayward girls.

"I doubt that Ella owned a hatpin, much less jewels and expensive trinkets," Tim said when Hope showed him the paper someone had brought from Omaha.

Even the *Police Gazette* in distant New York had taken notice of the affair, announcing in one of its typical bumptious headlines that BLASPHEMING BORDER BEAUTY BARBAROUSLY BOOSTED BRANCHWARD.

"Oh, isn't that just awful!" Hope said.

"Aye, but at least they admit she was barbarously murdered," Tim said. "The papers here pretend she was given a decent scaffold and a proper hanging."

"And now the killers are out—all free men."

"Maybe not forever. There are three witnesses all willin' to talk."

But by the following day there were only two witnesses. Frank Buchanan had disappeared. That brave and resourceful young man, who had tried single-handedly to save the victims, had now, according to the Cheyenne Ring's lackey, fled the territory because he didn't dare testify to the lies he had told about those good and honest men who had done for the vicious rustlers.

"Bull!" was Pat Cox's opinion. "Those bastards have done him in."

Hope thought so too. Buchanan was dangerous to the Cheyenne Ring, so they had seen to it that he died and his body wasn't found.

"They can commit murder over and over again and nothing can be done under the present political system," she had said to Amy and Joe Andrews when they stopped by on their way to Fort McKinney near Buffalo to sell the produce they raised in their truck garden.

"The only way to change things is through political action," Amy said.

"Oh Lord, here we go again," Joe said. "Amy has been on a campaign to change the world ever since she turned fifty."

"Not the world," the older woman said, fondly ruffling her husband's sparse hair. "Just Wyoming."

"Well, it certainly needs changing. When I think of those monsters sitting back laughing at us, I could scream."

"More than laughing," Joe said. "Plotting revenge."

"Yes, and Frank Buchanan seems to have already suffered from their revenge. Tim O'Callahan has been on leave from Sussex Ranch for a week searching for him."

"Couldn't he have become frightened and run off?" Amy asked.

"Not Frank. He was one of the really brave men I've known. When everyone else was paralyzed with fear, he tried to rescue Jim and Ella. He wouldn't turn yellow now."

Joe patted her shoulder as they prepared to leave. "There's still the trial, you know. Maybe..."

Hope sighed. "Yes, and we still have two witnesses who should be able to convince a jury, but everything depends on those two."

A week later they didn't have two.

Hope knew there was something wrong the minute she saw Tim ride up to the Lazy H ranch house. She ran to meet him as he dismounted and he took her in his arms but there was none of the usual Irish good humor in his face or manner. His green eyes were bleak and she could feel the suppressed anger in the tense muscles of his back and arms.

She looked up at him anxiously. "You didn't find Frank?"

"No, and for the last few days I've not been lookin' for him. I've been trying to find John de Corey."

"Oh no, not him too!"

"He was in Steamboat Springs, Colorado, on August 30, but he disappeared before I got there and no one knows where he's gone."

"Do you think he ran away?"

Tim shrugged tiredly. "Who knows? Either that or the ring had him killed, and 'tis to their advantage no matter which. I think they're responsible, because there's a couple other things that seem to tie in."

"Like what?"

"Ralph Cole, for one. He wasn't one of the main witnesses because all he saw was Jim being forced into the buckboard with Ella, but they killed him just the same."

"Killed him?" Hope could hardly believe her ears. "When? How?"

"Sometime last week he must have gotten his wind up, because he suddenly gave up his job in a Casper livery stable and hightailed it out of town."

"Had he been threatened?"

Tim shrugged again, moved out of Hope's embrace and slumped down into the porch swing. For once there was none of the ebullience and energy that made him everybody's choice as leader in a dangerous enterprise. He looked exhausted and totally discouraged. "It seems he got as far as a surveyors' camp near the Union Pacific. He spent the night with them and next morning headed for the railroad station, but he was overtaken by a rider the surveyors had seen stalking him shortly after he left camp. He was shot in the back and his body left for the coyotes, and the description the surveyors gave of the killer fits George Henderson perfectly."

"Yes, Henderson would do that! I knew the first time I looked into those snake eyes of his how dangerous he was!"

Tim grinned wryly at her vehemence. "That why you drew down on him?"

"No, because he wanted to check the brand on my cows."

The grim lines around the Irishman's mouth deepened. "They're going to be doing that to everybody's cows. The association is talkin' about holdin' one big roundup to do away with rustlin' and brand-blotting. Their people will be makin' all the decisions about whose cattle have been rustled, of course."

"We should start our own association," Hope said angrily.

"Sure now, and maybe we should, but how many of the large ranchers who haven't taken part in the Stock Growers' shenanigans do ye think would stand for that? Even Fenwick is talkin' about becomin' active in the association again and I'm sure 'tis because he's under pressure to do so."

"Pressure from whom? His wife?"

Tim cocked an eyebrow at Hope. "Ye don't care much for Anne, do ye, macushla?"

"No," she admitted.

"Why?"

"Because you call her Anne," she said, knowing this was not the time to delve deeper into that emotionally charged area.

"Oh. Well, the pressure on Morton is not her doing. 'Tis

comin' from his neighbors, who claim he's makin' it easy on rustlers by not takin' part in association activities." He leaned forward and took her hand in both of his. "But that's not the worst of what I came to tell you. Gene Crowder is sick."

"Sick? How sick? He's only fourteen."

Tim nodded. "I know, and I just found out he's been living with a family over near Douglas—a family with connections to the Cheyenne Ring."

"What? How did that happen? He has a father. I heard Justice Carter tell him to go home to his pa."

"Yes, but his father is a drunk, very rarely sober, so kindly Judge Blinder decided he wasn't getting proper care and placed him in a 'foster' home. Shortly after that, Gene began showin' symptoms of an illness called Bright's disease. The Kenmore family says he's always been a sickly boy."

"But that's absolute nonsense!" Hope exploded. "He was the healthiest, hardest-working, most apple-cheeked youngster I ever met! What have they done to him?"

Tim spread his hands helplessly.

Hope got to her feet and began pacing, fists clenched at her sides. "We can't let them do that boy harm! It's not just a matter of needing him for a witness! Three men are dead already and now a child's life is threatened!"

O'Callahan got slowly to his feet, squaring his shoulders. "Well, I can make sure one person does no more damage. I'm going after Henderson."

"No, Tim, no!" Hope said, instantly alarmed. "That would be murder!"

"Self-defense. I know that bastard means to shoot me in the back one of these days. If I get him now, I'll be safe and so will all the others on his list."

"He's not doing these things on his own, Tim. You know that. He's acting on orders from men like Bothwell and Frank Canton and H. B. Ijams. If you kill Henderson, they can hire a dozen more just like him. You would have committed murder for nothing."

"No, 'twould be a fair fight. I'd face and brace him till

he went for his gun, then I'd improve the atmosphere of this territory for all of us."

"Tim, don't you care for me at all?"

"I love you," he said so simply and so sincerely that it took her breath away.

She smiled at him tremulously, praying she could find the right words to dissuade him from this folly. Above all else, she wanted to keep him alive. "If you do love me, you'll give up this idea of forcing a gunfight on Henderson."

"And then what? Are you after havin' any better ideas, lass?"

"No. Well, yes, maybe. Let's try to get Gene away from those Kenmores. I don't believe he's really sick. They must be doing something to him."

"They have a court order from His Dishonor Judge Blinder. If we interfere, we'll be breakin' the law."

"And what would you be doing if you shot Henderson?"

A faint grin touched his lips. "You think we can just walk in there and tell those folks we want the boy?"

"No, but we could say we're taking him to see Doc Helms in Casper."

"And if they still say no? They're not like to let him out of their hands if they're really responsible for his illness, you know."

"If worst comes to worst, you draw your gun. We have to get that child out of there."

"Child? You're only nineteen yourself."

Hope laughed. "I feel like I was fifty when I was born and have been growing ever since."

"Well now, that accounts for the fact that you're the smartest girl I've ever known."

Hope beamed at him and then asked impulsively, "What do you think of women in politics?"

He stared blankly for a moment and then started to smile. "Well now, I—"

"I'm serious. I think what's wrong with this territory is its political setup. If decent people were elected to office, we would have better government."

"But first Wyoming has to become a state. Washington

can't regulate or control what goes on here until the territory becomes a state."

"No, the first order of business is to push through women's suffrage, then apply for statehood."

Tim regarded her with a bemused expression. "Faith, lass, I've ne'er given thought to a female gettin' mixed up in politics. The men involved in it are such an unsavory gang of thieves and scoundrels that—"

"Do you think Mr. Lincoln was a thief and a scoundrel?"

"Of course not. He was president, not a politician."

"He was both," Hope said, "and Robert E. Lee wasn't any thief or scoundrel either."

"Well, no, but he was a soldier."

Hope sighed. "All right, let it go for now. Do you agree we should try to get Gene away from the Kenmores?"

"Yes, I think you're right," Tim said, sounding more like himself. "We have to do something. I'll meet you at the Crossings tomorrow morning with a buckboard. I'll be seein' if Nate Champion can come with us."

"Nate Champion?" Hope had heard the name but had never met the man. Like many other cowboys who had started to run a few cattle of their own, Nate had been blackballed by the Stock Growers Association and frequently accused of being a rustler.

"I figure Nate is in pretty much the spot I am," Tim said. "He's crossed the cattle barons and sooner or later they'll hire some back-shootin' son of a bitch to get rid of him. Anything he does to hurt 'em in the meantime is more or less a free ride. They can't kill him twice."

Hope put her arms around Tim and hugged him fiercely. "They're not going to kill you at all if I have anything to do with it!"

Tim kissed her soundly, and as he was about to let her go, she wrapped her arms around his neck and kissed his ear, teasing it with her tongue.

"Hey," he said, the tension lines in his face easing a little. "Is that—"

She laughed throatily. "That's a proposition from a lady who loves you."

"And this is an acceptance," he whispered, crushing her to him on the swing. "Hmmmm. There's Irish nectar in those kisses. Every one is like a drop o' sweet poteen."

"Well then, you're going to be drunk before this night is over," she murmured, moving against him sensuously.

Chapter 22

SHORTLY AFTER DAWN the following morning, Hope rode into Three Crossings and found Tim waiting for her in a buckboard with another man on the seat beside him.

Nate Champion was a medium-sized, dark-haired man with a neatly trimmed moustache curving down either side of his upper lip. He was dressed for the early-morning chill in a sheepskin coat, checked shirt, breeches, and well-shined boots. He also wore a gun strapped to his lean hip.

"Glad to meet you, Miss Hope," he said, smiling. "I hear you singed the beard of that scoundrel Henderson."

Hope grinned. "If he'd had a beard worth singing, I might have done it."

They started in the direction of Fort Fetterman and Douglas, which was fifty miles from Casper, but only had to travel part of the road to reach the small town of Glenrock, where the Kenmores lived. It seemed to Hope that the Cheyenne Ring had stashed young Gene as far away from the center of things as possible.

When she remarked on it, however, Nate Champion shook

his head. "If they intend to kill him, they don't need to do that. They could do it right on the street in Cheyenne at high noon and no one would even bother to call the town marshal."

Hope's lips tightened. "One of these days, Mr. Champion, there's going to be real justice in Wyoming."

"I doubt any of us will live to see it," Champion said, and she wasn't sure whether he meant it was a long way off or that none of them had long to live—or even both.

They reached the tiny hamlet shortly before noon. Glenrock consisted of one street, perhaps a dozen houses, a livery stable, and three bars. An old black man, loading hay on a wagon with the help of two husky youths who appeared to be his sons, directed them to the Kenmore place.

"Last house on the street, two or three lots away from the others. Folks don' like to be around 'em any more than they likes to be around other folks."

"Don't they ever have visitors?" Hope asked.

"Nobody 'cept one fella name of—Henry? Hendricks? Plumb mean man. Can't recollect his name."

"Was it Henderson—George Henderson, by any chance?"

"Yes'm, that's it. Heared 'em call him George oncet. He come once or twice a week with a lil' black bag like a sawbones. Never see a man with eyes like that one."

"Is there a young boy living with the Kenmores?" Tim asked.

"Sure is, suh. Nice young fella, but sickly. Seemed healthy when he first come, but been sinkin' ever since. Don' know what ails him but they never have a doctor 'ceptin' that Henderson and he don' look like no proper doctor to me."

They thanked the man and drove on toward the Kenmore house, the men exchanging grim glances and Hope trying to hide her apprehension. Reaching the small, unpainted clapboard house, they picked their way past the splintered picket fence and through the weed-grown yard to reach the front door. There was no smoke coming from the stove pipe sticking through the roof, all the blinds were drawn, and there was an unlived-in feel to the place.

Nate Champion drew his revolver and pounded on the

door with it. There was no sound from inside, the silence broken only by the ganging of a broken shutter in the wind.

"They must have seen us coming," Hope said.

"Nate, go around to the back door," Tim said. "I'm going to break this one in."

Hope pulled her Colt and stood to one side as Nate dashed to the rear and Tim threw his shoulder against the door. The old rotten wood splintered with a loud cracking sound and flew open. It was pitch dark inside except for the streak of dusty light from the broken door. Hope could see a few pieces of furniture—a table, some chairs, and a potbelly stove.

Tim looked at her as though wanting to tell her to stay outside, but then shrugged and moved into what seemed to be the living room just as they heard Nate kicking in the back door and letting in another streak of light from the lean-to kitchen.

"There's another room over here," Tim said as Champion joined them in the uninhabited living room. "If anyone's in ambush, they'll be behind that."

"You want to put a few slugs through it?" Nate asked.

"No," Hope said. "They might be using Gene for a shield."

"Cover me," Tim said, moving up to the door and trying the handle. Finding it unlocked, he shoved it open and stepped back quickly.

Nothing—no flurry of gunfire; no one standing with raised hands; only the musty darkness and a faintly offensive smell Hope didn't recognize at first.

"There, on the bed," Champion said as their eyes adjusted to the dark.

A brass bed was the only item of furniture, and lying on the quilt that covered it was a body.

It was Gene Crowder. He looked as though he had died peacefully just lying there waiting for something.

"No gunshot wounds, no blood," Nate reported after a brief examination. "Must have been here a couple of days. Might have died in his sleep from the way he looks."

"The Kenmores' job was over and they took off as soon as they realized he was dead," Hope said with a catch in her voice as she backed out of the room into the relatively fresh air of the living room.

"It had to be poison," Tim said as he and Nate joined her. "His body is just wasted away. 'Tis my guess they used arsenic."

Hope's eyes were closed, her fists tightly clenched, and she was cursing steadily under her breath.

"They'll stop at nothing," Nate said. "Don't see how we can ever win against them."

Hope opened her eyes and turned their blue fire on him. "It's either find a way to beat them or be run out of the territory! When the people of Wyoming finally realize what those vile creatures are doing, they'll get rid of them!"

Nate nodded and looked away, obviously unbelieving. "Guess I better go find someone who knows where the nearest coroner is."

The grand jury met in Rawlins on October 14, a week after the first snowfall. The prosecutor asked for indictments against Albert J. Bothwell, W. B. Connor, John Durbin, R. M. Galbraith, Ernest McLain, and Tom Sun on the charge of murder. The accused men were represented by the law firm of Corlett, Lacey, and Piner, for many years the leading attorneys for the Wyoming Stock Growers Association.

Mr. Attorney Corlett, in a neat black suit and black string tie, stood up and faced Judge Blinder. "Your honor, the prosecution has produced no witnesses to the fact that any murders took place, much less any evidence that our clients had anything to do with them. I move that the defendants be freed and bail set aside."

"Your honor," Justice of the Peace Carter said, speaking as attorney for Ella Watson's father and Jim Averell's brother, "we have no witnesses because they were all murdered or run out of the territory by the defendants or men working for them."

The judge banged his gavel, told Carter he was out of order, declared that the six men were innocent of any wrongdoing, and ordered that their bail be set aside.

"Something has to be done," Hope said in a determined voice as she and Tim left the courthouse. "I am going to see to it that changes are made in the way our system is run."

"Short of a second American Revolution, I don't see how that can be accomplished," Tim said.

"We can elect people to office who will not permit such a travesty of justice ever to occur again. People like you or me."

"I doubt I could be elected mayor of Sussex Ranch," Tim said. "The boss thinks I already spend too much time makin' trouble for folks too powerful to take chances of offendin'."

"Well, I don't have a boss to tell me what I can or can't do, and I intend to go right on making trouble for them until they pull in their horns."

"Don't ye be so quick to write me off," Tim said, adjusting his gun belt. "I never said I was quittin', but 'tis thinkin' I am of changin' me tactics."

"Guns won't help. I told you that before."

"They will if all else fails."

She let the subject drop until they were on the stage headed for Buffalo and Powder River. Since they were the only passengers, there was no one to overhear them.

"You're worried because Fenwick is upset, aren't you?" she asked.

"I think the world of Morton," Tim said quietly. "He took me in when I was a drifter right out of the army and paid me top wages from the very beginning. Six months later, when old Jake Towley got all broken up in a fall from a bronc, he made me his foreman. 'Tis that grateful I am to him, and I can understand his point of view up to a point, but I have me own conscience to live with, too."

"It will be all right, darling," she said, squeezing his arm. "Five people have been murdered and the people of Wyoming will not let their deaths go unnoticed and unpunished."

"They will as long as the newspapers are in the pay of

the Cheyenne Ring," Tim said morosely, "and keep telling them nothing happened, or if it did, it happened to thieves who deserved it."

Leaving the stagecoach at Buffalo, they retrieved their horses from the livery stable and started toward home, but after they'd gone a few miles, Hope reached over and pulled on Tim's reins. "Pap doesn't expect me home until tomorrow night," she said. "We thought there would be more of a hearing than that and I told him I'd stay over at the hotel."

He lifted an eyebrow, and she went on. "There's an abandoned line camp down near Crazy Woman Creek with a fireplace and plenty of driftwood around."

"Yes." He seemed preoccupied and slow to catch her meaning.

"Well!" she said with mock indignation, "I never thought I'd be reduced to inviting a gentleman to spend the night with me and having him turn me down!"

He reached for her, plucking her out of the saddle. "Sure and 'tis yours truly who's slow on the draw, not yerself who's forward."

Then he was kissing her, those sweet thrilling kisses that she could feel from the crown of her head to the soles of her feet.

"Oh Lordy, when you kiss me like that, you tickle my toes," she said, sliding her arms around his neck.

"'Tis more than ticklin' your toes I'll be doin' when I get you in that bunk in the cabin," he promised.

The line cabin had been empty since the cattle had been driven farther south for the coming winter to more sheltered pastures, but it had been left clean and stocked with food for any passerby who might get caught in a storm.

"Well now, all the comforts of home," Tim said, taking down the frying pan from its nail beside the fireplace and picking up the coffeepot. "I don't suppose you know how—"

"I haven't cooked a meal since we left Texas," Hope said, lying back on the bunk with her head pillowed on her arms. "Comes of having a Chinese cook who knows his business."

Tim shook his head and checked the food supply. "I could do better if I had some pratties, but I guess I can manage biscuits, beans, and salt pork."

"You're going to make some girl a wonderful husband," she teased. "If she can catch you."

"I'm not so hard to catch," he said, setting the coffeepot on its place over the blazing logs.

"Not so hard to rope, but hard to hog-tie," she said languidly, stretching her arms over her head and arching her back.

He glanced at her and then looked back at the biscuits and beans cooking over the coals. "If you want supper, young lady, you might try to stop lookin' more temptin' than the food."

"Hmmm. I didn't think anything could come between a cowboy and his supper."

"Don't try me," he laughed. "We need food to keep our strength up... there's a long night ahead of us."

"I expect it'll seem very short and wonderful."

Actually it was a moderately long October night, with rain and sleet pounding on the roof and making them grateful for the snugness of the cabin. It was also the first whole night they had spent together and their first time in anything resembling a bed.

Lying naked under the blankets, without the worry of possibly being surprised by someone, was an entirely different experience, so much more intimate, and making it so easy to experiment. They spent the hours learning all kinds of new things about each other's bodies and how they responded to new and different stimuli. Tim never seemed to run out of vitality or imagination in his lovemaking.

Once during the night, while they were resting, he looked down at her in the dying firelight. "We have to do something about this, you know."

"About what?" she asked, tracing the line of his jaw with the tip of a finger.

"About us," he said, capturing the caressing hand and kissing each finger in turn. "When I'm not with you, I spend all me time thinkin' about you."

She slid the hand he was kissing around his neck and pulled his head down. "Being with me is better than thinking about me, isn't it?" she murmured against his lips and then stabbed her tongue deep into his mouth in sudden demand.

"Aye, lass, it sure is," he said when he had gotten his breath back.

"Then what was it you were thinking we should do about us—find a way we could spend lots of long autumn nights together?"

"Yes, I've ideas along that line, but there's a thing or two to be taken care of before we make plans."

"What things?"

"Uh . . . personal things . . . leftover things. Loose ends, ye might say."

Instinct told Hope he was talking about Anne Fenwick. What the devil could be the hold the woman had over him?

Her concern about and resentment of Anne faded into the background as Tim pulled her to him and began kissing her as though he would never let her go. Her lips, her neck and shoulders, the inside of her elbows, were all set afire by his tender yet demanding lips. And that, of course, was only the beginning in an explosion of passion that lifted her into banks of swirling pink clouds and then gently wafted her to earth before once again skyrocketing her toward the stars.

"Where, oh, where did you learn that?" she gasped as his lips moved from her breasts to her ribcage, her navel, down the curve of her hips to the outside of her thighs and calves and ankles, then up the inside of her thighs. "Did they teach you that in the army?"

"No." His voice was muffled by the caressing that was driving her crazy. "An aristocratic southern lady who owned a plantation down New Orleans way taught me that during the war. Her husband hadn't yet come back from prison camp, and she was used to giving orders about what she wanted done and how."

"Oh, damn her! But bless her, too!" Hope moaned and then shrieked in pleasure as the exquisite torture ended in an explosive burst of rapturous joy.

Afterward, she lay with her head on his bare chest, still cooing with delight, then raised her head to whisper in his ear, "When I get to be governor of Wyoming, I'm going to keep you chained to the governor's official chair behind the big desk so you can do that once a day and twice on Sunday."

He grinned at her wickedly. "'Tis not legal on Sunday, love. Is that what you suffragettes plan after you get the vote, to make us men your slaves?"

"Ha! If we do, we'll only be shifting the chains from us to you."

"Why don't we just get married instead?"

"What?" She sat up and looked at him in the last light of the fire. "What did you say?"

"I said, why don't we get married instead?"

"Yes, I thought that was what you said."

"Why the surprise? I've been hintin' about it for weeks—or haven't you noticed?"

"I heard some talk, but it was never very definite, and you said earlier tonight that you had things to settle first."

"Well, they are going to get settled fast," he said, "because I'm tired of not being with you all the time."

"That's how I feel, too," she said.

The rain had slackened to a quiet dripping along toward daybreak, and Tim sighed regretfully. "'Twill be dawn soon, macushla."

"Yes, and I wish it would never come," she said, suddenly fearful. This had been the most thrilling night of her life and the most fulfilling. Coming so soon after the tragedy of Gene Crowder and the travesty of justice they had called a hearing, it had been a reaffirmation of life and now it was all going to end. She fought against it.

"No, let's not let it end," she said, rolling over on top of him.

"Well now, lassie—"

"Shut up and kiss me," she said.

As it happened, it was almost ten o'clock before Tim was ready to go. "I'll ride over to the Seventy-six," he said. "Then I'll settle things as fast as I can and come back so we can make those plans we spoke of."

She was about to acquiesce, but then said impulsively, "Tim, I'd like to ride on to the Sussex with you. It's not all that much farther and I've got this funny feeling that . . ."

"That what?"

She shook her head. "I don't know. I just want to go with you."

"Not afraid that I'll be runnin' away, are you?" he laughed. "You put your brand on me for good last night, lass."

"Brands have been blotted out before," she said, trying to laugh along with him but finding that she couldn't.

There were signs of trouble shortly after they forded Powder River at Three Crossings and headed up the muddy road to Sussex House. As they passed through the second gate at the ranch, they saw cowboys rushing around without hats or ponchos and others saddling horses that would have preferred to stay in the corral on such a miserable day.

"Somethin's wrong," Tim said, spurring his black stallion forward. "Hey, Jed, what is it? What's happened?"

He grabbed the straw boss by the shirt to keep him from dashing off without answering. "Jed, what's going on?"

"Tim? Tim, is that you?" the man said, blinking against the rain. "You've been gone so much, I wasn't sure it was you."

"Never mind that now. What's going on?"

"Rustlers ran off a hundred and fifty head in the west pasture and Mr. Fenwick's been shot."

"What?"

"One of the night guard came galloping in early this morning to report that a dozen masked men had driven off the guards and rounded up our cattle."

"How did Fenwick get shot?"

"You weren't here, so he said he'd take the men out after them himself. They ran into an ambush and he took a hot one through the chest. Shorty Norris is dead and old man Stein, the wrangler, got a slug in his arm."

"How is Fenwick?"

"Don't know. Doc Seldes is with him."

"Gather all the men you can find," Tim ordered. "And

send a rider to Buffalo to tell Sheriff Angus. I'll—"

"Mr. Tim, Mr. Tim!" The usually imperturbable butler came running toward them, holding a poncho over his bald pate.

"Yes, what is it, Turner?"

"The master, sir. He's sinking fast, and Mrs. Fenwick is having—" he paused to catch his breath. "—what one would call hysterics if she wasn't a great lady."

"I'd better get up to Fenwick's room," Tim said, sliding off his horse and starting for the house at a run, leaving Turner and Hope trailing along after him.

This was what she had been fearing, Hope thought. This was what had been causing her feeling of apprehension, but she had never expected such a disaster.

Jed Bratsford seemed to be blaming it on Tim for not being on hand when he was needed. That was unfair; Tim had been away doing his duty in the cause of law and justice... well, except for last night and this morning.

But what about the raid? Were there really rustlers in the area now, and not just the mavericking that so incensed the Stock Growers Association? Was it possible that a band of thieves had drifted into the territory, or—and she hoped with all her heart this wasn't it—had some of the locals gotten so tired of being pushed around that they had decided to strike back? But why at Sussex Ranch? It was the only large spread that wasn't leaning on the smaller ones.

What concerned her more at the moment was Tim and how he would react to the situation. Would it make a difference to what they had promised each other last night? Would it change the plans they had been going to make?

She followed the butler into the house. Tim had shed his wet slicker on the polished floor of the entry hall and was taking the broad, curving stairway two steps at a time.

He certainly was familiar with the big house, Hope thought, and she tried to keep from speculating about whether that was because he had been summoned to Anne's bedroom so often while the man of the house was absent or asleep. She was ashamed of wondering about that when a man lay wounded and probably dying in the room Tim was now entering, but she couldn't help herself. Anne Fenwick had become an obsession with her, an obstacle that stood between her and the man she wanted.

She followed Tim up the stairs and heard the sound of sobbing coming from beyond the open door of Morton Fenwick's bedroom. She was unwilling to enter but felt driven toward the door by a compulsion to see Tim with the woman; she knew it was a terrible intrusion on a dying man, but she also knew she had to see Tim and Anne together.

Hope stepped inside just in time to see the doctor pull the sheet up over Fenwick's face and Anne turn and throw herself into Tim's arms.

"There, there," she heard Tim mumble against the woman's dark hair. "'Tis hard to bear, I know, but try to be brave."

Anne sobbed wildly and pressed closer to him, her arms encircling his neck. "Stay close to me, Tim! Please don't leave me! I'll die if you do! You're all I have left in the world!"

Hope's fists doubled up in the pockets of her slicker. Sure he is, she thought bitterly, except for a ranch covering tens of thousands of acres, twenty to thirty thousand head of cattle, and a million dollars in the bank.

Feeling sick, she started backing out of the room, but not quickly enough to miss hearing Tim say softly, "I'll be right here, Anne. I'll take care of you."

Suppressing a scream of rage and frustration, Hope raced down the stairs and out through the front door without a word to the servants gathered in the hallway. Once outside on the veranda, she halted as a veritable cloudburst hit the area and the rain came down in sheets.

A hundred feet or so away, nearly fifty cowboys were mounted and ready to ride, waiting for Tim to lead them. And Tim, damn his cheating Irish heart, was up there in the dead man's bedroom, holding the dead man's wife in his arms while she was undoubtedly whispering in his ear how it would be for them from now on with Morton's money.

Rollo was tied to the hitching post where Hope had left

him, drenched and miserable, but waiting patiently for his mistress. The rain began to slacken, but Hope had to speak to Tim before she left for home. She needed to know just how completely her world had been shattered.

She didn't have to wait long. Whatever endearments and promises he had exchanged with Anne Fenwick had been hurried. He had work to do, and only a few minutes later he emerged from the house. His slicker was over his arm and he was carrying an expensive sporting rifle, a weapon that, like Anne, had once belonged to Morton Fenwick but now was Timothy O'Callahan's.

He saw Hope at once and hurried to her despite a shout of impatience from Jed. "Hope darlin'," he said, and tried to put his arms around her.

She backed away from him, chin lifted proudly. "How is the bereaved widow?"

"She's totally distraught, but the doctor has given her a sleeping powder so she can get some rest."

"Why didn't you stay and cuddle her?"

"I have work to do. Please, Hope, try to understand. I know we'll have to change our plans, but—"

"*Change* them? Don't you mean abandon them?"

"No, that's not what I mean. We can still see each other. In time, we'll be able to—"

"Don't talk like an idiot! It's over and you know it! The beautiful rich lady needs you—"

"Of course Anne needs me."

"And I don't?"

He looked unhappy. "Macushla, 'tis not a matter of my wantin' or not wantin' to do this. 'Tis my duty to a man who was my friend as well as my employer."

"Some friend you were . . . you and his wife."

"Hope, please don't. Morton is dead and 'tis partly my fault. I should have been here to lead the men. He was killed because instead of being here to do the job I was hired to do, I was—"

"You were with me," she finished the sentence for him. "The blame is mine, not yours. I'm the one responsible. They killed him because I was fighting them. They killed him as deliberately as they lynched Jim and Ella."

That surprised her, but his suspicion that association gunmen had shot Fenwick wasn't her main concern right now. What mattered was that her love didn't mean as much to him as Anne and her ranch.

"So now you think you have to stay here and protect his widow."

"Hope, I must do my duty. I owe it to Morton."

"Do you love her?"

"No, damnit! I love *you!*"

"Have you slept with her?"

"Yes! But before I met you. Fenwick was an older man. She needed love, she begged me over and over—"

"Oh, spare me the vile details," she said, turning away and starting down the veranda steps.

"Please, Hope, don't let this ruin what we have. I love you!"

"But you're going to stay here at Sussex with her?"

"I have to for a while. Just for a few months, until—"

"Then go to her and kiss her rich ass! I never want to see you again! I could have forgiven the past, but this is the present and I can't forgive your ruining everything we had planned together. Just leave me alone. I never want to see you again!"

Half-blinded by tears, she ran to Rollo, leaped into the saddle, and headed north toward the rain-swollen Powder. She could hear Tim clattering down the steps behind her, vaulting onto his horse, and riding off with the waiting cowboys.

All the way to the river and across it, Hope lay with her head on Rollo's wet mane, her tears mingling with the raindrops of the weeping heavens.

Now, eight months later, lying in the straw of the Andrews' wagon on the way home from Cheyenne, there were tears in her eyes again at the poignant memory of that unhappy day.

Chapter 23

HOPE HAD BEEN in a state of emotional shock for some time after her parting with Tim that day at Sussex House. She had thrown herself into the hard physical work of the ranch, spending long hours in the saddle, going from sunup to sundown so she wouldn't have time to think and could fall asleep from sheer exhaustion the minute her head touched the pillow.

Sometime during that period she had written to Jebel Mason just to keep her father from nagging at her about it. In his reply, he had told her of the many important friends he had made in Washington who were urging him to run for Congress as soon as Wyoming became a state. He also said he still loved her and wanted to have a serious talk with her when he returned to Cheyenne to confer with Democratic leaders, who had promised to support him in the event of a move toward statehood. As her grief and bitterness at what she considered her betrayal by Timothy O'Callahan began to fade a little, she began to look forward to seeing Jebel again.

After the demonstration and her appearance before the legislature, she began to run into Edgar Potter everywhere. Those were restless months during which she found herself filled with needs she didn't completely understand, and Potter seemed to sense that and began to appear frequently at the Lazy H, despite Pat's outspoken hostility.

She had no admiration for the silver-haired, silken-tongued minister, but he always seemed to be around when she was troubled or feeling depressed. Several times he helped her with problems connected with the Stock Growers Association. That had been easy for him because he was in with the men who ran it: solid, prosperous men who owned broad lands and vast herds; men who were Harvard graduates, well-born Bostonians, or scions of Wall Street banking families. These were the types who headed the association that protected the large landowners and did everything possible to discourage the small ranchers and dirt farmers by using tactics including murder.

Oh, they were fine men, the members of the Cheyenne Ring, and Potter was unofficial chaplain of the association. He presided over their meetings, married their sons and daughters, buried their friends, and advised them in their dealings with the peasants who owned small parcels of land along Powder River and around the town of Buffalo.

So Hope accepted his company and didn't send him packing as her father suggested.

"All preachers are no-good bums, and he makes the others look good," Pat said. "What's he hangin' around you for when he's got a wife at home and God knows how many lady friends among his parishioners?"

"We don't know that for sure," Hope said absently, her mind on Timothy, not Potter. She had run into Tim while out riding the day before, the first time she had seen him in a year, and it had been anything but a pleasure because of who was with him.

Anne Fenwick had been dressed in a light gray riding habit with a small matching top hat and a veil over her face. Timothy had been trailing along behind her, looking odd in fancy coat and riding breeches. His face had broken into his usual magnificent smile at sight of Hope, but it faded quickly as Hope merely nodded and rode on, fully aware of the malicious glance Anne cast her way.

Later she heard that Tim was no longer foreman of the Sussex but manager, a position held by men who ran ranches for absentee landowners.

"Well, I guess old Tim has gone back on us," Nate Champion said to her and John Tisdale, a Canadian who had been in the area almost as long as the Fenwicks, when they happened to meet at the Buffalo post office.

"He took care of George Henderson first, though," Tisdale said.

"What?" Hope asked, fear gripping her heart like a cold hand. "He didn't—"

"No, but he hunted him down, braced him, and told him to either draw or stay away from Powder River. Told him he knew for a fact that he had murdered young Gene Crowder, and if he didn't leave this area, he was going to put a bullet through every button of his vest. Old Henderson must have believed him because he quit his job at the Quarter-Circle and skedaddled on down to Cheyenne and hasn't left the town since."

"Tim is just the hairpin who could do that," Nate said. "There's nobody in Wyoming who can outshoot or outride that Irisher."

In spite of herself Hope felt a glow of pride hearing these men praise Tim. It was as though he were still her man.

"That's one reason I hate to see him marry that Fenwick woman," Tisdale went on.

A wave of nausea swept through Hope. Marry Anne Fenwick? Somehow she had assumed the woman would eventually tire of her cowboy lover and go back east. Not that she expected to get Tim back when it happened. Damn-it, she didn't want him! She never wanted to see him again! But marriage to that woman? Impossible! She must be at least five years older than he was.

"I hear he's living in the castle right now," the postmaster stuck in his two cents' worth. "Maybe they figure they got to get married for appearances' sake."

Hope started to turn away, not wanting to hear any more. "I guess I'd better be getting on back to the ranch."

"There's something I wanted to talk to you about, Miss Hope," Champion said. "You know we're thinking of starting a Northern Wyoming Stock Raisers Association and holding our own roundups?"

"I'm with you right down the line," she said, relieved that the subject had been changed.

"Since the Cheyenne Ring started excluding us from the roundup—"

"Which they ain't got no right to do," interjected Tisdale. "The roundup and cattle shipping is a state affair, not an association matter, and they've no right to exclude anybody."

"But you know that anyone who runs cattle in a small way is a rustler in their eyes, and they say they don't want rustlers in the roundup," Champion said.

"How about murderers?" Hope asked.

"They don't matter," Champion said with a grim smile. "If they eliminated killers, they might not have anyone there. But what we want to do is hold our roundup a month ahead of theirs."

"Oh, my! Will that ever set them to buzzing like a hornet's nest!" Hope said.

An early roundup would give Powder River folks first chance at the mavericks and calves the Cheyenne Ring considered their natural right.

"Yeah, and we were wondering how the Seventy-six would stand on it. If we could get them and a couple other big ranches, we'd have a better foothold, especially if it goes to court."

"Well, with your place, John," Champion said—Tisdale and his brother owned two of the larger places north of the river—"and the Seventy-six, along with a couple of others, we wouldn't look like a bunch of little outfits trying to steal the cattle companies' calves."

"Miss Hope, we were wondering if you could talk to Tim O'Callahan," Tisdale said. "All I've been able to get out of him is that he'd have to ask Mrs. Fenwick and her lawyer about it. You and him used to be friends, and we thought—"

"I'm sorry, boys, but I couldn't possibly talk to Tim. We had a misunderstanding about a filly back a ways and haven't been speaking since."

"Some filly," her father had snorted when she told him about it later. "A fancy-assed two-legged filly. And you behaved like a balky filly yourself. That fella was so plumb in love with you that he couldn't keep his eyes straight, and what do you do? You lose your temper and run him right into the arms of that blue-blooded bitch."

"I didn't run him there," Hope said defensively. "I found him there."

"What do you expect a man to do when a woman throws herself in his arms overwhelmed with grief at her husband's death? Let her swoon on the floor? Push her out a window?"

"No, but I didn't expect him to feel he has to take care of her for the rest of her life. No, what I told the boys goes. I am not going to ask O'Callahan to join with us."

"Then I will," Pat said, getting to his feet carefully because of the bad leg he'd developed after a fall from a new horse. "I'll ride over there first thing in the morning and have a talk with Tim and Mrs. Fenwick."

"That will do a lot of good. I doubt the woman will talk to you any more than she would to me."

"Don't you be too sure now," Pat said. "You know I used to be quite a hand with the ladies, and this lady is too old for O'Callahan, so maybe—"

"Oh, Pap, you couldn't even hold on to Ma," she said, exasperated by his joking. Everything that touched on Tim O'Callahan and Anne Fenwick either exasperated her or made her want to cry, she realized, but she didn't know what to do about it except avoid the subject altogether.

The next day, while she was watering the stock with Juan and his younger brother, who had made his way north from San Antonio to work for her, Pat dressed up in his best town clothes, slicked down his hair, and rode off in the direction of Three Crossings.

He returned in late afternoon, suit covered with dust and

hair mussed by the wind, looking somewhat less pleased with himself than he had when he left.

"Well," Hope said. "Did you propose to Mrs. Fenwick and offer to take her away from it all?"

"No, but I was invited to have lunch with her and Timothy and an aunt who came out a few months ago to stay with her."

"As chaperon?" Hope asked, raising an eyebrow.

"Not exactly. Anne was mooning over poor Tim right in front of her and the old girl didn't say a word. She looked a lot of words, but she didn't say none of 'em."

"And did the lady of the manor agree to join with us?"

"No. The answer was no, but it was a pretty polite no. In fact, Anne said she felt sorry for the way some of her smaller neighbors had been treated, but she had to side with members of her own class. There wasn't anything personal about it, but that's the way it was."

"And Tim just sat and listened to that crap?"

"Yep, but he walked out with me afterward and told me he hadn't known it himself, but Fenwick didn't own the Sussex place outright. Seems like he had shareholders back in New York like some of them downstate spreads. It seems that Anne would have to consider their best interests, and if they were shut out of the association roundup they would lose money."

"*They* would lose money? What about us? We stand to lose everything if we're shut out."

"Yeah," Pat said, "and we stand to have a range war if we start our own roundup and shipping . . . and, honey chil', it's a hundred and twenty-five miles to the nearest railhead."

"Yes, but the railroad would be brought on through to Buffalo if it were profitable, and if we had enough cattle to ship it *would* be profitable."

Pat made himself more comfortable in his rocking chair by the window. "You know the railroad barons work hand in glove with the cattle barons and the steel barons and the press barons and all the other high mucky-mucks, not only in this state but in the whole country. We could get run over and smashed as flat as if we'd been hit by one of them steamrollers they use back east."

"Yes, we could as long as we have no political power," Hope agreed, "or newspaper power. That's where the real power lies, and the other side has got it all."

"So? Are you gonna ask one of them to change sides?"

"No," Hope said, "but I'm thinking of buying a paper in Buffalo."

"You don't mean that one old Joe Archon owns, the *Powder River Call,* do you?"

"I sure do. All I got to do is get eight hundred dollars together, buy the paper, keep Joe to run it for me, and we'll have a voice to answer the *Cheyenne Sun* and the *Ledger* and the rest the Cheyenne Ring owns."

"Sounds like a peashooter replying to a ten-inch gun," Pat said, peering out the window at a buggy off in the distance. "And here comes that preacher friend of yours. Why don't you tell him all about your brilliant idea?"

"No . . . no, I don't think I trust Edgar that much," Hope said, "but I'll think of something."

"Humph! Maybe he'll get his friends in the ring to loan you the money to buy a paper to use against them."

"Do you think they would?" she asked, grinning.

"I was joking," Pat said, easing out of his chair and going into the kitchen so he wouldn't have to be civil to Potter.

Hope stood thinking while she waited for Potter's vehicle to come down the road. The idea of tricking the Cheyenne Ring into putting up the money to buy a paper that would be used against them intrigued her. But how could she swing it? She'd have to use Potter, of course, since he was her only available link to them, and the only reason he was available was because he lived in hope that one day she would give in and let him have his lecherous way with her. There must be some way she could use what she knew about him and his colleagues to get what she wanted. If there wasn't, she wasn't nearly as smart as she'd always thought she was.

Hearing the buggy pull up in front, she ran to the mirror and inspected herself. She was wearing a denim skirt and a blue-and-white print blouse, and she had time to brush her blond hair into a soft halo around her face and pinch her cheeks into rosiness before there was a knock on the door.

"Well now, Edgar Potter," she said in mock surprise. "Whatever brings you up here to Powder River country?"

He beamed at her, looking as though he had stepped right out of an advertisement in a Sears, Roebuck catalogue. His silver hair was carefully combed and pomaded, and he was dressed in a pin-striped suit, complete with vest and four-in-hand tie. He was holding a derby in his hand, and his smile was as brilliant as the all-gold one she once had seen on a gambler in Abilene.

"I was making my weekly calls on the good people of my church who live in Johnson County, and when I was through and about to get back on the stage, I told myself I just had to see Miss Hope Cox, and digging into my own pocket, I rented this surrey and headed out here from Buffalo."

"My, my. Since you came all that way and paid for a buggy out of your own pocket, I guess I have to say you're welcome."

"Well, I hoped you would," he said. "I've felt there was an understanding growing between us, since we got over our disagreement on the suffrage matter, that might lead to a stronger bond than simple friendship."

She wanted to puncture his bubble by inquiring about his wife, but decided against it and swung the door wide. "Come in, come in. Of course you're welcome. I'll get you some lemonade."

"I'd appreciate that, Miss Hope, I surely would." He came inside and sat down in Pat's favorite chair.

She had seen Chou Li bring ice up from the icehouse a short time before and knew there was squeezed lemon juice ready to use. "Do you want one or two spoons of sugar?"

He was sitting straight as a ramrod in the chair, his hat

balanced on his knee. "Just one, if you please. I'm hoping for something sweeter later on."

He looked right at her lips as he spoke, and she had to swallow to keep from laughing. He was about as subtle as a bucking bronco, and she had known he had seduction in mind from the moment he eyed her during the suffrage hearings.

As she fixed the glasses of lemonade, she thought about his weekly trips on the stage from Cheyenne, usually on Wednesdays, and how he went from house to house, talking to people about religion but also gossiping about who was running how many cattle and how many cowboys blacklisted by the association were working little spreads of their own along Powder River and just generally nosing into folks' private business.

Nothing any preacher wouldn't have done, Hope thought, but knowing his connections, she had to suspect that Edgar was a spy for the association. She was sure he had already gotten an earful about the plans of Nate Champion, John Tisdale, and Ranger Jones to start a group of their own, and she would bet his report on the idea of an early roundup had caused his friends at the Cheyenne Club to choke on their fancy victuals.

When she handed him the chilled glass into which she had dumped three heaping spoonsful of sugar, he tried to take her hand, saying, "May I look forward to something sweeter later?"

"Drink your lemonade," Hope advised. "I think that will take care of your sweet tooth for a while."

He sipped at the concoction and almost choked. "Ah yes, sweet—very sweet."

"How are things at the Cheyenne Club, Reverend?" she asked. "Are the boys still enjoying their haute cuisine?"

"Why, uh—I haven't been to dinner there for some time, but I understand they have the same fine chef—"

"I meant, how are their appetites? Exasperation can ruin a person's appetite, you know, and they've been pretty exasperated with us lately."

He frowned slightly. "Frankly, my dear, I've been hoping to talk to you about the Johnson County rustlers."

"What about them?"

"Well . . . I think you and your father should keep your distance from those local inhabitants who have a reputation for rustling."

"You think something might happen to us if we don't?" she asked, staring at him with big, wide-open, innocent-looking eyes.

"Well, I—" He was twitching in his chair as he looked at her slightly parted lips.

She moved her chair a little closer to his so he could catch a whiff of the lily-of-the-valley perfume Jebel had sent her. "You know, I was thinking along those same lines, only my thought was that the association ought to separate itself from men like George Henderson who have a reputation for murdering."

Potter jumped as though she had stuck him with a hatpin. "Why, how can you say such a thing? Mr. Henderson is head of the association's range detectives."

"And he helped lynch Ella Watson and Jim Averell, and he poisoned young Gene Crowder and shot two or three other men in the back."

"Oh, Hope. My dear, dear Hope." He set down his glass and took both of her hands in his. "Your mind has been turned against the upstanding and honorable men in the Stock Growers Association by the locals. Why, my dear, those men attend my church, I visit at their homes, and they entertain me at their club. You just don't understand them, Hope."

She was beginning to see a way to use Potter's connection with the Cheyenne Ring for the benefit of her friends, so she temporized. "Well, I still must say I've never heard anything good about any of those fellows."

"You do them an injustice out of ignorance, dear girl," Potter said, his fingers playing games with the palms of Hope's hands.

She gave no indication she knew what the movements meant and was very careful not to tighten her fingers in an answering squeeze. She had no intention of promising him anything, and if he misinterpreted the fact that she was allowing the tickling to continue, that was his fault, not hers.

"There aren't many folks in these parts who see two sides to this fight," she told him. "That's why I'm kind of sorry to see the *Powder River Call* go out of business. It accepted advertising from Cheyenne merchants and didn't always call the Stock Growers crooks."

"The *Call* is going out of business?"

She nodded. "Yes, the owner has run out of operating funds."

"Hm. You know, I might be able to help that fellow . . . what's his name?"

"Archon," she said, pleased that he seemed to be nibbling at the bait. "Joe Archon."

"Yes. There are men with money, you know, who would have no trouble financing a small newspaper like that."

"I don't think Johnson County folks would buy a newspaper financed by anyone connected with the association," she said.

"No, I don't suppose they would," he said, and bent his silver head over the hands he still held, touching his lips and then his tongue to the palms.

"My, my, Reverend, you do crave sugar, don't you? Did I get some on my hands?"

"No, no. It's just that being so close to the sweet youthfulness of you—touching your warm flesh—gets me kind of light-headed. What was I saying?"

"That folks wouldn't trust a paper run by an outsider."

"Oh, yes. I'll have to think about that. It seems to me that if someone who lives in the vicinity ran the paper and there was no apparent connection to the association, people would have more faith in the opinions it expressed."

"You planning on moving up to Johnson County, Reverend?"

"No, I had someone else in mind," he said, raising his head and looking at her with glazed eyes. "Miss Hope, that perfume of yours is going to my head and . . . and I really would like to talk to you some more. Would you let me take you for a buggy ride out on the prairie?"

She had expected him to ask for more than that and knew the question she dreaded would come sooner or later. Well, she would deal with it when it happened. Right now, she had to keep Reverend Edgar Potter on the hook, not only as a source of information about the Cheyenne Ring, but as a possible source of funds to buy a newspaper to fight them.

"Why, of course, Reverend," she said, taking her hands away from him and crossing her fingers behind her back. "I would love to take a buggy ride with you."

Chapter 24

HOPE WAS SURE she knew what Edgar Potter wanted, but she wasn't sure how much she was going to let him have. She knew now that she was still in love with Tim O'Callahan; she couldn't doubt it after the storm of emotion that had shaken her following her father's visit to Sussex House and his story about how Anne had been mooning around Tim. And the talk about the probability of his marrying Anne had only made her feel worse. Maybe the only cure for what ailed her was another man.

Now here she was sitting in a buggy on a warm evening as the horse ambled along without guidance because Reverend Potter's arms were wrapped around her.

He was an attractive man, she had to admit, but no more attractive than Jebel Mason, and Jebel was a decent, hardworking man, not a two-timing hypocrite of a preacher. But Jebel was far away in Washington, D.C., and Edgar Potter was right here beside her.

"I could help you with a lot of things," he was saying. "I am friendly with the men who run the association and I know what they intend to do about the rustling in Johnson County."

That got Hope's full attention. "I'll bet you do. They keep your collection plate filled every Sunday while the other ministers in the area barely get by. Tell me, Reverend, what do you do for them—pray their way into heaven in spite of their crimes?" She hadn't meant to say that. She had planned to play along with him and use him in any way she could to help her against the barons.

"Hope, that's no way to talk, and please call me Edgar. You know how I feel about you."

"Do I? I didn't know you had any feeling for anyone but your cohorts in the association."

That had slipped out too, but she couldn't help it. It was one of those things she had to say. She was not the kind of woman who gave in to domination; that was one of the reasons she had come into conflict with the association in the first place. She considered herself the equal of any man in the territory. She had a vote and could run for office and refused to cringe like most folks did when the Stock Growers issued their orders.

"Damn you, you little temptress, I'll show you feeling!" Edgar said, crushing her to him, his full, soft lips closing over hers.

"This is it—this is what love is." He shoved her down onto the seat and stretched across her as the surrey came to a stop under a tree. Through the layers of cloth between them, she could feel the bulging maleness of him and was alarmed at the almost automatic response from her body. She didn't want any feeling to interfere with what she intended to do. But she had been without a man since Timothy and that was too long when you were twenty and warm-blooded and resented an ancient moral code that still turned a blind eye to men who satisfied their passions outside marriage but condemned the women who provided the outlet for that passion. "Ladies" could only sit at home and wait passively for a man to propose.

Hope declined to sit home and wait for anything. She needed a weapon with which to fight the association, something better than guns. The eight hundred dollars that stood between her and ownership of the *Powder River Call* was important to her, and so was a source of inside information about the activities of the Cheyenne Ring. Potter was the key to both, and she had to use the advantages nature had given her to deal with him; how far to go was the only question, and no emotion the only restriction.

"I can do more than help you, Hope," he was whispering now. "We can help each other. I've watched you, and I know that if anyone is ever going to break the power of the association, it will be you."

This really startled her. She had always thought he was perfectly content to ride along with the Stock Growers. She had never thought of him as having ambitions of his own.

"I'm not sure I know what you mean," she said as he pressed hot, damp kisses on the fabric that covered her breasts, making her acutely aware that her body might betray her in spite of her determination.

"I mean you and I against the rustlers in Johnson County and against the association. You've spoken about running for office, and it is my opinion that you could be elected and that I could, too. If we worked together, we could become a real power in this territory, a power that could replace the association."

She put her hands on his shoulders and pushed him away a little. "Ah! Are you saying you'd sell out your principals and your principles?"

He threw back his head and laughed, silver hair gleaming in the moonlight. "In a way, Hope, I'm very much like you. I have neither." He had completely misunderstood her. She was smart, certainly, and worked hard to get ahead, but she had principles. Maybe, like Uncle John Chisum, she trimmed them a little, but they were very much there. But, of course, there was no reason to let Potter know that.

She smiled. "I have sometimes suspected that, but wasn't your struggle against the suffrage movement something you believed in?"

"You cannot be a minister of the gospel and be too particular about what you believe in," he said with a disarming frankness she had never noticed in him before. "I thought the antisuffrage cause was a sure winner because it always was in the East. I thought it would fill my empty pews."

"And your empty pockets?"

"For a minister, my dear, they are one and the same."

She had known all along that he was a scoundrel, and now that he had admitted it he didn't offend her quite as much. "Just what did you have in mind about our cooperating?" she asked, letting him kiss her neck and fondle her breasts, but firmly stopping the progress of the hand creeping up her thigh.

"Well, you know that the association is determined to rid Johnson County of those they consider rustlers, which frankly, is anyone who has given them any trouble. They have a shooting list, or perhaps you might call it a hanging list, or both. It won't be long before they start checking names off wholesale."

Hope's breath was coming faster now, but it wasn't because of his lovemaking. "How high is my name on that list?"

"Well, I haven't actually seen the list. I've just heard a lot of talk about it, but I doubt that your name is on it. You're a woman."

"They hanged Ella Watson, didn't they?"

"Yes, but she was a common thing, not a lady. Besides, I can protect you. If you and I were friends, really close friends, I could do more than that." He had worked the buttons of her blouse open and was sliding a hand in under her bodice to touch her breasts.

He sucked in his breath when he found the nipple; she gritted her teeth but didn't push his hand away. She realized she might have to go farther than she had intended to accomplish her purpose. "What kind of friends did you have in mind?" she asked, fighting down the excitement she felt rising as his palm moved over her nipples.

"This kind of friends," he said, kissing her again and plunging his tongue deep into her mouth. For a moment she stiffened, but then her lips relaxed and let his roam at will.

"And there would be other things, ways in which we two together, with help from other people, could eventually topple the domination of the cattle barons."

Her ears heard his words but her thoughts were on his hands, one cupping her breasts, squeezing it lightly and toying with the nipple, the other trying to get free of her restraining grasp.

"You and I could go far, little Hope. All the way to the governor's house in a year or two, after Wyoming becomes a state."

"You and I and your little wife?" she couldn't resist asking.

"Mable isn't made for this country in the way you are," Edgar said with no embarrassment. "One of these days she's going to give up and go back east to her parents."

Just like my mother did, Hope thought. There were women, and men too, who couldn't take the hardships imposed by this rugged land, but she doubted seriously if that was the problem between Edgar and his wife. The most probable bone of contention was his inability to keep his hands off other women.

"Marriage might even be possible for us," he said, as though it were a prize of great worth.

"Hmmm." Hope didn't want marriage with this silver fox. She wasn't sure she wanted an alliance with him against the cattle barons; she preferred the allies she had. If only she could get her hands on a newspaper, she knew she could write the kind of editorials that would prick the fat bottoms of the members of the Cheyenne Club and wake up the people to what was really going on. Who knows, she might be able to get her name well known enough to enable her to run for political office, although she realized her oft-stated ambition to be governor was unrealistic. All she wanted for now was a base of power from which to fight her sworn enemies.

The way Edgar was so expertly caressing her breasts, taking his time and skillfully moving through the stages of arousal, made Hope wonder how many of the prim and proper ladies of his congregation had been the recipients of his adulterous attentions. She shivered slightly. She didn't honestly care what he did when he wasn't preaching the hypocritical morality he specialized in, but it would be interesting to know which ladies were indulging in illicit passion while turning up their noses at social contact with small ranchers and squatters. God, what she couldn't do with knowledge like that to hint at in the society column of the *Powder River Call,* once it was hers.

Had Mrs. James Ainsworth, the nose-in-air wife of an Englishman whose past was a trifle murky but whose present and future in Wyoming seemed very bright, bounced her proud British arse on a mattress for Edgar Potter? Had plump and haughty Lucy Barton, wife of John Barton, current head of the association, laid bare her proper Boston Brahmin pussy for the reverend's pleasure? The mental picture of such activities made Hope giggle against the demand of Edgar's kisses, and he drew away and looked at her in surprise. "Is something amusing? I can't imagine what you would find laughable at a time like this."

"It's nothing. I just happened to recall that you said politics would take away a woman's femininity."

"Oh well, as I said, just because I am a minister of the gospel doesn't mean everything I say is gospel."

"No, I suppose not," she said, remembering all the other things he had said and comparing them with what she knew about him now. What kind of a life would a woman have with a man so totally without principles?

But did Timothy have principles? After all, he'd been bedding the Fenwick woman at the same time he was telling her he loved her. In his way and on a smaller scale, he was as two-faced as Potter. When a rich woman had beckoned, he had danced right into her arms. So what difference was there between one man and another? What difference did it make whose lips were on hers or whose body she responded to in the moonlight, especially if by doing so she could help herself and perhaps save her friends and neighbors from being murdered in cold blood?

"Let me touch you," he was pleading. "I want to feel your femininity—your sex."

"Haven't you forgotten I lost it when I got to keep the vote?"

"Please, my dearest one, do not hold that silliness against me. I need you so much! Touch me and feel how much I need you."

"That might be interesting," she said. "Then I'd know for sure why the front pews of your church are filled every Sunday with big-bosomed ladies in large hats and fashionable bustles."

He had her blouse fully open now and his tongue was caressing her nipples while the hand under her skirt tried to get past the barrier she had placed in its way.

"I really don't think you should keep bringing up what might have taken place between me and certain ladies of my congregation."

"Why not? I find it interesting. If I knew more about your affairs, I might be able to decide how far I can trust you."

"Trust?" He looked up at her in apparent distress. "I—why, Hope, I thought you knew. I'm in love with you. You're so young and lovely and vibrant. I've never felt about anyone the way I feel about you."

"Ummm," she said skeptically. "How about poor Mabel back in Cheyenne?"

"She . . . I must confess this, my dear—she was a dreadful mistake. It happened when I was young, just out of the seminary and called to a church in Temperance, Minnesota. She was pretty and sang in the choir and . . . well, we were intimate and she stupidly became pregnant—"

"And you had to marry her." Hope again pushed away the hand that tried to dart above her knee. "I was unaware there were any little Potters at home."

"The unfortunate child took ill and passed away while we were on our way to a larger church in Duluth."

"A larger church in Duluth? Then why on earth did you come out to this wilderness?" she asked, making no move to keep him from kissing her breasts and pressing against her urgently, but not letting him see that it was affecting her in any way.

"There was a little trouble—I lost my post—"

"You mean you got caught with the wife of a deacon and came west to make a new start, with your faithful wife trotting along beside you. How touching. Now, shall we talk about the ladies of the First Church of Cheyenne?"

"Hope, you must forget this notion of yours that I have anything to do with the ladies of my congregation. Some of them are the wives of our most prominent men, and I would be extremely foolish to engage in any—"

"Any hanky-panky like you're engaging in right now."

"But, Hope, you're an unmarried girl, and not connected with any people..." He stopped, realizing he had said the wrong thing.

"That's the truth of it, isn't it?" she remarked. "I'm a person of no importance, a female you can toy with and toss aside whenever it suits you."

"No, Hope, no! That isn't true! I want you, need you. You've got to let me love you, Hope, you've got to! I'm half insane with the desire for you."

"That's because you've been wasting your talents on the likes of Lucy Barton and Felice Ainsworth, whose English puss has long since been frozen by the chill of her family tree. Or perhaps with Tilly Martin, whose husband used to be a butcher back in St. Louis and now struts around in a plug hat and sends out gunmen to shoot people he claims have stolen the cows he stole in the first place. How is it with her, Potter, my love? Is it wildly exciting to kiss that moustache of hers?"

Her mockery had taken the fire out of Potter and was helping her suppress the last lingering physical reactions he had aroused in her. Just picturing him with those women caused a wave of revulsion to flood through her. She pushed him away with both hands and calmly buttoned up her blouse.

"Hope, you can't refuse me this way after you've gotten me all excited. Only a tease would do that, and I don't believe you are one."

"I'm not," she assured him, sitting up and kissing him lightly. "But neither do I intend to become just one more in your long list of conquests. You're too handsome and too glib, Edgar. I can understand why women fall over themselves to please you, but I'm not going to . . . at least not until I feel that we have a real commitment to each other."

"But I love you, Hope! Please—please." He took one of her hands in his and began kissing it passionately.

"Not now, not yet. Not tonight, anyway," she said. "I want to be sure."

"But I've told you I love you. Isn't that enough?"

"Didn't you ever tell any of the others that you loved them? Your wife? That nameless woman in Duluth? Those women in Cheyenne?"

"Not and meant it!" he blurted, and then had the grace to look embarrassed.

"Do you mean it now?"

"Yes, yes, my dearest one. Honestly and from the bottom of my heart, I mean it!" He emphasized the words by thumping his chest with his fist at every other word.

"Well . . . I don't know." Hope sounded hesitant, but she was in full control of herself now and knew exactly what she was doing. "I just don't know."

"Isn't there anything I can do to convince you that this one time—that this time for the first time in my life, I am genuinely in love and totally sincere in everything I've said to you?"

"Well, we'll see. Perhaps in a few months or a year, we can—"

"Hope, I couldn't stand that!" he said, sounding on the verge of tears. "I couldn't stand doing without you for even a few weeks, much less months or a year . . . oh God, a year!"

He bowed his head over her hands and she felt a wetness on them that could only be tears. She had heard of actors who could produce real tears on demand. Could Edgar act as well as that? It was nice to be able to sit back and observe him in action. One could see a person so much more clearly when one's emotions weren't involved.

"Please tell me, dearest Hope, that there is some chance

you might change your mind earlier than in a year."

She didn't want to push him in the direction she wanted him to go because when the denouement came she wanted him to think it had been his idea, not hers.

"I think perhaps after several months have passed and I can see that you are really sincere, I could see my way clear to give myself to you—even though you are married. It would have to be a proper period of time, though. And you would have to convince me that your marriage was forced on you and that therefore it would not be too sinful for us to join together in the sight of the Lord."

"I can't wait. I really can't, Hope," he said brokenly. "Can't you see I'm going crazy with wanting you?"

"I understand," she said sympathetically, patting his head, "but I can't help the way I feel. Now that I know about the other women, I can't take a chance on being used and left behind, as they were."

He groaned, and the sound seemed to come clear from his boots.

"I wish there was some way of resolving this," she said, "but I fear it is a dilemma beyond our ability to solve."

He grunted and looked up. "Hope, I think I know a way to prove to you I am sincere."

Remembering the cynical statements he had made about how a minister had to operate, she doubted if he knew the meaning of sincerity but managed to look interested. "You have?"

"Yes. Do you recollect what we were saying about that newspaper in Buffalo? The one that's for sale?"

"Yes, of course."

"Suppose I were able to arrange a loan for you from the Frontier Bank of Cheyenne so you could buy it? Wouldn't that prove I really cared for you?"

She pretended to think about it. "Well, maybe, but I don't think anyone in Johnson County would have much faith in a publisher financed by the bank known to have connections to the Cheyenne Ring."

"Then suppose I arranged for a personal loan?"

She shook her head after a thoughtful pause. "No, someone would be sure to discover there were loan papers."

He looked crestfallen for a minute and then said triumphantly, "I've got it! An outright gift! Eight hundred dollars, all in little bills, as if you'd been saving it up! The gentlemen of the club would be glad to contribute that much to have a newspaper in Buffalo that would present their side of the case."

"I would promise only to write nothing but the truth—the whole truth."

"That's good enough. Once you and I are one and are working together against both sides to become powerful in Wyoming, I'm sure you'll see that my way of dealing with things is the right way."

She smiled at him. "You are very persuasive, Edgar. Very persuasive."

Chapter 25

A WEEK LATER, Edgar delivered the money. More than he had promised, in fact; one thousand dollars rather than the eight hundred Hope needed.

"No strings attached to this?" she asked.

"No strings. The association trusts me and I trust you."

"Then take this back," she said, counting out two hundred dollars and handing them to him. "The *Call* costs only eight hundred, and that's all I need."

"The gentlemen at the club thought perhaps the extra money would be helpful. Something for yourself."

"I don't want anything for myself," she said, thrusting the money into his pocket. "They can't buy me for two hundred dollars. Take it back to them."

He reached for her hand. "Hope, *now* can you and I—"

"Not right now, Edgar," she said. "I've got to ride into town and see Joe Archon about the paper. That's what you and I want, isn't it?"

"Yes, I suppose so, but..."

He was so obviously disappointed that she relented enough to give him a big smile and a peck on the cheek. "I'll see you on your next trip to Johnson County, Edgar dear."

As soon as he had left to visit Fred Hesse and Frank Canton, two strong supporters of the association in Johnson County, she was up on Sally's back and heading into Buffalo.

"Here's the eight hundred, Joe," she said to the grizzly old character with leg-of-mutton whiskers. "You can pay off your debts and still have a few hundred to live on. I'll pay you forty and found for operating the press for me."

He wiped his hands on his long green apron and straightened the false sleeves he wore to protect the shirt that was already spotted with ink. "Done," he said, taking the stack of bills. "As long as you don't get yourself blown up by association dynamiters."

"I can't promise anything, Joe, but I'll do my damnedest to see that they don't get close enough to do it. Besides, we'll lay low on that subject for a while and work on my plans to run for office."

"Run for office? You're a woman!"

"You got strong objections to that, you better state 'em now, Joe."

"Naw, I don't care who runs. Politics is a bunch of cow puke anyway."

Then, just a few weeks after her twenty-first birthday, Jebel Mason returned, and Hope was faced with the decisions she'd known all along she'd have to make eventually. One of them was whether to go ahead and marry Jebel when he asked her; a second was whether she should launch a campaign for public office for him as well as for herself. Those questions had occupied her somewhat all the time she was running the ranch, starting the newspaper, and still yearning for Tim O'Callahan, but now they would have to take precedence.

Suddenly Jebel was there, standing on the doorstep of her house, hat in hand, black curly hair slicked down, boots shined, and dressed like an eastern dude.

She threw her arms around him with an enthusiasm that surprised both her and Pat. "Glad to have you back, Jebel. How's the government doing in Washington?"

"Well—" he began, and then paused to kiss her, doing such a thorough job of it that she found it extremely enjoyable, even if it didn't quite come up to Tim's efforts.

"Well," he started over again when he finally released her, "the Democrats are in control of the Senate and that means Wyoming's request for statehood is sure to get a favorable reception."

"Good!" she said. "That will give us the chance we need. Once we have statehood, we can really have a go at those bastards in the Cheyenne Ring."

"Yes, and there's something else. As I told you, I made a good impression on some influential Democrats and I've been promised party support for any office I want in Wyoming or the Congress. I am thinking of running for the Senate."

"I think the state legislature would be better," Hope said. "That way you'll be closer to things in the state when it comes time to run for governor."

"Governor?" He grinned at her. "I thought that was going to be your job."

"I'm going to run for justice of the peace in Buffalo first," she said. "There's a lot of things that have to be cleared up in and around that town. So if you run for the legislature and I for justice of the peace, we'll have a pro-Johnson County slate all ready to go."

"Hope," Jebel said, grinning down at her from his six-foot-two height, "I was wondering if we couldn't run together in another way—a more personal way."

"I've been wondering that myself," she said, making the long-deferred decision on the spot. It was now or never. She had been without a man too long and she certainly did have an abiding affection for Jebel.

"You mean—"

"I mean the answer is yes," she said. "Pap can give the bride away, Juan can be best man, and we can spend our honeymoon launching our campaign for public office."

But it didn't work out the way she had it planned. Following the statehood vote in Washington, the man picked to run for Congress in the first election was Clint Werth. He was the choice of Johnson County citizens to run against the Stock Growers' tame representative.

"I hope he has a bodyguard," Jebel said to Hope the day after their wedding.

"I hear Nate Champion already has the job," Hope said, "but he might need an undertaker unless he keeps Nate handy at all times."

Two weeks later, three association gunmen tried to kill Clint Werth. The attempt ended with one of them dead, one wounded, and Clint Werth thoroughly intimidated. And the day after Hope and Jebel returned from a honeymoon trip to St. Louis, Jebel announced that he was going to run in Clint's place.

"Don't do it, Jebel," Hope pleaded. "They'll kill you just like they tried to kill Clint."

"I don't think they really wanted to kill Werth," Jeb said with a grin. "They only wanted to scare him off and they succeeded. That won't work with me."

"But I . . . we just got married," she protested. She had found that she liked having a husband around and she didn't want him traipsing off to Washington again. Nor did she want to risk his being killed during the election.

"Hope, you're the one who's always saying what a gang of tyrants the members of the association are and ranting about ideals and democracy, and now you're telling me I shouldn't run against their puppet. That doesn't make sense."

"It makes plenty of sense for a new bride," Hope said. "But you're right. If you don't do what you believe in, no one else is going to do it for you. We'll up the *Call* to twice a week and print what we know about Kenny Bentley, including when and why he quit beating his wife."

"He could sue us," Jebel cautioned.

"In Powder River country, my dear husband, people do not sue each other. Either they shoot the person who slanders them or they just forget the whole thing."

To their surprise, Jebel was elected to Congress without

once having to use his gun to protect his life. Fed up and disgusted with the machinations of the Cheyenne Ring, Johnson County rose up almost as one man and one woman to vote for Jebel Mason.

"You ought to run for office, too, Miz Hope," Nate Champion said.

"How about yourself, Nate?" Hope countered. Nate was now referred to by the kept press of the cattle barons as the King of Johnson County or the King of the Cattle Thieves. "Folks around here swear by you."

The dark-haired man shrugged and smiled. "But you know what they say about me downstate. They don't think there's a cow in Wyoming that's safe from my long rope and running brand."

"The *Call* will support you right down the line," she promised.

"You got a better chance yourself," Champion said. "Folks remember how you and Tim O'Callahan stood up to the ring after they murdered Jim Averell and Ella Watson and the three witnesses."

"Yes, and how Tim ran George Henderson out of this part of the state. But now he and that soon-to-be bride of his are on the other side of the fence."

"I don't know about that," Nate said. "Seems like they're more neutral, if that's possible. I heard they are going back east to her folks' home to get married later this year."

"Really?" She tried not to show how that bit of news made her feel, telling herself she had no right to react to it at all. She was married, wasn't she? Why shouldn't Tim marry his rich boss?

"The reason I think you got a good chance is because you're such a good writer and you got the *Call*. I figure you was the one got Jeb elected. Folks downstate might even vote for you if you ran."

Hope forced herself to smile and stop thinking about Tim. "I'll allow as how I've been thinking about it, but the office I was considering was justice of the peace, or maybe the state senate now that we got ourselves a state."

"Just the same, Miss Hope, you ought to start running right away for some office. The state senate can come next year."

Hope thought that over and then nodded. "All right, how about justice of the peace?"

The expression on Nate's face told her he didn't think much of that suggestion. In places like Johnson County, the justice of the peace had to deal with the more unpleasant aspects of running government—the sentencing of people to jail or to death.

"If I got that job, I could keep on running my ranch and the *Call*. What's wrong with justice of the peace, Nate?"

"Nothing's wrong with it, but it's kind of a job for a man. I mean, with a bunch of cussing, tobacco-chewing, gallus-snapping lawyers hanging around the courtroom, and the jury not much better... well, it just ain't no place for a lady."

"I thought everybody agreed a long time ago that Calamity Jane and Hope Cox Mason are women but not ladies," she said with a grin.

"Still, it ain't no place for a member of the gentler sex, a courtroom ain't. Why, you'd have to—"

"Send people to jail or order them hanged if twelve good men and true convicted them?"

"Yes, ma'am, and other things too."

"Tell me, Nate, how did you feel about the women's suffrage issue when it came up?"

Nate kicked at the dust for a minute and then looked up and grinned. "I didn't feel anything about it, Miss Hope. I didn't even know about it. I was too busy doing some mavericking over near the Big Horns to pay much attention. Afterward, I just figured it didn't make much difference 'cause most folks voted with their feet or their guns anyway."

"How do you feel about it now?"

"I figure we need folks like you voting and running for office or there'll always be a Cheyenne Ring running the state. And if you insist on running for justice of the peace, remember that job does carry a lot of power. If there was an Indian raid or something like that, you'd even have the power to call out the militia."

"Hey, that's right. I never thought of that and it's another good reason to run. What with hanging around army bases when Pap was in the Dragoons, I've got as much military experience as anyone around here, so I ought to be just the person to have the power to call out the militia."

Despite Nate's doubts as to the suitability of a woman's holding such a position, Nate and most of the other foes of the Stock Growers supported Hope and she got the job. And just in time, as it happened.

The long, smoldering feud between the association and the small ranchers was building to a climax, and the first sign of it was the killing of Ranger Jones and John Tisdale. Both were shot in the back under similar circumstances. Each had driven into Buffalo to put in supplies for the winter and on the way back to his ranch was bushwhacked. Sheriff Angus looked bad in both cases because his deputies had failed to trail the man or men, who had killed Tisdale even though there were fresh tracks.

A witness had come forward, however, who testified to seeing a masked man mounted on Frank Canton's horse Fred. Perhaps the fastest horse in the area, Fred was well known and easily identified by his white face and long racehorse legs.

Canton had given several alibis, none of which held up under cross-questioning when the witness came before Hope. She was in the process of drawing up an indictment on Canton when the body of Ranger Jones was brought in. Fred Hesse and Frank Canton were immediate suspects. They fled the county two days before the warrants were to be served by Sheriff Angus, and reported to their bosses in Cheyenne to make preparations to return with an army.

The night it happened, Hope was lying awake beside Jebel, her thoughts on something that had occurred earlier in the day. She had been coming out of the office of the *Call* on her way back to the ranch, when an elegant carriage pulled by four horses and with a footman and a driver had come rolling down the street, seemingly headed for the stagecoach station.

Riding in the open carriage was Anne Fenwick, dressed in a mauve traveling dress with matching hat and holding a parasol against the sun. Beside her was Timothy O'Callahan in black morning coat, white shirt with stiff collar, bow tie, and patterned silk waistcoat. When he stepped down from the carriage in front of the state line office, Hope saw that he was also wearing gray striped trousers.

"Oh Lord, Timmy lad," she muttered to herself. "What has she done to you?"

They obviously were heading east, just as Nate had heard, and would be getting married there. It was unlikely that Hope would ever see Tim again.

What difference does it make? she asked herself as she lay beside Jebel and watched the moon set. She had her husband, he was on his way to greatness, and she would be beside him, exercising power for the good of the people of their state. She didn't need anything else! She didn't! Let Anne have Tim; she'd had him in everything but name for almost two years.

The sound of a horse approaching at a gallop brought Hope straight up in bed and caused Jebel to stir. Before it stopped at their door, she was up and into a robe.

Booted feet strode across the porch and then a fist was pounding at the door.

"Congressman Mason! Miss Hope! Wake up!" the horseman was shouting. "There's trouble! A whole mess of trouble! A trainload of gunmen pulled into Johnson County from Cheyenne! We been invaded! Nate Champion and another man have been murdered, and all hell is breaking loose!"

Chapter 26

NATE CHAMPION DEAD? She should have known that would happen, Hope thought as she took down a rifle and a shotgun from the rack in the bedroom, handed the shotgun to Jebel, and expertly flipped a cartridge into the chamber of the Winchester. That had been coming ever since Nate, Tisdale, and Ranger Jones had decided to found the Northern Wyoming Farmers' and Stockmen's Association and announced there would be a roundup independent of, and preceding, the Stock Growers Association event.

The trouble between Powder River people and those in the south had always been over one thing—that pesky little critter called the maverick and who was going to get first chance to put their brand on him.

Before the new maverick law had passed through the territorial legislature during the last days before Wyoming was granted statehood, the small outfits had been allowed to work the strays along with the barons and had occasionally gotten their fair share. After the law was passed, only the major spreads were to get the mavericks, the rationale being that most of the calves were offspring of their cows. The small cattle ranchers of the north would soon have gone out of business at that rate, and they had taken to branding anything they found, which resulted in increased shouts from the south that nothing but rustlers lived in Johnson County.

Hope knew of at least two previous attempts by the barons, or their hired guns, to kill Champion, and of course Tisdale and Ranger Jones had both been bushwhacked, ostensibly over personal grudges. Everybody in the county, however, including Sheriff Red Angus and Justice of the Peach Hope Cox Mason, knew it had been done by Fred Hesse and Frank Canton, who had fled to the protection of their friends in Cheyenne. Now it appeared that the Stock Growers Association was making a concentrated effort to wipe out the small ranchers and farmers. Edgar Potter had told Hope that the association had a list of people in Johnson County they wanted out of the way. Champion had certainly been at the top of that list, and now he was dead. An invasion of gunmen from the south could only mean they were now ready to dispose of the rest of those who opposed them.

It had seemed that the ballot had won the day when Jebel had been elected to Congress and she had become justice of the peace, but now it looked as though bullets would decide the issue after all. Well, Johnson County was armed and ready.

None of this came as a surprise. Hope had known that the Stock Growers Association, which had ruled the territory before Wyoming became a state, would not give in to democracy and depart peacefully.

What she didn't know was that twenty Texas gunfighters had been brought in on a special train made up to transport fifty heavily armed men and their horses from Cheyenne to Casper. From Casper, the invaders planned to fan out across the upper part of the state to "liquidate all the rustlers in Wyoming along with their local supporters." The expedition had been held up briefly by the refusal of Horace G. Burt, a railroad manager, who had told the association leaders, "This railroad will have nothing to do with an expedition of this kind, nor will I, and my advice to you gentlemen is to drop what amounts to an insurrection that even the present administration in Washington won't be able to ignore."

But the men who ran the association claimed that the insurrection was in Johnson County, where people dared to defy them, the natural leaders of Wyoming; that it must be put down and no railroad official was going to stand in the way by refusing them access to his track. So the cattle barons had circumvented Burt's objections and his portion of the railroad system and had moved their special train—curtains drawn, lights darkened, and armed guards on the coal tender and caboose—without his help.

"About five-thirty we pulled out," Dr. Penrose, a physician who accompanied the expedition wrote later, "none but the initiated knowing that such an expedition had left Cheyenne. For days, the bustle of preparation had been going on in the yards, the branding of horses, stowing of gear and loading of wagons, while uptown the gun store favored with the patronage of the Stock Association members had been doing a land office business."

The landing and departure of the "special" hadn't been nearly as secret as the association members had assumed. There was hardly anyone in Cheyenne who didn't know that something was brewing and those with any knowledge of recent events knew what it was. Several politicians with sympathies or connections in the northern part of the state had become aware of what was about to take place and had hired a messenger to ride to Buffalo. Miss Violet Mechin, schoolteacher and women's vote advocate, after talking to several of the larger boys in her classes, had put on a neat little bonnet and hurried downtown to the telegraph office.

"I want to send a telegram to Justice of the Peace Mason in Buffalo," she announced.

But while the clerk was taking the message, the manager, shifting his cigar from one side of his mouth to the other and jingling association cartwheels in his pocket, stepped in, took the paper away, and crumpled it up.

"Sorry, Miss Mechin," he said. "All lines are down north of Casper."

"How can that be, Mr. Bowder?" she demanded.

"Wind and snowstorms," he said.

"In April?"

"In April," he said, knowing that by the time anyone got around to checking, the lines would be down, because teams of association cowboys had been sent out to throw ropes around the poles and pull them down with teams of horses as fast as the telegraph linemen could put them up.

The train arrived at the outskirts of Casper in the dark at four o'clock in the morning of April 6. The horses were led off, each man picking out his own and galloping away, except for the few who stayed behind to unload the wagons of supplies and weapons taken along to arm the hundred or so supporters who were expected to rise up and join the invasion in Johnson County itself. That expectation was to prove to be an error of judgment.

As Hope was dressing, she remembered she had asked Edgar if her name was on the association death list. He had told her that in the West men did not kill women, and she had laughed and reminded him of Ella Watson.

Pulling chaps on over her divided riding skirt, setting a Stetson on her head, and strapping a six-gun around her waist, she thought again of how she had tricked Potter into obtaining eight hundred dollars of association funds so she could buy the *Powder River Call* and use that newspaper against them. That in itself was enough for them to want her dead, that and the fact that she had been largely instrumental in running Frank Canton and Fred Hesse out of Johnson County by pointing them out as the killers of Ranger Jones and John Tisdale.

"This is revolution," Hope had said then. "They'll kill anyone they want to and worry about explaining or covering up later."

And now it had come, and there was a man on her front porch babbling excitedly about the invasion of Johnson County.

"Easy, easy, Bill," Jebel was saying to Bill Walker, an out-of-work cowhand who, along with a chuck-wagon cook named Ben Jones, had been trapping along the Yellowstone to get through the winter and had only recently come south to sell his pelts. "Just tell us what happened."

"There must have been sixty or seventy of them, all armed to the teeth," Walker said. "Ben and I laid over for the night at the KC, where Nate Champion and Nick Ray, who works for him, gave us grub."

"Who were the armed men?" Hope interrupted, although she thought she already knew.

"Stock Association ranch owners, range detectives, and hired guns from down Texas way. Major Wolcott and Frank Canton are in command, with Tom Smith leading the Texans."

"What happened after the men came?" Jebel asked, fingering the revolver in his holster. As a United States congressman, he was as involved in this as anyone else in Johnson County.

"It was morning, and Ben went out to get water to make coffee. Nate and Nick Ray were still asleep, and Ben didn't come back. He's an old man so I went to look for him, and just as I got down by the barn, half a dozen Winchesters were poked in my face and Major Wolcott started yelling at me, asking who I was and what I was doing at that nest of rustlers, the KC. I didn't know what to say so I told them that Ben and I were freighters who had stopped overnight and didn't know nothing about no rustlers. I think the major was going to order us shot—they already had Ben tied up—but Smith and a couple of the young fellows, the hired Texans, spoke up and said we weren't on the shooting list, so Wolcott said we was to hang around—that we weren't to go anywhere until it was all over."

"Then what?"

"We heard them talking about how they was going to wipe out all the rustlers in Johnson County and end the trouble once and for all," he said. "And pretty soon, Nick, he came out of the house and started down toward the barn. He had gone 'bout twenty paces when a dozen men must of opened fire and he fell. He should of been dead, but somehow he managed to crawl up to the porch of the house. Nate Champion opened the door and blazed away at the gunmen in and around the barn, then dragged him inside."

"And then?" Hope prodded impatiently when the man paused for breath.

"Why, all of them started blazing away at poor Nate, trapped in that log house of his. There must have been thirty or forty Winchesters firing steadily, with him taking a potshot back at them now and then. Pretty soon the invaders realized they couldn't get him that way and sent men off for dynamite. About that time, a man and a boy came along the road in a buckboard and someone shouted that it was Jack Flagg and his kid and that Jack was wanted along with Nate and the others. Several of them went for him and Flagg managed to get his buckboard turned around and raced off. They gave chase and came back with his buckboard, but not him or the kid."

"The first thing I had better do," Jebel said, "is go into town and get off a message to the governor asking for troops. It sounds like they intend to kill every man in the county if they get half a chance."

"You won't get any state troops," Hope said, and remembered that the Sixth U.S. Cavalry under Colonel Van Horn had recently returned to Fort McKinney, to the cheers of the people of Johnson County. The relationship between the troops and the inhabitants had always been warm and friendly, and she wondered if they would be willing to help under the circumstances.

"I'll ask for troops as a U.S. congressman and as the nominee of the Democratic party for governor," Jebel said.

"You won't get them, but Company C, under Captain Menardi, is stationed in the Buffalo area. As justice of the peace, and with the agreement of Sheriff Angus, I can order them out to support the civil authorities."

"Them fellows is headed right for Buffalo," Bill Walker said. "Heard 'em talking about it. First thing they gonna do is seize the courthouse and the militia's arms stored there."

"Call Juan to get our horses," Hope said. "We better get into town." She turned back to Walker. "What about Nate?"

"They burned him out, using that Flagg fellow's wagon

to set the cabin on fire. He burst out of the building running like hell with his Winchester in his hand, but he didn't get far. Half a dozen slugs was pumped into him before he got more than a hundred feet from his burning house."

Juan came running with the horses and Hope leaped into the saddle. "Let's get into Buffalo, wake up Red Angus, and rouse the county before it's too late."

"After they got through with Nate, they all piled into wagons and left," Walker said. "I got away, took Ben to the closest ranch, and came on to alert you folks."

Jebel was in his saddle only a second behind Hope.

"Keep going, Bill," she shouted as they rode off. "Ride to the other ranches! Tell the men to get their guns and come into Buffalo! Those who don't have guns, ride anyway! I'm going to call out the militia!"

It was a thirty-five-minute ride into Buffalo over roads turned to mush by April storms. Hope and Jebel made it in twenty minutes flat but found others had preceded them.

Jack Flagg and his son, whom Bill Walker had seen fleeing from association gunmen, had not been killed, as Bill had assumed. Flagg had abandoned his wagon, cut loose one of the horses, and ridden into town to spread the alarm. Nor had he been the only one. Shooting on the scale that had accompanied the murders of Nate Champion and Nick Ray was bound to attract attention, and a neighboring rancher, Jeff Smith, had witnessed the events at the KC from a nearby hill and also ridden for help.

Sheriff Red Angus and a posse of ten men were already mounted when Hope and Jebel arrived.

"Heard there's trouble at the KC," the big, freckle-faced, redheaded sheriff told them. "Going to ride out and see. Something about invaders from down south."

"You'll need more men than that," Hope said as Jebel rushed to the telegraph office to get off a message asking for state troops. "There must be fifty or sixty armed men headed for Buffalo right now."

"I asked the captain here for troops," Red Angus said, nodding toward Captain Menardi of Company C, Wyoming

National Guard. "He says he can't do it."

Hope turned to the dark-haired young man. "What's this?"

"Direct orders from Cheyenne," Menardi said. "Governor says no troops are to be turned out without his direct orders."

"To hell with that," Red Angus said. "There's been murders committed in this county and it's my duty to arrest the murderers. Come on, boys, let's ride!"

Jebel came hurrying from the telegraph office. "The wires have been cut. We're out of communication with Cheyenne, Casper, and Denver."

"I guess we should have expected that," Hope said. "But it wouldn't have done any good to ask the acting governor for state troopers anyway. He's in the pay of the Stock Growers Association too." She turned to the steadily growing crowd around them. "What we have to do, boys, is elect our own governor, and he's standing right here beside me—Congressman Jebel Mason!"

"That's fine for next year," someone shouted, "but what about now?"

"Well, for now there are fifty or sixty invaders marching on Buffalo, and probably another fifty locals who support the Cheyenne Ring will join them before they get here. So for now, we got to fight."

"They're all armed to the teeth," Jack Flagg said. "I got two bullet holes in my coat and my boy has a graze on his arm. Where we gonna get guns?"

"I have an idea," Hope said. "Come on, let's open up the courthouse. I'm going to convene court right now."

"What for? This ain't no time to issue injunctions," the mayor said.

"Come along and I'll show you," Hope said, hurrying on ahead, boots thumping along the boardwalk.

As soon as the doors of the courtroom where she presided as justice of the peace of Johnson County were opened, she pulled on her judicial robe over her riding skirt and chaps and began pounding her gavel. "This court is now in session, sitting on the subject of the state of insurrection that is known to exist in Johnson County. This court is convened for the purpose of calling on the state military to join with the court in putting down said insurrection."

A gasp went up from the packed room, and Captain Menardi started to protest. Ben James, a lawyer known to represent some members of the association, also objected, saying, "I have not seen any insurrection, Justice Mason."

"I have the governor's orders," Menardi insisted.

"I am now calling witnesses to the state of insurrection. Jack Flagg, Billy Flagg, Jeff Smith, and Bill Walker will please step forward and be sworn in. Are they in court, Marshal Malder?"

Bill Malder stepped up front and called out the names while the court clerk hurriedly pulled on his coat and went for the Bible to swear them in.

"Do you, Jack Flagg, swear to tell the truth, the whole truth, and nothing but the truth?"

"I do."

"Did you observe an armed insurrection in process in the vicinity of the KC ranch? Did you see two citizens of this county murdered? Were you and your son set upon by the same insurrectionaries?" Hope rapped out the questions staccato fashion.

"Yes, and yes," Jack Flagg replied, and the other three answered just as quickly and decisively, as they began to understand what she was about.

"All right," Hope said, pounding her gavel. "This court finds that a state of insurrection exists in Johnson County and orders that the militia be summoned to support the civil authorities as set forth in the Constitution of the State of Wyoming."

A whoop went up from the crowd, and Hope turned to Captain Menardi. "As Commander of Company C of the Wyoming National Guard, you are hereby ordered, Captain Menardi, to support the civil authority as represented by Sheriff Angus with all the force at your command."

"But I have the governor's orders," Menardi said again.

"Are you in contempt of this court, Captain?" Hope asked.

"No, ma'am—your honor."

"Then call out your men and enlist the men in this room, pass out weapons, and stand ready to defend Buffalo against the invaders and insurrectionaries."

"But there are no insurrectionaries," the captain said. "Those are some of the leading ranchers of this state."

"They are in arms against the constituted authority of this county and have murdered at least two citizens thereof," Hope said firmly. "It does not matter what their social status is. Jefferson Davis and Robert E. Lee were gentlemen of the first order but they were insurrectionaries and the United States Army was ordered to put them down. I so order the Wyoming National Guard to put down this insurrection."

"All right, boys," Menardi said, taking the keys to the Guard armory in the basement of the courthouse out of his pocket. "Come and get your guns and sign the articles of war and you're enlisted."

Another whoop went up and most of the spectators tramped out of the courtroom on the captain's heels. Hope turned to the court clerk and the marshal. "Is the telegraph still operating between here and Fort McKinney?"

The manager of the telegraph office answered. "It was, last we heard. The military telegraph officer signaled that they were waiting for a message from Governor Barber."

Hope grimaced. "Has the message come through?"

"It just did, your honor," the man said, handing her a telegraph form.

Hope took it and quickly scanned its contents.

AN INSURRECTION EXISTS IN JOHNSON COUNTY IN THE STATE OF WYOMING, IN THE IMMEDIATE VICINITY OF FORT MCKINNEY, AGAINST THE GOVERNMENT OF SAID STATE. THE LEGISLATURE IS NOT IN SESSION AND CANNOT BE CONVENED IN TIME TO AFFORD ANY RELIEF WHATEVER OR TO TAKE ANY ACTION THEREON. OPEN HOSTILITIES EXIST AND LARGE BODIES OF ARMED MEN ARE ENGAGED IN BATTLE. A COMPANY OF THE STATE MILITIA IS LOCATED AT THE CITY OF BUFFALO NEAR THE SCENE OF SAID ACTION BUT ITS CONTINUED PRESENCE IN THE CITY IS ABSOLUTELY REQUIRED FOR THE

PURPOSE OF PROTECTING LIFE AND PROPERTY THEREIN. THE SCENE OF ACTION IS 125 MILES FROM THE NEAREST RAILROAD POINT FROM WHICH OTHER PORTIONS OF THE STATE MILITIA COULD BE SENT. NO RELIEF CAN BE AFFORDED BY STATE MILITIA AND THE CIVIL AUTHORITIES ARE WHOLLY UNABLE TO AFFORD ANY RELIEF WHATEVER. UNITED STATES TROOPS ARE LOCATED AT FORT MCKINNEY, WHICH IS THIRTEEN MILES FROM THE SCENE OF ACTION, WHICH IS KNOWN AS THE TA RANCH. I APPLY TO YOU ON BEHALF OF THE STATE OF WYOMING TO DIRECT THE UNITED STATES TROOPS AT FORT MCKINNEY TO ASSIST IN SUPPRESSING THIS INSURRECTION. LIVES OF A LARGE NUMBER OF PERSONS ARE IN IMMINENT DANGER.

AMOS W. BARBER, ACTING GOVERNOR

The telegram was addressed to President Benjamin Harrison with a copy to Colonel Van Horn.

Hope pondered the situation. So the invaders were at the TA ranch. That figured, since the TA was a large spread owned by a supporter of the association. They were probably waiting there for reinforcements, and Sheriff Angus was probably nearby keeping an eye on them. Barber was obviously trying to arrange for federal troops to support the invaders, and Harrison might give such an order, since he was a notorious partisan of big business, East or West. But suppose the telegram didn't get through to Colonel Van Horn and he heard the truth of the matter from another source? The officers and men of the 6th U.S. Cavalry had an excellent relationship with the people of Johnson County. Several officers and dozens of men were courting local girls. She doubted that Colonel Van Horn would be fooled by the acting governor's message to President Harrison, but the War Department might be. Just to be on the safe side, it might be better if the telegram didn't get through.

"You know, Sam," she said to the telegraph office manager, "just before we came in here, a fellow came riding into town and said the telegraph between here and Fort McKinney was down. He saw some men throw a lasso over the lines and pull with their horses until two poles and both lines went down. I think what I'll do is send this message along with one I'm going to write by courier to the fort."

"Whatever you say, your honor," the manager said, giving no indication he knew she had made up the story on the spot.

Hope nodded and went to her judge's bench for a sheet of court paper. On it she wrote:

> Franklin Van Horn, Colonel Commanding 6th United States Cavalry.
>
> Dear Colonel Van Horn,
>
> This is to inform you that a state of insurrection has broken out in Johnson County following the invasion of fifty to sixty armed revolutionaries...

She paused and thought about that last word. Yes, it was a good description, despite the fact that the people involved were among the richest in the state.

> ...and conspirators with the intention of overthrowing the existing civil authority of this county. A state of siege has been declared by Justice of the Peace Hope Cox Mason. We the undersigned urge you to dispatch troops to the aid of the civil authorities in repelling and bringing to justice the invading revolutionaries.
>
> Hope Cox Mason, Justice of the Peace
> Charles I. Hogerson, Mayor, Buffalo Township
> Red Angus, Sheriff, Johnson County
> Jebel Mason, United States Congressman

When the document had been signed by all except Red Angus, who was off with the posse, Hope signed it herself and affixed the county seal to it. Then she asked Jack Flagg to carry the message to Fort McKinney.

"What about that other message?" he asked. "The one from the governor?"

"I think this one will be enough. We don't want anyone to get confused by hearing two sides of what is a very simple matter . . . armed insurrection." Flagg grinned, nodded, and hurried off with the message for Fort McKinney.

"Now, boys, let's get going and join Sheriff Angus down at the TA ranch," Hope said.

A wild cheer went up from the forty to fifty heavily armed men gathered around the court house.

"I think I had better take command in the field, my dear," Jebel said. "You stay here in Buffalo, send on reinforcements, and wait for news from the fort and Cheyenne."

Hope shook her head. "Red Angus will give the orders for the actual fighting," she said. Angus wasn't much of a leader for a desperate affair like this, but they had no one else to depend on now that Nate Champion was dead. "I think you should stay here and represent the authority of the U.S. government as far as Fort McKinney is concerned."

"Does anyone really have to do that?" Jebel asked.

"He does if he wants to be elected governor of Wyoming next year," she said. "You've got to be in the public eye. You've got to be here when the representatives of the press start arriving. *You* have to be the one who makes the announcement that the people of Johnson County are resisting armed invasion in the spirit of the Minutemen of Concord and Lexington."

"Aren't you making a little much of this, Hope?" Jebel asked.

"Hell, no! This is war! War to the death, but it is also politics. If they win, we all better run for it. If we win, we'll win the election next year and they had better run. You're our candidate, and you have to be in all the headlines as the hero of Buffalo."

"While you go off and do the actual fighting," Jebel grumbled. "That makes me some hero."

"Did Robert E. Lee personally lead the charge at Gettysburg or did Pickett?" Hope asked. "You're the commander in chief. I—Red Angus is the field commander."

"But you're my wife, not my field commander."

"Maybe, but you're still the commander in chief and, like Grant after the war, you're going to get the credit and the votes for it," she told him.

Reluctantly, Jebel agreed to stay behind in Buffalo and do the organizing and political work while Hope rode off with seventy men to reinforce the sheriff and his posse at the TA ranch.

When she arrived, Hope found that her estimation of Red Angus as a leader of men had been close to the mark. He had ridden up with his ten-man posse in full daylight and been greeted by overwhelming fire from the main house of the ranch. Apparently fifty to sixty men were barricaded inside while another group occupied the bunkhouse and barn. Several of Angus's men had been wounded; he was pinned down by heavy fire and mighty glad to see reinforcements. Unfortunately, the arrival of the force from Buffalo didn't help much at first, because the panic that had seized the posse now spread to the new arrivals.

"Stand your ground, boys! Stand your ground!" Hope shouted, emptying her Winchester in the direction of the smoke-obscured TA bunkhouse. "We have them outnumbered!"

"Yeah, but they got us outgunned and they're professionals," one of the deputies said loud enough for everyone to hear, and no rebuke came from Angus, who was sitting with his back to a tree shoving bullets, one by one, into his six-shooter.

Hope was beginning to regret her decision to leave Jebel in Buffalo. She knew what should be done, but would they listen to a woman when it came down to guns and sudden death?

"Spread out, boys, and keep your heads down!" she shouted as a volley of slugs tore through the trees and spattered off nearby rocks, and she hit the dust behind a felled log.

Almost all the firing was coming from the ranch. Her men had scattered and were staying low—too low. They weren't shooting back; they were just protecting their hides. If the men at the TA decided to make a sortie, they would break through the thin lines Angus had stretched around the buildings with ease.

"I think they're getting ready to counterattack," Bill Wandering said. "Look at that wagon over there between the house and the bunkhouse. They've turned it into a moving fort with logs and bags of sand. If they push that toward us, we'll never be able to stop it."

"Sure you will! We've got 'em outnumbered!" Hope yelled.

"YOU OUT THERE! SHERIFF ANGUS, THIS IS MAJOR WOLCOTT," a voice bellowed through a megaphone. "I HAVE SEVENTY MEN HERE AND WE EXPECT LARGE REINFORCEMENTS WITHIN THE NEXT HOUR FROM THE LOCAL RANCHES. DISBAND YOUR MEN AND LEAVE THE AREA AT ONCE!"

"You go to hell!" Angus shouted back, but gave no orders to see that they did.

"I think they're getting ready to rush us," Bill Wandering said, and the fire from the house and bunkhouse doubled in intensity. Two men cried out and fell, wounded.

"Here they come . . . here they come!" yelled one of the farmers who had joined the Johnson County force. Hope saw other men along the line start to drift away toward the rear, where the horses were being held.

"There are riders coming along the river road," Menardi reported. "I think they're from Sussex Ranch."

That would be the final blow, Hope thought. If the Sussex forces, who had remained aloof until now, allied themselves with the invasion, all was lost.

"They're attacking from the house!" Angus yelled, standing up and emptying his gun at a line of men who had appeared behind the wagon being pushed in their direction.

"Pour it on, boys, pour it on!" Hope shouted, but her voice barely carried over the sound of firing. She could see that only a few of her men were responding. Most of the firing was coming from the house, and now also from the riders bursting through the woods and galloping down toward the battle.

Then she was seeing something she didn't believe possible, something she told herself was an illusion born of her need. She thought she saw a very tall, redheaded man on a black stallion, waving his hat with one hand and firing with the other at the association gunmen who were pouring out of the house. She thought she saw him leading twenty men she recognized as Seventy-six cowboys and all of them were shooting at the suddenly faltering invaders.

"Get 'em, lads, go get 'em!" shouted a voice that sounded like Tim O'Callahan's. But Timothy was in St. Louis by now, or even farther east, on his way to marry Anne Fenwick. He couldn't be here leading Seventy-six cowboys against the Cheyenne Ring's hired guns.

Red Angus had come to life and was rounding up those of the posse and the military who had started to retreat. "Hey, get back where you were! We got help now! Let's get those fellows!"

Even if she was imagining it, Hope took heart from what she saw. She stood behind her log and poured round after round from her Winchester into the house and the wagon that had been advancing but was now abandoned, the men scattering back toward the house.

Then a horse halted near her, a man leaped from it, and a brawny arm was wrapped around her, pulling her down behind the log just as a particularly heavy volley of fire from the bunkhouse whistled overhead.

"What are you doing here?" she blurted as a Seventy-six wrangler grabbed the reins of the black stallion and several other horses and led them toward the rear, while Sussex Ranch cowboys scattered among the besiegers of the TA.

"Who, me?" Timothy said, resting his rifle on the log. "Why, to be sure, me love, I'm shootin' at them varmints in the house over there."

"I know that. I mean what are you doing in Wyoming? I thought you had gone east. I saw you getting into the stage to go to Casper to catch the train to get married."

"No, you saw me taking Anne to catch the train," Tim said, sighting along the barrel of his Winchester and putting three slugs through the window of the bunkhouse, promptly silencing the firing from that end of the building.

"But you were all dressed up like a dude in—"

"In me Sunday-to-meetin' clothes," he said. "Well, poor Anne liked me to look like a brass monkey when I was with her, but no son of the Auld Sod could stand to do that more than a couple of times a year and none of them the anniversary of the Battle of the Boyne."

"Then you're not going to marry her?"

"Never had any intention of it," he said. "And she finally got tired of pesterin' me about it."

"Oh, Lord, Tim. I'm married to Jebel Mason."

"And would you be thinkin' I didn't know that? 'Twas in all the papers, includin' your own."

"Oh, what are we going to do? Poor Jebel. Poor, dear Jebel."

"Poor nothin'," Timothy said, looking only at the house, where gunfire was slacking off under the steady fire from those around it. "Why, the man's going to be the next governor of the sovereign state of Wyoming, and he's married to the most beautiful lass in the world. Poor, indeed."

"But she doesn't love him, Tim. His wife doesn't really love him because she gave her heart to someone else a long time ago."

"Well now . . ." His voice was unexpectedly husky. "Well now, I guess that's something it would be better not to talk about, don't you?"

"Yes . . . yes, I suppose so," she said, unable to see where she was firing through the tears welling up in her eyes.

An hour later Sheriff Angus went toward the house with a flag of truce and demanded that those inside throw down their arms and submit to arrest by an authorized posse and the militia of the county. The demand was answered by curses from Major Wolcott and a volley of bullets from the invaders' Winchesters.

Red Angus hurriedly withdrew to the lines, and the fire

was returned by a hundred rifles. The outsiders must have realized by then that the entire county was up in arms and they would get no reinforcements from the locals. All they could do was sit tight and hope for rescue from Cheyenne or Fort McKinney.

Hope was also waiting to see what Fort McKinney would do. Would the troops side with the invaders or with the authorities of the county, who had always supported the fort and befriended its occupants? She couldn't predict what would happen. She could only wait.

"I didn't expect you to be on our side," she said to Tim once during the afternoon.

"I always have been, haven't I?"

"But Mrs. Fenwick—"

"I'm running the Seventy-six now, and the boys do what I tell 'em. She backs me up from a distance."

"Then you and she . . ."

"No," he said. "Nothing except what I told you."

"Oh," she said, feeling strangely happy but saying no more about it.

The siege continued on through Monday night and into Tuesday morning.

"We're not going to smoke them out of there with rifle fire," Red Angus said. "The logs of that ranch house and barn are too damn thick."

Bill Walker nodded. "And they'll never run out of ammunition with all they brought with them."

Hope questioned Jack Flagg when he joined them after his trip to the fort. "How did it go?"

"They finally got a telegraph line open and the colonel got a message from Cheyenne that had been sent by the President to Governor Barber. I got a copy from the signal corps sergeant," he said and handed her a folded paper.

She opened it and read: "I have, in compliance with your call for the aid of the United States forces to protect the state of Wyoming against domestic violence, ordered the Secretary of War to concentrate a sufficient force at the scene of the disturbance and to cooperate with your authorities."

"What authorities?" Hope asked.

Flagg shrugged but told her Colonel Van Horn had sent a message in return that was clearer. It read, "Entire county is aroused by killings at the KC ranch, and some of the best citizens are in the posse."

"So we don't really know which way the army is going to go, do we?" Hope said to Tim and Red Angus. "I guess we'll just have to wait and see."

"If they don't show up at all, this is going to be a standoff," Tim said, "and in a standoff, we lose because all the ammo and supplies we have is what we brought with us while Wolcott has an endless amount of both."

"Perhaps we should send out riders to ask folks—"

"Yeah, let's ask them to bring wagons and anything that will burn," Angus said. "Maybe we can burn them out."

Hope was sick at the prospect, knowing there would be dozens of casualties on both sides, but to let the invaders win now would mean that the association would continue to control Wyoming in the future and the upcoming election would be an exercise in futility. She agreed to the project reluctantly and kept out of the way while Angus and Tim made the arrangements to carry it out.

Early the next morning, wagons were brought up to the lines around the TA. By then, perhaps two hundred and fifty enraged Powder River farmers and ranchers had joined with Red Angus's posse, all armed with guns from the armory or the gun store in Buffalo.

Around seven A.M., when it was light enough for an assault, it was decided to push the wagons, loaded with combustibles, into the walls of the TA buildings and storm them. Pushed by a score of men each, the wagons started rolling forward into the heavy fire coming from the target structures.

"Hold it! Hold it!" Jack Flagg yelled suddenly from his watch station on a nearby hill. "Cavalry coming!"

Seconds later a trumpet sounded and two troops of cavalry, led by Colonel Van Horn, came marching up the road, the Stars and Stripes flying in front.

The firing from both sides ceased at the appearance of the soldiers, and the Johnson County forces stood staring, not knowing whether to cheer or give up in despair.

Hope leaped up onto the log behind which she had been firing and waved her hat. "The cavalry is here, boys! Let's give them a cheer! They'll save our county from the outlaws! Cheer them, boys, cheer them!"

Tim stepped up on one side of her and Sheriff Angus on the other, both redheads yelling as though greeting the arrival of a gold train. "Hooray for the U.S. Cavalry! Hooray for the Sixth Regiment! Hooray for Colonel Van Horn!"

Timothy leaned over and whispered to Hope, "Sure now, and they'd be a sour bunch if they didn't side with us after that greetin'!"

A trumpet sounded and the troops fell into line. At a second trumpet call, Colonel Van Horn and two of his captains rode toward the TA with guidons and the Stars and Stripes whipping in the wind on either side of them.

There were a few moments of silence and then a head appeared above the breastworks in front of the ranch house. It was followed by a hand fanning the air with a soiled rag, and at almost the same instant a white cloth fluttered from the door of the barn.

"You will come out," Colonel Van Horn called, "and lay down your arms at once."

Major Wolcott came into view, strutting out on his short bantam legs. "I will surrender to you, but not to that woman," he shouted, indicating Hope. "Never! I know her well! Rather than give up to her, we will all die here!"

The colonel replied that he was now in command and the invaders would be held for trial in the courts of the state.

"They'll never be convicted," Tim said.

"It doesn't matter," Hope said, trying not to look at him. "They're through in Wyoming. Everyone will know what they tried to do and will vote for Jebel for governor next year."

"Yes, he'll be winnin'," Timothy said. "The people of Johnson County did their votin' today with their feet and their guns. Next June, I'm athinkin', they'll be voting along the same lines and maybe a lot of other folks in the state will be too."

"You do remember Jebel, don't you?" she asked.

"Sure do. Nice fellow," Tim said. "He'll make a good governor. But I always thought you were the one who was going to be governor of Wyoming someday."

She laughed. "That was just a silly little-girl notion. No, it is Jebel who will be governor, and I'll be content to be the governor's wife."

Tim kissed her quickly on the cheek and turned away to gather the Sussex cowboys for the ride back to the ranch.

"I'll vote for your husband, Hope," he said, as he waved goodbye, "but I'll really be voting for you."

Oh, Tim . . . Tim . . . Tim, she sobbed in her heart as he rode off.

Chapter 27

BUT, AS IT happened, Jebel Mason was never elected governor of the state of Wyoming, although he was the unanimous nominee of the Democratic party the year following the official end of the Powder River war. That war seemed to have ended at the TA ranch when the army had marched between fifty and sixty Cattle Stock Association invaders off to Fort McKinney and locked them up to keep them safe from the aroused people of Johnson County.

The state courts, however, were still in the hands of association appointees, and their kept judges and corrupt press had gone to work to free the prisoners. One by one, the ranchers, their foremen, the Cheyenne Ring "detectives," and, finally, the hired Texas gunmen were liberated. The Texans were returned to their home state, most of them swearing they would never get mixed up again in a situation they didn't understand and expressing more sympathy for Johnson County people than for their corrupt former employers.

The association had not received its death blow, but as

a political power its days were numbered. Most of the officers who had created the disastrous policies that led to the war were voted out of power in the organization, which then gradually reverted to its original purpose of protecting cattle ranchers—*all* cattle ranchers.

But the men who had caused all the trouble did not go away. They stayed on in Cheyenne to fight the bid for office of Jebel Mason, the hero of Johnson County, and some of them were still willing to fight in the old way.

And so one day in May of the following year, Congressman Jebel Mason approached the gate to the Lazy H ranch and got out of his wagon to open it. As he reached for the top bar, there was a blinding explosion that fatally injured both horses and killed Jebel.

When Hope came running from the house, with Pat limping along behind her and Chou Li trailing in the rear, Jebel was already dead. Hope knelt beside him, weeping for the man she had never loved enough.

Pat stood patting her head as he had done when she was a very young girl. "There, there, sweetheart, there, there."

Chou Li shook his head sadly and went to tell Juan, who saddled up and rode into town to bring Sheriff Angus.

"He was such a good man, Pap . . . such a good husband. And all I ever thought about was seeing that he got to be governor."

"That's what you both wanted," Pat said, lifting her to her feet as another storm of sobbing shook her. "Shhh, now, shhh."

She gradually quieted and then suddenly her grief turned to anger and she pushed away from him, her turquoise eyes flashing. "They did it, Pap! I know they did it! They couldn't stop him one way, so they did it another. They killed Jebel!"

Pat didn't try to answer; he knew she was right. The Cheyenne Ring had struck once again. In danger of losing their hold on the state, they had committed one more crime. But this time, he thought, they had gone too far. If caught, they wouldn't be tried in courts still packed with their bought-and-paid-for judges. They would be tried in the federal courts, and they might find those tougher for their corporation lawyers to sway with money and lies.

Jebel Mason was buried with full honors, accompanied to the grave by an honor guard from Fort McKinney. Hundreds of people came to pay their respects. Two days after the funeral, Hope had to make an important decision.

Three carriages pulled up in front of her house, and pale but dry-eyed, she opened the door to greet the important gentlemen who had come to see her.

William H. Bright, the former saloonkeeper from South Pass who had pushed for the women's franchise amendment and was now a power in the Democratic party, spoke first.

"We have reconvened the nominating convention, Mrs. Mason. They are only waiting for word from you to substitute your name for Jebel's as our candidate for governor."

She wanted to tell them she couldn't do it. The guilt she felt because she had married Jebel without really loving him was made worse by the fact that it was she who had urged him to go into politics, to run for the office of governor; and that had led directly to his death.

"Miss Hope," Sheriff Angus said, "you know as well as I do who did in Mr. Jeb. You also know that if the opposition is elected, the Cheyenne Ring is going to have another four years to cover up that crime like they did the rest of their murders."

"This trial will be in the federal courts," Hope said tiredly. "This time it will be different."

"Will it?" Jack Flagg asked. "No one has even been arrested yet."

"The *Cheyenne Sun* is saying it was done by anarchists like the ones over in Europe," Red Angus said. "But I hear that a special federal marshal has been appointed to investigate on the suggestion of Colonel Van Horn."

"It won't make any difference what they find out or what happens at the trial," Bright said. "Some flunkey of the association will take the blame and the rest will be clear of it. We can beat them only if we win the election, and there is only one person in the state who could be elected—and that one person is justice of the peace of Johnson County, the widow of the late nominee, Hope Cox Mason!"

For the first time since Jebel's death, Hope almost smiled. Bright sounded as though he was making the nomination speech already. Still she hesitated. She had lost some of her enthusiasm for politics now that Jebel was dead. She only wanted to run her ranch and her newspaper. Maybe someday, when she could forgive herself, she would . . .

Two people who had been standing at the rear of the group, almost hidden by the men, now began to push to the fore. Hope was astonished to recognize Amy Andrews, who had recently lost her husband of more than fifty years, and Violet Mechin, the schoolteacher who had never married.

"Hope honey," Amy said, "I guess you don't remember how we felt that day when with the help of Mr. Bright and Mr. Lee we women got to keep the vote."

"Of course I do," Hope said, giving the elderly woman a hug. "I remember it very well."

"Well, Hope, we now have a chance to do something with that vote," Violet said. "We can vote in honest government in the form of a woman governor."

"Now, Madam Governor, are you going to turn your back on that?" Bright asked.

"No—no, I'm not," Hope said. "I will run if nominated and do my best to take my late husband's place."

The solemn faces and serious voices of the visitors dissolved into happy shouts and cheers.

"Hooray! Hip, hip, hooray!" Chow Li joined in the celebration, pounding on a frying pan. "Missy be governor and then president and Chou Li be citizen!"

"No, not president, Chou Li, just governor, but you certainly are going to be a citizen or I'll know the reason why," Hope said, and she hugged him, her father, and Juan before turning back to Bright and the two women who had come to show her the way.

"What do we do now, Mr. Bright?" she asked.

"I'll reconvene the convention and your name will be the only one presented in nomination and voted on. You'll make an acceptance speech and we'll start getting ready for the general election in November. Then we're going to run the last remnants of the Cheyenne Ring out of the Equality state of Wyoming."

"I'll be there," Hope promised. "I'll be there, as Jebel would have wanted me to be." What a shocking hypocrite I am, she thought. While he was alive I never gave much thought to what Jebel wanted. I don't think I'll ever forgive myself until his killers are brought to justice, and if I have to become governor—or secretary of the army—to do it, that's what I'll have to do.

After they had all drunk a glass of the champagne Bright had brought with him to show how sure he was of Hope's answer and the guests had departed, Hope sat down on the front steps. Pat rocked back and forth in the chair he seemed to spend so much time in lately. "We've come a long way, gal," he said.

"And we've got a long way to go, Pap. A long, hard way to victory."

She found out just how hard when she arrived in Cheyenne three days later for the convention and was met at the coach terminal by a process server, who handed her a summons.

"What's this?" she asked.

"That's a summons to appear as the defendant in an alienation-of-affections suit."

"A *what?*"

"An alienation-of-affections suit brought by Mrs. Mabel Potter," the man said with a sly smile.

Hope blindly shoved the paper into her pocket and went on toward the building where the nomination would take place, feeling as though she had been hit very hard. What should she do? She would have to tell the committee before the nomination. A woman accused of having stolen the affections of another woman's husband couldn't be elected president of a garden club, much less governor of a state.

She was still asking herself what she should do when she passed the Cheyenne Club and it suddenly occurred to her that the summons had come from there, just like most of the other problems that had shaken the territory and state of Wyoming the last few years. She turned her head to glare at the building and caught sight of a man she hadn't seen for several years standing on the veranda that swept around all four sides of the magnificent structure: the man who had murdered Gene Crowder and the other witnesses of the lynching of Jim Averell and Ella Watson—and now her husband.

That settled it, she thought, as she continued on her way. She had to become governor, no matter what. The subpoena could wait until after the nomination was hers.

She faced the three dozen men and three women who made up the nominating committee and told them how she felt. "My husband was murdered because he was a threat to the wielders of power in this state. I want to tell them very clearly, to give them fair warning, that I pose even more of a threat; that I intend not only to drive them from their places of power but also to see that many of them rot in jail for the rest of their lives or dangle from a scaffold for the crimes they have committed."

The convention voted twenty-nine to ten to give her the nomination.

The *Cheyenne Sun* reacted to her speech with a headline: "HOPE COX MASON THREATENS LYNCH LAW IN WYOMING. Firebrand From Johnson County Will Introduce Powder River Justice to Rest of State."

"Well, that certainly lost something in the translation, didn't it?" Violet Mechin said to Hope.

"That's about the standard for the press in this city," Hope said.

"Well I suppose he who pays the piper calls the tune," Violet said.

"What I'm worried about is what they're going to make of this," Hope said, handing her the summons.

Violet read it and looked at her aghast. "Oh my God, Hope! You didn't, did you?"

"Let's say I led him on. I couldn't have alienated his affections, since he hasn't any except for himself, but in order to strike a blow against the association, I let him think he was going to get what he wanted. I suppose that wasn't very ethical, but I felt the end justified the means."

Violet shrugged. "I doubt there's a woman in Cheyenne who hasn't been approached by Edgar Potter with the same thing in mind," she said, and Hope made a sound of surprise as she realized that her quiet friend must have been the target of one of the minister's campaigns.

"Hope, how do you suppose Mabel found out about you and the reverend?"

"He told her, of course. He told her and ordered her to bring suit against me. And he was ordered to do it by the Stock Growers in their effort to prevent my election."

After considering that for a minute, Violet nodded. "Yes, you must be right. A mouse like Mabel would never turn on her tormentor."

"This move could really hurt me, Violet. I cannot in all honesty stand up in court and deny that I led Potter on, and I'm sure a Cheyenne jury would not approve my motives."

"No, but at least it's a peaceful attack. Maybe it means they won't try to kill you now, or after you're elected."

"*If* I'm elected. This could make the voters turn their backs on me in droves."

"I doubt it. I really do. Too many people know what Potter is like."

"The people who know what Potter is like don't care," Hope said. "They own and operate him. And I question whether their approach will remain peaceful."

"Why?"

"Because I think I saw my assassin standing on the veranda of the Cheyenne Club."

"Your assassin?"

"George B. Henderson, the ring's top hired killer. He's the one who set up the lynching of Jim and Ella, killed the witnesses to it, and was probably implicated with Fred Hesse and Frank Canton in the murders of Ranger Jones and John Tisdale. There is nothing to connect him to Jebel's death, but he is supposed to be an expert with dynamite."

"Oh, Hope, no!" Violet was truly alarmed. "You've got to have protection!"

"I don't know who could provide it. There's only one

man Henderson is afraid of, and there are reasons he might not want to guard me."

"Nevertheless, something has to be done," Violet said. "Perhaps we could appeal to the city authorities. Wasn't poor Jebel's murder a federal offense? Didn't I hear that a special U.S. marshal was assigned to investigate it?"

"Yes, but no one has seen hide nor hair of him, or even knows who he is. He hasn't made his presence known at all, and, Violet, when I looked into George Henderson's eyes, they glittered like a copperhead's."

Someone tried to kill Hope as she was stepping out of her carriage on her way to a ball given by the Women's Democratic Club the next evening. The only thing that saved her was Juan's quick action in pushing her aside when he caught the reflection of gaslight off the barrel of a rifle just before it was fired.

"Henderson, without a doubt," Pat Cox said, pulling his old Dragoon pistol out of the holster that was partly hidden under the dress coat he had worn to the affair. "I'm going to kill that man."

"You may not have to," Violet said. "Mrs. Henry Houston, the wife of the justice of the peace for this county, told me in the strictest confidence that the federal marshal has arrived with a warrant for Henderson's arrest."

"Does he have a troop of federal cavalry with him?" Juan asked. "If not, he'll probably be dead before Miss Hope."

"I'd be dead right now if it hadn't been for you, *mi caballero,*" Hope said. "If you hadn't insisted on driving us yourself—"

"It is *nada, señorita,*" the young Mexican said. "You have helped me too many times in the past."

Later that evening, Hope decided to break the news to her supporters about the Potter suit. She did it in a private room off the ballroom, while the orchestra played "The Blue Danube" and men more used to boots than dancing slippers guided young women more used to gingham than silk dresses about the floor.

"What is it, Hope?" Jack Flagg asked when the door was

shut, cutting off the sounds of music and laughter.

"Someone tried to kill her as we came in," Pat said, "George Henderson, we think."

"My Lord," Bright said, looking around at the committee members. "This may come down to bullets instead of ballots after all."

"We've got guns too," another man said. "And we're not going to wait for them to pick us off one at a time."

"No, no, please, not that," Hope pleaded. "Besides, there's a more immediate obstacle standing in the way of my election."

"What's that?" Bright demanded.

Hope took a deep breath and looked at them each in turn as she said, "I'm being sued by Mabel Potter, the wife of the Reverend Edgar Potter of this city, for alienation of affections."

"It's a low-down dirty trick," Pat said.

"Of course it is," Juan said. "Señorita, I will testify that man never set foot on Lazy H."

"But you know he did, Juan," Hope said.

"Of course it's a trick," Flagg said. "We'll go to court and have it thrown out for lack of evidence."

"Here they own the courts," Bright reminded him. "We need another way out of this."

"The suit is intended to prevent my election, and it will easily accomplish that. The story will be in the *Sun* and the *Telegraph* and they are both association papers. They will play up the implication of the suit, which is that I committed adultery. And a woman accused of adultery couldn't be elected dogcatcher in this or any other state of the union."

"That's ridiculous," Bright argued. "It won't stand up for a minute. That worm Potter is after every woman who crosses his path. Why would his wife speak up now?"

"Because he ordered her to. And they can make it stand up. Mabel's chief witness will be her husband, and his testimony will be true as far as the actual charge of alienation of affections is concerned. I did lead the man on in hopes of getting information that would help our fight against the ring, but the implication will go far beyond his true testimony. It will be hinted and strongly suggested that I was actually intimate with that creature. And knowing his reputation with the women of Cheyenne, even an unprejudiced jury, if we can get one, will believe Potter."

"*Díos,* I will kill him!" Juan growled.

"We're beaten. Goddamnit, they found a way to beat us!" Jack Flagg said. "The only thing to do is avoid trial. When does it come up?"

"In two weeks," Hope said, "that is, if George Henderson doesn't kill me first."

But the next morning there was a new development. As though by magic, MAN WANTED posters appeared on strategically placed poles around Cheyenne offering a thousand-dollar reward for the capture of George B. Henderson, wanted by the federal government for the murder of Jebel Mason, U.S. Congressman from the 10th District of Wyoming.

"Good Lord, I didn't expect them to move so fast," Jack Flagg said.

"Chester Arthur is president now, and he's confounding the thieves and scoundrels who put him in office by his zeal for reform," Bright said. "This is probably the result of that."

"But will it make any real difference?" Violet Mechin asked. "This morning when I walked by the Cheyenne Club, one of the posters was tacked to the telegraph pole right out in front, and there was that Henderson fellow sitting with his feet up on the rail of the veranda, a big cigar in his mouth, looking as though he didn't have a care in the world."

"Well, he has, whether he knows it or not," Pat said. "I hear tell the special U.S. marshal is in town, and he's a man Henderson has reason to fear."

"What's that?" Hope asked. She had been staring gloomily at the desk at which she was seated, wondering if she shouldn't pick up the pen, dip it in the inkwell, and write out the withdrawal of her candidacy. "What did you say, Pap? Who is the special marshal?"

"Fella from up our way by name of Timothy O'Callahan. I hear he's gonna take Henderson in this morning—"

"Oh, Pap!" Hope was on her feet. "Why didn't you tell

me? He could be killed! Henderson is on his own territory—he could have a dozen gunmen with him!"

"Where are you going?" Bright asked as she rushed toward the bedroom of the suite she and Pat had taken at the Cheyenne Arms.

"I'm going to change my clothes and get my gun," she said over her shoulder. "Someone rent me a horse."

"Hope, are you crazy? You are the candidate for governor of this state. You can't go running around the streets of Cheyenne in jeans with a gun in your hand."

"All right, then call me a hack," she said. "I'll keep the gun out of sight in my reticule unless I have to use it."

Ten minutes later Hope, Pat, Jack, and Violet were crowded into a hack racing toward the Cheyenne Club, followed by a second vehicle carrying Juan Mendoza, Bill Bright, and two other party officials.

"The association won't let Henderson be brought to trial," Hope was saying. "They can't afford to, and Henderson won't let himself be taken. He'll come out shooting, probably with backup. Then he'll run for the Canadian border. Tim could be killed! I've got to get to him!"

"Calm down," Pat advised. "He knows what he's doing. Not that I see any reason why we can't side him, just in case."

When they arrived the drama had already begun. Twenty minutes after he finished breakfast in the home of a local federal judge, Timothy O'Callahan strolled down the street toward the Cheyenne Club with his coat off and his marshal's star pinned to his vest, his cross-draw holster in plain sight on his belt. There was the usual scattering of women and children when a gunfight was imminent, and the rush from barbershops and other places of business by men attracted by the excitement of a genuine draw down.

"Hey, you, George B. Henderson!" Timothy shouted as soon as he was situated in the middle of the street directly in front of the steps leading to the club's main entrance. "I'm Tim O'Callahan! You know me! I'm here to arrest you for the murder of Congressman Jebel Mason. Come out or I'm coming in to get you!"

There wasn't a sound from the club, but those watching got the impression that more than one pair of eyes was peering from behind drawn blinds.

"You'd better come on out, Henderson! I've got a train to catch at ten o'clock and I don't intend to wait very long!"

Still there was no reply, and the watchers hardly dared to breathe lest they miss some sound from the club or street.

"You big men of the association, if you're in there with Henderson, I'm givin' you warnin'! I'm comin' in there after him, and I'm comin' in shootin'. If you're in there breakfastin' with your fancy ladies, you'd better get under the table quick!"

A white napkin was waved as the door opened a crack, and the club's maître d' stepped out, contriving to look dignified, mortified, and terrified all at the same time.

"Mr. O'Callahan, I am instructed by the committee to inform you that this is a private club. You are not a member and are definitely not invited to enter."

O'Callahan roared with laughter, and he was still laughing when Hope and the others arrived on the scene. She wanted to call to him or rush to his side but was restrained by her friends.

"Ye can tell your committee that they are interferin' with a United States marshal in the performance of his duty and that if any of them happen to get killed or shot during the arrest of Henderson, they will be charged, dead or alive, as accessories to the assassination of a United States congressman!"

The maître d' went back inside to confer with club members and in a matter of seconds there was a shout.

"All right, O'Callahan, don't shoot! I'm coming out the front door with my hands up! Don't shoot!"

It was Henderson's voice, but to Hope it didn't sound as though it was coming from behind the stained-glass door.

"Look out, Tim, it's a trick!" she yelled as the door opened and a man, wearing a broad-brimmed hat that hid his face, stepped out onto the veranda with his hands up.

Tim braced himself with his legs spread, his head thrust forward as he tried to see the face of the man on the veranda.

A shot rang out from a clump of bushes on the left side of the building, and Tim, grabbing his leg, pitched forward.

Hope had broken away from those holding her and now saw that the unknown man had drawn a gun and was taking a step toward Tim just as Henderson, Winchester in hand, stepped from behind the bushes, throwing another round into the chamber preparatory to firing again.

Hope's shot went through the wrist and right thigh of the man on the steps, hurling him back across the veranda howling with pain. Before Henderson could get off another shot, Tim had fired from his prone position, and the killer's face disappeared in a welter of blood as the slug tore between his eyes.

It was all over so fast that most of the crowd that had gathered broke up in semidisappointment and wandered away to begin making up stories that in later years would exaggerate the slaughter until it almost equaled Custer's last stand.

Hope ran to Timothy. "Darling, are you all right?"

"Got me in the leg, the bloody bastard," Tim said, holding his thigh and trying to sit up, "I should have known that reptile would try a trick like that."

"Well, it was his last one," she said, nodding toward the body of George Henderson, stretched out on the lawn of the club, watering the grass with its blood.

"It hurts me pride more than it does me leg to know I let him get in the first shot. Me father would have taken me off to the woodshed for it."

She knelt beside him as a doctor came running to cut open his pants leg and examine the wound.

"How did you happen to take the marshal's job?" she asked.

"Because I know you. I knew you'd be feelin' guilty about Jebel 'cause you didn't love him, and I figured the only way to get rid of that guilt was to find the man who killed him."

She laughed shakily, blinking back tears. "I'm not sure I like a man knowing me that well."

"Sure now, love, and ye must have known we Irish have

the second sight and take a wee peek into the future now and again."

"Well then, maybe ye could be after tellin' me if I'll marry again," she said, imitating the accent he could put on and take off like a pair of boots.

"Sure and ye will, lassie, just as soon as ye've been elected governor of Wyoming, and to a fine fella ye used to know up in Johnson County."

"Oh, Tim, I might not be elected! There's something I have to tell you about myself and Reverend Potter." Hope's heart was in her mouth as she told him the whole story.

"Oh, so 'tis alienation of affections now. Well, well—" Whatever he had intended to say was cut off abruptly as the doctor began to probe for the bullet. He hit the bone and Timothy passed out.

An ambulance pulled by a frisky young colt arrived and the attendants loaded in the man Hope had shot on one side and Timothy on the other, with a city constable sitting between them.

Hope, standing in the middle of the street with tears in her eyes and her gun dangling from her fingers, was quietly surrounded by a crowd of well-wishers and advisers. She was escorted back to her hotel and informed that she had a week before the day of the trial and ought to be out campaigning.

"I'll take care of Mr. Timothy," Violet promised as Hope boarded a train that would take her on a campaign swing across the state. "You take care of the voters."

"But I don't know if he's forgiven me for the Potter thing," Hope said anxiously.

"He will when you're governor," Flagg assured her as the train began to move.

She didn't get back to Cheyenne until late on the evening before the hearing and had no opportunity to talk to Timothy before going to court the next morning. Violet met her there and assured her Timothy was recovering nicely and beginning to move around on crutches.

"But does he forgive me?" Hope asked just before they went inside the courtroom.

"I don't know. He's the quietest Irishman I've ever seen."

"That doesn't sound right," Hope said in alarm. "If there's one thing Tim isn't, it's quiet."

"He seems to be thinking about something all the time."

Hope bit her lip, her brow furrowed. "Maybe he's still upset because Henderson got in the first shot. Or maybe he's brooding about Potter and me."

Flagg had arrived in time to hear that. "You have to think about your reputation and about getting elected in spite of this suit. Forget about O'Callahan until it's over."

"I can't. . . and I don't think I care about the rest of it if Tim doesn't love me."

"He does, I'm sure he does," Flagg said, but somehow that didn't make Hope feel any better.

A jury of sour-faced men had been chosen, and as she looked at their cold eyes and drooping moustaches, Hope's heart sank to her boots. Aside from the possibility that they were in the pay of the Stock Growers Association, they looked plain mean.

The preliminaries didn't take long. Then the lawyer for the whey-faced, silent Mabel Potter called his first witness, Edgar Potter. Bandbox-neat in a white suit with a string tie, the reverend sauntered down toward the witness box, smiling and waving to acquaintances.

"He looks like he just swallowed two canaries," Violet whispered to Hope.

Hope ground her teeth, wishing she had found an excuse to shoot him years before.

"Do you, Edgar Potter, solemnly swear that you will tell the truth—" the court clerk began as Potter raised one hand and rested the other on the Bible.

"He doesn't know the meaning of the word," a voice said from the rear of the courtroom, and a tall, redheaded man on crutches came down toward the judge's bench.

"Order! Order in the court!" the judge said, rapping with his gavel. "What is the meaning of this, sir?"

"Your honor, forgive this interruption. I am Timothy O'Callahan, United States marshal, retired. I wish to state that the woman being defamed by this man is my fiancée.

Not only is her character without blemish, but I am, by most calculations, the fastest gun north of the Pecos. If any word is spoken in this court or elsewhere against her honor, I will personally kill the man who speaks the words, even if I hang for it."

Hope had been watching the arrogant smile on Potter's face as he was being sworn in, and now she saw him staring at Timothy in shock. He seemed actually to deflate and grow smaller, sinking down into the witness chair as though trying to hide there.

"Stand up," the clerk said. "You're not sworn in yet."

"And he's not going to be sworn in," Tim said. "He saw me kill George B. Henderson with one bullet between the eyes. He was watching from his room in the Cheyenne Club, where he was in bed with Susie Mathers, one of Madam Marge's soiled doves, and he knows I'll do the same thing to him."

"Order! Order! You are in contempt of court, young man! I don't care who you are!"

There was a collective gasp from the listeners and a buzz of conversation at the front of the courtroom. But this shock was nothing to what the audience felt when Mabel Potter suddenly stood up and began to speak in a voice that shook with barely suppressed fury. "Your honor, my husband has committed adultery with at least twenty women I know of, and I have never sued for alienation of affections prior to this. He has admitted to me that this particular woman is innocent of that sin. I do not care what he does to me—I will not go on with the suit. I will give you names, and if I do, people in very high places will be considerably embarrassed. What I prefer to do is withdraw this suit, apologize to Mrs. Mason, and tell her she has my best wishes in being elected governor of this state."

It was all over. A trembling, ashen-faced Potter had fled the witness stand and raced out the back door before Tim could reach him. Later they learned that he had not stopped running until he reached the railroad station. He stayed on the train until he reached New York City, where he went to work as chaplain for Boss Tweed's Good Government Committee.

"Case dismissed," the judge said, and then leveled his gavel at O'Callahan. "You, sir, are still guilty of contempt of court, and I hereby sentence you to six months in jail, to be served after your wound is healed."

"Thank ye, yer honor," Timothy said in his best Irish brogue. "But 'tis suspectin' I am that the new governor will pardon me ere I serve half o' that."

Then Hope was in his arms, Juan was shaking his hand, and the campaign manager was pounding him on the back.

Three weeks after the election, Hope was sworn in by the chief justice of Wyoming as the first woman governor of any state, with Timothy standing beside her, handcuffed to a marshal.

"What is the first thing you are going to do in office, Governor Mason?" a reporter asked when the ceremony was over.

"My first action will be to order the Cheyenne Club closed down as a hazard to public health and safety," Hope said. "After that, I'm going to..."

Timothy lifted his handcuffed wrist and shook it, a comical expression of pleading on his face.

"...And then I'm going to get married to a prisoner in the city jail," Hope finished, slanting her laughing turquoise eyes upward to meet Tim's ardent green gaze.